W9-BWL-759

THE DESERT

CRUCIBLE

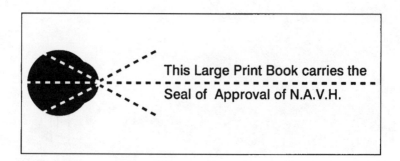

THE DESERT CRUCIBLE

A Western Story

ZANE GREY™

Thorndike Press • Waterville, Maine

Published in 2004 by arrangement with Golden West Literary
Agency.

Thorndike Press® Large Print Western.

The tree indicium is a trademark of Thorndike Press.

The text of this Large Print edition is unabridged.
Other aspects of the book may vary from the original edition.

Set in 16 pt. Plantin by Liana M. Walker.

Printed in the United States on permanent paper.

Library of Congress Cataloging-in-Publication Data

Grey, Zane, 1872–1939.
    The desert crucible : a western story / Zane Grey.
      p. cm.
    ISBN 0-7862-3767-8 (lg. print : hc : alk. paper)
    1. Mormons — Fiction. 2. Polygamy — Fiction.
3. Arizona — Fiction. 4. Large type books.
  I. Title.
PS3513.R6545D38 2004
  813'.52—dc22   2003065126

THE DESERT CRUCIBLE

As the Founder/CEO of NAVH, the only national health agency solely devoted to those who, although not totally blind, have an eye disease which could lead to serious visual impairment, I am pleased to recognize Thorndike Press* as one of the leading publishers in the large print field.

Founded in 1954 in San Francisco to prepare large print textbooks for partially seeing children, NAVH became the pioneer and standard setting agency in the preparation of large type.

Today, those publishers who meet our standards carry the prestigious "Seal of Approval" indicating high quality large print. We are delighted that Thorndike Press is one of the publishers whose titles meet these standards. We are also pleased to recognize the significant contribution Thorndike Press is making in this important and growing field.

Lorraine H. Marchi, L.H.D.
Founder/CEO
NAVH

* Thorndike Press encompasses the following imprints: Thorndike, Wheeler, Walker and Large Print Press.

Foreword

Frequently, when there is an immensely popular book in circulation, the cry goes out for a sequel. Such was the case for *Riders of the Purple Sage* (Harper, 1912), and Dad was only too happy to oblige. There have been several other sequels that followed memorable Zane Grey novels: *Majesty's Rancho* (Harper, 1942) after *The Light of Western Stars* (Harper, 1914), *Stairs of Sand* (Harper, 1943) after *Wanderer of the Wasteland* (Harper, 1923), *"Nevada"* (Harper, 1928) after *Forlorn River* (Harper, 1927), and *The Hash Knife Outfit* (Harper, 1933) that followed *The Drift Fence* (Harper, 1933). In at least one case, the sequel — *"Nevada"* — became more popular than the novel it succeeded. The novel for which this Foreword is written was published by Harper & Bros. in 1915 and quickly became a best seller — despite some of the startling omissions that were edited out of Dad's version and were discovered when reading the holographic manuscript.

This is by no means the only time that publishers saw fit to make editorial changes that have significantly altered the scope and thrust of some of Dad's books. In point of time of publication, this is only one of several we have discovered, and the original manuscript of *Riders of the Purple Sage*, I suspect, when examined, will show that significant editorial changes were made there as well — as, for example, in the details of the relationship between Jane Withersteen and her father and the relationship of Jane's father to Milly Erne. Whether or not the alterations in *The Desert Crucible* were made to render it "inoffensive" for the reading audience or were in response to pressure from an outside group is not known, as I have never found any correspondence on the subject. Yet, whatever the motive, Harper's action did assure that the practice of having sealed wives, once so intrinsic a part of Mormon polygamy after the practice was outlawed by the federal government, was something never openly stated in the book that Harper's titled *The Rainbow Trail*. Also in that version, Fay Larkin, the child who was rescued and reared by Lassiter and Jane Withersteen in Surprise Valley in *Riders of the Purple Sage,* is kidnapped by a band of Mormons and taken to one of their villages but only confined there under mysterious circumstances. Oddly in *The Rainbow Trail,* while it is known that Fay is visited at night in her cabin by one or more Mormon men, she is never said to be married and what took place between her and these men is passed over in silence.

In *The Desert Crucible,* the story as Zane Grey wrote it and now published for the first time anywhere, Fay becomes a sealed wife almost immediately, having been forced to marry a masked Mormon as the price for sparing Lassiter's life. In the subsequent trial, presided over by a federal Supreme Court judge in an attempt to expose those guilty of polygamy, Fay denies vehemently that she is married but does admit she has had a child who died shortly after birth. Although Fay and all the other sealed wives are acquitted for lack of evidence, Fay later does admit the truth about her Mormon marriage to John Shefford, the former minister who has come to northern Arizona to search for Lassiter and Jane and who is in love with her. Although Fay struggles with guilt and remorse over what she sees as a "sin", Shefford eventually is able to convince her that what happened to her is what many outside the Mormon circle would consider to be rape and that, certainly, she committed no unworthy offense.

What seemed incredible at the time *The Rainbow Trail* was published is how this girl could have lived for such a long time in a Mormon village, be regularly visited by men, and yet never have had sexual relations with any of them or have become pregnant. I was baffled by it when I read the book for the first time. My guess was that it was a fantasy Dad had imposed on gullible readers, but, as it has now turned out, this fantasy was imposed by the editors of the story and not by Zane Grey. *The Desert Crucible* continued Dad's searing indictment, first illustrated so forcibly in *Riders of the Purple Sage*, of the way Mormon men would kidnap Gentile women and then force them to become Mormon wives. Even the outlawing of polygamy did not stop this practice, but prompted instead the creation of these villages of sealed wives.

Sometime during, or even before, the writing of *The Desert Crucible*, an event occurred that came to form a significant part of the later portion of the story. This was Dad's discovery of the Rainbow Bridge, that awesome cathedral of red sandstone located just above the Utah border and north of Navajo Mountain, about twenty miles south of the Colorado River. It is the largest natural bridge in the world and is the second designated part of what eventually became the vast U.S. National Park system, being declared a national monument in 1910 by President William McKinley at the request of Theodore Roosevelt. It is one of the least-known natural wonders of America and might be even more obscure today if it had not been for the building of the Glen Cañon Dam on the Colorado River that brought the highest waters of Lake Powell to about twenty-seven feet and so to the very base of the bridge. Now, instead of a grueling horseback ride over many miles of rugged terrain, thousands of tourists take the easy two-hour daily boat trip from Page, Arizona to a special dock built by the Park Service, within a mile of the bridge.

I have been there five times and even the gleeful shouts of children swimming in the lake just under the bridge do not dim its magnificence. When Dad went there in 1913, with the trader John Wetherill and led by the Paiute, Nasja-Begay, who also guided the first white men, the Cummins-Wetherill expedition to the bridge in 1910, he was literally overwhelmed by what he saw. The character Nas-Ta-Bega in *The Desert Cru-*

cible was modeled on this Paiute guide. My father called the Rainbow Bridge Nonnezoshe. "Sound, movement, life seemed to have no fitness here," he wrote of his first encounter with it in an article for *Recreation* (2/15). "Ruin was there and desolation and decay. The meaning of the ages was flung at me. A man became nothing." When Nonnezoshe is visited by characters in *The Desert Crucible*, their reaction is much the same. "The spell of the desert comes back to me," Grey wrote in his original Foreword to this novel, "as it always will come. I see the veils like purple smoke in the cañons, and I feel the silence. And it seems that again I must try to pierce both and to get at the strange, wild life of the last American wilderness — wild still, almost, as it ever was."

The plot of this story has John Shefford and his party escape from the Mormons, who are pursuing them, follow the trail that leads down the Valley of the Rainbow to the Colorado River where they board a raft and drift down the river to the safety of Lee's Ferry. It apparently mattered little to Dad that the locale of the action of *Riders of the Purple Sage* was well north of the Colorado River and the rescue of Jane and Lassiter took place south of the river. At the time of the book the nearest possible crossing would have been more than forty miles downstream from where the party emerged. It is now known as The Crossing of the Fathers and is buried under 700 feet of water. But such is the fiction writer's prerogative, and one who has read *Riders of the Purple Sage* and also reads this book will probably not notice the difference. When one sees how Zane Grey, through the eyes of Shefford, was so awed and entranced by his encounter with this great cathedral-like edifice, one will understand why this had to be an essential aspect of the novel.

In *The Desert Crucible*, we have restored Dad's original title as well as his original text for this story. It surely deserves to be read as Zane Grey wrote it.

Loren Grey
Woodland Hills, California

Chapter One

Shefford halted his tired horse, and gazed with slowly realizing eyes. A league-long slope of sage rolled and billowed down to Red Lake, a dry red basin, denuded and glistening, a hollow in the desert, a lonely and desolate door to the vast, wild, and broken upland beyond.

All day Shefford had plodded onward with the clear horizon line a thing unattainable, and for days before that he had ridden the wild bare flats and climbed the rocky desert benches. The great colored reaches and steps had led endlessly onward and upward through dim and deceiving distance. A hundred miles of desert travel, with its mistakes and lessons and intimations, had not prepared him for what he now saw. He beheld what seemed a world that knew only magnitude. Wonder and awe fixed his gaze, and remained aloof. Then that dark and unknown northland flung a menace at him. An

14

irresistible call had drawn him to this seamed and peaked border of Arizona, this broken, battlemented wilderness of Utah upland, and at first sight it frowned upon him, as if to warn him not to search for what lay hidden beyond the ranges. But Shefford thrilled with both fear and exultation. That was the country that had been described to him. Far across the yellow range lay the wild cañon with its haunting secret.

Red Lake must be his Rubican. Either he must enter the unknown to seek, to strive, to find, or turn back and fail and never know and be always haunted. A friend's strange story had prompted his singular journey: a beautiful rainbow with its mystery and promise had decided him. Once in his life he had answered a wild call to the kingdom of adventure within him, and once in his life he had been happy. But here in the horizon-wide face of that upflung and cloven desert he grew cold, he faltered, even while he felt more fatally drawn.

As if impelled, Shefford started his horse down the sandy trail, but he avoided his former far-reaching gaze. It was the month of April and the waning sun lost heat and brightness. Long shadows crept down the slope ahead of him, and the scant sage deepened its gray. He watched the lizards shoot like brown streaks across the sand, leaving their slender tracks. He heard the rustle of pack rats as they darted into their brushy homes. The *whir* of a low-sailing hawk startled his horse.

Like ocean waves the slope rose and fell, its hollows choked with sand, its ridge tops showing scantier growth of sage and grass and weed. The last ridge was a sand dune, beautifully ribbed and scalloped and lined by the wind, and from its knife-sharp crest a thin, wavering sheet of sand blew, almost like smoke. Shefford wondered why the sand looked red at a distance, for here it seemed almost white. It rippled everywhere, clean and glistening, always leading down.

Suddenly Shefford became aware of a house looming out of the bareness of the slope. It dominated that long white incline. Grim, lonely, forbidding, how strangely it harmonized with the surroundings! The structure was octagon-shaped, built of uncut stone, and resembled a fort. There was no door on the sides exposed to Shefford's gaze, but small apertures two-thirds the way up probably served as windows and portholes. The roof appeared to be made of poles covered with red earth.

Like a huge cold rock on a wide plain this house stood there on the winding slope. It was an outpost of the trader Presbrey, of whom Shefford had heard at Flagstaff and Tuba. No living thing appeared in the limit of Shefford's vision. He gazed shudderingly at the unwelcoming habitation, at the dark eye-like windows, at the sweep of barren slope merging into the vast red valley, at the bold, bleak bluffs. Could anyone live there? The nature of that sinister valley forbade a home there, and the spirit of the place hovered in the silence and space. Shefford thought irresistibly of how his enemies would have consigned him to just such a hell. He thought bitterly and mockingly of the narrow congregation that had proved him a failure in the ministry, that had repudiated his ideas of religion and immortality and God, that had driven him, at the age of twenty four, from the calling forced upon him by his people. As a boy he had yearned to make himself an artist; his family had made him a clergyman; fate had made him a failure. A failure only so far in his life, something urged him to add — for in the lonely days and silent nights of the desert he had experienced a strange birth of hope. Adventure had called him, but it was a vague and spiritual hope, a dream of promise, a nameless attainment that fortified his wilder impulse.

17

As he rode around a corner of the stone house, his horse snorted and stopped. A lean, shaggy pony jumped at sight of him, almost displacing a red, long-haired blanket that had covered an Indian saddle. Quick *thuds* of hoofs in sand drew Shefford's attention to a corral made of peeled poles, and here he saw another pony.

Shefford heard subdued voices. He dismounted, and walked to an open door. In the dark interior he dimly descried a high counter, a stairway, a pile of bags of flour, blankets, and silver-ornamented objects, but the persons he had heard were not in that part of the house. Around another corner of the octagon-shaped wall he found another open door and, through it, saw goatskins and a mound of dirty sheep wool, black and brown and white. It was light in this part of the building. When he crossed the threshold, he was astounded to see a man struggling with a girl — an Indian girl. She was straining back from him, panting and uttering very low guttural sounds. The man's face was corded and dark with passion. This scene affected Shefford strangely. Primitive emotions were new to him.

Before Shefford could speak, the girl broke loose and turned to flee. She was an Indian and this place was the uncivilized desert, but Shefford knew terror when he saw it. Like a dog the man rushed after her. It was instinct that made Shefford strike, and his blow laid the man flat. He lay stunned a moment, then raised himself to a sitting posture, his hand to his face, and the gaze he fixed upon Shefford seemed to combine astonishment and rage.

"I hope you're not Presbrey," said Shefford slowly. He felt awkward, not sure of himself.

The man appeared about to burst into speech, but repressed it. There was blood on his mouth and his hand. Hastily he scrambled to his feet. Shefford saw this man's amaze and rage change to shame. He was tall and rather stout; he had a smooth, tanned face, soft of outline, with a weak chin; his eyes were dark. The look of him and his corduroys and his soft shoes gave Shefford an impression that he was not a man who worked hard. By contrast with the few other worn and rugged desert men Shefford had met, this stranger stood out strikingly. He stooped to pick up a soft felt hat, and, jamming it on his head, he hurried out. Shefford followed him, and watched him from the door. He went directly to the corral, mounted the pony, and rode out, to turn down the slope toward the south.

When he reached the level of the basin, where evidently the sand was hard, he put the pony to a lope, and gradually drew away.

"Well," ejaculated Shefford. He did not know what to make of this adventure. Presently he became aware that the Indian girl was sitting on a roll of blankets near the wall. With curious interest Shefford studied her appearance. She had long, raven-black hair, tangled and disheveled, and she wore a soiled white band of cord above her brow. The color of her face struck him; it was dark, but not red, or bronzed; almost it had a tinge of gold. Her profile was clean-cut, bold, almost stern. Long black eyelashes hid her eyes. She wore a tight-fitting waist garment resembling velveteen. It was ripped along her side, exposing a skin still more richly gold than that of her face. A string of silver ornaments and turquoise and white beads encircled her neck, and it moved gently up and down with the heaving of her full bosom. Her skirt was of some gaudy print goods, torn and stained and dusty. She had little feet, encased in brown moccasins, fitting like gloves and buttoning over the ankles with silver coins.

"Who was that man? Did he hurt you?" inquired Shefford, turning to gaze down the valley where a moving black object showed on the bare sand.

"No savvy," replied the Indian girl.

"Where's the trader, Presbrey?" asked Shefford.

She pointed straight down into the red valley. "Toh," she said.

In the center of the basin lay a small pool of water shining brightly in the sunset glow. Small objects moved around it, so small that Shefford thought he saw several dogs led by a child. But it was distance that deceived him. There was a man down there watering his horses. That reminded Shefford of the duty owing to his own tired and thirsty beast. Whereupon he untied his pack, took off the saddle, and was about ready to start down when the Indian girl grasped the bridle from his hand.

"Me go," she said.

He saw her eyes then, and they made her look different. They were as black as her hair. He was puzzled to decide whether or not he thought her handsome.

"Thanks, but I'll go," he replied, and, taking the bridle again, he started down the slope. At every step his horse sank into the deep, soft sand. Down a little way he came upon piles of tin cans; they were everywhere, buried, half buried, and lying loose;

21

and these gave evidence of how the trader lived. Presently Shefford discovered that the Indian girl was following him with her own pony. Looking upward at her against the light, he thought her slender, lithe, picturesque. At a distance he liked her.

He plodded on, at length glad to get out of the drifts of sand to the hard level floor of the valley. This, too, was sand, but dried and baked hard, and red in color. At some season of the year this immense flat must be covered with water. How wide it was, and empty! Shefford experienced again a feeling that had been novel to him — it was that he was loose, free, unanchored, ready to veer with the wind. From the foot of the slope the water hole had appeared to be a few hundred rods out in the valley. But the small size of the figures made Shefford doubt, and he had to travel many times a few hundred rods before these figures began to grow. Then Shefford made out that they were approaching him. Thereafter, they rapidly increased to normal proportions of man and beast. When Shefford met them, he saw a powerful, heavily built young man leading two ponies.

"You're Mister Presbrey, the trader?" Shefford inquired.

"Yes, I'm Presbrey, without the mister," he replied.

"My name's Shefford. I'm knocking about on the desert. Rode from Tuba today."

"Glad to see you," said Presbrey. He offered his hand. He was a stalwart man, clad in gray shirt, overalls, and boots. A shock of tumbled light hair covered his massive head; he was tanned, but not darkly, and there was red in his cheeks; under his shaggy eyebrows were deep keen eyes; his lips were hard and set, as if occasion for smiles or words was rare; and his big strong jaw seemed locked.

"Wish more travelers came knocking around Red Lake," he added. "Reckon here's the jumping off place."

"It's pretty . . . lonesome," said Shefford, hesitating, as if at a loss for words.

Then the Indian girl came up. Presbrey addressed her in her own language that Shefford did not understand. She seemed shy and would not answer; she stood with downcast face and eyes. Presbrey spoke again, at which she pointed down the valley, and then moved on with her pony toward the water hole.

Presbrey's keen eyes fixed on the receding black dot far down that oval expanse.

"That fellow left . . . rather abruptly," said Shefford constrainedly. "Who was he?"

"His name's Willetts. He's a missionary.

He rode in today with this Navajo girl. He was taking her to Blue Cañon where he lives and teaches the Indians. I've met him only a few times. You see not many white men ride in here. He's the first white man I've seen in six months, and you're the second. Both the same day! Red Lake's getting popular! It's queer, though, his leaving. He expected to stay all night. There's no other place to stay. Blue Cañon is fifty miles away."

"I'm sorry to say . . . no, I'm not sorry, either . . . but I must tell you I was the cause of Mister Willetts's leaving," replied Shefford.

"How so?" inquired the other.

Then Shefford related the incident following his arrival. "Perhaps my action was hasty," he concluded apologetically. "I didn't think. Indeed, I'm surprised at myself."

Presbrey made no comment, and his face was as hard to read as one of the distant bluffs.

"But what did the man mean?" asked Shefford, conscious of a little heat. "I'm a stranger out here. I'm ignorant of Indians . . . how they're controlled. Still I'm no fool. If Willetts didn't mean evil, at least he was brutal."

"He was teaching her religion," replied Presbrey. His tone held faint scorn and implied a joke, but his face did not change in the slightest.

Without understanding just why, Shefford felt his conviction justified and his action approved. Then he was sensible of a slight shock of wonder and disgust.

"I am . . . I was a minister of the Gospel," he said to Presbrey. "What you hint seems impossible. I can't believe it."

"I didn't hint," replied Presbrey bluntly, and it was evident that he was a sincere but close-mouthed man. "Shefford, so you're a preacher? Did you come out here to try to convert the Indians?"

"No. Said I *was* a minister. I am no longer. I'm just a . . . a wanderer."

"I see. Well, the desert's no place for missionaries, but it's good for wanderers. Go water your horse and take him up to the corral. You'll find some hay for him. I'll get grub ready."

Shefford went on with his horse to the pool. The water appeared thick, green, murky, and there was a line of salty crust extending around the margin of the pool. The thirsty horse splashed in and eagerly bent his head, but he did not like the taste. Many times he refused to drink, yet always lowered his nose again. Finally he drank, although not his fill. Shefford saw the Indian girl drink from her hand. He scooped up a handful and found it too sour to swallow. When he turned to retrace his steps, she mounted her pony and followed him.

A golden flare lit up the western sky, and silhouetted dark and lonely against it stood the trading post. Upon his return Shefford found the wind rising, and it chilled him. When he reached the slope, thin gray sheets of sand were blowing low, rising, whipping, falling, sweeping along with soft silken rustle. Sometimes the gray veils hid his boots. It was a long, toilsome climb up that yielding, dragging ascent, and he had already been lame and tired. By the time he had put his horse away, twilight was everywhere, except in the west. The Indian girl left her pony in the corral, and came like a shadow toward the house.

Shefford had difficulty in finding the foot of the stairway. He climbed to enter a large loft, lighted by two lamps. Presbrey was there, kneading biscuit dough in a pan.

"Make yourself comfortable," he said. The huge loft was the shape of a half octagon. A door opened upon the valley side, and here, too, there were windows. How attractive the place was in comparison with impressions gained from the outside! The furnishings consisted of Indian blankets on the floor, two beds, a desk and table, several chairs and a couch, a gun rack full of rifles, innumerable silver-ornamented belts, bridles, and other Indian articles upon the walls, and in one corner a wood-burning stove with tea kettle steaming, and a great cupboard with shelves full of canned foods.

Shefford leaned in the doorway and looked out. Beneath him on a roll of blankets sat the Indian girl, silent and motionless. He wondered what was in her mind, what she would do, how the trader would treat her. The slope now was a long slant of sheeted, moving shadows of sand. Dusk had gathered in the valley. The bluffs loomed black beyond. A pale star twinkled above. Shefford suddenly became aware of the intense nature of the stillness about him. Yet, as he listened to this silence, he heard an intermittent and immeasurably low moan, a fitful mournful murmur. Assuredly it was only the wind. Nevertheless, it made his blood run cold. It was a different wind from that which had made music under the eaves of his Illinois home. This was a lonely, haunting wind, with desert hunger in it, and more that he could not name. Shefford listened to this spirit-brooding sound while he watched night envelop the valley. How black, how thick the mantle! Yet it brought no comforting sense of close-folded protection, of walls, soft sleep, of a home. Instead, there was the feeling of space, of emptiness, of an infinite hall down which a mournful wind swept streams of murmuring sand.

"Well, grub's about ready," said Presbrey.

"Got any water?" asked Shefford.

"Sure. There in the bucket. It's rain water. I have a tank here."

Shefford's sore and blistered face felt better after he had washed off the sand and alkali dust.

"Better not wash your face often while you're in the desert. Bad plan," went on Presbrey, noting how gingerly his visitor had gone about his ablutions. "Well, come and eat."

Shefford marked that, if the trader did live a lonely life, he fared well. There was more on the table than twice two men could have eaten. It was the first time in four days that Shefford had sat at a table and he made up for lost opportunity. His host's actions manifested delight, yet the strange, hard face never relaxed, never changed. When the meal was finished, Presbrey declined assistance, had a generous thought of the Indian girl, who, he said, would have a place to eat and sleep downstairs — and then with the skill and dispatch of an accomplished

28

housewife cleared the table, after which work he filled a pipe and evidently prepared to listen.

It took only one question for Shefford to find that the trader was starved for news of the outside world, and for an hour Shefford fed that appetite. But when he had talked himself out, there seemed indication of Presbrey's being more than a good listener.

"How'd you come in?" he asked.

"By Flagstaff . . . across Little Colorado . . . and through Moencopie."

"Did you stop at Moen Ave?"

"No, what place is that?"

"A missionary lives there. Did you stop at Tuba?"

"Only long enough to drink and water my horse. That was a wonderful spring for the desert."

"You said you were a wanderer. Do you want a job? I'll give you one."

"No, thank you, Presbrey."

"I saw your pack. That's no pack to travel with in this country. Your horse won't last, either. Have you any money?"

"Yes, plenty of money."

"Well, that's good. Not that a white man out here would ever take a dollar from you. But you can buy from the Indians as you go. Where are you making for, anyhow?"

Shefford hesitated, debating in mind whether to tell his purpose or not. His host did not press the question.

"I see. Just footloose and wandering around," went on Presbrey. "I can understand how the desert appeals to you. Preachers lead easy, safe, crowded, bound lives. They're shut up in a church with a Bible and good people. When once in a lifetime, they get loose . . . they break out."

"Yes, I'm broken out . . . beyond all bounds," replied Shefford sadly. He seemed retrospective for a moment, unaware of the trader's keen and sympathetic glance, and then he caught himself. "I want to see some wildlife. Do you know the country north of here?"

"Only what little the Navajos tell me. And they're not much to talk. There's a trail goes north, but I've never traveled it. It's a new trail every time an Indian goes that way, for here the sand blows and covers old tracks. But few Navajos ride in from the north. My trade is mostly with Indians up and down the valley."

"How about water and grass?"

"We've had rain and snow. There's sure to be water. Can't say about grass, though the sheep and ponies from the north are always fat. But, say, Shefford, if you'll excuse me for advising you . . . don't go north."

"Why?" asked Shefford, and it was certain that he thrilled.

"It's unknown country, terribly broken as you can see from here, and there are bad Indians hiding in the cañons. I've never met a man who has been over the pass between here and Kayenta. The trip's been made, so there must be a trail. But it's a dangerous trip for any man, let alone a tenderfoot. You're not even packing a gun."

"What's this place . . . Kayenta?" asked Shefford.

"It's a spring. Kayenta means bottomless spring. There's a little trading post, the last and the wildest in northern Arizona. Withers, the trader who keeps it, hauls his supplies in from Colorado and New Mexico. He's never come down this way. I never saw him. Know nothing of him except hearsay. Reckon he's a nervy and strong man to hold that post. If you want to go there, better go by way of Keams Cañon, and then around the foot of Black Mesa. It'll be a long ride . . . maybe two hundred miles."

"How far straight north over the pass?"

"Can't say. Upward of seventy-five miles over rough trails, if there are trails at all. I've heard rumors of a fine tribe of Navajos

31

living in there, rich in sheep and horses. It may be true, and it may not. But I do know there are bad Indians, half-breeds and outcasts, hiding in there. Some of them have visited me here. Bad customers! More than that you'll be going close to the Utah line, and the Mormons over there are unfriendly these days."

"Why?" queried Shefford, again with that curious thrill.

"They are being persecuted by the government for polygamy."

Shefford asked no more questions, and his host vouchsafed no more information on that score. The conversation lagged. Then Shefford inquired about the Indian girl, and learned that she lived up the valley somewhere. Presbrey had never seen her before Willetts came with her to Red Lake. This query brought out the fact that Presbrey was comparatively new to Red Lake and vicinity. Shefford wondered why a lonely six months there had not made the trader old in experience. Probably the desert did not readily give up its secrets. Moreover, this Red Lake house was only an occasionally used branch of Presbrey's main trading post, situated at Willow Springs, fifty miles westward over the mesa.

"I'm closing up here soon for a spell," said

Presbrey, and now his face lost its set hardness and seemed singularly changed. It was a difference of light and softness. "Won't be so lonesome over at Willow Springs. I'm being married soon."

"That's fine," replied Shefford warmly. He was glad for the sake of this lonely desert man. What good a wife would bring into a trader's life!

Presbrey's naïve admission, however, appeared to detach him from his present surroundings, and with his massive head enveloped by a cloud of smoke he lived in dreams. Shefford respected his host's serene abstraction. Indeed, he was grateful for silence. Not for many nights had the past impinged so closely upon the present. The wound in his soul had not healed and to speak of himself made it bleed anew. Memory was too poignant — the past was too close — he wanted to forget till he had toiled into the heart of this forbidding wilderness, till time had gone by, and he dared to face his unquiet soul. Then he listened to the steadily rising roar of the wind. How strange and hollow! That wind was freighted with heavy sand, and he heard it sweep, sweep, sweep by in gusts, and then blow with dull steady blast against the walls. The sound was provocative of thought. This moan and rush of wind was no dream — this presence of his in a night-enshrouded and sand-besieged house of the lonely desert was a reality — this adventure was not one of fancy. True, indeed, then must be the wild strange story that had led him hither. He was going on to seek, to strive, to find. Somewhere northward in the broken fastness lay hidden a valley walled-in from the world. Would they be there, those lost fugitives whose story had thrilled him? After twelve years would she be alive, a child grown to womanhood in the solitude of a beautiful cañon? Incredible! Yet he believed his friend's story, and he, indeed, knew how strange and tragic life was. He fancied he heard her voice on the sweeping wind. She called to him, haunted him. He admitted the improbability of her existence, but lost nothing of the persistent intangible hope that drove him. He believed himself a man stricken in soul, unworthy through doubt of God to minister to the people who had banished him. Perhaps a labor of Hercules, a mighty and perilous work of rescue, the saving of this lost and imprisoned girl, would help him in his trouble. She might be salvation — who could tell? Always as a boy and as a man he had fared forth to find the treasure at the foot of the rainbow.

Chapter Two

Next morning the Indian girl was gone. The tracks of her pony led north. Shefford's first thought was to wonder if he could overtake her on the trail, and this surprised him with the proof of how unconsciously his resolve to go on had formed. Presbrey made no further attempt to turn Shefford back, but he insisted on replenishing the pack and that Shefford take weapons. Finally Shefford was persuaded to accept a revolver. The trader bade him good bye and stood in the door while Shefford led his horse down the slope toward the water hole. Perhaps the trader believed he was watching the departure of a man who would never return. He was still standing at the door of the post when Shefford halted at the pool.

Upon the level floor of the valley lay thin patches of snow that had fallen during the night. The air was biting cold, yet stimulated Shefford while it stung him. His horse drank rather slowly and disgustedly. Then Shefford mounted and reluctantly turned his back upon the trading post.

As he rode away from the pool, he saw a large flock of sheep approaching. They were very closely, even densely, packed in a solid, slow-moving mass and coming with a precision almost like a march. This fact surprised Shefford for there was not an Indian in sight. Presently he saw that a dog was leading the flock, and a little later he discovered another dog in the rear of the sheep. They were splendid long-haired dogs, of a wild-looking shepherd breed. He halted his horse to watch the procession pass by. The flock covered fully an acre of ground and the sheep were black, white, and brown. They passed him making a little pattering roar on the hard-caked sand. The dogs were taking the sheep to water.

Shefford went on and was drawing close to the other side of the basin, where the flat red level was broken by rising dunes and ridges, when he espied a bunch of ponies. A shrill whistle told him that they had seen him. They were wild, shaggy, with long manes and tails. They stopped, threw up their heads, and watched him. Shefford certainly returned the attention. There was no Indian with them. Presently with a snort the leader, which appeared to be a stallion, trotted behind the others, seemed to be driving them, and went clear around the band to get in the lead again. He was taking them in to water, the same as the dogs had taken the sheep.

These incidents were new and pleasing to Shefford. How ignorant he had been of life in the wilderness. Once more he received subtle intimations of what he might learn out in the open, and it was with a less weighted heart that he faced the gateway between the huge yellow bluffs on his left and the slow rise of ground to the black mesa on his right. He looked back in time to see the trading post, bleak and lonely on the bare slope, pass out of sight behind the bluffs. Shefford felt no fear — he really had little experience of physical fear — but it was certain that he gritted his teeth and welcomed whatever was to come to him. He had lived a narrow, insulated life with his mind on spiritual things: his family and his congregation and his friends — except that one new friend whose story had enthralled him. These were people of quiet religious habit. The man deep down in him had never had a chance. He breathed hard as he tried to imagine the world opening to him and almost dared to be glad for the doubt that had sent him adrift.

The tracks of the Indian girl's pony were plain in the sand. Also there were other tracks, not so plain, and these Shefford decided had been made by Willetts and the girl the day before. He climbed a ridge, half soft sand and half hard, and saw right before him, rising in striking form, two great yellow buttes, like elephant legs. He rode between them, amazed at their height. Then before him stretched a slowly ascending valley walled on one side by the black mesa and on the other by low bluffs. For miles a dark green growth of greasewood covered the valley, and Shefford could see where the green thinned and failed, to give place to sand. He trotted his horse and made good time on this stretch.

The day contrasted greatly with any he had yet experienced. Gray clouds obscured the walls of rock a few miles to the west and Shefford saw squalls of huge veils like snow dropping down and spreading out. The wind cut with the keenness of a knife. Soon he was chilled to the bone. A squall swooped and roared down upon him, and the wind that bore the driving white pellets of snow, almost like hail, was so freezing, bitterly cold, that the former wind seemed warm in comparison. The squall passed as swiftly as it had come, and it left Shefford so be-numbed he could not hold the bridle. He tumbled off his horse, and walked. By and by the sun came out and soon warmed him and melted the thin layer of snow on the sand. He was still on the trail of the Indian girl, but hers were now the only tracks he could see.

All morning he gradually climbed, with limited view, till at last he mounted to a point where the country lay open to his sight on all sides except where the endless black mesa ranged on into the north. A rugged yellow peak dominated the landscape to the fore, but it was far away. Red and ragged country extended westward to a huge flat-topped wall of gray rock. Lowering swift clouds swept across the sky, like drooping mantles, and they darkened the sun. Shefford built a little fire out of dead greasewood sticks, and with his blanket around his shoulders he hung over the blaze, scorching his clothes and hands. He had been cold before in his life, but he had never before appreciated fire. Thin desert blasts pierced him. The squall enveloped him, thicker and colder and windier than the other, but being better fortified he did not suffer so much. It howled away, hiding the mesa, and leaving a white desert behind.

Shefford walked on, leading his horse, till the exercise and the sun had once more warmed him.

This last squall had rendered the Indian girl's trail difficult to follow. The snow did not quickly melt, and, besides, sheep tracks and the tracks of horses gave him trouble till at last he was compelled to admit that he could not follow her any longer. A faint path or trail led north, however, and, following that, he soon forgot the girl. Every sur-mounted ridge held a surprise for him. The desert seemed never to change in the vast whole that encompassed him, yet near him it was always changing. From Red Lake he had seen a peaked, walled, and cañoned country, as rough as a stormy sea, but when he rode into that country, the sharp and broken features held to the distance.

He was glad to get out of the sand. Long narrow flats, gray with grass and dotted with patches of greasewood and lined by low bare ridges of yellow rock, stretched away from him, leading toward the yellow peak that seemed never to be gained upon. Shefford had pictures in his mind, pictures of stone walls and wild valleys and domed buttes, all of which had been painted in col-orful and vivid words by his friend, Bern Venters. He believed he would recognize the

40

distinctive and remarkable landmarks Venters had portrayed, and he was certain that he had not yet come upon one of them. This was his second lonely day of travel and he had grown more and more susceptible to the influences of horizon and the different prominent points. He attributed a gradual change in his feelings to the loneliness and the increasing wildness. Between Tuba and Flagstaff he had met Indians and an occasional prospector and teamster. Here he was alone, and, although he felt some strange gladness, he could not help but see the difference.

He rode on during the gray, lowering, chilly day, and toward evening the clouds broke in the west and a setting sun shone through the rift, burnishing the desert to red and gold. Shefford's instinctive but deadened love of the beautiful in nature stirred into life, and the moment of its rebirth was a melancholy and sweet one. Too late for the artist's work, but not too late for his soul.

For a place to make camp he halted near a low area of rock that lay like an island in a sea of grass. There was an abundance of dead greasewood for a campfire, and after searching over the rock he found little pools of melted snow in the depressions. He took off the saddle and pack, watered his horse, and, hobbling him as well as his inexperience permitted, he turned him loose on the grass.

Then, while he built a fire and prepared a meal, the night came down upon him. In the lee of the rock he was well sheltered from the wind, but the air was bitterly cold. He gathered all the dead greasewood in the vicinity, replenished the fire, and rolled in his blanket, back to the blaze. The loneliness and the coyotes did not bother him this night. He was too tired and cold. He went to sleep at once and did not awaken till the fire died out. Then he rebuilt it and went to sleep again. Every half hour all night long he repeated this, and was glad, indeed, when the dawn broke.

The day began with misfortune. His horse was gone. It had been stolen, or had worked out of sight, or had broken the hobbles and made off. From a high stone ridge Shefford searched the grassy flats and slopes, all to no purpose. Then he tried to track the horse, but this was equally futile. He had expected disasters, and the first one did not daunt him. He tied most of his pack in the blanket, threw the canteen across his shoulder, and set forth, sure at least of one thing — that he was a very much better traveler on foot than on horseback.

Walking did not afford him the leisure to study the surrounding country. However, from time to time when he surmounted a bench, he scanned the different landmarks that had grown familiar. It took hours of steady walking to reach and pass the yellow peak that had been a kind of goal. He saw many sheep trails and horse tracks in the vicinity of this mountain, and once he was sure he espied an Indian watching him from a bold ridge top.

The day was bright and warm, with air so clear it magnified objects he knew to be far away. The ascent was gradual. There were many narrow flats connected by steps, and the grass grew thicker and longer. At noon, Shefford halted under the first cedar tree, a lonely dwarfed shrub that seemed to have had a hard life. From this point the rise of ground was more perceptible, and straggling cedars led the eye on to a purple slope that merged into green of piñon and pine. Could that purple be the sage Venters had so feelingly described, or was it merely the purple of deceiving distance? Whatever it might be, it gave Shefford a thrill and made him think of the strange, shy, and lovely woman Venters had won out here in this purple sage country.

He calculated that he had ridden thirty

miles the day before and had already traveled ten miles today, and, therefore, could hope to be in the pass before night. Shefford resumed his journey with too much energy and enthusiasm to think of being tired. He discovered presently that the straggling cedars and the slope beyond were much closer than he had judged them to be. He reached the sage to find it gray instead of purple. Yet it was always purple a little way ahead, and, if he half shut his eyes, it was purple near at hand. He was surprised to find that he could not breathe freely, or it seemed so, and soon made the discovery that the sweet, pungent, penetrating fragrance of sage and cedar had this strange effect upon him. It was an exceedingly dry and odorous forest, where every open space between the clumps of cedars was choked with luxuriant sage. The piñons were higher up on the mesa and the pines still higher. Shefford appeared to lose himself. There were no trails. The black mesa on the right and the wall of stone on the left could not be seen, but he pushed on with what was either singular confidence or rash impulse. He did not know whether that slope was long or short.

Once at the summit he saw with surprise that it broke abruptly and the descent was very steep and short on that side. Through the trees he once more saw the black mesa, rising to the dignity of a mountain, and he had glimpses of another flat, narrow valley, this time with a red wall running parallel with the mesa. He could not help but hurry down to get an unobstructed view. His eagerness was rewarded by a splendid scene, yet to his regret he could not force himself to believe it had any relation to the pictured scenes in his mind. The valley was half a mile wide, perhaps several miles long, and it extended in a curve between the cedar-sloped mesa and a looming wall of red stone. There was not a bird or a beast in sight. He found a well-defined trail, but it had not been recently used. He passed a low structure made of peeled logs and mud, with a dark opening like a door. It did not take him many minutes to learn that the valley was longer than he had calculated. He walked swiftly and steadily, in spite of the fact that the pack had become burdensome. What lay beyond the jutting corner of the mesa had increasing fascination for him and acted as a spur. At last, he turned the corner only to be disappointed at sight of another cedar slope. He had a glimpse of a single black shaft of rock rising far in the distance, and it disappeared as his striding forward made the crest of the slope rise toward the sky.

Again his view became restricted, and he lost the sense of a slow and gradual uplift of rock and an increase in the scale of proportion. Halfway up this ascent he was compelled to rest, and the sun was slanting low when he entered the cedar forest. Soon he was descending, and he suddenly came into the open to face a scene that made his heart beat thick and fast.

He saw lofty crags and cathedral spires, and a wonderful cañon winding between huge, beetling red walls. He heard the murmur of flowing water. The trail led down to the cañon floor. It appeared to be level and green and was cut by deep washes in red earth. Could this cañon be the mouth of Deception Pass? It bore no resemblance to any place Shefford had heard described, yet somehow he felt rather than saw that it was the portal to the wild fastness he had traveled so far to enter.

Not till he had descended the trail and had dropped his pack did he realize how weary and footsore he was. Then he rested. But his eyes roved to and fro, and his mind was active. What a wild and lonesome spot. The low murmur of shallow water came up to him from a deep narrow cleft. Shadows were already making the cañon seem full of blue haze. He saw a bare slope of stone out of which cedar trees were growing. As he looked about him, he became aware of a singular and very perceptible change in the light and shade. The sun was setting. The crags were gold-tipped, the shadows crept upward, the sky seemed to darken swiftly, then the gold changed to red, slowly dulled, and the grays and purples stood out. Shefford was entranced with the beautiful changing effects and watched till the walls turned black and the sky grew steely and a faint star peeped out. Then he set about the necessary camp tasks.

Dead cedars right at hand assured him a comfortable night with steady fire, and, when he had satisfied his hunger, he arranged an easy seat before the blazing logs and gave his mind over to thought of his weird, lonely environment. The murmur of running water mingled in harmonious accompaniment with the moan of wind in the cedars, wild sweet sounds that were balm to his wounded spirit. They seemed a part of the silence, rather than a break in it, or a hindrance to the feeling of it. But suddenly that silence did break to the rattle of a rock. Shefford listened, thinking some wild animal was prowling around. He felt no alarm. Presently he heard the sound again, and again. Then he recognized the crack of unshod hoofs upon rock. A horse was coming down the trail. Shefford rather resented the interruption, although he still felt no alarm. He believed he was perfectly safe. As a matter of fact, he had never in his life been anything but safe and padded around with wool, hence never having experienced peril, he did not know what fear was.

Presently he saw a horse and rider come into dark prominence on the ridge just above his camp. They were silhouetted against the starry sky. The horseman stopped, and he and his steed made a magnificent black statue, somehow wild and strange in Shefford's sight. Then he came on, vanished in the darkness under the ridge, presently to emerge into the circle of campfire light.

He rode to within twenty feet of Shefford and the fire. The horse was dark, wild-looking, and seemed ready to run. The rider appeared to be an Indian and yet had something about him suggesting the cowboy. At once Shefford remembered what Presbrey had said about half-breeds. A little shock, inexplicable to Shefford, rippled over him.

He greeted his visitor but received no answer. Shefford saw a dark, squat figure, bending forward in the saddle. The man was tense. All about him was dark except the glint of a rifle across the saddle. The face under the sombrero was only a shadow. Shefford kicked the fire logs so a brighter blaze lighted the scene. Then he saw this stranger a little more clearly and made out an unusually large head, broad dark face, a sinister, tightly shut mouth, and gleaming black eyes.

Those eyes were unmistakably hostile. They roved searchingly over Shefford's pack, and then over his person. Shefford felt for the gun that Presbrey had given him, but it was gone. He had left it back where he had lost his horse and had not thought of it since. Then a strange, slow-coming, cold agitation possessed Shefford. Something gripped his throat.

Suddenly Shefford was stricken at a menacing movement on the part of the horseman. He had drawn a gun. Shefford saw it shine darkly in the firelight. The Indian meant to murder him. Shefford saw the grim dark face in a kind of horrible amaze. He felt the meaning of that drawn weapon as he had never felt anything before in his life, and he collapsed back into his seat with an icy, sickening terror. In a second he was dripping wet with cold sweat. Lightning swift thoughts flashed through his mind. It had been one of his platitudes that he was not afraid of death. Yet here he was a shaking, helpless coward. What had he learned about either life or death? Would this dark savage plunge him into the unknown? It was then that Shefford realized his hollow philosophy and the bittersweetness of life. He had a brain and a soul and between them he might have worked out his salvation. But what were they to this ruthless night murderer, this raw and horrible wildness of the desert?

Incapable of voluntary movement, with tongue cleaving to the roof of his mouth, Shefford watched the horseman and the half-poised gun. It was not yet leveled. Then it dawned upon Shefford that the stranger's head was turned a little, his ear to the wind. He was listening. His horse was listening. Suddenly he straightened up, wheeled his horse, and trotted away into the darkness. But he did not climb the ridge by which he had come.

Shefford heard the *click* of hoofs up on the stony trail. Other horses and riders were descending into the cañon. They had been the cause of his deliverance, and in the relaxation of feeling he almost fainted. Then he sat there, slowly recovering, slowly ceasing to tremble, divining that this situation was somehow to change his attitude toward life.

Three horses, two with riders, moved in dark shapes across the skyline above the ridge, disappeared as had Shefford's first visitor, and then rode into the light. Shefford saw two Indians, a man and a woman, then with surprise recognized the latter to be the girl he had met at Red Lake. He was still more surprised to recognize the third horse, the one he had lost at the last camp. Shefford rose, a little shaky in his legs, to thank these Indians for a double service. The man slipped from his saddle, and his moccasined feet thudded lightly. He was tall, lithe, erect, a singularly graceful figure, and, as he advanced, Shefford saw a dark face and sharp, dark eyes. The Indian was bare-headed with his hair bound by a band. He resembled the girl but appeared to have a finer face.

"How do," he said in a voice low and distinct. He extended his hand, and Shefford felt a grip of steel. He returned the greeting. Then the Indian gave Shefford the bridle of the horse, and made signs that appeared to indicate the horse had broken his hobbles and strayed. Shefford thanked him. Thereupon, the Indian unsaddled and led the horses away, evidently to water them. The girl remained behind. Shefford addressed her, but she was shy and did not respond. He then set about cooking a meal for his visitors, and was busily engaged at this when the Indian returned without the horses. Presently Shefford resumed his seat by the fire and watched the two eat what he had prepared. They certainly were hungry and soon had the pans and cups empty. Then the girl drew back a little into the shadow while the man sat with his legs crossed and his feet tucked under him.

His dark face was smooth, yet it seemed to have lines under the surface. Shefford was impressed. He had never seen an Indian who interested him as this one. Looked at superficially, he appeared young, wild, silent, locked in his primeval apathy, just a healthy savage, but looked at more attentively he appeared matured, even old, a strange, sad, brooding figure with a burden on his shoulders. Shefford found himself growing curious.

"What place?" asked Shefford, waving his hand toward the dark opening between the black cliffs.

"Sagi," replied the Indian.

That did not mean anything to Shefford, and he asked if the Sagi was the pass, but the Indian shook his head again.

"*Bi-la*," he said.

52

"What you mean?" asked Shefford. "What *bi-la?*"

"Sister," replied the Indian. He spoke the word reluctantly, as if the white man's language did not please him, but the clearness and correct pronunciation surprised Shefford.

"What name . . . what call her?" Shefford asked.

"Glen-Nas-Pa."

"What your name?" inquired Shefford, indicating the Indian.

"Nas-Ta-Bega," answered the Indian.

"Navajo?"

The Indian bowed with what seemed pride and stately dignity.

"My name John Shefford. Come far . . . way back toward rising sun. Come stay here long."

Nas-Ta-Bega's dark eyes were fixed steadily upon Shefford. He reflected that he could not remember having ever felt so penetrating a gaze, but neither the Indian's eyes nor face gave any clue to his thoughts.

"Navajo no savvy Jesus Christ," said the Indian, and his voice rolled out, low and deep.

Shefford felt both amaze and pain. The Indian had taken him for a missionary.

"No! Me no missionary," cried Shefford,

and he flung up a passionately repudiating hand.

A singular flash shot from the Indian's dark eyes. It struck Shefford even at this stinging moment when the past came back.

"Trade . . . buy wool . . . blanket?" queried Nas-Ta-Bega.

"No," replied Shefford. "Me want ride . . . walk far." He moved his hand to indicate a wide sweep of territory. "Me sick."

Nas-Ta-Bega laid a significant finger upon his lungs.

"No," replied Shefford. "Me strong. Sick here." With motions of his hands he tried to show that his was a trouble of the heart.

Shefford received instant impression of this Indian's intelligent comprehension, but he could not tell just what had given him the feeling. Nas-Ta-Bega rose then, and walked away into the shadow. Shefford heard him working around the dead cedar tree, where he had probably gone to get firewood. Then Shefford heard a splintering crash, which was followed by a crunching, bumping sound. Presently he was astounded to see the Indian enter the lighted circle dragging the whole cedar tree trunk first. Shefford would have doubted the ability of two men to drag that tree, and here came Nas-Ta-Bega managing it easily. Nas-Ta-Bega laid the trunk on the fire, and then proceeded to break off small branches, to place them advantageously where the red coals kindled them into a blaze.

The Indian's next move was to place his saddle, which he evidently meant to use for a pillow. Then he spread a great skin on the ground, lay down upon it, with his back to the fire, and, pulling a long-haired saddle blanket over his shoulders, he relaxed and became motionless. His sister Glen-Nas-Pa did likewise, except that she stayed farther away from the fire, and she had a larger blanket, which covered her well. It appeared to Shefford that they went to sleep at once.

Shefford felt as tired as he had ever been, but he did not think he could soon drop into slumber, and, in fact, he did not want to.

There was something in the companionship of these Indians that he had not experienced before. He still had a strange and weak feeling — the aftermath of that fear which had sickened him with its horrible, icy grip. Nas-Ta-Bega's arrival had frightened away that dark and silent prowler of the night, and Shefford was convinced the Indian had saved his life. The measure of his gratitude was a source of wonder to him. Had he cared so much for life? Yes, he had, when face to face with death. That was something to know. It helped him. And he gathered from his strange feelings that the romantic quest that had brought him into the wilderness might turn out to be an antidote for the morbid bitterness of heart.

With new sensations had come new thoughts. Right then it was very pleasant to sit in the warmth and light of the burning cedar fire. There was a deep-seated ache of fatigue in his bones. What joy it was to rest. He had felt the dry scorch of desert thirst and the pang of hunger. How wonderful to learn the real meaning of water and food. He had just finished the longest, hardest day's work of his life. Had that anything to do with something almost like peace that seemed to hover near in the shadows, trying to come to him? He had befriended an Indian girl, and now her brother had paid back the service. Both the giving and receiving were somehow sweet to Shefford. They opened up hitherto vague channels of thought. For ten years he had imagined he was serving people, when he had never lifted a hand. A blow given in the defense of an Indian girl had somehow operated to make a change in John Shefford's existence. It had liberated a spirit in him. Moreover, it had worked its influence outside his mind. The Indian girl and her brother had followed his trail to return his horse, perhaps to guide him safely, but, unknowingly perhaps, they had done infinitely more than that for him. As Shefford's eye wandered over the dark, still figures of the sleepers, he had a strange, dreamy premonition, or perhaps only a fancy, that there was to be more come of this fortunate meeting. For the rest it was good to be there in the speaking silence, to feel the heat on his outstretched palms and the cold wind on his cheek, to see the black wall lifting its bold outline and the crags reaching for the white stars.

Chapter Three

The stamping of horses awoke Shefford. He saw a towering crag, rosy in the morning light, like a huge red spear splitting the clear blue of sky. He got up, feeling cramped and sore, yet with unfamiliar exhilaration. The nipping air made him stretch his hands to the fire. An odor of coffee and broiled meat mingled with the fragrance of wood smoke. Glen-Nas-Pa was on her knees, broiling a rabbit on a stick over the coals. Nas-Ta-Bega was saddling the ponies. The cañon appeared to be full of purple shadows under one side of dark cliffs and golden streaks of mist on the other where the sun struck high up on the walls.

"Good morning," said Shefford.

Glen-Nas-Pa shyly replied in Navajo.

"How," was Nas-Ta-Bega's greeting.

In daylight the Indian lost some of the dark somberness of face that had impressed Shefford. He had a noble head, in poise like that of an eagle, a bold, clean-cut profile and stern, close-shut lips. His eyes were the most attractive and striking feature about him. They were coal-black and piercing. The intent look out of them seemed to come from a keen and inquisitive mind.

Shefford ate breakfast with the Indians, and then helped with the few preparations for departure. Before they mounted, Nas-Ta-Bega pointed to horse tracks in the dust. They were those that had been made by Shefford's threatening visitor of the night before. Shefford explained by word and sign, and succeeded at least in showing that he had been in danger. Nas-Ta-Bega followed the tracks a little way, and presently returned.

"Shadd," he said with an ominous shake of his head. Shefford did not understand whether he meant the name of his visitor or something else, but the menace connected with the word was clear enough.

Glen-Nas-Pa mounted her pony, and it was a graceful action that pleased Shefford. He climbed a little stiffly into his own saddle. Then Nas-Ta-Bega got up, and pointed northward.

"Kayenta?" he inquired.

Shefford nodded, and then they were off with Glen-Nas-Pa in the lead. They did not climb the trail that they had descended but took one leading to the right along the base of the slope. Shefford saw down into the red wash that bisected the cañon floor. It was a sheer wall of red clay or loam, a hundred feet high, and at the bottom ran a swift shallow stream of reddish water. Then for a time a high growth of greasewood hid the surroundings from Shefford's sight. Presently the trail led out into the open, and Shefford saw he was at the neck of a wonderful valley that gradually widened with great, jagged, red peaks on the left and the black mesa, now a mountain, running away to the right. He turned to find that the opening of the Sagi could no longer be seen, and he was conscious of a strong desire to return and explore that cañon.

Soon Glen-Nas-Pa put her pony to a long, easy, swinging canter, and her followers did likewise. As they got outward into the valley, Shefford lost the sense of being overshadowed and crowded by the nearness of huge walls and crags. The trail appeared level underfoot, but at a distance it was seen to climb. Shefford found where it disappeared over the foot of a slope that formed a graceful, rising line up to the cedared flank of the mesa. The valley floor, widening away to the north, remained level and green. Beyond rose the jagged range of red peaks, all strangely cut and slanting. These distant, deceiving features of the country held Shefford's gaze till the Indian drew his attention to things near at hand. Then Shefford saw flocks of sheep dotting the gray-green valley and bands of beautiful, long-maned, long-tailed ponies.

For several miles the scene did not change except that Shefford imagined he came to see where the upland plain ended, or at least broke its level. He was right, for presently the Indians pointed, and Shefford went on to halt upon the edge of a steep slope leading down into a valley vast in its barren gray reaches.

"Kayenta," said Nas-Ta-Bega.

Shefford at first saw nothing except the monotonous gray valley reaching far to strange grotesque monuments of yellow cliffs. Then close under the foot of the slope he espied two squat houses with red roofs and a corral with a pool of water shining in the sun.

The trail leading down was steep and sandy, but it was not long. Shefford's sweeping eyes appeared to take in everything at once, the crude stone structures with their earthen roofs, the piles of dirty wool, the Indians lolling around, the tents and wagons and horses, little lazy burros and dogs, and scattered everywhere saddles, blankets, guns, and packs.

There a white man came out of the door. He waved a hand and shouted. Dust and wool and flour were thick upon him. He was muscular and weather-beaten, and appeared young in activity rather than face. A gun swung at his hip and a row of brass-tipped cartridges showed in his belt. Shefford looked into a face that he thought he had seen before, till he realized the similarity was only the bronze and hard line and rugged cast common to desert men. The gray, searching eyes went right through him.

"Glad to see you. Get down and come in. Just heard from an Indian you were coming. I'm the trader, Withers," he said to Shefford. His voice was welcoming, and the grip of his hand made Shefford's ache.

Shefford told his name, and said he was as glad as he was lucky to arrive at Kayenta.

"Hello! Nas-Ta-Bega!" exclaimed Withers. His tone expressed a surprise his face did not show. "Did this Indian bring you in?"

Withers shook hands with the Navajo while Shefford briefly related what he owed to him. Then Withers looked at Nas-Ta-Bega and spoke to him in the Indian tongue.

"Shadd," said Nas-Ta-Bega.

Withers let out a dry little laugh, and his strong hand tugged at his mustache.

"Who's Shadd?" asked Shefford.

"He's a half-breed Ute . . . bad Indian, outlaw, murderer. He's in with a gang of outlaws who hide in the San Juan country. Reckon you're lucky. How'd you come to be there in the Sagi alone?"

"I traveled from Red Lake. Presbrey, the trader there, advised against it, but I came anyway."

"Well." Wither's gray glance was kind if it did express the foolhardiness of Shefford's act. "Come into the house. Never mind the horse. My wife will sure be glad to see you."

Withers led Shefford by the first stone house, which evidently was the trading store, into the second. The room Shefford entered was large, with logs smoldering in a huge open fireplace, blankets covering every foot of floor space, and Indian baskets and silver ornaments everywhere, with strange Indian designs painted upon the white-washed walls. Withers called his wife and made her acquainted with Shefford. She was a slight comely little woman, with keen, earnest, dark eyes. She seemed to be serious and quiet, but she made Shefford feel at home immediately. He refused, however, to accept the room offered him, saying that he meant to sleep out under the open sky. Withers laughed at this and said he understood. Shefford, remembering Presbrey's hunger for news of the outside world, told this trader and his wife all he could think of, and he was listened to with that close attention a traveler always gained in the remote places.

"Sure am glad you rode in," said Withers for the fourth time. "Now, you make yourself at home. Stay here . . . come over to the store . . . do what you like. I've got work. Tonight we'll talk."

Shefford went out with his host. The store was as interesting as Presbrey's although much smaller and more primitive. It was full of everything and smelled strongly of sheep and goats. There was a narrow aisle between sacks of flour and blankets on one side and a high counter on the other. Behind this counter Withers stood to wait upon Indian customers. They sold blankets and skins and bags of wool, and in exchange took silver money. Then they lingered and with slow staid reluctance bought one thing and then another — flour, sugar, canned goods, coffee, tobacco, ammunition. The counter was never without two or three Indians leaning on their dark, silver-braceleted arms. But as they were slow to sell and buy and go, so were others slow to come in. Their voices were soft and low, and it seemed to Shefford they were whispering. He liked to hear them and to look at the banded beads, the long, twisted rolls of black hair tied with white cords, the still, dark faces and watchful eyes, the silver earrings, the slender, shapely brown hands, the lean and sinewy shapes, the corduroys with a belt and gun, and the small, close-fitting buckskin moccasins buttoned with coins. These Indians all appeared young, and under the quiet, slow demeanor there was fierce blood and fire.

By and by two women came in, evidently squaw and daughter. The former was a huge, stout Indian with a face that was certainly pleasant, if not jolly. She had the corners of a blanket tied under her chin and in the folds behind on her broad back was a naked Indian baby, round and black of head, brown-skinned, with eyes as bright as beads. When the youngster caught sight of Shefford, he made a startled dive into the sack of the blanket. Manifestly, however, curiosity got the better of fear, for presently Shefford caught a pair of wondering dark eyes peeping at him.

"They're good spenders, but slow," said

Withers. "The Navajos are careful and cautious. That's why they're rich. This squaw, Yan-As-Pa, has flocks of sheep and more mustangs than she knows about."

"Mustangs. So that's what you call the ponies," replied Shefford.

"Yep. They're mustangs and mostly wild as jack rabbits."

Shefford strolled outside and made the acquaintance of Withers's helper, a Mormon named Whisner. He was a stockily built man past maturity, and his sun-blistered face and watery eyes told of the open desert. He was engaged in weighing sacks of wool brought in by the Indians. Nearby stood a framework of poles from which an immense bag was suspended. From the top of this bag protruded the head and shoulders of an Indian who appeared to be stamping and packing wool with his feet. He grinned at the curious Shefford, but Shefford was more interested in the Mormon. So far as he knew, Whisner was the first man of that creed he had ever met and he could scarcely hide his eagerness. Venters's stories had been of a long-past generation of Mormons, fanatical, ruthless, and unchangeable. Shefford did not expect to meet Mormons of this kind, but any man of that religion would have interested him.

Besides, this Whisner seemed to bring him closer to that wild, secret cañon he had come West to find. Shefford was somewhat amazed and discomfited to have his polite and friendly overtures repulsed. Whisner might have been an Indian. He was cold, incommunicative, aloof, and there was something about him that made the sensitive Shefford feel his presence was resented.

Presently Shefford strolled to a corral that was full of shaggy mustangs. They snorted and kicked at him. He had a half-formed wish that he would never be called upon to ride any of those wild brutes, and then he found himself thinking that he would ride one of them, and after a while any of them. Shefford did not understand himself, but he fought his natural instinctive reluctance to meet obstacles, peril, suffering.

He traced the white-bordered little stream that made the pool in the corral, and, when he came to where it oozed out of the sand under the bluff, he decided it was not the spring that had made Kayenta famous. Down below the trading post he saw a trough from which burros were drinking. Here he found the spring, a deep well of eddying water walled in by stones, and the overflow made a shallow stream meandering away between its borders of alkali, like a crust of salt. Shefford tasted the water. It bit, but it was good.

Shefford had no trouble in making friends with the lazy, sleepy-eyed burros. They let him pull their long ears and rub their noses, but the mustangs standing around were unapproachable. They had wild eyes, raised long ears, and looked vicious. He let them alone.

Evidently this trading post was a great deal busier than Red Lake. Shefford counted a dozen Indians lounging outside, and there were others riding away. Big wagons told how the bags of wool were transported out of the wilds and how supplies were brought in. A wide, hard-packed road led off to the east, and another, not so clearly defined, wound away to the north. Indian trails streaked off in all directions. Shefford discovered, however, when he had walked off a mile or so across the valley to lose sight of the post, that the feeling of wildness and loneliness returned to him. It was a wonderful country. It held something for him besides the possible rescue of an imprisoned girl from a wild cañon.

That night after supper, when Withers and Shefford sat alone before the blazing logs in the huge fireplace, the trader laid his

hands on Shefford's and said with directness and force: "I've lived my life in the
desert. I've met many men and have been a
friend to most. You're no prospector or
trader or missionary?"

"No," replied Shefford.

"You've had trouble?"

"Yes."

"Have you come in here to hide? Don't be
afraid to tell me. I won't give you away."

"I didn't come to hide."

"Then no one is after you? You've done
no wrong?"

"Perhaps I wronged myself, but no one
else," replied Shefford steadily.

"I reckoned so. Well, tell me, or keep your
secret . . . it's all one to me."

Shefford felt a desire to unburden himself. This man was strong, persuasive,
kindly. He drew Shefford.

"You're welcome in Kayenta," went on
Withers. "Stay as long as you like. I take no
pay from a white man. If you want work, I
have it aplenty."

"Thank you. That is good. I need to work.
We'll talk of it later. But just yet I can't tell
you why I came to Kayenta, what I want to
do, how long I shall stay. My thoughts put in
words would seem so like dreams. Maybe
they are dreams. Perhaps I'm only chasing a

phantom . . . perhaps I'm only hunting the treasure at the foot of the rainbow."

"Well, this is the country for rainbows." Withers laughed. "In summer from June to August, when it storms, we may have rainbows that'll make you think you're in another world. The Navajos have rainbow mountains, rainbow cañons, rainbow bridges of stone. It sure is rainbow country."

That deep and mystic chord in Shefford thrilled. Here it was again — something tangible at the bottom of his dream.

Withers did not wait for Shefford to say any more, and, almost as if he read his visitor's mind, he began to talk about the wild country he called home. He had lived at Kayenta for several years — hard and profitless years by reason of marauding outlaws. He could not have lived here at all but for the protection of the Indians. His father-in-law had been friendly with the Navajos and Paiutes for many years, and his wife had been brought up among them. She was held in peculiar reverence and affection by both tribes in that part of the country. Probably she knew more of the Indians' habits, religion, and life than any white person in the West. Both tribes were friendly and peaceable, but there were bad Indians, half-breeds and outlaws, that made the trading post a venture Withers had long considered precarious, and he wanted to move and intended to someday. His nearest neighbors in New Mexico and Colorado were a hundred miles distant, and at some seasons the roads were impassable. In the north, however, twenty miles or so from Kayenta was situated a Mormon village named Stonebridge. It lay across the Utah line. Withers did some business with this village, but scarcely enough to warrant the risks he had to run. During the last year he had lost several pack trains, one of which he had never heard of after it left Stonebridge.

"Stonebridge!" exclaimed Shefford, and he trembled. He had heard that name. In his memory it had a place beside the name of another village. Shefford longed to speak of it to this trader.

"Yes . . . Stonebridge," replied Withers. "Ever heard the name?"

"I think so. Are there other villages in . . . in that part of the country?"

"A few, but not close. Glaze is now only a water hole. Bluff and Monticello are far north across the San Juan. There used to be another village . . . but that wouldn't interest you."

"Maybe it would," replied Shefford quietly.

But his hint was not taken by the trader. Withers suddenly showed a semblance of the aloofness Shefford had observed in Whisner.

"Withers, pardon an impertinence . . . I am deeply serious. Are you a Mormon?"

"Indeed, I'm not," replied the trader instantly.

"Are you for the Mormons or against them?"

"Neither. I get along with them. I know them. I believe they are a misunderstood people."

"That's being for them."

"No. I'm only fair-minded."

Shefford paused, trying to curb his thrilling impulse, but it was too strong. "You said there used to be another village. Was the name of it . . . Cottonwoods?"

Withers gave a start, and faced around to stare at Shefford in blank astonishment. "Say, did you give me a straight story about yourself?" he queried sharply.

"So far as I went," replied Shefford.

"You're no spy on the look-out for sealed wives?"

"Absolutely not. I don't even know what you mean by sealed wives."

"Well, it's damned strange that you'd know the name Cottonwoods. Yes, that's the name of the village I meant . . . the one that used to be. It's gone now, all except a few stone walls."

"What became of it?"

"Torn down by Mormons years ago. They destroyed it, and moved away. I've heard Indians talk about a grand spring that was there once. It's gone, too. Its name was . . . let me see."

"Amber Spring," interrupted Shefford.

"By George, you're right," rejoined the trader, again amazed. "Shefford, this beats me. I haven't heard that name for ten years. I can't help seeing what a tenderfoot . . . stranger . . . you are to the desert. Yet, here you are . . . speaking of what you should know nothing of. There's more behind this."

Shefford rose, unable to conceal his agitation. "Did you ever hear of a rider named Venters?"

"Rider? You mean cowboy? Venters . . . Venters. No, I never heard that name."

"Did you ever hear of a gunman named Lassiter?" queried Shefford with increasing emotion.

"No."

"Did you ever hear of a Mormon woman named Jane Withersteen?"

"No."

Shefford drew his breath sharply. He had followed a gleam — he had caught a fleeting glimpse of it. "Did you ever hear of a child . . . a girl . . . a woman . . . called Fay Larkin?"

Withers rose slowly with a paling face. "If you're a spy, it'll go hard with you . . . though I'm no Mormon," he said grimly.

Shefford lifted a shaking hand. "I *was* a clergyman. Now I'm nothing . . . a wanderer . . . least of all a spy."

Withers leaned closer to see into the other man's eyes. He looked long, and then appeared satisfied. "I've heard the name Fay Larkin," he said slowly. "I reckon that's all I'll say till you tell your story."

Shefford stood with his back to the fire, and he turned the palms of his hands to catch the warmth. He felt cold. Withers had affected him strangely. What was the meaning of the trader's somber gravity? Why was the very mention of Mormons attended by something austere and secret? "My name is John Shefford. I am twenty-seven," he began. "My family. . . ."

Here a knock on the door interrupted Shefford.

"Come in!" called Withers.

The door opened, and like a shadow Nas-Ta-Bega slipped in. He said something in

Navajo to the trader. "How," he said to Shefford, and extended his hand. He was stately, but there was no mistaking his friendliness. Then he sat down before the fire, doubled his legs under him after the Indian fashion, and with dark eyes on the blazing logs seemed to lose himself in meditation.

"He likes the fire," explained Withers. "Whenever he comes to Kayenta, he always visits me like this. Don't mind him. Go on with your story."

"My family were plain people, well-to-do, and very religious," Shefford resumed. "When I was a boy, we moved from the country to a town called Beaumont, Illinois. There was a college in Beaumont, and eventually I was sent to it to study for the ministry. I wanted to be . . . but never mind that. By the time I was twenty-two, I was ready for my career as a clergyman. I preached for a year around at different places, and then got a church in my hometown of Beaumont. I became exceedingly good friends with a man named Bern Venters, who had recently come to Beaumont. He was a singular man. His wife was a strange, beautiful woman, very reserved, and she had wonderful dark eyes that always seemed to be haunted. They had money and were devoted to each other, and perfectly happy. They owned the finest horses ever seen in Illinois, and their particular enjoyment seemed to be riding. They were always taking long rides. It was something worth going far for to see Missus Venters on a horse.

"It was through my own love of horses that I became friendly with Venters. He and his wife attended my church, and I got to see more of them, so gradually we grew intimate. And it was not till I did get intimate with them that I realized that both seemed to be haunted by the past. They were sometimes sad even in their happiness. They drifted off into dreams. They lived back in another world. They seemed to be listening. Indeed, they were a singularly interesting couple, and I grew genuinely fond of them. By and by they had a little girl who they named Jane. The coming of the baby made a change in my friends. They were happier, and I observed that the haunting shadow did not so often return. Venters had often spoken of a journey West that he and his wife meant to take sometime, but after the baby came, he never mentioned his wife in connection with the trip. I gathered that he felt compelled to go to clear up a mystery or to find something . . . I did not make out just what. But eventually . . . it was about a year ago . . . he told me his story . . . the strangest, wildest, and most tragic I have ever heard.

"I can't tell it all now. Suffice to say that fifteen years before he had been a rider for a rich Mormon woman named Jane Withersteen of the village, Cottonwoods. She had adopted a beautiful Gentile child named Fay Larkin. Her interest in Gentiles earned the displeasure of her churchmen, and, as she was proud, there came a breach. Venters and a gunman named Lassiter became involved in her quarrel. Finally Venters took to the cañons. Here in the wilds he found the strange girl he eventually married. For a long time they lived in a wonderful hidden valley, the narrow entrance to which was guarded by a huge balancing rock. Venters got away with the girl. But Lassiter and Jane Withersteen and the child Fay Larkin were driven into the cañon. They escaped to the valley where Venters had lived. Lassiter rolled the balancing rock, and crashing down the narrow trail it loosened the weathered walls, and closed the narrow outlet forever."

Chapter Four

Shefford ended his narrative out of breath, pale, and dripping with sweat. Withers sat leaning forward with an expression of intense interest. Nas-Ta-Bega's easy, graceful pose had succeeded to one of strained rigidity. He seemed a statue of bronze. Could a few intelligible words, Shefford wondered, have created that strange listening posture?

"Venters got out of Utah, of course, as you know," Shefford went on. "He got out knowing . . . as I feel I would have known . . . that Jane, Lassiter, and little Fay Larkin were shut up, walled up in Surprise Valley. For years Venters considered it would not have been safe for him to venture to rescue them. He had no fears for their lives. They could live in Surprise Valley, but Venters always intended to come back with Bess and find the valley and his friends. No wonder he and Bess were haunted. However, when his wife had the baby, that made a difference. It meant he had to go alone. He was thinking seriously of starting when I . . . when there were developments that made it desirable for me to leave Beaumont. Venters's story haunted me as he had been haunted. I dreamed of that wild valley . . . of little Fay Larkin grown to womanhood . . . such a woman as Bess Venters was. The longing to come was great . . . and Withers . . . here I am."

"Listen to this. I wish I could help you. Life is a queer deal . . . Shefford, I've got to trust you. Over here in the wild cañon country there's a village of Mormons' sealed wives. It's in Arizona, perhaps twenty miles from here, and near the Utah line. When the United States government began to persecute, or prosecute, the Mormons for polygamy, the Mormons over here in Stonebridge took their sealed wives and moved them out of Utah, just across the line. They built houses, established a village there. I'm the only Gentile who knows about it, and I pack supplies every few weeks in to these women. There are perhaps fifty women, mostly young . . . second or third or fourth wives of Mormons . . . sealed wives. I want you to understand that sealed means *sealed* in all that religion or loyalty can get out of the word. There are also some

79

old women and old men in the village, but they hardly count. There's a flock of the finest children you ever saw in your life.

"The idea of the Mormons must have been to escape prosecution. The law of the government is one wife for each man . . . no more. All over Utah polygamists have been arrested. The Mormons are deeply concerned. I believe they are a good, law-abiding people, but this law is a direct blow at their religion. In my opinion they can't obey both, and, therefore, they have not altogether given up plural wives. Perhaps they will someday. I have no proof, but I believe the Mormons of Stonebridge pay secret night visits to their sealed wives across the line in the lonely hidden village.

"Now, once, over in Stonebridge, I overheard some Mormons talking about a girl who was named Fay Larkin. I never forgot the name. Later, I heard the name in this sealed-wife village. But as I told you, I never heard of Lassiter or Jane Withersteen. Still, if Mormons had found them, I would never have heard of it. Deception Pass . . . that might be the Sagi . . . I'm not surprised at your rainbow-chasing adventure. It's a great story. This Fay Larkin I've heard of *might* be your Fay Larkin . . . I almost believe so. Shefford, I'll help you find out."

"Yes, yes . . . I must know," replied Shefford. "Oh, I hope, I pray we can find her. But . . . I'd rather she was dead . . . if she's not still hidden in the valley."

"Naturally. You've dreamed yourself into rescuing this lost Fay Larkin, but, Shefford, you're old enough to know life doesn't work out as you want it to. One way or another, I fear, you're in for bitter disappointment."

"Withers, take me to the village."

"Shefford, you're liable to get in bad out here," said the trader gravely.

"I couldn't be any more ruined than I am now," replied Shefford passionately.

"But there's risk in this . . . risk such as you never had," persisted Withers.

"I'll risk anything."

"Reckon this is a funny deal for a sheep trader to have on his hands. Shefford, I like you. I've a mind to see you through this. It's a damned strange story. I'll tell you what . . . I will help you. I'll give you a job packing supplies in to the village. I meant to turn that over to a Mormon cowboy . . . Joe Lake. The job shall be yours, and I'll go with you first trip. Here's my hand on it. Now, Shefford, I'm more curious about you than I was before you told your story. What ruined you? As we're to be partners, you can tell me now. I'll keep your secret.

Maybe I can do you good."

Shefford wanted to confess, yet it was hard. Perhaps had he not been so agitated, he would not have answered to impulse. But this trader was a man, a man of the desert, and he would understand.

"I told you I was a clergyman," said Shefford in a low voice. "I didn't want to be one, but they made me one. I did my best. I failed. I had doubts of religion . . . of the Bible . . . in God, as my church believed in them. As I grew older, thought and study convinced me of the narrowness of religion as my congregation lived it. I preached what I believed. I alienated them. They put me out, took my calling from me, disgraced me, ruined me."

"So that's all!" exclaimed Withers slowly. "You didn't believe in the God of the Bible. Well, I've been in the desert long enough to know there *is* a God, but probably not the one your church worships. Shefford, go to the Navajo for a faith."

Shefford had forgotten the presence of Nas-Ta-Bega, and perhaps Withers had likewise. At this juncture the Indian rose to his full height, and he folded his arms to stand with the somber pride of a chieftain while his dark, inscrutable eyes were riveted upon Shefford. At that moment he seemed magnificent. How infinitely more he seemed than just a common Indian who had chanced to befriend a white man. The difference was obscure to Shefford, but he felt that it was there in the Navajo's mind. Nas-Ta-Bega's strange look was not to be interpreted. Now he turned and passed from the room.

"By George!" cried Withers suddenly, and he pounded his knee with his fist. "I'd forgotten."

"What?" ejaculated Shefford.

"Why, that Indian understood every word we said. He knows English. He's educated. Well, if this doesn't beat me. . . . Let me tell you about Nas-Ta-Bega." Withers appeared to be recalling something half forgotten. "Years ago, in 'Fifty-Seven I think, Kit Carson with his soldiers chased the Navajo tribes and rounded them up to be put on reservations. But he failed to catch all the members of one tribe. They escaped up into wild cañons like the Sagi. The descendants of these fugitives live there now and are the finest Indians on earth . . . the finest because unspoiled by the white man. Well, as I got the story, years after Carson's roundup, one of his soldiers guided some interested travelers in here. When they left, they took an Indian boy with them to educate. From what I know of Navajos, I'm inclined to think the boy was taken against his parents' wishes. Anyway, he was taken. That boy was Nas-Ta-Bega. The story goes that he was educated somewhere. Years afterward, and perhaps not long before I came here, he returned to his people. There have been missionaries and other interested fools who have given Indians a white man's education. In all the instances I know of, these educated Indians returned to their tribes, repudiating the white man's knowledge, habits, life, and religion. I've heard that Nas-Ta-Bega came back, laid down the white man's clothes along with the education, and never again showed that he had known either.

"You have just seen how strangely he acted. It's almost certain he heard our conversation. Well, it doesn't matter. He won't tell. He can hardly be made to use an English word. Besides, he's a noble red man, if there ever was one. He's been a friend in need to me. If you stay long out here, you'll learn something from the Indians. Nas-Ta-Bega has befriended you, too, it seems. I thought he showed unusual interest in you."

"Perhaps that was because I saved his sister . . . well, to be charitable . . . from the rather rude advances of a white man," said Shefford, and he proceeded to tell of the incident that had occurred at Red Lake.

"Willetts!" exclaimed Withers with much the same expression that Presbrey had used. "I've never met him. But I know about him. He's . . . well, the Indians don't like him much. Most of the missionaries are good men . . . good for the Indians, in a way, but sometimes one drifts out here who is bad. A bad missionary teaching religion to supposed savages! Queer, isn't it? The queerest part is the white people's blindness . . . the blindness of those who send the missionaries. Well, I dare say, Willetts isn't very good. When Presbrey said that was Willetts's way of teaching religion, he meant just what he said. If Willetts drifts over here, he'll be risking much. What you've told me explains Nas-Ta-Bega's friendliness toward you, and also his bringing his sister Glen-Nas-Pa to live with relatives up in the pass. She had been living near Red Lake."

"Do you mean Nas-Ta-Bega wants to keep his sister far removed from Willetts?" inquired Shefford.

"I mean that," replied Withers, "and I hope he's not too late."

Later Shefford went outdoors to walk and think. There was no moon, but the stars made light enough to cast his shadow on the ground. The dark, illimitable expanse of blue sky seemed to be glittering with numberless points of fire. The air was cold and still. A dreaming silence lay over the land. Shefford saw and felt all these things, and their effect was continuous and remained with him and helped calm him. He was conscious of a burden removed from his mind. Confession of his secret had been like tearing a thorn from his flesh, but once done it afforded him relief and a singular realization that out here it did not matter much. In a crowd of men, all looking at him and judging him by their standards, he had been made to suffer. Here, if he were judged at all, it would be by what he could do, how he sustained himself and helped others.

He walked far across the valley toward the low bluffs, but they did not seem to get any closer. Finally he stopped beside a stone, and looked around at the strange horizon and up at the heavens. He did not feel utterly aloof from them, nor alone in a wasteland, nor a useless atom amid incomprehensible forces. Something like a loosened mantle fell from about him, dropping down at his feet, and all at once he was conscious of freedom. He did not understand in the least why abasement left him, but it was so. He had come a long way, in bitterness, in despair, believing himself to be what men had called him. The desert and the stars and the wind, the silence of the night, the loneliness of this vast country where there was room for a thousand cities, these somehow vaguely yet surely bade him lift his head. They withheld their secret, but they made a promise. The thing that he had been feeling every day and every night was a strange, enveloping comfort. It was at this moment that Shefford, divining whence his help was to come, embraced all that wild and speaking nature around and above him, and surrendered himself utterly.

"I'm young. I am free. I have my life to live," he said. "I'll be a man. I'll take what comes. Let me learn here!"

When he had spoken out, settled once and forever his attitude toward his future, he seemed to be born again, wonderfully alive to the influences around him, ready to trust what yet remained a mystery.

Then his thoughts reverted to Fay Larkin. Could this girl be known to Mormons? It was possible. Fay Larkin was an unusual name. Deeply into Shefford's heart had sunk the story Venters had told. Shefford found that he had unconsciously created a like romance — he had been loving a wild and strange and lonely girl, like beautiful

Bess Venters. It was a shock to learn the truth, but as it had been only a dream, it could hardly be vital.

Shefford retraced his steps toward the post. Halfway back he espied a tall, dark figure moving toward him, and presently the shape and the step seemed familiar. Then he recognized Nas-Ta-Bega. Soon they were face to face. Shefford felt that the Indian had been trailing him over the sand, and that this was to be a significant meeting. Remembering Withers's revelation about the Navajo, Shefford knew how to approach him now. There was no difference to be made out in Nas-Ta-Bega's dark face and inscrutable eyes, yet there was a difference to be felt in his presence. The Indian did not speak, and turned to walk by Shefford's side. Shefford could not long be silent.

"Nas-Ta-Bega, were you looking for me?" he asked.

"You had no gun," replied the Indian. But for his very low voice, his slow speaking of the words, Shefford would have thought him a white man. For Shefford there was, indeed, an instinct in this meeting, and he turned to face the Navajo.

"Withers told me that you had been educated . . . that you came back to the desert . . . that you never showed your training.

Nas-Ta-Bega, did you understand all I had told Withers?"

"Yes," replied the Indian.

"You won't betray me?"

"I am a Navajo."

"Nas-Ta-Bega, you trail me . . . you say I have no gun." Shefford wanted to ask this Indian if he cared to be the white man's friend, but the question was not easy to put and, besides, seemed unnecessary. "I am alone and strange in this wild country. I must learn."

"Nas-Ta-Bega will show you the trails and the water holes and how to hide from Shadd."

"For money . . . for silver you will do this?" inquired Shefford.

Shefford felt that the Indian's silence was a rebuke. He remembered Withers's singular praise of this red man. He realized he must change his idea of Indians. "Nas-Ta-Bega, I know nothing. I feel like a child in the wilderness. When I speak, it is out of the mouths of those who have taught me. I must find a new voice and a new life. You heard my story to Withers. I am an outcast from my own people. If you will be my friend . . . be so."

The Indian clasped Shefford's hand, and held it in a response that was more beautiful for its silence. So they stood for a moment in the starlight, and Shefford felt born in him brotherhood for Nas-Ta-Bega.

"Nas-Ta-Bega, what did Withers mean when he said go to the Navajos for a faith?" asked Shefford.

"He meant the desert is my mother. Will you go with Nas-Ta-Bega into the cañons and the mountains?"

"Indeed, I will."

They unclasped hands, and turned toward the trading post.

"Nas-Ta-Bega, have you spoken my tongue to any other white man since you returned to your home?" asked Shefford.

"No."

"Why do you . . . why are you different with me?"

The Indian maintained silence.

"Is it because of . . . of Glen-Nas-Pa?" inquired Shefford.

Nas-Ta-Bega stalked on, still silent, but Shefford divined that, although his service to Glen-Nas-Pa never would be forgotten, still it was not wholly responsible for the Indian's subtle sympathy.

"*Bi-nai* . . . the Navajo will call his white friend *bi-nai* . . . brother," said Nas-Ta-Bega, and he spoke haltingly, not as if words were hard to find but strange to speak. "I was stolen from my mother's hogan and taken to California. They kept me ten years in a mission at San Bernardino and four years in a school. They said my color and my hair were all that was left of the Indian in me, but they could not see my heart. They took fourteen years of my life. They wanted to make me a missionary among my own people, but the white man's ways and his life and his God are not the Indian's. They never can be."

How strangely productive of thought for Shefford to hear the Indian talk. What fatality in this meeting and friendship. Upon Nas-Ta-Bega had been forced education, training, religion that had made him something more and something less than an Indian. It was something assimilated from the white man which made the Indian unhappy and alien in his own home — something meant to be good for him and his kind that had ruined him. Shefford felt the passion and the tragedy of this Navajo.

"*Bi-nai,* the Indian is dying!" Nas-Ta-Bega's low voice was deep and wonderful with its intensity of feeling. "The white man robbed the Indian of lands and homes, drove him into the deserts, made him a gaunt and sleepless spiller of blood. The blood is all spilled now for the Indian is broken. But the white man sells him rum and seduces his daughters. He will not leave the Indian in peace with his own God! *Binai*, the Indian is dying."

That night Shefford lay in his blankets out under the open sky and the stars. The earth had never meant much to him and now it was a bed. He had preached of the heavens, but till now had never studied them. An Indian slept beside him, and not till the gray of morning had blotted out the starlight did Shefford close his eyes.

With the break of the next day came full, varied, and stirring incidents for Shefford. He was strong, although unskillful at most kinds of outdoor tasks. Withers had work for ten men, if they could have been found. Shefford dug and packed and lifted till he was so sore and tired that rest was a blessing.

He never succeeded in getting on a friendly footing with the Mormon, Whisner, although he kept up his agreeable and kindly advances. He listened to the trader's wife as she told him about the Indians, and what he learned he did not forget. His wonder and respect increased in proportion to his knowledge.

One day the Mormon for whom Withers had been waiting rode into Kayenta. His name was Joe Lake. He appeared young and slipped off his superb bay with a grace and activity that was astounding in one of his huge bulk. He had a still, smooth face the color of red bronze and the expression of a cherub, big, soft, dark eyes, and a winning smile. He was surprisingly different from Whisner, or any Mormon character that Shefford had imagined. His costume was that of a cowboy on active service, and he packed a gun at his hip. The handshake he gave Shefford was an ordeal for that young man and left him with his whole right side momentarily benumbed.

"I sure am glad to meet you," he said in lazy, mild voice. He was taking friendly stock of Shefford when the bay mustang reached with vicious muzzle to bite at him. Lake gave a jerk on the bridle that almost brought the mustang to his knees. He reared then, snorted, and came down to plant his forefeet widely apart, and watch his master with defiant eyes. This mustang was the finest horse Shefford had ever seen. He appeared quite large for his species, was almost red in color, had a racy and powerful build, and a fine Thorough-bred head with dark, fiery eyes. He did not look mean, but he had spirit.

"Navvy, you've sure got bad manners," said Lake, shaking the mustang's bridle. He spoke as if he were chiding a refractory little boy. "Didn't I break you better'n that? What's this gentleman goin' to think of you? Tryin' to bite my ear off!"

Lake had arrived about the middle of the forenoon, and Withers announced his intention of packing at once for Rainbow Cañon. Indians were sent out on the ranges to drive in burros and mustangs. Shefford had his thrilling expectancy somewhat chilled by what he considered must have been Lake's reception of the trader's plan. Lake seemed to oppose him, and evidently it took vehemence and argument on Withers's part to make the Mormon tractable. "You fellows got to be good friends," he said. "You'll have charge of my pack trains. Nas-Ta-Bega wants to go with you. I'll feel safer about my supplies and stock than I've ever been. Joe, I'll back this stranger for all I'm worth. He's square . . . and, Shefford, Joe Lake is a Mormon of the younger generation. I meant to start you right. You can trust him as you trust me. He's white clean through. And he's the best horse wrangler in Utah."

It was Lake who again offered his hand,

and Shefford made haste to meet it with his own. Neither of them spoke. Shefford intuitively felt an alteration in Lake's regard, or at least a singular increase of interest. Lake had been told that Shefford had been a clergyman, was now a wanderer without any religion. Again it seemed to Shefford that he owed a forming of friendship to this singular fact. It hurt him, but strangely it came to him that he had taken a liking to a Mormon.

About one o'clock the pack train left Kayenta. Nas-Ta-Bega led the way up the slope. Following him climbed half a dozen patient, plodding, heavily laden burros. Withers came next, and he turned in his saddle to wave good bye to his wife. Joe Lake appeared to be busy keeping a red mule and a wild gray mustang and a couple of restive blacks on the trail. Shefford brought up the rear.

His mount was a beautiful black mustang with three white feet, a white spot on his nose, and a mane that swept to his knees. "His name's Nack-Yal," Withers had said. "It means two-bits, or twenty-five cents. He ain't worth more." To look at Nack-Yal had pleased Shefford very much, indeed, but once upon his back Shefford grew dubious. The mustang acted queerly. He actually looked back at Shefford, and it was a look of speculation and disdain. Shefford took exception to Nack-Yal's manner and to his reluctance to go, and especially to a habit the mustang had of turning off the trail to the left. Shefford had managed some rather spirited horses back in Illinois, and, although he was willing and eager to learn all over again, he did not enjoy the prospect of Lake and Withers seeing this black mustang show what a novice he was. He guessed that was just what Nack-Yal intended to do. However, once up over the hill with Kayenta out of sight, Nack-Yal trotted along fairly well, needing only now and then to be pulled back from his strange swinging to the left off the trail.

The pack train traveled steadily and soon crossed the upland plain to descend into the valley again. Shefford saw the jagged red peaks with an emotion he could not name. The cañons between them were purple in the shadows. The great walls and slopes brightened to red, and the tips were golden in the sun. Shefford forgot all about his mustang and the trail. Suddenly with a pound of hoofs Nack-Yal seemed to rise. He leaped sidewise out of the trail, came down stiff-legged. Then Shefford shot out of the saddle. He landed so hard that he was stunned for an instant. Sitting up, he saw the mustang, bent down, eyes and ears showing fight, and his forefeet spread. He appeared to be looking at something in the trail. Shefford got up, and soon saw what had been the trouble. A long crooked stick, rather thick and black and yellow, lay in the trail, and any mustang looking for an excuse to jump might have mistaken it for a rattlesnake. Nack-Yal appeared disposed to be satisfied and gave Shefford no trouble in mounting. The incident increased Shefford's dubiousness. These Arizona Mustangs were unknown quantities.

Thereafter, Shefford had an eye for the trail rather than the scenery, and this procedure held till the pack train entered the mouth of the Sagi. Then those wonderful lofty cliffs with their peaks and towers and spires loomed, so close and so beautiful, that he did not care if Nack-Yal did throw him. Along here, however, the mustang behaved well, and Shefford decided that, if it had been otherwise, he would have walked. The trail suddenly stood on end and led down into the deep wash where some days before he had seen the stream of reddish water. This day there appeared to be less water and it was not so red. Nack-Yal sank deeply as he took short and careful steps down. The burros and the other mustangs were drinking, and Nack-Yal followed suit. The Indian, with a hand clutching his mustang's mane, rode up a steep sandy slope on the other side that Shefford would not have believed any horse could climb. The burros plodded up and over the rim with Withers calling to them. Joe Lake swung his rope and cracked the flanks of the gray mare and the red mule, and the way the two kicked was a revelation and a warning to Shefford. When his turn came to climb the trail, he got off and walked, an action that Nack-Yal appeared fully to appreciate.

From the head of this wash the trail wound away up the widening cañon, through greasewood flats and over grassy levels, and across sandy stretches. The looming walls made the valley look narrow, yet it must have been half a mile wide. The slopes under the cliffs were dotted with huge stones and cedar trees. There were deep indentations in the walls, running back to form box cañons, choked with green of cedar and spruce and piñon. These notches haunted Shefford, and he was ever on the look-out for more of them.

Withers came back to ride alongside and began to talk. "Reckon this Sagi Cañon is your Deception Pass," he said. "It's sure a queer hole. I've been lost more than once hunting mustangs in here. I've an idea Nas-

Ta-Bega knows all this country. He just pointed out a cliff dwelling to me. See it . . . there, 'way up in the cave of the wall?"

Shefford saw a steep, rough slope leading up to a bridge of the cliff, and finally he made out strange little houses with dark, eye-like windows. He wanted to climb up there. Withers called his attention to more caves with what he believed were the ruins of cliff dwellings. As they rode along, the trader showed him remarkable formations of rock where the elements were slowly hollowing out a bridge. They came presently to a region of intersecting cañons, and here the breaking of the trail up and down the deep washes took Withers back to his task with the burros and gave Shefford more concern than he liked with Nack-Yal. The mustang grew unruly and was continuously turning to the left. Sometimes he tried to climb the steep slope. He had to be pulled hard away from the opening cañons on the left. It was strange to Shefford that the mustang never swerved to the right. This habit of Nack-Yal's and the increasing caution needed on the trail took all of Shefford's attention. When he dismounted, however, he had a chance to gaze around, and more and more he grew amazed at the increasing proportions and wildness of the Sagi.

He came at length to a place where a fallen tree blocked the trail. All the rest of the pack train had jumped the log. Nack-Yal balked. Shefford dismounted, pulled the bridle over the mustang's head, and tried to lead him. Nack-Yal refused to budge. Whereupon Shefford got a stick, and, re-mounting, he gave the balking mustang a cut across the flank. Then something violent happened. Mostly it was swift movement. Shefford received a sudden, propelling jolt, and then he was rising into the air, and then falling. Before he alighted he had a clear image of Nack-Yal in the air above him, bent double, and seemingly possessed of the devil. Then Shefford hit the ground with no light *thud*. He was thoroughly angry when he got dizzily upon his feet, but he was not quick enough to catch the mustang. Nack-Yal leaped easily over the log and went on ahead, dragging his bridle. Shefford hurried after him, and the faster he went, just by so much the cunning Nack-Yal accelerated his gait. As the pack train was out of sight some-where ahead, Shefford could not call to his companions to halt his mount, so he gave up trying and walked on now with free and growing appreciation of his surroundings.

The afternoon had waned. The sun blazed low in the west in a notch of the cañon ramparts, and one wall was darkening into purple shadow while the other shown through a golden haze. It was a weird, wild world to Shefford and every four strides he caught his breath and tried to realize actuality was not a dream.

Nack-Yal kept about a hundred paces to the fore, and ever and anon he looked back to see how his new master was progressing. He diversified these occasions by reaching down and nipping a tuft of grass. Evidently he was too intelligent to go on fast enough to be caught by Withers. Also he kept continually looking up the slope to the left as if seeking a way to climb out of the valley in that direction. Shefford thought it was well the trail lay at the foot of a steep slope that ran up to unbroken bluffs.

The sun set, and the cañon lost its red and its gold and deepened its purple. Shefford calculated he had walked five miles, and, although he did not mind the effort, he would rather have ridden Nack-Yal into camp. He mounted a cedar ridge, crossed some sandy washes, turned a corner of bold wall to enter a wide green level. The mustangs were rolling and snorting. He heard the bray of burros. A bright blaze of campfire greeted him, and the dark figure of the Indian approached to intercept and catch Nack-Yal.

When he stalked into camp, Withers wore a beaming smile, and Joe Lake, who was on his knees making biscuit dough in a pan, stopped proceedings and drawled: "Reckon Nack-Yal bucked you off."

"Bucked! Was that it? Well, he separated himself from me in a new and somewhat painful manner . . . to me."

"Sure I saw that in his eye," replied Lake, and Withers laughed with him.

"Nack-Yal never was well broke," Withers said. "But he's a good mustang, nothing like Joe's Navvy, or that gray mare, Dynamite. All this Indian stock will buck on a man once in a while."

"I'll take the bucking along with the rest," said Shefford.

Both men liked his reply, and the Indian smiled for the first time.

Soon they all sat around a spread tarpaulin and ate like wolves. After supper came the rest and talk before the campfire. Joe Lake was droll. He said the most serious things in a way to make Shefford wonder if he were not joking. Withers talked about the cañon, the Indians, the mustangs, the scorpions running out of the heated sand, and to Shefford it was all like a fascinating book. Nas-Ta-Bega smoked in silence, his brooding eyes upon the fire.

Chapter Five

Shefford was awakened next morning by a sound he had never heard before — the plunging of hobbled horses in soft turf. It was clear daylight with a ruddy color in the sky and a tinge of red along the cañon rim. He saw Withers, Lake, and the Indian driving the mustangs toward camp.

The burros appeared lazy yet willing, but the mustangs and the mule Withers called Red and the gray mare, Dynamite, were determined not to be driven into camp. It was astonishing how much action they had, how much ground they could cover with their forefeet hobbled together. They were exceedingly skillful. They lifted both forefeet at once, and then plunged. They all went in different directions. Nas-Ta-Bega darted in here and there to head off escape.

Shefford pulled on his boots and went out to help. He got too close to the gray mare, and, warned by a yell from Withers, he jumped back just in time to avoid her vicious heels. Then Shefford turned his attention to Nack-Yal and chased him all over the flat in a futile effort to catch him. Nas-Ta-Bega came to Shefford's assistance and put a rope over Nack-Yal's head.

"Don't ever get below one of these mustangs," said Withers warningly, as Shefford came up. "You might be killed. Eat your bite now. We'll soon be out of here."

Shefford had been late in awakening. The others had breakfasted. He found eating somewhat difficult in the excitement that ensued. Nas-Ta-Bega held ropes that were around the necks of Red and Dynamite. The mule showed his cunning and always appeared to present his heels to Withers who tried to approach him with a pack saddle. The patience of the trader was a revelation to Shefford. At length Red was cornered by the three men, the pack saddle was strapped on, and then the packs. Red promptly bucked the packs off, and the work had to be done over again. Then Red dropped his long ears and seemed ready to be tractable.

When Shefford turned his attention to Dynamite, he decided that this was his first sight of a wild horse. The gray mare had wild eyes that rolled and showed the white. She jumped straight up, screamed, pawed, bit, and then plunged down to throw her hind hoofs into the air, as high as her head had been. She was amazingly agile, and she seemed mad to kill something. She dragged the Indian about, and, when Joe Lake got a rope on her hind leg, she dragged them both. They lashed her with the ends of the lassoes which action only made her kick harder. She plunged into camp, drove Shefford flying for his life, knocked down two of the burros, and played havoc with the unstrapped packs. Withers ran to the assistance of Lake, and the two of them hauled back with all their strength and weight. They were both powerful and heavy men. Dynamite circled around and finally, after kicking the campfire to bits, fell down on her haunches in the hot embers. "Let . . . her . . . set . . . there!" panted Withers. Joe Lake shouted: "Blow up, you durn' coyote!" Both men appeared delighted that she had brought upon herself just punishment. Dynamite sat in the remains of the fire long enough to get burned, and then she got up, and meekly allowed Withers to throw a tarpaulin and a roll of blankets over her and tie them fast.

Lake and Withers were sweating freely when this job was finished.

"Say, is that a usual morning's task with

the pack animals?" asked Shefford.

"They're all pretty decent today, except Dynamite," said Withers. "She's got to be worked out."

Shefford felt both amusement and consternation. The sun was just rising over the ramparts of the cañon, and he had already seen more difficult and dangerous work accomplished than half a dozen men of his type could do in a whole day. He liked the outlook of his new job as Withers's assistant, but he felt helplessly inefficient. Still, all he needed was experience. He passed over what he anticipated would be pain and peril; the cost was of no moment.

Soon the pack train was on the move with the Indian leading. This morning Nack-Yal began his strange swinging off to the left, precisely as he had done the day before. It got to be annoying to Shefford, and he lost patience with the mustang and jerked him sharply around. This, however, had no great effect on Nack-Yal.

As the train headed straight up the cañon, Joe Lake dropped back to ride beside Shefford. The Mormon had been amiable and friendly.

"Flock of deer up that draw," he said, pointing up a narrow side cañon. Shefford gazed to see a half dozen small, brown, long-eared objects, very like burros, watching the pack train pass.

"Are they deer?" he asked delightedly.

"Sure are," replied Joe sincerely. "Get down and shoot one. There's a rifle in your saddle sheath."

Shefford had already discovered that he had been armed this morning, a matter that had caused him reflection. These animals certainly looked like deer. He had seen a few deer, although not in their native wild haunts, and he experienced the thrill of the hunter. Dismounting, he drew the rifle out of the sheath and started toward the little cañon.

"Hyar! Where you going with that gun?" yelled Withers. "That's a bunch of burros. Joe's up to his old tricks. Shefford, look out for Joe!"

Rather sheepishly Shefford returned to his mustang and sheathed the rifle, and then took a long look at the animals up the draw. They resembled deer, but upon second glance they sure were burros.

"Durn me! Now if I didn't think they sure were deer!" exclaimed Joe. He appeared absolutely sincere and innocent. Shefford hardly knew how to take this likeable Mormon, but vowed he would be on his guard in the future.

Nas-Ta-Bega soon led the pack train toward the left wall of the cañon, and evidently intended to scale it. Shefford could not see any trail, and the wall appeared steep and insurmountable. But upon nearing the cliff, he saw a narrow broken trail leading zigzag up over smooth rock, weathered slope, and through cracks.

"Spread out, and careful now!" yelled Withers.

The need of this advice soon became manifest to Shefford. The burros started stones to rolling, making danger for those below. Shefford dismounted and led Nack-Yal and turned aside many a rolling rock. The Indian and the burros with the red mule leading climbed steadily, but the mustangs had trouble. Joe's spirited bay had to be coaxed to face the ascent. Nack-Yal balked at every difficult step. Dynamite slipped on a flat slant of rock and slid down forty feet. Withers and Lake with ropes hauled the mare out of the dangerous position. Shefford, who brought up the rear, saw all the action, and it was exciting, but his pleasure in the climb was spoiled by sight of blood and hair on the stones. The climb was crooked, steep, and long, and, when Shefford reached the top of the wall, he was glad to rest. It made him gasp to look down and see what he had surmounted. The cañon floor, green and level, laid a thousand feet below, and the wild burros that had followed on the trail looked like rabbits.

Shefford mounted presently, and rode out upon the wide, smooth trail leading into a cedar forest. There were bunches of gray sage in the open places. The air was cool and crisp, laden with a sweet fragrance. He saw Lake and Withers bobbing along, now on one side of the trail, now on the other, and they kept to a steady trot. Occasionally the Indian and his bright red saddle blanket showed in an opening of the cedars.

It was level country, and there was nothing for Shefford to see except cedar and sage, an outcropping of red rock in places, and the winding trail. Mockingbirds made melody everywhere. Shefford seemed full of a strange pleasure, and the hours flew by. Yet Nack-Yal wanted to be everlastingly turning off the trail, and, moreover, now he wanted to go faster. He was eager, restless, dissatisfied.

At noon the pack train descended into a deep draw, well covered with cedar and sage. There was plenty of grass and shade, but no water. Shefford was surprised to see that every pack was removed. However, the blanket roll was left on Dynamite.

The men made a fire and began to cook a noonday meal. Shefford, tired and warm, sat in a shady spot and watched. He had become all eyes. He had almost forgotten Fay Larkin. He had forgotten his trouble, and the present seemed sweet and full. Soon his ears were filled by a pattering roar, and, looking up the draw, he saw two streams of sheep and goats coming down. Soon an Indian shepherd appeared, and he rode a fine mustang. A cream-colored colt bounded along behind, and then a shaggy dog came in sight. The Indian dismounted at the camp, and his flock spread by in the white and black streams. The dog went with them. Withers and Joe shook hands with the Indian, who Joe called Na-Voy, and Shefford lost no time in doing likewise. Then Nas-Ta-Bega came in, and he and the Navajo talked. When the meal was ready, all of them sat down around the canvas. The shepherd did not tie his horse.

Shefford noticed that Nack-Yal had returned to camp and was acting strangely. Evidently he was attracted by the Indian's mustang or the cream-colored colt. At any rate, Nack-Yal hung around, tossed his head, whinnied in a low nervous manner, and looked strangely eager and wild. Shefford was at first amused, then curious.

Nack-Yal approached too close to the mother of the colt, and she gave him a re-sounding kick in the ribs. Nack-Yal uttered a plaintive snort, and backed away to stand crest-fallen, with all his eagerness and fire vanished.

Nas-Ta-Bega pointed to the mustang and said something in his own tongue. Then Withers addressed the visiting Indian, and they exchanged some words, whereupon the trader turned to Shefford.

"I bought Nack-Yal from this Indian three years ago. This mare is Nack-Yal's mother. He was born over here to the south. That's why he always swings left off the trail. He wants to go home. Just now he recognized his mother, and she whaled away and gave him a whack for his pains. She's got a colt now and probably didn't recognize Nack-Yal. But he's broken-hearted."

The trader laughed, and Joe said: "You can't tell what these durn' mustangs will do." Shefford felt sorry for Nack-Yal and, when it came time to saddle him again, found him easier to handle than ever before. Nack-Yal stood with head down, broken-spirited.

Shefford was the first to ride up out of the draw, and once upon the top of the ridge he halted to gaze, wide-eyed and entranced. A rolling endless plain sloped down beneath him and led on to a distant, round-topped mountain. To the right a red cañon opened its jagged jaws, and away to the north rose a whorled and strange sea of curved ridges, crags, and domes.

Nas-Ta-Bega rode up then, leading the pack train.

"*Bi-nai,* that is Na-Tsis-An," he said, pointing to the mountain. "Navajo Mountain. And there in the north are the cañons."

Shefford followed the Indian down the trail, and soon lost sight of that wide green and red wilderness. Nas-Ta-Bega turned at an intersecting trail, rode down into the cañon, and climbed out on the other side. Shefford got a glimpse now and then of the black domes of the mountains, but for the most part the distant points of the country were hidden. They crossed many trails, and went up and down the sides of many shallow cañons. Troops of wild mustangs whistled at them, stood on ridge tops to watch, and then dash away with manes and tails flying.

Withers rode forward and halted the pack train. He had some conversation with Nas-Ta-Bega, whereupon the Indian turned his horse and trotted back to disappear in the cedars.

"I'm some worried," explained Withers.

"Joe thinks he saw a bunch of horsemen trailing us. My eyes are bad, and I can't see far. The Indian will find out. I took a round-about way to reach the village 'cause I'm always dodging Shadd."

This communication lent an added zest to the journey. Shefford could hardly believe the truth that his eyes and his ears brought to his consciousness. He turned in behind Withers, and rode down the rough trail, helping the mustang with all in his power. It occurred to him that Nack-Yal had been entirely different since that meeting with his mother in the draw. He turned no more off the trail. He answered readily to the rein. He did not look afar from every ridge. Shefford conceived a liking for the mustang.

Withers turned sidewise in his saddle and let his mustang pick the way. "Another time we'd go up around the base of the mountain where you can look down on the grandest scene in the world," he said. "Two hundred miles of wind-worn rock, all smooth and bare, without a single straight line . . . cañons, caves, bridges . . . the most wonderful country in the world. Even the Indians haven't explored it. It's haunted for them, and they have strange gods. The Navajos will hunt on this side of the mountain, but not on the other. That north side is consecrated ground. My wife has long been trying to get the Navajos to tell her the secret of Nonnezoshe. Nonnezoshe means rainbow bridge. The Indians worship it, but as far as she can find out only a few have ever seen it. I imagine it'd be worth some trouble."

"Maybe that's the bridge Venters talked about . . . the one arching over the entrance to Surprise Valley," said Shefford.

"It might be," replied the trader. "You've got a good chance of finding out. Nas-Ta-Bega is the man. You stick to that Indian. Well, we start down here into this cañon, and we go down *some,* I reckon. In half an hour you'll see sago lilies and Indian paintbrush and vermilion cactus."

About the middle of the afternoon the pack train and its drivers arrived at the hidden Mormon village. Nas-Ta-Bega had not returned from his scout, back along the trail. Shefford's sensibilities had all been overly strained, but he had left in him enthusiasm and appreciation that made the situation of this village a fairyland. It was a valley, a cañon floor, so long that he could not see the end. It was perhaps a quarter of a mile wide. The air was hot, still, and sweetly odorous of unfamiliar flowers. Piñon and cedar trees surrounded the little log and stone houses, and along the walls of the cañon stood sharp-pointed, dark-green spruce trees. These walls were singular of shape and color. They were not imposing in height, but they waved like the long, undulating swell of a sea. Every foot of surface was perfectly smooth, and the long, curved lines of darker tinge that streaked the red followed the rounded line of the shape at the top. Far above and back, yet overhanging, were great yellow crags and peaks, and between these, still higher, showed the pine-fringed slope of Navajo Mountain with snow in the sheltered places and glistening streams, like silver threads, running down.

All this Shefford noticed as he entered the valley from around a corner of wall. Upon nearer view he saw and heard a host of children, who, looking up to see the intruders, scattered like frightened quail. Long gray grass covered the ground, and here and there wide, smooth paths had been worn. A swift and murmuring brook ran through the middle of the valley, and its banks were bordered with flowers.

Withers led the way to one side near the wall where a clump of cedar trees and a dark, swift spring boiling out of the rocks, and banks of amber moss with purple blossoms made a beautiful campsite. Here the mustangs were unsaddled, and turned loose without hobbles. It was certainly unlikely that they would leave such a spot. Some of the burros were unpacked, and the others Withers drove off into the village.

"Sure's pretty nice," said Joe, wiping his sweaty face. "I'll never want to leave. It suits me to lie on this moss. Take a drink of that spring."

Shefford complied with alacrity and found the water cool and sweet, and he seemed to feel it all through him. Then he returned to the mossy bank. He did not reply to Joe. In fact, all his faculties were absorbed in watching and feeling, and he lay there long after Joe went off to the village. The murmur of water, the hum of bees, the songs of strange birds, the sweet warm air, the dreamy summer somnolence of the valley — all these added drowsiness to Shefford's weary lassitude, and he fell asleep. When he awoke Nas-Ta-Bega was sitting near him, and Joe was busy around a campfire.

"Hello, Nas-Ta-Bega," said Shefford. "Was there anyone trailing us?"

The Navajo nodded. Joe raised his head and with forceful brevity said: "Shadd."

"Shadd," echoed Shefford, remembering

the dark sinister face of his visitor that night in the Sagi. "Joe, is it serious . . . his trailing us?"

"Well, I don't know how durn' serious it is, but I'm scared to death," replied Lake. "He and his gang will hold us up somewhere on the way home."

Shefford regarded Joe with both concern and doubt. Joe's words were at variance with his looks.

"Say, pard, can you shoot a rifle?" queried Joe.

"Yes. I'm a fair shot at targets."

The Mormon nodded his head as if pleased. "That's good. These outlaws are all poor shots with a rifle. So'm I. But I can handle a six-shooter. I reckon we'll make Shadd sweat if he pushes us."

Withers returned then, driving the burros, all of which had been unpacked down to the saddles. Two gray-bearded men accompanied him. One of them appeared to be very old and vulnerable, and walked with a stick. The other had a sad-lined face and kind, mild eyes. Shefford observed that Lake seemed unusually respectful. Withers introduced these Mormons merely as Smith and Henninger. They were very cordial and pleasant in their greetings to Shefford. Then another, somewhat younger man joined the group, a stalwart, jovial fellow with a ruddy face. There was certainly no mistaking his kindly welcome as he shook Shefford's hand. His name was Beal. The three Mormons stood around the campfire for a while, evidently glad of the presence of fellowmen and to hear news from the outside. Finally they went away, taking Joe with them.

Withers took up the task of getting supper where Joe had left it. "Shefford, listen," he said, as he knelt before the fire. "I told them right out that you'd been a Gentile clergyman . . . that you'd gone back on your religion. It impressed them, and you've been well received. I'll tell the same thing over at Stonebridge. You'll get in right. Of course, I don't expect they'll make a Mormon of you, but they'll try to. Meanwhile, you can be square and friendly, all the time you're trying to find your Fay Larkin. Tomorrow you'll meet some of the women. They're good souls, but like any woman . . . crazy for news. Think what it is to be shut in here between these walls."

"Withers, I'm intensely interested," replied Shefford, "and excited, too. Shall we stay here long?"

"I'll stay a couple of days, then go to Stonebridge with Joe. He'll come back here, and, when you both feel like leaving, and, if

Nas-Ta-Bega thinks it safe, you'll take a trail over to some Indian hogans and pack me out a load of skins and blankets. My boy, you've all the time there is, and I wish you luck. This isn't a bad place to loaf. I always get sentimental over here. Maybe it's the women. Some of them are pretty, and one of them . . . Shefford, I call her Sago Lily. Her first name is Lily, I'm told. Don't know her last name. She's lovely. And I'll bet you'll forget Fay Larkin in a flash. Only . . . be careful. You drop in here with rather peculiar credentials, so to speak . . . as my helper and as a man with no religion. You'll not only be fully trusted, but you'll be welcome to these lonely women. So be careful. Remember, it's my secret belief they are sealed wives and are visited occasionally at night by their husbands. I don't *know* this, but I believe it. And you're not supposed to dream of that."

"How many men in the village?" asked Shefford.

"Three. You've met them."

"Have they wives?" asked Shefford curiously.

"Wives! Well, I guess. But only one each that I know of. Joe Lake is the only unmarried Mormon I've met."

"And no men . . . strangers, cowboys, outlaws ever come to this village?"

"Except to the Indians, it seems to be a secret so far," replied the trader earnestly. "But it can't be kept secret. I've said that time after time even in Stonebridge. With Mormons it's . . . 'sufficient unto the day is the evil thereof'."

"What'll happen when outsiders do learn and ride in here?"

"There'll be trouble . . . maybe bloodshed. Mormon women are absolutely good, but they're human and want and need a little life. And, strange to say, Mormon men are pig-headedly jealous. Why, if some of the cowboys I knew in Durango would ride over here, there'd simply be hell. But that's a long way, and probably this village will be deserted before news of it ever reaches Colorado. There's more danger of Shadd and his gang coming in. Shadd's half Paiute. He must know of this place. And he's got some white outlaws in his gang. Come on. Grub's ready and I'm too hungry to talk."

Later, when shadows began to gather in the valley and the lofty peaks above were golden in the sunset glow, Withers left camp to look after the straying mustangs, and Shefford strolled to and fro under the cedars. The lights and shades in the Sagi that first night had moved him to enthusiastic watchfulness, but here they were so weird and beautiful that he was enraptured. He actually saw great shafts of gold and shadows of purple streaming from the peaks down into the valley. It was day on the heights and twilight in the valley. The swiftly changing colors were like rainbows.

While he strolled up and down, several women came to the spring and filled their buckets. They wore shawls or hoods, and their garments were somber, but nevertheless they appeared to have youth and comeliness. They saw him, looked at him curiously, and then, without speaking, went back on the well-trodden path. Then down the path appeared a woman — a girl in lighter garb. It was almost white. She was shapely and walked with free, graceful step, reminding him of the Indian girl, Glen-Nas-Pa. This Mormon wore a hood shaped like a huge sunbonnet, and it concealed her face. She carried a huge bucket. When she reached the spring and went down the few stone steps, Shefford saw that she did not have on shoes. As she braced herself to lift the bucket, her bare foot clung to the mossy stone. It was a strong, sinewy, beautiful foot, instinct with youth. He was curious enough, he thought, but the awakening artist in him made him more so. She dragged at the full bucket and had difficulty in lifting it out of the hole. Shefford strode forward and took the bucket handle from her.

"Won't you let me help you?" he said, lifting the bucket. "Indeed . . . it's very heavy."

"Oh . . . thank you," she said, without raising her head. Her voice seemed singularly young and sweet. He had not heard a voice like it. She moved down the path, and he walked beside her.

He felt embarrassed, yet more curious than ever. He wanted to say something, to turn and look at her, but he kept on for a dozen paces without making up his mind. Finally he said: "Do you really carry this heavy bucket? Why, it makes my arm ache."

"Twice every day . . . morning and evening," she replied. "I'm very strong."

He stole a look out of the corner of his eye and, seeing that her face was hidden from him by the hood, he turned to observe her at better advantage. A long braid of hair hung down her back. In the twilight it gleamed a dull gold. She came up to his shoulder. The sleeve nearest him was rolled up to her elbow, revealing a fine round arm. Her hand, like her foot, was brown, strong, and well-shaped. It was a hand that had been de-

122

veloped by labor. She was full-bosomed, yet slender, and she walked with a free stride that made Shefford admire and wonder.

They passed several of the little stone and log houses, and women greeted them as they went by, and children peered shyly from the doors. He kept trying to think of something to say and, failing in that, determined to have one good look under the hood before he left her.

"You walk lame," she said solicitously. "Let me carry the bucket now . . . please. My house is near."

"Am I lame? Guess so, a little," he replied. "It was a hard ride for me. But I'll carry the bucket just the same."

They went on under some piñon trees, down a path to a little house identical with the others, except that it had a stone porch. Shefford smelled fragrant wood smoke, and saw a column curling from the low flat stone chimney. Then he set the bucket down on the porch.

"Thank you, Mister Shefford," she said.

"You know my name?" he asked.

"Yes, Mister Withers spoke to my nearest neighbor about you, and she told me."

"Oh, I see. And you . . . ?"

He did not go on, and she did not reply. When she stepped upon the porch and turned, he was able to see under the hood. The face there was in shadow, and for that very reason he answered to ungovernable impulse and took a step closer to her. Dark, grave, sad eyes looked down at him, and he felt as if he could never draw his own glance away. He seemed not to see the rest of her face and yet felt that it was lovely. Then a downward movement of the hood hid from him the strange eyes and the shadowy loveliness.

"I . . . I beg your pardon," he said, quickly drawing back. "I'm rude. Withers told me about a girl he called . . . he said looked like a sago lily. That's no excuse to stare under your hood. But I . . . I was curious . . . I wondered if. . . ."

He hesitated, realizing how utterly foolish his talk was. She stood a moment, probably watching him, but he could not be sure, for her face was hidden.

"They call me that," she said. "But my name is Mary."

"Mary . . . what?" he asked.

"Just Mary," she said simply. "Good night."

He did not say good night and could not have told why. She took the bucket, and went into the dark house. Shefford hurried away into the gathering darkness.

Chapter Six

Without having a good view of her face, Shefford was more interested in a woman than he had ever been before. Still, he reflected, as he returned to camp, he had long been off his balance. He was unduly excited by this new and adventurous life and the mystery of this Mormon village and its sealed wives were perhaps accountable for a state of mind that could not last.

He rolled in his blankets on the soft bed of moss, and he saw the stars through the needle-like fringe of the piñons. It seemed impossible to fall asleep. The two domed peaks split the sky, and back of them, looming dark and shadowy, rose other mountains. There was something cold, austere, and majestic in their lofty presence, and they made him feel alone, yet not alone. He raised himself to see the quiet forms of Withers and Nas-Ta-Bega prone in the starlight, and their slow, deep breathing was that of tired men. A bell on a mustang rang somewhere off in the valley, and it made a low, strange, hollow, reverberating echo from wall to wall. When it ceased, a silence fell that was deader than any silence he had ever felt, but gradually he became aware of the low murmur of the brook. For the rest there was no sough of wind, no bark of dog, or yelp of coyote, no sound of voices in the village.

He tried to sleep, and instead thought of this girl who was called Sago Lily. He recalled everything incident to their meeting and the walk to her home. Her swift, free step, her graceful poise, her shapely form, the long braid of hair, dull gold in the twilight, the beautiful bare foot, and the strong round arm — these he thought of and recalled vividly. But of her face he had no idea, except the shadowy, haunting loveliness, and that grew more and more difficult to remember. The tone of her voice and what she had said — how the one had thrilled him, and the other mystified! It was her voice that had most attracted him. There was something in it besides music — what he could not tell — sadness, depth, something like that in Nas-Ta-Bega — a beauty springing from disuse. But this seemed absurd. Why should he imagine her voice one that had not been used as freely as any other woman's? She was a Mormon; very likely, almost surely, she was a sealed wife. His interest, too, was absurd, and he tried to throw it off, or imagine it something he might have felt about any other of these strange women of the hidden village. Shefford's intelligence and his good sense, which became operative when he was fully aroused and set a situation clearly before his eyes, had no effect upon his deeper, mystic, and primitive feelings. He saw the truth, and he felt something that he could not name. He would not be a fool, but there was no harm in dreaming. Unquestionably, beyond all doubt, the dream and the romance that had lured him to the wilderness were here, hanging over him like the shadows of the great peaks. His heart swelled with emotion when he thought of how the black and incessant despair of the past was gone. So he embraced any attraction that made him forget and think and feel; some instinct stronger than intelligence bade him drift.

Joe's rolling voice awoke him next morning, and he rose with a singular zest. When or where in his life had he awakened in such a beautiful place? Almost he understood why Venters and Bess had been haunted by memories of Surprise Valley. The morning was cool, clear, sweet; the peaks were dim and soft in rosy cloud; shafts of golden sunlight shot down into the purple shadows. Mockingbirds were singing. His body was sore and tired from the unaccustomed travel, but his heart was full, happy. His spirit wanted to run, and he knew there was something out there waiting to meet it. The Indian and the trader and the Mormon all meant more to him this morning. He had grown a little over night. Nas-Ta-Bega's deep — *"Bi-nai."* — rang in his ears, and the smiles of Withers and Joe were greetings. He had friends; he had work; there was a rich, strange, and helpful life to live. There was even a difference in the mustang, Nack-Yal. He came readily; he did not look wild; he had a friendly eye. Shefford liked him more.

"What's there to do?" asked Shefford, feeling equal to a hundred tasks.

"No work," replied the trader with a laugh. "I'm in no hurry. I like it here. And Joe never wants to leave. Today you can meet the women. Make yourself popular. I've already made you that. These women are 'most all young and lonesome. Talk to them. Make them like you. Then, someday, you may be safe to ask questions. Last night

128

I wanted to ask old Mother Smith if she ever heard the name Fay Larkin, but I thought better of it. If there's a girl here or at Stonebridge of that name, we'll learn it. If there's mystery, we'd better go slow. Mormons are hell on secret and mystery, and to pry into their affairs is to estrange yourself. My advice is . . . just be as nice as you can be, and let things happen."

Fay Larkin! All in a night Shefford had forgotten her. Why? He pondered over the matter, and then the old thrill, the old desire came back.

"Shefford, what do you think Nas-Ta-Bega said to me last night?" asked Withers, in lower voice.

"Haven't any idea," replied Shefford curiously.

"We were sitting beside the fire. I saw you walking under the cedars. You seemed thoughtful. That keen Indian watched you, and he said to me in Navajo . . . '*Bi-nai* has lost his God. He has come far to find a wife. Nas-Ta-Bega is his brother.' He meant he'll find both God and a wife for you. I don't know about that, but I say take the Indian as he thinks he is . . . your brother. Long before I knew Nas-Ta-Bega well, my wife used to tell me about him. He's a sage and a poet . . . the very spirit of this desert. He's worth cultivating for his own sake. But more . . . remember, if Fay Larkin is still shut up in that valley, the Navajo will find her for you."

"I shall take Nas-Ta-Bega as my brother . . . and be proud," replied Shefford. "There's another thing. Might I confide in Joe?"

"Well, that might be a good plan, but wait till you know him better, and he knows you. He's ready to fight for you now. He's takin' your trouble to heart. You wouldn't think Joe is deeply religious. Yet he is. He may never breathe a word about religion to you. All the same he's capable of doing anything to make you a Mormon. Now, Shefford, go ahead. You've struck a trail. It's rough, but it'll make a man of you. It'll lead somewhere."

"I'm singularly fortunate . . . I . . . who had lost all friends. Withers, I am grateful. I'll prove it. I'll show. . . ."

Withers's upheld hand checked further speech, and Shefford realized that beneath the rough exterior of this desert trader there was fine feeling. These men of crude torsion and wild surroundings were beginning to loom up large in Shefford's mind.

The day began leisurely. The men were yet at breakfast when the women of the village began to come, one by one, to the

130

spring. Joe Lake made friendly and joking remarks to each. As each one passed on down the path, he poised a biscuit in one hand and a cup of coffee in the other, and with his head cocked sidewise like an owl he said: "Reckon I've got to get me a woman like her."

Shefford saw and heard, yet he was all the time, half unconsciously, watching with strange eagerness for a white figure to appear. At last he saw her, the same girl with the hood, the same swift step. A little shock or quiver passed over him, and at the moment all that was explicable about it was something associated with regret.

Joe Lake whistled and stared. "I haven't met her," he muttered.

"That's Sago Lily," said Withers.

"Reckon I'm going to carry that bucket," went on Joe.

"And queer yourself with all the other women who've been to the spring? Don't do it, Joe," advised the trader.

"But her bucket's bigger," protested Joe weakly.

"That's true. But you ought to know Mormons. If she'd come first, all right. As she didn't . . . don't single her out."

Joe kept his seat. The girl came on to the spring. A low — "Good morning." —

came from under the hood. Then she filled her bucket, and started home. Shefford observed that this time she wore moccasins and she carried the heavy bucket with ease. When she disappeared, he had again that vague, inexplicable sensation of regret.

Joe Lake breathed heavily. "Reckon I've got to get me a woman like her," he said. But the former jocose tone was lacking, and he appeared thoughtful.

Withers first took Shefford to the building used for a school. It was somewhat larger than the other houses, had only one room with two doors and several windows. It was full of children of all sizes and ages, sitting on rude board benches. There were half a hundred of them, sturdy, healthy, rosy boys and girls, clad in home-made garments. The young woman teacher was as embarrassed as her pupils were shy, and the visitors withdrew without having heard a word of lessons.

Withers then called upon Smith, Henninger, and Beal, and their wives. Shefford found himself cordially received, and what little he did say showed him how he would be listened to when he cared to talk. These folk were plain and kindly, and he found that there was nothing about them to dislike. The men appeared mild and quiet and, when not conversing, seemed austere. The repose of the women was only on the surface; underneath he felt their intensity. Especially in many of the younger women, who he met in the succeeding hour, did he feel this power of restrained emotion. This surprised him as did also the fact that almost every one of them was attractive and some of them were exceedingly pretty. He became so interested in them all as a whole that he could not individualize one. They were as widely different in appearance and temperament as women of any other class, but it seemed to Shefford that one common trait united them — it was a strange, checked yearning for something that he could not discover. Was it happiness? They certainly seemed to be happy, far more so than those millions of women who were chasing phantoms. Were they really sealed wives, as Withers believed, and was this unnatural wifehood responsible for the strange intensity? At any rate, he returned to camp with the conviction that he had stumbled upon a remarkable situation.

He had been told the last names of only three women, and their husbands were in the village. The names of the others were Ruth, Rebecca, Joan — he could not recall them all. They were the mothers of these beautiful children. The fathers, as far as he was concerned, were as intangible as myths. Shefford was an educated clergyman, a man of the world, and as such knew women in his way. Mormons might be strange and different, yet the fundamental truth was that all over the world mothers of children were wives; there was a relation between wife and mother that did not need to be named to be felt. He divined from this that whatever the situation of these lonely and hidden women they knew themselves to be wives. Shefford absolutely satisfied himself on that score. If they were miserable, they certainly did not show it, and the question came to him how just was the criticism of uninformed men? His judgment of Mormons had been established by what he had heard and read, rather than what he knew. He wanted now to have an open mind. He had studied the totemism and exogomy of the primitive races, and here was his opportunity to understand polygamy. One wife for one man — that was the law. Mormons broke it openly. Gentiles broke it secretly. The Mormons acknowledged all their wives and protected their children. Gentiles acknowledged one wife only. Unquestionably the Mormons were wrong, but were not the Gentiles still more wrong?

The following day Joe Lake appeared reluctant to start for Stonebridge with Withers.

"Joe, you'd better come along," said the trader dryly. "I reckon you've seen a little too much of Sago Lily."

Lake offered no reply, but it was evident from his sober face that Withers had not hit short of the mark. Withers rode off with a parting word to Shefford, and finally Joe somberly mounted his bay and trotted down the valley. As Nas-Ta-Bega had gone off somewhere to visit Indians, Shefford was left alone.

He went into the village and made himself useful and agreeable. He made friends with the children, and he talked to the women till he was hoarse. Their ignorance of the world was a spur to him, and never in his life had he had such an attentive audience. As he showed no curiosity, asked no difficult questions, gradually what reserve he had noted wore away, and the end of the day saw him on a footing with them that Withers had predicted.

By the time several like days had passed, it seemed from the interest and friendliness of

135

these women that he might have lived long among them. He was possessed of wit and eloquence and information, which he freely gave and not with selfish motive. He liked these women; he liked to see the somber shade pass from their faces, to see them brighten. He had met the girl, Mary, at the spring and along the path, but he had not yet seen her face. He was always looking for her, hoping to meet her, and confirmed to himself that the best of the day for him were the morning and evening visits she made to the spring. Nevertheless, for some reason hard to divine, he was reluctant to seek her deliberately. Always, while he had listened to her neighbors talk, he had hoped they might let fall something about her, but they did not. He received the impression that she was not so intimate with the others as he had supposed. They all composed one big family. Still she seemed a little outside. He could bring no proof to strengthen this idea. He had merely felt it, and many of his feelings were independent of intelligent reason. Something had surely been added to his curiosity.

It was his habit to call upon Mother Smith in the afternoons. From the first, her talk to him hinted of a leaning toward thought of making him a Mormon. Her husband and the other men took up her cue and spoke of their religion, casually at first, but gradually opening their minds to free and simple discussion of their faith. Shefford lent respectful attention. He would rather have been a Mormon than an atheist, and apparently they considered him the latter and were earnest to save his soul. Shefford knew that he could never be one any more than the other. He was just at sea. But he listened, and he found them simple in faith, blind perhaps, but loyal and good. It was noteworthy that Mother Smith happened to be the only woman in the village who had ever mentioned religion to him. She was old, of a past generation; the young women belonged to the present. Shefford pondered the significant difference.

Every day made more steadfast his impression of the great mystery that was like a turning shadow around these women, yet in the same time many little ideas shifted and many new characteristics became manifest. This last was, of course, the result of acquaintance. He was learning more about the villagers. He gathered from keen interpretation, of subtle words and looks, that here, in this lonely village the same as in all the rest of the world where women were together, there were cliques, quarrels, dislikes, loves, and jealousies. The truth, once known to him, made him feel natural and fortified his confidence to meet the demands of an increasingly interesting position. He discovered, with a somewhat grim amusement, that a clergyman's experience in a church full of women had not been entirely useless.

One afternoon he let fall a careless remark that was a subtle question in regard to Sago Lily. In response he received an answer couched in the sweet poisoned honey of woman's jealousy. He said no more. Certain ideas of his were strengthened, and straightaway he became thoughtful.

Next afternoon late, as he did his camp chores, he watched for her, but she did not come. Then he decided to go to see her. But even the decision and the strange thrill it imparted did not change his reluctance.

Twilight was darkening the valley when he reached her house, and the shadows were thick under the piñons. There was no light in the door or window. He saw a white shape on the porch, and, as he came down the path, it rose. She was there and appeared startled.

"Good evening," he said. "It's Shefford. May I stay and talk a little while?"

She was silent for so long that he began to

feel awkward. "I'd be glad to have you," she said then.

There was a bench on the porch, but he preferred to sit upon a blanket on the step. "I've been getting acquainted with every-body . . . except you," he said.

"I have been here," she replied.

That might have been a woman's speech, but it certainly had been made in a girl's voice. She was neither shy nor embarrassed or self-conscious. As she stood back from him, he could not see her face in the dense twilight.

"I've been wanting to call on you."

She made some slight movement.

Shefford felt a strange calm. He knew the moment was big and potent. "Won't you sit here?" he asked.

She complied with his wish, and then he saw her face, although dimly, in the twilight. It struck him mute. He had no glimpse such as had flashed upon him from under her hood that other night. He thought of a white flower in shadow and received his first impression of the rare and perfect lily Withers had said graced the wild cañons. She was only a girl. She sat very still, looking straight before her, and seemed to be waiting, listening. Shefford saw the quick rise and fall of her bosom.

"I want to talk," he began swiftly, hoping to put her at her ease. "Everyone here has been good to me, and I've talked . . . oh, for hours and hours. But the thing in my mind I haven't spoken of. I've never asked any questions. That makes my part so strange. I want to tell why I came out here. I need someone who will keep my secret, and perhaps help me. Would you?"

"Yes, if I could," she replied.

"You see, I've got to trust you, or one of these other women. You're all Mormons. I don't mean that's anything against you. I believe you're all good and noble. But the fact makes . . . well, makes liberty of speech impossible. What can I do?"

Her silence probably meant that she did not know. Shefford sensed less strain in her and more excitement. He believed he was on the right track and did not regret his impulse. Even had he regretted it, he would have gone on, for opposed to caution and intelligence was his driving mystic force. Then he told her the truth about his boyhood, his ambition to be an artist, his renunciation to his father's hope, his career as a clergyman, his failure in religion, and the disgrace that had made him a wanderer.

"Oh, I'm sorry," she said. The faint starlight shown on her face, in her eyes, and if he ever saw beauty and soul, he saw them then. She seemed deeply moved. She had forgotten herself. She betrayed her girlhood — all the quick sympathy, the wonder, the sweetness of a heart innocent and untutored. She looked at him with great, starry, questioning eyes, as if they had just become aware of his presence, as if a man had been strange to her.

"Thank you. It's good of you to be sorry," he said. "My instinct guided me right. Perhaps you'll be my friend."

"I will be . . . if I can," she said.

"But *can* you be?"

"I don't know. I never had a friend. I . . . but, sir, I mustn't talk of myself. Oh, I'm afraid I can't help you."

How strange the pathos of her voice! Almost, he believed, she was in need of help or sympathy or love, but he could not wholly trust a judgment formed from observations of a class different from his. "Maybe you *can* help me. Let's see," he said. "I don't seek to make you talk of yourself. But . . . you're a human being . . . a girl . . . almost a woman. You're not dumb. Even a nun can talk."

"A nun? What is that?"

"Well . . . a nun is a sister of mercy . . . a woman consecrated to God who has renounced the world. In some ways, you

141

Mormon women here resemble nuns. It is sacrifice that nails you in this lonely valley. You see . . . how I talk! One word . . . one thought brings another, and I speak what perhaps should be unsaid. And it's hard, because I feel I could unburden myself to you."

"Tell me what you want," she said.

Shefford hesitated, and became aware of the rapid pound of his heart. More than anything he wanted to be fair to this girl. He saw that she was warming to his influence. Her shadowy eyes were fixed upon him. The starlight, growing brighter, shone on her golden hair and white face.

"I'll tell you presently," he said. "I've trusted you. I'll trust you with all. But let me have my own time. This is so strange a thing . . . my wanting to confide in you. It's selfish, perhaps. I have my own axe to grind. I hope I won't wrong you. That's why I'm going to be perfectly frank. I might wait for days to get better acquainted. But the impulse is in me. I've been so interested in all you Mormon women. The fact . . . the meaning of this hidden village is so . . . so terrible to me. But that's none of my business. I have spent my afternoons and evenings with these women, at the different cottages. You do not mingle with them. They are lonely, but have not such loneliness as yours. I have passed here every night. No light . . . no sound. I can't help thinking. Don't censure me or be afraid or draw within yourself just because I must think. I may be all wrong. But I'm curious. I wonder about you. Who are you? Mary . . . Mary what? Maybe I really don't want to know. I came with selfish motive, and now I'd like to . . . to . . . what shall I say? . . . make your life a little less lonely for the while I'm here. That's all. It needn't offend. And if you accept it, how much easier I can tell you my secret. You are a Mormon, and I . . . well, I am only a wanderer in these wilds. But . . . we might help each other. Have I made a mistake?"

"No . . . no!" she cried, almost wildly.

"We can be friends then . . . you will trust me, help me?"

"Yes, if I dare."

"Surely you may dare what the other women would?"

She was silent, and the wistfulness of her silence touched him. He felt contrition. He did not stop to analyze his own emotions, but he had an inkling that, once this strange situation was ended, he would have food for reflection. What struck him most now was the girl's blanched face, the strong, nervous clasp of her hands, the visible tumult of her bosom. Excitement alone could not account for this. He had not divined a cause for such agitation. He was puzzled, troubled, and drawn irresistibly. He had not said what he had planned to say. The moment had given birth to his speech, and it had flowed. What was guiding him?

"Mary," he said earnestly, "tell me . . . have you mother, father, sister, brother? Something prompts me to ask that."

"All dead . . . gone . . . years ago," she answered.

"How old are you?"

"Eighteen, I think. I'm not sure."

"You *are* lonely."

His words were gentle and divining.

"Oh, God!" she cried. "Lonely!"

Then as a man in a dream he beheld her weeping. There was in her the unconsciousness of a child and the passion of a woman. He gazed out into the dark shadows and up at the white stars, and then at the bowed head with its mass of glistening hair. But her agitation was no longer strange to him. A few gentle and kind words had proved her undoing. He knew then that, whatever her life was, no kindness or sympathy entered it. Presently she recovered, and sat as before, only whiter of face, it seemed, and with something tragic in her dark eyes. She was

144

growing cold and still again, aloof, more like those other Mormon women.

"I understand," he said. "I'm not sorry I spoke. I felt your trouble, whatever it is . . . do not retreat into your cold Mormon shell, I beg of you. Let me trust you with my secret."

He saw her shake out of the cold apathy. She wavered. He felt an inexplicable sweetness in the power his voice seemed to have upon her. She bowed her head in acquiescence, and so Shefford began his story. Did she grow still, like stone, or was that only his avid imagination? He told her of Venters and Bess — of Lassiter and Jane — of little Fay Larkin — of the romance and then the tragedy of Surprise Valley.

"So, when my church disowned me," he concluded, "I conceived the idea of wandering into the wilds of Utah to save Fay Larkin from that cañon prison. It grew to be the best and strongest desire of my life. I think, if I could save her, that it would save me. I never loved any girl. I can't say that I love Fay Larkin. How could I when I've never seen her . . . when she's only a dream girl? But I believe if she were to become a reality . . . a flesh and blood girl . . . that I would love her!"

That was more than Shefford had ever

confessed to anyone, and it stirred him to his depths. Mary bent her head on her hands in strange, stone-like rigidity.

"So here I am in the cañon country," he continued. "Withers tells me it is a country of rainbows, both in the evanescent air and in the changeless stone. Always as a boy there has been for me some haunting promise, some treasure at the foot of the rainbow. I shall expect the curve of a rainbow to lead me down into Surprise Valley. A dreamer you will call me. But I have had strange dreams come true. Mary, do you think *this* dream will come true?"

She was silent so long that he repeated his question.

"Only in heaven," she whispered.

He took her reply strangely, and a chill crept over him.

"You think my plan to seek, to strive, to find . . . you think that idle, vain?"

"I think it noble. Thank God I've met a man like you."

"Don't praise me!" he exclaimed hastily. "Only help me. Mary, will you answer a few little questions, if I swear by my honor I'll never reveal what you tell me?"

"I'll try."

He moistened his lips. Why did she seem so strange, so far away? The hovering shadows made him nervous. Always he had been afraid of the dark. His word now admitted of unreal fancies. "Have you ever heard of Fay Larkin?" he asked in a very low voice.

"Yes."

"Was there only one Fay Larkin?"

"Only one."

"Did you . . . ever see her?"

"Yes," came the faint reply.

He was grateful. How she might be breaking faith with creed or duty! He had not dared to hope so much from any Mormon. All his inner being trembled at the portent of his next query. He had not dreamed it would be so hard to put, or would affect him so powerfully. A warmth, a glow, a happiness pervaded his spirit, and the chill, the gloom were as if they had never been.

"Where is Fay Larkin now?" he asked huskily.

He bent over her, touched her, leaned close to catch her whisper.

"She is . . . dead!"

Slowly Shefford rose with a sickening shock, and then in bitter pain he strode away into the starlight.

Chapter Seven

The Indian returned to camp that night, and early next day, which was Sunday, Withers rode in, accompanied by a stout, gray-bearded personage wearing a long black coat.

"Bishop Kane, this is my new man John Shefford," said the trader.

Shefford acknowledged the introduction with the respectful courtesy evidently in order, and found himself being studied instantly by clear blue eyes. The bishop appeared old, dry, and absorbed in thought; he spoke quaintly, using in every speech some Biblical word or phrase, and he had an air of authority. He asked Shefford to hear him preach at the morning service, and then he went off into the village.

"Guess he liked your looks," remarked Withers.

"He certainly sized me up," replied Shefford.

"Well, what could you expect? Sure, I

never heard of a deal like this . . . a handsome young fellow left alone with a lot of pretty Mormon women! You'll understand when you learn to know Mormons. Bishop Kane's a square old chap. Crazy in religion, maybe, but otherwise a good fellow. I made the best stand I could for you. The Mormons over at Stonebridge were huffy because I hadn't consulted them before fetching you over here. If I had, of course, you'd never have gotten here. It was Joe Lake who made it all right with them. Joe's well thought of, and he certainly stood up for you."

"I owe him something, then," replied Shefford. "Hope my obligations don't grow beyond me."

"Yes. He wanted to stay, and I had work there that'll keep him a while. Shefford, we got news of Shadd, bad news. The halfbreed's cutting up rough. His gang shot up some Paiutes over here across the line. Then he got run out of Durango a few weeks ago for murder. A posse of cowboys trailed him, but he slipped them. He's a fox. You know he was trailing us here. He left the trail, Nas-Ta-Bega said. I learned at Stonebridge that Shadd is well disposed toward Mormons. It takes the Mormons to handle Indians. Shadd knows of their village and that's why he shunted off our trail. But he might hang down in the pass and wait for us. I think I'd better go back to Kayenta alone, across country. You stay here till Joe and the Indian think it safe to leave. You'll be going up on the slope of Navajo to load a pack train, and from there it may be well to go down West Cañon to Red Lake, and home over the divide, the way you came. Joe'll decide what's best. And you might as well buckle on a gun and get used to it. Sooner or later you'll have to shoot your way through."

Shefford did not respond with his usual enthusiasm, and the omission caused the trader to scrutinize him closely.

"What's the matter?" he queried. "There's no light in your eye today. You look a little shady."

"I didn't rest well last night," replied Shefford. "I'm depressed this morning. But I'll cheer up directly."

"Did you get along well with the women?"

"Very well, indeed. And I've enjoyed myself. It's a strange, beautiful place."

"Do you like the women?"

"Yes."

"Have you seen much of Sago Lily?"

"No. I carried her bucket one night and saw her only once again. I've been with the other women most of the time."

"It's just as well you didn't run often into Mary. Joe's sick over her. I never saw a girl with a face and form to equal hers. There's danger here for any man, Shefford. Even for you who think you've turned your back on the world. Any of these Mormon women may fall in love with you. They *can't* love their husbands. That's how I figure it. Religion holds them, not love. And the peculiar thing is this. They're second, third, or fourth wives, all sealed. That means their husbands are old, have picked them out for youth and physical charms, have chosen the very opposite to their first wives, and then have hidden them here in this lonely hole. Did you ever imagine as terrible a thing?"

"No, Withers, I did not."

"Maybe that's what depressed you. Anyway, my hunch is worth taking. Be as nice as you can, Shefford. Lord knows it would be good for these poor women if every last one of them fell in love with you. That won't hurt them so long as you keep your head. Savvy? Perhaps I seem rough and coarse to a man of your class. Well, that may be. But human nature is human nature. And in this strange and beautiful place you might love an Indian girl, let alone Sago Lily. That's all. I sure feel better with that off my conscience. Hope I don't offend."

"No, indeed. I thank you, Withers," replied Shefford with his hand on the trader's shoulder. "You are right to caution me. I seem to be wild . . . thirsting for adventure . . . chasing a gleam. In these unstable days I can't answer for my heart. But I can for my honor. These unfortunate women are as safe with me as . . . as they are with you and Joe."

Withers uttered a blunt laugh. "See here, son, look things square in the eye. Men of violent, lonely, toilsome lives store up hunger for the love of woman. Love of a *strange* woman, if you want to put it that way. It's nature. It seems all the beautiful young women in Utah are corralled in this valley. When I come over here, I feel natural, but I'm not happy. I'd like to make love to . . . to that flower-faced girl. And I'm not ashamed to own it. I've told Molly, my wife, and she understands. As for Joe, it's much harder for him. Joe never has had a wife or sweetheart. I tell you he's sick, and, if I'd stay here a month, I'd be sick."

Withers had spoken with fire in his eyes, with grim humor on his lips, with uncompromising, brutal truth. What he admitted was astounding to Shefford, but once spoken, not at all strange. The trader was a man who spoke his inmost thought. What he said suddenly focused Shefford's mental vision clearly and wholly upon the appalling significance of the tragedy of these women, especially of the girl whose life was lonelier, sadder, darker than that of the others.

"Withers, trust me," replied Shefford.

"All right. Make the best of a bad job," said the trader, and went off about his tasks.

Shefford and Withers attended the morning service, which was held in the schoolhouse. Exclusive of the children every inhabitant of the village was there. The women, except the few oldest, were dressed in white and look exceedingly well. Manifestly they had bestowed care upon this Sabbath morning's toilet. One thing surely this dress occasion brought out, evidence that the Mormon women were not poor, whatever their misfortunes might be. Jewelry was not wanting, or fine lace. They all wore beautiful wild flowers of a kind unknown to Shefford. He received many a bright smile. He looked for Mary, hoping to see her face for the first time in the daylight, but she sat far forward and did not turn. He saw her graceful white neck, the fine lines of her throat, and her colorless cheek. He recognized her, yet in the light she seemed a stranger.

The service began with a short prayer and was followed by the singing of a hymn. Nowhere had Shefford heard better music or sweeter voices. How deeply they affected him. Had any man ever fallen into a stranger adventure than this? He had only to shut his eyes to believe it all a creation of his fancy — the square log cabin with its red mud between the chinks and a roof like an Indian Hogan; the old bishop in his black coat, standing solemnly, his hand beating time to the tune; the few old women, dignified and stately, the many young women, fresh and handsome, lifting their voices.

Shefford listened intently to the bishop's sermon. In some respects it was the best he had ever heard. In others it was impossible for an intelligent man to regard seriously. It was very long, lasting an hour and a half, and the parts that were helpful to Shefford came from the experience and wisdom of a man who had grown old in the desert. The physical things that had molded character of iron, the obstacles that only strong, patient men could have overcome, the making of homes in a wilderness showed the greatness of this alien band of Mormons. Shefford conceded greatness to them. But the strange religion, the narrowing down of the world to the soil of Utah, the intimations of prophets on earth who had direct converse with God, the austere, self-conscious omnipotence of this old bishop — these were matters that Shefford felt he must understand better and see more favorably, if he were not to consider them impossible.

Immediately after the service, forgetting that his intention had been to get the look he had long waited for of Mary in the light of sun, Shefford hurried back to camp and to a secluded spot among the cedars. Strikingly it had come to him that the fault he had found in Gentile religion he now found in the Mormon religion. An old question returned to haunt him — were all religions the same in blindness? As far as he could see, religion existed to uphold the founders of a church, a creed. The church of his own kind was a place where narrow men and women went to think of their own salvation. They did not go there to think of others. Now Shefford's keen mind saw something more of Mormonism and found it wanting. Bishop Kane was a sincere, good, mistaken man. He believed what he preached, but that would not stand logic. He taught blindness, and mostly it appeared to be directed at the women. Was there no religion divorced from power, no religion as good for one man as another, no religion in the spirit of brotherly love? Nas-Ta-Bega's *"Bi-nai."* That was love, if not religion, and perhaps the one and the other were the same. Shefford kept in mind an intention to ask Nas-Ta-Bega what he thought of the Mormons.

Later, when opportunity afforded, he did speak to the Indian. Nas-Ta-Bega threw away his cigarette and made an impressive gesture that conveyed as much sorrow as scorn.

"The first Mormon said God spoke to him and told him to go to a certain place and dig. He went there and found the Book of Mormon. It said follow me . . . marry many wives . . . go into the desert and multiply . . . send your sons out into the world and bring us young women, many young women. And when the first Mormon became strong with many followers he said again . . . give to me part of your labor . . . of your cattle and sheep . . . of your silver that I may build great cathedrals for you to worship in. And I will commune with God and make it right and good that you have more wives. That is what the bishop preached. That is Mormonism."

"Nas-Ta-Bega, you mean the Mormons are a great and good people blindly following a leader?"

"Yes. And the leader builds for himself . . . not for them."

"That is not religion. He has no god but himself."

"They have no god. They are blind like the Hopis who have the creeping growths on their eyes. They have no god they can see and hear and feel, who is with them day and night."

It was late in the afternoon when Bishop Kane rode through the camp, and halted on his way to speak to Shefford. He was kindly and fatherly.

"Young man, are you open to faith?" he questioned gravely.

"I think I am," replied Shefford, thankful he could answer readily.

"Then come into the fold. You are a lost sheep. Away on the desert I heard its cry. God bless you. Visit with me when you ride to Stonebridge."

He flicked his horse with a cedar branch and trotted away beside the trader, and presently the green-choked neck of the valley hid them from view. Shefford could not have said that he was glad to be left behind, and yet neither was he sorry.

That Sabbath evening, as he sat quietly with Nas-Ta-Bega watching the sunset gilding the peaks, he was visited by three of the young Mormon women — Ruth, Joan, and Hester. They deliberately sought him and merrily led him off to the village, and to the evening service of singing and prayer. Afterward, he was surrounded and made much of. He had been popular before, but this was different. When he thoughtfully wended his way toward camp under the quiet stars, he realized that the coming of Bishop Kane had made a subtle change in the women. That change was at first hard to define, but from every point by which he approached he came to the same conclusion — the bishop had not objected to his presence in the village. The women became natural, free, and unrestrained. A dozen or twenty young and attractive women thrown much into companionship with one man, he might become a Mormon. The idea made him laugh. But upon reflection it was not funny; it sobered him. What a situation! He felt instinctively that he ought to fly from this hidden valley. But he could not have done it, even had he not been in the trader's employ. The thing was provokingly seductive. It was like an Arabian Nights' Tale. What would these strange, fatally bound women do? Would any one of them become involved with him. He was no fool. Already eyes had flashed, and lips had smiled.

A thousand like thoughts whirled through his mind. When he had calmed down somewhat, two things were not lost upon him — an intricate and fascinating situation, with no end to its possibilities, threatened and attracted him, and the certainty that whatever change the bishop had inaugurated, it had made these poor women happier. The latter fact weighed more with Shefford than fears for himself. His word was given to Withers. He would have felt just the same without having bound himself. Still, in the light of the trader's blunt philosophy, and of his own assurance that he was no fool, Shefford felt it incumbent upon him to accept a belief that there were situations no man could resist without an anchor. The ingenuity of man could not have devised a stranger, a more enticing, a more overpoweringly fatal situation. Fatal in that it could not be left untried! Shefford gave in and clicked his teeth as he let himself go, and suddenly he thought of her who these bitter women called Sago Lily.

The regret that had been his returned with thought of her. The saddest disillusion of his life, the keenest disappointment, the strangest pain would always be associated with her. He had meant to see her face clearly in the sunlight, so that he could always remember it, and then never go near her again. Now it came to him that, if he did see much of her, these other women would find him like the stone wall in the valley. Folly! Perhaps it was, but she would be safe, maybe happier. When he decided, it was certain that he trembled. Then he buried the memory of Fay Larkin.

Next day Shefford threw himself with all the boy left in him into the work and play of the village. He helped the women and made games for the children. He talked or listened. In the early evening he called on Ruth, chatted a while, and went on to see Joan, and from her to another. When the valley became shrouded in darkness, he went unseen down the path to Mary's lonely home.

She was there, a white shadow against the black. When she replied to his greeting, her voice seemed full, broken, eager to express something that would not come. She was happier to see him than she should have been, Shefford thought. He talked swiftly, eloquently, about whatever he believed would interest her. He stayed long, and finally left, not having seen her face except in pale starlight and shadow, and the strong clasp of her hand remained with him as he went away under the piñons.

Days passed swiftly. Joe Lake did not return. The Indian rode in and out of camp, watered and guarded the pack burros and the mustangs. Shefford grew strong and active. He made a garden for the women; he cut cords of firewood; he dammed the brook, and made an irrigation ditch; he learned to love these fatherless children, and they loved him.

In the afternoons there was leisure for him and for the women. He had no favorites, and let the occasion decide what he should do and with whom he should be. They had little parties at the cottages and picnics under the cedars. He rode up and down the valley with Ruth, who could ride a horse as no other girl he had ever seen. He climbed with Hester. He walked with Joan. Mostly he continued to include several at once in the little excursions, although it was not rare for him to be out alone with one.

It was not a game he was playing. More and more, as he learned to know these young women, he liked them better, he pitied them, he was good for them. It shamed him, hurt him somehow to see how they tried to forget something when they were with him. Not improbably a little of it was coquetry, as natural as a laugh to any pretty woman. But that was not what hurt him. It was to see Ruth or Rebecca, as the case might be, full of life and fun, thoroughly enjoying some jest or play, all of a sudden be strangely recalled from the wholesome pleasure of a girl to become a deep and somber woman.

The crimes in the name of religion! How he thought of the blood and the ruin laid at the door of religion! He wondered if that were so with Nas-Ta-Bega's religion, and he meant to find out someday. The women he liked best he imagined the least religious, and they made less effort to attract him.

Every night in the dark he went to Mary's home and sat with her on the porch. He never went inside. For all he knew his visits were unknown to her neighbors. Still it did not matter to him if they found out. To her he could talk as he had never talked to anyone. She liberated all his thought and fancy. He filled her mind.

As there had been a change in the other women, so was there in Mary. However, it had no relation to the bishop's visit. The time came when Shefford could not but see that she lived and dragged through the long day for the sake of these few hours in the shadows of the stars with him. She seldom spoke. She listened. Wonderful to him, sometimes she laughed, and it seemed the sound was a ghost of childhood pleasure. When he stopped to consider that she might fall in love with him, he drove the thought from him. When he realized that his folly had become sweet and that the sweetness imperiously drew him, he likewise cast off that thought. The present was enough. If he had any treasures of mind and heart, he gave them to her.

She never asked him to stay, but she showed that she wanted him to. That made it hard to go. Still he never stayed late. The moment of parting was like a break. Her good bye was sweet low music; it lingered in his ear; it bade him come tomorrow night; it sent him away into the valley to walk under the stars, a man fighting against himself.

One night at parting, as he tried to see her face in the wan glow of a clouded moon, he said: "I've been trying to find a sago lily."

"Have you never seen one?" she asked.

"No." He meant to say something with a double meaning, in reference to her face and the name of the flower, but her unconsciousness made him hold his tongue. She was wholly unlike the other Mormon women.

"I'll show you where the lilies grow," she said.

"When?"

"Tomorrow. Early in the afternoon I'll come to the spring. Then I'll take you."

Next morning Joe Lake returned and imparted news that was perturbing to Shefford. Reports of Shadd had come in to Stonebridge from different Indian villages. Joe was not inclined to linger long at the camp and favored taking the trail with the pack train.

Shefford discovered that he did not want to leave the valley, and the knowledge made him reflective. That morning he did not go into the village and stayed in camp alone. A depression weighed upon him. It was dispelled, however, early in the afternoon by the sight of a slender figure in white swiftly coming down the path to the spring. He had an appointment with Mary to go to see the sago lilies. Everything else slipped his mind.

Mary wore the long black hood that effectually concealed her face. It made of her a woman, a Mormon woman, and strangely belied the lithe form and the braid of gold hair.

"Good day," she said, putting down her

bucket. "Do you still want to go . . . to see the lilies?"

"Yes," replied Shefford with a short laugh.

"Can you climb?"

"I'll go where you go."

Then she set off under the cedars, and Shefford stalked at her side. He was aware that Nas-Ta-Bega watched them walk away. This day, so far at least, Shefford did not feel talkative, and Mary had always been one who mostly listened. They came, at length, to a place where the wall rose in low smooth swells, not steep, but certainly at an angle Shefford would not of his own accord have attempted to scale.

Light, quick, and sure as a mountain sheep Mary went up the first swell to an offset above. Shefford in amaze and admiration watched the little moccasins as they flashed and held on to the smooth rock.

When he essayed to follow her, he slipped and came to grief. A second attempt resulted in like failure. Then he backed away from the wall, to run forward first, and up the slope, only to slip halfway up, and fall again.

He made light of the incident, but she was solicitous. When he assured her he was unhurt, she said he had agreed to go where she went.

"But I'm not a . . . a bird," he protested.

"Take off your boots. Then you can climb. When we get over the wall, it'll be easy," she said.

In his stocking feet he had no great difficulty walking up the first bulge of the wall. From there she led him up the strange waves of wind-worn rock. He could not attend to anything save the red, polished rock under him and so saw little. The ascent was longer than he would have imagined and steep enough to make him pant, but at last a huge round summit was reached.

From here he saw down into the valley where the village lay. But for the lazy columns of blue smoke curling up from the piñons, the place would have seemed uninhabited. The wall on the other side was about level with the one on which he stood. Beyond rose other walls and cliffs, up and up to the great towering peaks, between which the green and black mountains loomed. Facing the other way, Shefford had only a restricted view. There were low crags and smooth stone ridges between which were aisles green with cedar and piñon. Shefford's companion headed toward one of these, and, when he had followed her a few steps, he could no longer see down into the valley. The Mormon village where she

166

lived was as if it were lost, and, when it vanished, Shefford felt a difference. Scarcely had the thought passed when Mary removed the dark hood. Her small head glistened like gold in the sunlight.

Shefford caught up with her and walked at her side, but could not bring himself at once deliberately to look at her. They entered a narrow, low-walled lane where cedars and piñons grew thickly, their fragrance heavy in the warm air, and flowers began to show in the grassy patches.

"This is Indian paintbrush," she said, pointing to little low scarlet flowers. A gray sagebrush with beautiful purple blossoms she called purple sage, another bush with yellow flowers she named buck brush, and there were vermilion cactus and low flat mounds of lavender daisies that she said had no name. A whole mossy bank was covered with lace-like green leaves and tiny blossoms the color of violets which she called loco.

"Loco? Is this what makes the horses go crazy when they eat it?"

"It is, indeed," she said, laughing.

When she laughed, it was impossible not to look at her. She walked a little in advance. Her white cheek and temple seemed framed in the gold of her hair. How white was her skin, but faintly veined and flushed. The profile, clean-cut and pure, appeared cold, almost stern. He knew now that she was singularly beautiful, although he had yet to see her full face.

They walked on. Quite suddenly the lane opened out between two rounded bluffs, and Shefford looked down upon a grander and more awe-inspiring scene than ever he had viewed in his dreams. What appeared to be a green mountainside sloped endlessly down to a plain, and that rolled and billowed away to a boundless region of strangely carved rock. The greatness of the scene could not be grasped in a glance. The slope was long; the plain not as level as it seemed to be on first sight; here and there round red rocks, isolated and strange, like lonely castles, rose out of the green. Beyond the green all the earth seemed naked, showing smooth glistening bones. It was a formidable wall of rock that flung itself up in the distance, carved into a thousand cañons and walls and domes and peaks, and there was not a straight or a broken or a jagged line in all that wildness. The color low down was red, dark blue, and purple in the clefts, yellow upon the heights, and in the distance rainbow-hued. A land of curves and colors!

Shefford uttered an exclamation.

"That's Utah," said Mary. "I come often to sit here. You see that winding blue line. There . . . that's San Juan Cañon. And that other dark line, that's Escalante Cañon. They wind down into this great purple chasm . . . 'way over here to the left . . . and that's the Grand Cañon. They say not even the Indians have been in there."

Shefford had nothing to say. The moment was one of subtle and vital assimilation. Such places as this unknown to men, what strength, what wonder, what help, what glory, just to sit here an hour, slowly and appallingly to realize. Something came to Shefford from the distance, out of the purple cañons and from those dim wind-worn peaks. He resolved to come here to this promontory again and again, alone and in humble spirit, and learn to know why he had been silenced, why peace pervaded his soul.

It was with this emotion upon him that he turned to find his companion watching him. Then for the first time he saw her face fully, and was thrilled that chance had reserved the privilege for this moment. It was a girl's face he saw, flower-like, lovely, and pure as a Madonna's, and strangely, tragically sad. The eyes were large, dark-gray, the color of sage. They were as clear as the air that made distant things close, and yet they seemed full of shadows, like a ruffled pool under midnight stars. They disturbed him. Her mouth had the sweet curves and redness of youth, but it showed bitterness, pain, and repression.

"Where are the sago lilies?" he asked suddenly.

"Farther down. It's too cold up here for them. Come," she said.

He followed her down a winding trail — down and down till the green plain rose to blot out the scrawled wall of rock, down into a verdant cañon where a brook made swift music over stones, where the air was sultry and hot, laden with the fragrant breath of flowers and leaves. This was a cañon of summer, and it bloomed.

The girl bent, and plucked something from the grass.

"Here's a white lily," she said. "There are three colors. The yellow and pink ones are deeper down in the cañons."

Shefford took the flower, and regarded it with great interest. He had never seen such an exquisite thing. It had three large petals, curving cup-like, of whiteness purer than new-fallen snow, and a heart of rich warm gold. Its fragrance was so faint as to be almost indistinguishable, yet of a haunting unforgettable sweetness. Even while he looked at it, the petals drooped and their whiteness shaded and the gold paled. In a moment the flower was wilted.

"I don't like to pluck the lilies," said Mary. "They die so swiftly."

Shefford saw the white flowers everywhere in the open sunny places along the brook. They swayed with stately grace in the slow warm wind. They seemed like three-pointed stars shining out of the green. He bent over one with a particularly lofty stem, and after a close survey of it he rose to look at her face. His action was plainly one of comparison. She laughed, and said it was foolish for the women to call her Sago Lily. She had no coquetry; she spoke as she would have spoken of the stones at her feet; she did not know that she was beautiful. Shefford imagined there was some resemblance in her to the lily — the same whiteness, the same rich gold, and more striking than either a strange rare quality of beauty, of life, intangible as something fleeting, the spirit that had swiftly faded from the plucked flowers. When had the girl been born? What had her life been? Shefford was intensely curious about her. She seemed as different from any other woman he had known as this rare cañon lily was different from the tame flowers at home.

On the return up the slope she outstripped him. She climbed lightly and tirelessly. When he reached her upon the promontory, there was a stain of red in her cheeks and her expression had changed.

"Let's go back up over the rocks," she said. "I've not climbed for . . . for so long."

"I'll go where you go," he replied.

Then she was off, and he followed. She took to the curves of the bare rocks and climbed. He sensed a spirit released in her. It was so strange, so keen, so wonderful to be with her, and, when he did catch her, he feared to speak lest he break this mood. Her eyes grew dark and daring, and, after she stopped, she looked away across the wavy sea of stones to something beyond the great walls. When they got high, the wind blew her hair loose, and it flew out, a golden stream, with the sun brightly upon it. He saw that she changed her direction, which had been in line with the two peaks, and now she climbed toward the heights. They came to a more difficult ascent, where the stone still held to the smooth curves yet was marked by deep bulges and slants and crevices. Here she became a wild thing. She ran, she leaped, she would have left him far be-

172

hind had he not called. Then she appeared to remember him, and waited.

Her face had now lost its whiteness; it was flushed, rosy, warm.

"Where . . . did you . . . ever learn . . . to run over rocks . . . this way?" he panted.

"All my life I've climbed," she said. "Oh! It's so good to be up on the walls again . . . to feel the wind . . . to see!"

Thereafter, he kept close to her, no matter what the effort. He would not miss a moment of her, if he could help it. She was wonderful. He imagined she must be like an Indian girl, a savage who loved the lofty places and the silence. When she leaped, she uttered a strange, low, sweet cry of wildness and exultation. Shefford guessed she was a girl freed from her prison, forgetting herself, living again youthful hours. Still, she did not forget him at the bad places, lent him a strong hand, and sometimes let it stay long in his clasp. Tireless and agile, sure-footed as a goat, fleet and wild, she leaped and climbed and ran till Shefford marveled at her. This adventure was, indeed, fulfillment of a dream. Perhaps she might lead him to the treasure at the foot of the rainbow. But that thought with memory daring forth from its grave was irrevocably linked with a girl who was dead. He could not remember her, in the presence of this wonderful creature who was as strange as she was beautiful. When Shefford reached for the brown hand stretched forth to help him in a leap, when he felt its strong clasp, the youth and vitality and life of it, he had the fear of a man who was running toward a precipice and who could not turn back. This was a climb, a lark, a wild race to the Mormon girl, bound now in the village, and by the very freedom of it she betrayed her bonds. To Shefford it was also a wild race, but toward one sure goal he dared not name.

They went on, and at length, hand in hand, even where no steep step or wide fissure to give reason for the clasp, but she seemed unconscious. They were nearing the last height, a bare eminence, when she broke from him and ran up the smooth stone. When he surmounted it, she was standing on the very summit, her arms wide, her full breast heaving, her slender body straight as an Indian's, her hair flying in the wind and blazing in the sun. She seemed to embrace the west, to reach for something afar, to offer herself to the wind and the distance. Her face was scarlet from the exertion of the climb and her broad brow was moist. Her eyes had the piercing light of an eagle's, although now they were dark. Shefford intuitively grasped the essence of this strange spirit upon her, and it was wildness. She was not the woman who had met him at the spring. She had dropped some side of her with that Mormon hood, and now she stood totally strange.

She belonged up here, he divined. She was a part of the wildness. She must have been born and brought up in loneliness, where the wind blew and the peaks loomed and silence held dominion. The sinking sun touched the rim of the distant wall and, as if in parting regret, shone with renewed golden fire. The girl was crowned as with a glory.

Shefford loved her then. Realizing it, he thought he might have loved her before, but that did not matter when he was certain of it now. He trembled a little, fearfully, although without regret. Everything pertaining to his desert experience had been strange — this the strangest of all.

The sun sank swiftly, and instantly there was a change in the golden light. Quickly it died out. The girl changed as swiftly. She seemed to remember herself and sat down as if suddenly weary. Shefford went closer, and seated himself beside her.

"The sun has set. We must go," she said.

But she made no movement.

"Whenever you are ready," he replied.

Just as the blaze had died out of her eyes, so the flush faded out of her face. The whiteness stole back and with it the sadness. He had to bite his tongue to keep from telling her what he felt, to keep from pouring out a thousand questions. But the privilege of having seen her, of having been with her when she had forgotten herself — that, he believed, was enough. It had been wonderful; it had made him love her. But it need not add to the tragedy of her life, whatever that was. He tried to eliminate himself, and he watched her.

Her eyes were fixed upon the gold-rimmed ramparts of the distant wall in the west. Plain it was how she loved that wild upland. There seemed to be some haunting memory of the past in her gaze, some happy part of life, agonizing to think of now.

"We must go," she said, and rose.

Shefford arose to accompany her. She looked at him, and her haunting eyes seemed to want him to know that he had helped her to forget the present, to remember girlhood, and that somehow she would always associate a wonderful, happy afternoon with him. He divined that her silence then was a Mormon seal on lips.

"Mary, this has been the happiest, the best, the most revealing day of my life," he said simply.

Swiftly, as if startled, she turned and faced down the slope. At the top of the wall above the village she put on the dark hood and with it that somber something which was Mormon.

Twilight had descended into the valley, and shadows were so thick Shefford had difficulty in finding Mary's bucket. He filled it at the spring, and made offer to carry it home for her, which she declined.

"You'll come tonight . . . later?" she asked.

"Yes!" he replied, hurriedly promising. Then he watched her white form slowly glide down the path to disappear in the shadows.

Nas-Ta-Bega and Joe were busy at the campfire. Shefford joined them. This night he was uncommunicative. Joe peered curiously at him in the flare of the blaze. Later, after the meal, when Shefford appeared restless and strode to and fro, Joe spoke up gruffly.

"Better hang around camp tonight."

Shefford heard, but did not heed. Nevertheless, the purport of this remark, which was either jealousy or admonition, haunted him with the possibility of its meaning.

He walked away from the campfire, under the dark piñons, out into the starry open, and every step was hard to take, unless it pointed toward the home of the girl whose beauty and sadness and mystery had bewitched him. After what seemed hours, he took the well-known path toward her cabin, and then every step seemed lighter. He divined he was rushing to some fate — he knew not what.

The porch was in shadow. He peered in vain for the white form against the dark background. In the silence he seemed to hear his heartbeats thick and muffled. Then a tiny, high-pitched wail pierced him. He listened breathlessly — heard it again — and never would have recognized what made it but for a sweet low song in a voice he would never forget. A baby and Mary's voice! He had never dreamed she had a child. She was singing it to sleep.

He fled swifter than he had come. Some distance down the path he heard the sounds of hoofs. Withdrawing into the gloom of a cedar, he watched. Soon he made out moving horses with riders. They filed past him to the number of half a score. Like a flash of fire the truth burned him: Mormons come on one of their mysterious night visits to sealed wives!

Shefford stalked far down the valley, into the lonely silence and the night shadows under the walls.

Chapter Eight

The home of Nas-Ta-Bega lay far up the cedared slope, with the craggy, yellowed cliffs and the black cañons, and the pine-fringed top of Navajo Mountain behind, and to the fore the vast, rolling descent of cedar groves and sage flats and sandy washes. No dim dark range made bold outline along the horizon. The stretch of gray and purple and green extended to the blue line of sky.

Down the length of one sage level Shefford saw a long lane where the brush and grass had been beaten flat. This, the Navajo said, was a track where the young braves had raced their mustangs and had striven for supremacy before the eyes of maidens and the old people of the tribe.

"Nas-Ta-Bega, did you ever race here?" asked Shefford.

"I am a chief by birth. But I was stolen from my home, and now I cannot ride well enough to race the braves of my tribe," the

Indian replied bitterly.

In another place Joe Lake halted his horse and called Shefford's attention to a big, yellow rock lying along the trail. Then he spoke in Navajo to the Indian.

"I've heard of this stone . . . Isende Aha," said Joe after Nas-Ta-Bega had spoken. "Get down, and let's see."

Shefford dismounted, but the Indian kept his seat in the saddle.

Joe placed a big hand on the stone and tried to move it. According to Shefford's eye measurement the stone was nearly oval, perhaps three feet high by a little over two in width. Joe threw off his sombrero, took a deep breath, and, bending over, clasped the stone in his arms. He was an exceedingly heavy and powerful man, and it was plain to Shefford that he meant to lift the stone, if that were possible. Joe's broad shoulders strained, flattened; his arms bulged, his joints cracked, his neck corded, and his face turned black. By gigantic effort he lifted the stone and moved it about six inches. Then as he released his hold, he fell, and, when he sat up, his face was wet with sweat.

"Try it," he said to Shefford with his lazy smile. "See if you can heave it."

Shefford was strong, and there had been a time when he took pride in his strength.

Something in Joe's supreme effort and in the gloom of the Indian's eyes made Shefford curious about this stone. He bent over and grasped it as Joe had done. He braced himself and lifted with all his power, till a red blur obscured his sight and shooting stars seemed to explode in his head. But he could not even stir the stone.

"Shefford, maybe you'll be able to heft it someday," observed Joe. Then he pointed to the stone and addressed Nas-Ta-Bega. The Indian shook his head and did not speak.

"This is the Isende Aha of the Navajos," explained Joe. "The young braves are always trying to carry this stone. As soon as one of them can carry it, he is a man. He who carries it farthest is the biggest man. And just so soon as any Indian can no longer lift it, he is old. Nas-Ta-Bega says the stone has been carried two miles in his lifetime. His own father carried it the length of six steps."

"Well, it's plain to me that I am not a man," said Shefford, "or else I am old."

Joe Lake drawled his lazy laugh and, mounting, rode up the trail. Shefford lingered beside the Indian.

"*Bi-nai*," said Nas-Ta-Bega, "I am a chief of my tribe, but I have never been a man. I never lifted that stone. See what the paleface education has done for the Indian!"

182

The Navajo's bitterness made Shefford thoughtful. Could greater injury be done to man than this — to rob him of his heritage of strength?

Joe drove the bobbing pack train of burros into the cedars where the smoke of the hogans curled upward, and soon the whistling of mustangs, the barking of dogs, the bleating of sheep told of his reception. Presently Shefford was in the midst of an animated scene. Great, wooly, fierce dogs, like wolves, ran out to meet the visitors. Sheep and goats were everywhere, and little lambs scarcely able to walk along with others that were frisky and frolicsome. There were pure white lambs, and some that appeared to be painted, they were so beautiful with their fleecy white all except black faces or ears or tails or hoofs. They ran right under Nack-Yal's legs and bumped against Shefford, and kept bleating their thin-piped welcome. Under the cedars surrounding the several hogans were mustangs that took Shefford's eye. He saw an iron-gray with white mane and tail sweeping to the ground; a fiery black, wilder than any other beast he had ever seen; a pinto as wonderfully painted as the little lambs; most striking of all, a pure, cream-colored mustang with grace and fine lines and beautiful mane and tail and, strange to see, eyes as blue as azure. This albino mustang came right up to Shefford, an action in singular contrast with that of the others, and showed a tame and friendly spirit toward him and Nack-Yal. Indeed, Shefford had reason to feel ashamed of Nack-Yal's temper or jealousy.

The first Indians to put in an appearance were a flock of children, half-naked, with tangled manes of raven black hair and skin like gold bronze. They appeared shy and bold by turns. Then a little sinewy man, old and beaten and gray, came out of the principal hogan. He wore a blanket around his bent shoulders. His name was Hosteen Doetin and it meant gentle man. His fine, old, wrinkled face lighted with a smile of kindly interest. His squaw followed him, and she was as venerable as he. Shefford caught a glimpse of the shy, dark Glen-Nas-Pa, Nas-Ta-Bega's sister, but she did not come out. The other Indians appeared coming from adjacent hogans.

Nas-Ta-Bega turned the mustangs loose in among those that Shefford already had noticed, and there rose a snorting, whistling, kicking, plunging mêlée. A cloud of dust hid them somewhat, and then a thudding of swift hoofs told of a run through the cedars. Joe Lake began picking over stacks of goatskins and bags of wool that were piled against the hogan.

"Reckon we'll have one grand job packing out this load," he growled. "It's not so heavy, but awkward to pack."

It developed, from talk with the old Navajo, that this pile was only a half of the load to be packed to Kayenta, and the other half was around the corner of the mountain in a camp of Paiutes. Hosteen Doetin said he would send to the camp and have the Paiutes bring their share over. The suggestion suited Joe, who wanted to save his burros as much as possible. Accordingly a messenger was dispatched to the Paiute camp. Shefford, with time on his hands and poignant memory to combat, decided to recall his keen interest in the Navajo, and learn if possible, what the Indian's life was like. What would a day of his natural life be?

In the gray of dawn, when the hush of the desert still lay deeply over the land, the Navajo stirred in his blanket and began his chant to the morning light. It began very softly and low, a strange, broken murmur, like the music of a brook, and, as it swelled, the weird and mournful tone was slowly lost in one of hope and joy. The Indian's soul was coming out of night's blackness, the sleep that resembled death, and into the day, the light that was life. Then he stood in the door of his hogan, his blanket around him, and faced the east.

Night was lifting out of the clefts and ravines. The rolling cedar ridges and the sage flats were softly gray, with thin veils like smoke mysteriously rising and vanishing. The colorless rocks were changing. A long, horizon-wide gleam of light, rosiest in the center, lay low down in the east and momentarily brightened. One by one the stars in the deep blue sky paled and went out, and the blue dome changed and lightened. Night had vanished on invisible wings, and silence broke to the music of a mockingbird. The rose in the east deepened; a wisp of cloud turned gold; dim, distant mountains showed dark against the red; low down in a notch a rim of fire appeared. Over the soft ridges and valleys crept a wondrous transfiguration. It was as if every blade of grass, every leaf of sage, every twig of cedar, the flowers, and the rocks came to life at sight of the sun. The red disc rose, and a golden fire burned over the glowing face of that lonely waste.

The Navajo, dark, stately, inscrutable, faced the sun — his god. This was his Great Spirit. The desert was his mother, but the sun was his life. To the keeper of the winds and rams, to the master of light, to the maker of fire, to the giver of life the Navajo sent up his prayer.

> Of all the good things of the earth,
>   let me always have plenty,
> Of all the beautiful things of the earth,
>   let me always have plenty.
> Peacefully let my horses go
>   and peacefully let my sheep go.
> God of the heavens,
>   give me many sheep and horses.
> God of the heavens,
>   help me to talk straight.
> Goddess of the earth, my mother,
>   let me walk straight.
> Now all is well, now all is well,
>   now all is well, now all is well.

Hope and faith were his. A chief would be born to save the vanishing tribe of Navajos. A bride would rise from a wind kiss of the lilies in the moonlight. He drank from the clear cold spring bubbling from under mossy rocks.

Nas-Ta-Bega went into the cedars, and the tracks on the trails told him of the visitors in the night. His mustangs whistled to him from the ridge tops, standing clear with heads up and manes flying, and then trooped down through the sage. The shepherd dogs, guardians of the flocks, barked him a welcome, and the sheep bleated and the lambs pattered around him.

In the hogan by the warm red fire his women baked his bread and cooked his meat. He satisfied his hunger. Then he took choice meat to the hogan of a sick relative, and joined in the song and the dance and the prayer that drove away the evil spirit of illness. Down in the valley, in a sandy, sunny place was his cornfield, and here he turned in the water from the ditch, and worked a while, and went his contented way.

He loved his people, his women, and his children. To his son he said: "Be bold and brave. Grow like the pine. Work and ride and play that you may be strong. Talk straight. Love your brother. Give half to your friend. Honor your wife. Pray and listen to our gods."

Then with his gun and his mustang he climbed the slope of the mountain. He loved the solitude, but he was never alone. There were voices in the wind and steps on his trail. The lofty pine, the lichened rock, the tiny bluebell, the seared crag — all whispered their secrets. For him their spirits spoke. In the morning light Old Stone Face, the mountain, was a red god calling him to the chase. He was a brother of the eagle, at home on the heights where the winds swept and the earth lay revealed below.

In the golden afternoon, with the warm sun on his back and the blue cañons at his feet, he knew the joy of doing nothing. He did not need rest, for he was never tired. The sage, sweet breath of the open, was thick in his nostrils, the silence that had so many whisperings was all about him, the loneliness of the wild was his. His falcon eye saw mustang and sheep, the puff of dust down on the cedar level, the Indian riding on a distant ridge, the gray walls and the blue clefts. Here was home, still free, still wild, still untainted. He saw with the eyes of his ancestors. He felt them around him. They had gone into the elements from which their voices came on the wind. They were the watchers on his trails.

At sunset he faced the west, and this was his prayer:

> Great Spirit, God of my fathers,
> Keep my horses in the night.
> Keep my sheep in the night.
> Keep my family in the night.
> Let me wake to the day.
> Let me be worthy of the light.
> Now all is well, now all is well.
> Now all is well, now all is well.

He watched the sun go down and the gold sink from the peaks and the red die out of the west and the gray shadows creep out of the cañons to meet the twilight, and the slow silent mysterious approach of night with its gift of stars.

Night fell. The white stars blinked. The wind sighed in the cedars. The sheep bleated. The shepherd dogs bayed the mourning coyotes. The Indian lay down in his blankets with his dark face tranquil in the starlight. All was well in his lonely world. Phantoms hovered, illness lingered, injury and pain and death were there, the shadow of a strange white hand flitted across the face of the moon, but now all was well — the Navajo had prayed to the God of his fathers. Now all was well!

This, thought Shefford in revolt, was what the white man had killed in the Indian tribes, was reaching out now to kill in this wild remnant of the Navajos. The *padre*, the trapper, the trader, the prospector, and the missionary — so the white man had come, some of him good, no doubt, but more of him evil, and the young brave learned a thirst that could never be quenched at the cold sweet spring of his forefathers, and the young maiden burned with a fever in her blood and lost the sweet, strange, wild fancies of her tribe.

Joe Lake came to Shefford and said: "Withers told me you had a mix-up with a missionary at Red Lake."

"Yes, I regret to say," replied Shefford.

"About Glen-Nas-Pa?"

"Yes, Nas-Ta-Bega's sister."

"Withers just mentioned it. Who was the missionary?"

"Willetts, so Presbrey, the trader, said."

"What'd he look like?"

Shefford recalled the smooth brown face, the dark eyes, the weak chin, the mild expression, and the soft lax figure of the missionary.

"Can't tell by what you said," went on Joe. "But I'll bet a *peso* to a horse hair that's the fellow who's been here. Old Hosteen Doetin just told me. First visits he ever had from the Priest With The Long Gown. That's what he called the missionary. These old fellows will never forget what's come down from father to son about the Spanish *padre* . . . well, anyway, Willetts has been here twice after Glen-Nas-Pa. The old chief is impressed, but he doesn't want to let the girl go. I'm inclined to think Glen-Nas-Pa would as lief go as stay. She may be a Navajo, but she's a girl.

She won't talk much."

"Where's Nas-Ta-Bega?" asked Shefford.

"He rode off somewhere yesterday. Perhaps to the Paiute camp. These Indians are slow. They may take a week to pack that load over here. But if Nas-Ta-Bega or someone doesn't come with a message today, I'll ride over there myself."

"Joe, what do you think about this missionary?" queried Shefford bluntly.

"Reckon there's not much to think, unless you see him or find out something. I heard of Willetts before Withers spoke of him. He's friendly with Mormons. I understand he's worked for Mormon interests, someway or other. That's on the quiet, savvy? This matter of him coming after Glen-Nas-Pa, reckon that's all right. The missionaries all go after the young people. What'd be the use to try to convert the old Indians? No, the missionary's work is to educate the Indian, and, of course, the younger he is the better."

"You approve of the missionary?"

"Shefford, if you understood a Mormon you wouldn't ask that. Did you ever read or hear of Jacob Hamblin? Well, he was a Mormon missionary among the Navajos. The Navajos were as fierce as Apaches till Hamblin worked among them. He made them friendly to the white man."

"That doesn't prove he made converts of them," replied Shefford still bluntly.

"No. For the matter of that Hamblin let religion alone. He made presents, then traded with them, then taught them useful knowledge. Mormon or not, Shefford, I'll admit this . . . a good man, strong with his body and learned in ways with his hands, with some knowledge of medicine, can better the condition of these Indians. But just as soon as he begins to preach his religion, then his influence wanes. That's natural. These heathens have their ideals, their gods."

"Which the white man should leave them!" replied Shefford feelingly.

"That's a matter of opinion. But don't let's argue. Willetts is after Glen-Nas-Pa. And if I know Indian girls, he'll persuade her to go to his school."

"Persuade her!" Then Shefford broke off and related the incident that had occurred at Red Lake.

"Reckon any means justifies the end," replied Joe imperturbably. "Let him talk love to her or rope her or beat her."

Shefford felt a sensation of heat in his neck and had difficulty in controlling himself. From this single point of view the

Mormon was impossible to reason with.

"That, too, is a matter of opinion. We won't discuss it," continued Shefford. "But if old Hosteen Doetin objects to the girl's leaving and, if Nas-Ta-Bega does the same, won't that end the matter?"

"Reckon not. The end of the matter is Glen-Nas-Pa. If she wants to go, she'll go."

Shefford thought best to drop the discussion. For the first time he had occasion to be repelled by something in this kind and genial Mormon, and he wanted to forget it. Just as he had never talked about men to the sealed wives in the hidden valley, so he could not talk of women to Joe Lake.

Nas-Ta-Bega did not return that day, but next morning a messenger came calling Lake to the Paiute camp. Shefford spent the morning high on the slope, learning more with every hour in the silence and loneliness, that he was stronger of soul than he had dared to hope, and that the added pain which had come to him could be borne.

Upon his return toward camp in the cedar grove, he caught sight of Glen-Nas-Pa with a white man. They did not see him. When Shefford recognized Willetts, an embarrassment as well as an instinct made him halt and step behind a bushy, low-branched cedar. It was not his intention to spy on them. He merely wanted to avoid a meeting. But the missionary's hand on the girl's arm, and her uplifted head, her pretty face strange, intent, troubled, struck Shefford with an unusual and an irresistible curiosity. Willetts was talking earnestly. Glen-Nas-Pa was listening intently. Shefford watched long enough to see that the girl loved the missionary, and that he reciprocated. Perhaps he was pretending, but his manner scarcely savored of pretense, Shefford concluded, as he slipped away under the trees.

He did not go at once into camp. He felt troubled and wished that he had not encountered the two. His duty in the matter, of course, was to tell Nas-Ta-Bega what he had seen. Upon reflection, Shefford decided to give the missionary the benefit of a doubt, and, if he really cared for the Indian girl, and admitted or betrayed it, to think all the better of him for the fact. Glen-Nas-Pa was certainly pretty enough and probably lovable enough to please any lonely man in this desert. The pain and the yearning in Shefford's heart made him lenient. He had to fight himself — not to forget, for that was impossible — but to keep rational and sane when a white flower-like face haunted him and a voice called.

The cracking of hard hoofs on stones

caused him to turn toward camp, and, as he emerged from the cedar grove, he saw three Indian horsemen ride into the cleared space before the hogans. They were superbly mounted and well armed, and impressed him as being different from Navajos. Perhaps they were Paiutes. They dismounted, and led the mustangs down to the pool below the spring. Shefford saw another mustang, standing bridle down, and carrying a pack behind the saddle. Some squaws with children hanging behind their skirts were standing at the door of Hosteen Doetin's hogan. Shefford glanced in to see Glen-Nas-Pa, pale, quiet, almost sullen. Willetts stood with his hands spread. The old Navajo's seamed face worked convulsively as he tried to lift his bent form to some semblance of dignity, and his voice rolled out sonorously. "Me no savvy Jesus Christ! Me hungry! Me no eat Jesus Christ!"

Shefford drew back as if he had received a blow. That had been Hosteen Doetin's reply to the importunities of the missionary. The old Navajo could work no longer. His sons were gone. His squaw was worn out. He had no one save Glen-Nas-Pa to help him. She was young, strong. He was hungry. What was the white man's religion to him?

With long swift strides Shefford entered

the hogan. Willetts, seeing him, did not look so mild as Shefford had him pictured in memory, nor did he appear surprised. Shefford touched Hosteen Doetin's shoulder and said: "Tell me."

The aged Navajo lifted a shaking hand. "Me no savvy Jesus Christ! Me hungry! Me no eat Jesus Christ!"

Shefford then made signs that indicated the missionary's intention to take the girl away.

"Him come . . . big talk . . . Jesus . . . all Jesus. Me no want Glen-Nas-Pa go," replied the Indian.

Shefford turned to the missionary. "Willetts, is he a relative of the girl?"

"There's some blood tie, I don't know what. But it's not close," replied Willetts.

"Then don't you think you better wait till Nas-Ta-Bega returns? He's her brother."

"What for?" demanded Willetts. "That Indian may be gone a week. She's willing to go."

Shefford looked at the girl. "Glen-Nas-Pa, do you want to go?"

She was shy, ashamed, and silent, but manifestly willing to accompany the missionary. Shefford pondered a moment. How he hoped Nas-Ta-Bega would come back! It was thought of the Indian that made

Shefford stubborn. What his stand ought to be was hard to define, unless he answered to impulse, and here in the wilds he had become imbued with the idea that his impulses and instincts were no longer false.

"Willetts, what do you want with the girl?" queried Shefford coolly, and at the question he seemed to find himself. He peered deliberately and searchingly into the other's face. The missionary's gaze shifted and a tinge of red crept up from under his collar.

"Absurd thing to ask a missionary!" he burst out impatiently.

"Do you care for Glen-Nas-Pa?"

"I care as God's disciple . . . who cares to save the soul of heathens," he replied with the lofty tone of prayer.

"Has Glen-Nas-Pa no . . . no other interest in you . . . except to be taught religion?"

The missionary's face flamed, and his violent tremor showed that under his exterior there was a different man. "What right have you to question me?" he demanded. "You're an adventurer . . . an outcast. I've my duty here. I am a missionary with church and state and government behind me."

"Yes, I'm an outcast," replied Shefford bitterly. "And you may be all you say. But we're alone now out here on the desert, and this girl's brother is absent. You haven't answered me yet. Is there anything between you and Glen-Nas-Pa except religion?"

"No, you insulting beggar!"

Shefford had forced the reply that he had expected and which damned the missionary beyond any consideration. "Willetts, you are a liar!" said Shefford steadily.

"And what are you?" cried Willetts in shrill fury. "I've heard all about you. Heretic! Atheist! Driven from your church! Hated and scorned for your blasphemy!"

Then he gave way to ungovernable rage and cursed Shefford as a religious fanatic might have cursed the most debased of sinners. Shefford heard with the blood beating, strangling the pulse in his ears. Somehow this missionary had learned his secret — most likely from the Mormons in Stonebridge — and the terms of disgrace were coals of fire upon Shefford's head. Strangely, however, he did not bow to them, as had been his humble way in the past when his calumniators had arraigned and flayed him. Passion burned in him now, and hate, for the first time in his life, made a tiger of him. These raw emotions, new to him, were difficult of control.

"You can't take the girl," he replied, when

the other had ceased. "Not without her brother's consent."

"I will take her!"

Shefford threw him out of the hogan and strode after him. Willetts had stumbled. When he straightened up, he was white and shaken. He groped for the bridle of his horse while keeping his eyes upon Shefford, and, when he found it, he whirled quickly, mounted, and rode off. Shefford saw him halt a moment under the cedars to speak with the three strange Indians, and then he galloped away. It came to Shefford then that he had been unconscious of the last strained moment of that encounter. He seemed all cold, tight, locked, and was amazed to find his hand on his gun. Verily the wild environment had liberated strange instincts and impulses, which he had answered. That he had no regrets proved how he had changed.

Shefford heard the old woman scolding. Peering into the Hogan, he saw Glen-Nas-Pa flounce down in a sullen fret, for all the world like any other thwarted girl. Hosteen Doetin came out and pointed down the slope at the departing missionary.

"Heap talk Jesus . . . all talk . . . Jesus!" he exclaimed contemptuously. Then he gave Shefford a hard rap on the chest. "Small talk . . . heap man!"

The matter appeared to be adjusted for the present. But Shefford felt that he had made a bitter enemy, and perhaps a powerful one.

He prepared and ate his supper alone that evening, for Joe Lake and Nas-Ta-Bega did not put in an appearance. He observed that the three strange Indians, who he took for Paiutes, kept to themselves, and so far as he knew had no intercourse with anyone at the camp. This would not have seemed unusual, considering the taciturn habit of Indians, had he not remembered seeing Willetts speak to the trio. What had he to do with them? Shefford was considering the situation with vague doubts when to his relief the three strangers rode off into the twilight. Then he went to bed.

He was awakened by violence. It was the gray hour before dawn. Dark forms knelt over him. A cloth pressed down hard over his mouth. Strong hands bound it while other strong hands held him. He could not cry out. He could not struggle. A heavy weight, evidently a man, held down his feet. Then he was rolled over, securely bound, and carried, to be thrown like a rock over the back of a horse.

All this happened so swiftly as to be bewildering. He was too astounded to be frightened. As he hung head downward, he saw the legs of a horse and a dim trail. A stirrup swung to and fro, hitting him in the face. He began to feel exceedingly uncomfortable, with a rush of blood to his head and cramps in his arms and legs. This kept on and grew worse for what seemed a long time. Then the horse was stopped, and a rude hand tumbled him to the ground. Again, he was rolled over on his face. Strong fingers plucked at his clothes, and he believed he was being searched. His captors were as silent as if they had been dumb. He felt when they took his pocketbook and his knife and all that he had, that they cut, tore, and stripped off all his clothing. He was lifted, carried a few steps, and dropped upon what seemed a soft, low mound, and left lying there, still tied and naked. Shefford heard the rustle of sage and the dull *thud* of hoofs as his assailants went away.

His first sensation was one of immeasurable relief. He had not been murdered. Robbery was nothing. Although roughly handled he had not been hurt. He associated the assault with the three strange visitors of the preceding day. Still he had no proof of that. Not the slightest clue remained to help him be certain who had attacked him.

It might have been a short while or a long one, his mind was so filled with growing conjectures, but a time came when he felt cold. As he lay face down, only his back felt cold at first. He was grateful that he had not been thrown upon the rocks. The ground under him appeared soft, spongy, and gave somewhat as he breathed. He had really sunk down a little in this pile of soft earth. The day was not far off, as he could tell by the brightening of the gray. He began to suffer with the cold, and then slowly he seemed to freeze and grow numb. In an effort to roll over upon his back he discovered that his position or his being bound or the numbness of his muscles was responsible for the fact that he could not move. Here was a predicament. It began to look serious. What would a few hours of the powerful sun do to his uncovered skin? Somebody would trail and find him, still he might not be found soon.

He saw the sky lighten, turn rosy, and then gold. The sun shone upon him, but some time elapsed before he felt its warmth. All of a sudden a pain, like a sting, shot through his shoulder. He could not see what caused it, probably a bee. Then he felt another upon his leg, and almost simultaneously with it a tiny, fiery stab in his side. A sickening sensation pervaded his body, slowly moving, as if poison had entered the blood of his veins. Then a puncture, as from a hot wire, entered the skin of his breast. Unmistakably it was a bite. By dint of great effort he twisted his head to see a big red ant on his breast. Then he heard a faint sound, so exceedingly faint that he could not tell what it was like, but his straining ears detected a low, swift-rustling, creeping sound, like the slipping rattle of an infinite number of tiny bits of moving gravel. Then it was a sound like the seeping of wind-blown mud. Several hot bites occurred at once. With his head twisted he saw a red stream of ants pour out of the mound and spill over his quivering flesh.

In an instant he realized his position. He had been dropped intentionally on an ant heap, which had sunk with his weight, wedging him between the crusts, at the mercy of those terrible desert ants! A frantic effort to roll out proved futile, as did another and another. His violent muscular contractions infuriated the ants, and in an instant he was writhing in pain so horrible and so unendurable that he nearly fainted. But he was too strong to faint suddenly. A bath of vitriol, a stripping of his skin, and red embers of fire thrown upon raw flesh could not have equaled this. There was fury in the bites and poison in the fangs of these ants. Was this an Indian's brutal trick or was it the missionary's revenge? Shefford realized that it would kill him soon. He sweat what seemed blood, although perhaps the blood came from the bites. A strange, hollow buzzing roar filled his ears, and it must have been the pouring of the angry ants from their mound. There followed a time that was hell, worse than fire, for fire would have given merciful death, agony under which his physical being began spasmodically to jerk and retch and his eyeballs turned and his breast caved in.

A cry rang through the roar in his ears. *"Bi-nai! Bi-nai!"*

His fading sight seemed to fix on the dark face of Nas-Ta-Bega. Then powerful hands dragged him from the mound, through the grass and sage, rolled him over and over, and brushed his burning skin with strong, swift sweeps.

Chapter Nine

That hard experience was but the beginning of many cruel trials for John Shefford. He never knew who his assailants were, or their motive, other than robbery, and they had gotten little for they had not found the large sum of money sewed in the lining of his coat. Joe Lake declared it was Shadd's mark, and the Mormon showed the stern nature that lay hidden under his habitual mild manner. Nas-Ta-Bega shook his head and would not tell what he thought, but a somber fire burned in his eyes.

The three started with a heavily laden pack train and went down the mountain slope into West Cañon. The second day they were shot at from the rim walls. Lake was wounded, hindering the swift flight necessary to escape deeper into the cañon. Here they hid for days, while the Mormon recovered and the Indian took stealthy trips to try to locate the enemy. Lack of water and grass for the burros drove them on. They climbed out of a side cañon, losing several burros on a rough trail, and had proceeded to within half a day's journey of Red Lake when they were attacked while making camp in a cedar grove. Shefford sustained an exceedingly painful injury to his leg, but fortunately the bullet went through without breaking a bone. With that burning pain there came to Shefford the meaning of fight and his rifle grew hot in his hands. Might alone saved the trio from certain fatality. Under the cover of darkness the Indian helped Shefford to escape. Joe Lake looked out for himself. The pack train was lost.

Shefford learned what it meant to be out at night, listening for pursuit, cold to his marrow, sick with dread, and enduring frightful pain from a ragged bullet hole. Next day the Indian half dragged and half carried him down into the red basin, where the sun shone hot and the sand reflected the heat. They had no water. A wind arose, and the valley became a place of flying sand. Through a heavy, stifling pall Nas-Ta-Bega somehow got Shefford to the trading post at Red Lake. Presbrey attended to Shefford's injury and made him comfortable. Next day Joe Lake limped in, surly and somber, with the news that Shadd and eight or ten of his outlaw gang had gotten away with the pack train.

In short time Shefford was able to ride and with his companions went over the pass to Kayenta. Withers already knew of his loss and all he said was that he hoped to meet Shadd someday.

Shefford showed a reluctance to go again to the hidden village in the silent cañon with the rounded walls. The trader appeared surprised, but did not press the point. Shefford meant sooner or later to tell him, yet never quite reached the point. The early summer brought more work for the little post, and Shefford toiled with the others. He liked the outdoor tasks, and at night was grateful that he was too tired to think. Then followed trips to Durango and Bluff and Monticello. He rode fifty miles a day for many days. He knew how a man fared who packed light and rode far and fast. When the Indian was with him, he got along well, but Nas-Ta-Bega would not go near the towns. Thus many mishaps were Shefford's fortune.

Many and many a mile he trailed his mustang, for Nack-Yal never forgot the Sagi, and always headed for it when he broke his hobbles. Shefford accompanied an Indian teamster into Durango with a wagon and four wild mustangs. Upon the return, with a

heavy load of supplies, accident put
Shefford in charge of the outfit. In despair
he had to face the hardest task that could
have been given him — to take care of a
crippled Indian, catch, water, feed, harness,
and drive four wild mustangs that did not
know him and tried to kill him at every turn,
and to get that precious load of supplies
home to Kayenta. That he accomplished it
proved to him the possibilities of a man,
both for endurance and patience. From that
time he never gave up in the front of any
duty.

In the absence of an available Indian he
rode to Durango and back in record time.
Upon one occasion he was lost in a cañon
for days with no food and little water. Upon
another he bore out a sand storm in the
open desert, facing it for forty miles and
keeping to the trail. When he rode into
Kayenta that night, the trader in grim fraise
said there was no worse to endure.

At Monticello, Shefford and Nas-Ta-
Bega stood off a band of desperadoes, and
this time Shefford experienced a strange
sickening shock in the killing, or at least the
wounding, of a man. Later he had other
fights, but in none of them did he know
whether or not he had shed blood.

The heat of midsummer came, when the

blistering sun shone and a hot blast blew across the sand, and the furious storms made floods in the washes. Day and night Shefford was always in the open, and anyone who had ever known him in the past would have failed to recognize him now.

In the early fall, with Nas-Ta-Bega as companion, he set out to the south of Kayenta upon long neglected business of the trader. They visited Red Lake, Blue Cañon, Kearn's Cañon, Orbi, the Hopi villages, Tuba, Meoncopi, and Moen Ave. This trip took many weeks and gave Shefford all the opportunity he wanted to study the Indians and conditions nearer to the border of civilization. He learned the truth about the Indians and the missionaries.

Upon the return trip he rode over the trail he had followed alone to Red Lake and thence on to the Sagi, and it seemed that years had passed since he had first entered the wild region that had come to be home, years that had molded him in the stern and fiery crucible of the desert.

Chapter Ten

In October Shefford arranged for a hunt in the Cresaw Mountains with Joe Lake and Nas-Ta-Bega. The Indian had gone home for a short visit, and upon his return the party expected to start. But Nas-Ta-Bega did not come back. Then the arrival of a Paiute with news that excited Withers and greatly perturbed Lake convinced Shefford that something was wrong.

The little trading post seldom saw much disorder. Certainly Shefford had never known the trader to neglect work. Joe Lake threw a saddle on a mustang he would have scorned to notice in an ordinary moment, and without a word of explanation or farewell rode hard to the north on the Stonebridge trail.

Shefford had long since acquired patience. He was curious, but he did not care particularly what was in the wind. However, when Withers came out and sent an Indian to drive up the horses, Shefford could not refrain from a query.

"I hate to tell you," replied the trader.

"Go on," added Shefford quietly.

"Did I tell you about the government sending a Supreme Court judge out to Utah to prosecute the polygamists?"

"No," replied Shefford.

"I forgot to, I reckon. You've been away a lot. Well, there's been hell up in Utah for six months. Lately this judge and his men have worked down into southern Utah. He visited Bluff and Monticello a few weeks ago. Now, what do you think? Willetts is allied with the judge."

"Willetts! Will he be going to Stonebridge?"

"He's there now. Someone betrayed the whereabouts of the hidden village over in the cañon. All the women have been arrested. The trial begins today."

"Arrested?" echoed Shefford blankly. "Those poor lonely good women? What on earth for?"

"Sealed wives!" exclaimed Withers tersely. "This judge is after the polygamists. They say he's absolutely relentless."

"But . . . women can't be polygamists. Their husbands are the ones responsible."

"Sure, but the prosecutors have got to

find the sealed wives . . . the second wives
. . . to find the law-breaking husbands.
That'll be a job, or I don't know Mormons.
Are you willing to ride over to Stonebridge
with me? That's where the trial is being
held."

Shefford shrank at the idea. Months of
toil and pain and travail had not been
enough to make him forget the strange girl
he had loved, but he had remembered only
at weak and poignant intervals, and a long
time had made thought of her a memory,
like that sad dream that had lured him into
the desert. With the query of the trader returned a bittersweet regret.

"Better come with me," said Withers.
"Have you forgotten Sago Lily? She'll be
put on trial. That girl . . . that child!
Shefford, you know she hasn't any friends.
And now no Mormon man dare protect her
for fear of prosecution."

"I'll go," replied Shefford shortly.

The Indian brought up the horses. Nack-
Yal was thin from his long travel during the
hot summer, but he was as hard as iron, and
the way he pointed his keen nose toward the
Sagi showed how he wanted to make for the
upland country with its clear springs and
valleys of grass. Withers mounted his bay
and with hurried farewell to his wife spurred

the mustang onto the trail. Shefford took time to get his weapons and the light pack he always carried, and then rode out after the trader.

The pace Withers set was the long steady lope to which these Indian mustangs had been trained all their lives. In an hour they reached the mouth of the Sagi, and sight of it made it seem to Shefford that the hard, half year of suffering since he had been there had never been. Withers, to Shefford's regret, did not enter the Sagi. He turned off to the north and took a wild trail into a split of the red wall, and wound in and out, and climbed a crack so narrow that the light was obscured and the cliffs could be touched from both sides of a horse.

Once up on the wild plateau Shefford felt again in a different world from the barren desert he had latterly known. The desert had crucified him, and had left him to die or survive, according to his spirit and his strength. If he had loved the glare, the endless level and deceiving distance, the shifting sand, it had certainly not been as he loved this softer, wilder, more intimate upland. With the red peaks shining up into the blue, and the fragrance of cedar and piñon, and the purple sage and flowers and grass, and splash of clear water over stones —

with these there came back to him something that he had lost and which had haunted him.

It seemed that he had returned to this wild upland of color and cañons and lofty crags and green valleys and silent places with a spirit gained from victory over himself in the harsher and sterner desert below. And strange to him he found his old self, the dreamer, the artist, the lover of beauty, the searcher for he knew not what came to meet him on the fragrant wind. He felt this, saw the old wildness with glad eyes, yet the greater part of his mind was given over to the thought of the unfortunate women he expected to see in Stonebridge.

Withers was harder to follow, to keep up with than an Indian. For one thing, he was a steady and tireless rider, and for another there were times when he had no mercy on a horse. Then an Indian always found easier steps in a trail and shorter cuts. Withers put his mount to some bad slopes, and Shefford had no choice but to follow. However, they crossed the great broken bench of upland without mishap and came out upon a promontory of the plateau, from which Shefford saw a wide valley and dark green alfalfa fields. Stonebridge lay in the center of this fertile valley surrounded by pink cliffs. It must have been a very old town, certainly far older than Bluff or Monticello, although smaller, and evidently it had been built to last. There was one main street, very wide, that divided the town and was crossed at right angles by a stream spanned by a small natural stone bridge. A line of poplar trees shaded each footpath. The little log cabins and stone houses and cottages were half hidden in foliage now tinted with autumn colors. Toward the center of the town the houses and stores and shops fronted upon the street and along one side of a green square, or plaza. Here were situated several edifices, the most prominent of which was a church built of wood, whitewashed, and re-markable, according to Withers, for the fact that not a nail had been used in its construc-tion. Beyond the church was a large, low structure of stone with a split shingle roof, and evidently this was the town hall.

Shefford saw before he reached the square that this day in Stonebridge was one of singular action and excitement for a Mormon village. The town was full of people, and, judging from the horses hitched everywhere and the big canvas-covered wagons, many of the people were visitors. A crowd surrounded the hall, a dusty, booted, spurred, shirt-sleeved, and sombreroed assemblage that did not wear the hallmark Shefford had come to associate with Mormons. They were riders, cowboys, horse wranglers, and some of them Shefford had seen in Durango. Navajos and Paiutes were present, also, but they loitered in the background.

Withers drew Shefford off to the side, where under a tree they hitched their horses.

"Never saw Stonebridge full of a riff-raff gang like is here today," said Withers. "I'll bet the Mormons are wild. There's a tough outfit from Durango. If they can get anything to drink, or if they've got it . . . Stonebridge will see smoke today! Come on, let's get in that hall."

But before Withers reached the hall, he started violently and pulled up short, then with apparent unconcern turned to lay a hand upon Shefford. The trader's face had blanched, and his eyes grew hard and shiny, like flint. He gripped Shefford's arm.

"Look. Over to your left," he whispered. "See that gang of Indians there . . . by the big wagon. See the short Indian with the chaps. He's got a face big as a ham, dark, fierce. That's Shadd. You ought to know him. Shadd and his outfit here. How's that for nerve? But he pulls a rein with the Mormons."

Shefford's keen eye took in a lounging group of ten or twelve Indians and several white men. They did not present any great contrast to the other groups, except that they were isolated, appeared quiet and watchful, and were all armed. A bunch of lean, racy mustangs, restive and spirited, stood nearby in charge of an Indian. Shefford had to take a second and closer glance to distinguish the half-breed. At once he recognized in Shadd the broad-faced, squat Indian who had paid him a threatening visit that night long ago in the mouth of the Sagi. A fire ran along Shefford's veins and seemed to concentrate in his breast. Shadd's dark, piercing eyes alighted upon Shefford and rested there. Then the half-breed spoke to one of his white outlaws, and pointed at Shefford. His action attracted the attention of others in the gang, and for a moment Shefford and Withers were treated to a keen-edged stare.

The trader cursed low. "Maybe I would like to mix it with that damned 'breed," he said. "But what chance have we with that gang? Besides, we're here on other and more important business. All the same, before I forget, let me remind you that Shadd has had you spotted ever since you came out here. A friendly Paiute told me that only

218

lately. Shefford, did any Indian between here and Flagstaff ever see that money you persist in carrying?"

"Why, yes, I suppose so . . . way back in Tuba, when I first came out," replied Shefford.

"Huh! Well, Shadd's after that. Come on, now, let's get inside the hall."

The crowd opened for the trader, who appeared known to everybody. A huge man with a bushy head blocked the way to a shut door.

"Hello, Meade," said Withers. "Let us in."

The man opened the door, permitted Withers and Shefford to enter, and then closed it.

Shefford, coming out of the bright glare of sun into the hall, could not see distinctly at first. His eyes blurred. He heard a subdued murmur of many voices. Withers appeared to be affected with the same kind of blindness, for he stood bewildered a moment. But he recovered sooner than Shefford. Gradually the darkness shrouding many obscure forms lifted. Withers drew him through a crowd of men and women to one side of the hall, and squeezed along a wall to a railing where progress was stopped. Then Shefford raised his head to look with bated breath and strange curiosity.

The hall was large and had many windows. Men were in conversation upon a platform. Women to the number of twenty sat close together upon benches. Back of them stood another crowd, but the women on the benches held Shefford's gaze. They were the prisoners. They made a somber group. Some were hooded, some veiled, all clad in dark garments except one on the front bench, and she was dressed in white. She wore a long hood that concealed her face. Shefford recognized the hood and then the slender shape. She was Mary — she who her jealous neighbors had named Sago Lily. At sight of her a sharp pain pierced Shefford's breast. His eyes were blurred when he forced them away from her, and it took a moment for him to see clearly.

Withers was whispering to him or to someone near at hand, but Shefford did not catch the meaning of what was said. He paid more attention. However, Withers ceased speaking. Shefford gazed upon the crowd back of him. The women were hooded, and it was not possible to see what they looked like. There were many stalwart, clean-cut young Mormons of Joe Lake's type, and these men appeared troubled, even distressed and conjecturing. There was little about them resembling the stern, quiet, somber austerity of the more matured men, and nothing at all of the strange, aloof, serene impassiveness of the gray-bearded old patriarchs. These venerable men were the Mormons of the old school, the sons of the pioneers, the ruthless fanatics. Instinctively Shefford felt that it was in them that polygamy was embodied; they were the husbands of the sealed wives. He conceived an absorbing curiosity to learn if his instinct was correct and hard upon that followed a hot, hateful eagerness to see which one was the husband of Mary.

"There's Bishop Kane," whispered Withers, nudging Shefford. "And there's Waggoner with him."

Shefford saw the bishop, and then beside him a man of striking presence.

"Who's Waggoner?" asked Shefford, as he looked.

"He owns more than any Mormon in southern Utah," replied the trader. "He's the biggest man in Stonebridge, that's sure. But I don't know his relation to the church. They don't call him elder or bishop. But I'll bet he's some pumpkin. He never had any use for me, or any Gentile. A close-fisted, tight-lipped Mormon . . . a skinflint if I ever saw one. Just look him over."

Shefford had been looking and considered it unlikely that he would ever forget this individual called Waggoner. He seemed old, sixty at least, yet, at that, only in the prime of a wonderful physical life. Unlike most of the others he wore his grizzled beard close-cropped, so close that it showed the lean, wolfish line of his jaw. All his features were of striking sharpness. His eyes, of a singularly brilliant blue, were yet cold and pale. The brow had a serious, thoughtful cast, long furrows sloping down the cheeks. It was a strange, secretive face, full of a power that Shefford had not seen in another man's, full of intelligence and thought that had not been used as Shefford had known them used among men. The face mystified him. It had so much more than the strange aloofness so characteristic of his fellows.

"Waggoner had five wives and fifty-five children before the law went into effect," whispered Withers. "Nobody knows and nobody ever will know how many he's got now. That's my private opinion."

Somehow, after Withers said that, Shefford seemed to understand the strange power in Waggoner's face. Absolutely it was of the force, the strength given to a man from his years of control of men. Shefford, long schooled now in his fair-mindedness, fought down the feelings of other years, and waited with patience. Who was he to judge Waggoner or any other Mormon? But whenever his glance strayed back to the quiet, slender form in white, when he realized again and again the appalling nature of this court, his heart beat heavily and labored within his breast.

Then a bustle among the men upon the platform appeared to indicate that proceedings were about to begin. Some men left the platform; several sat down at a table upon which were books and papers, and others remained standing. These last were all roughly garbed, in riding boots and spurs, and Shefford's keen eye detected the bulge of hidden weapons. They looked like deputy marshals on duty.

Somebody whispered that the judge's name was Stone. The name fitted him. He was not young and looked a man suited to the prosecution of these secret Mormons. He had a ponderous brow, a deep, cavernous eye that emitted gleams but betrayed no color or expression. His mouth was the saving human feature of his strong face.

Shefford took the man upon the judge's right hand to be a lawyer, and the one on his left an officer of court, perhaps a prosecuting attorney. Presently this fellow pounded on the table and stood up as if to address a courtroom. Certainly he silenced that hall full of people. Then he perfunctorily and briefly stated that certain women had been arrested upon suspicion of being sealed wives of Mormon polygamists and were to be herewith tried by a judge of the United States Supreme Court. Shefford felt how the impressive words affected the silent hall of listeners, but he gathered from the brief preliminaries that the trial could not be otherwise than a crude, rapid investigation, and perhaps for that the more sinister.

The first woman on the foremost bench was led forward by a deputy to a vacant chair on the platform just in front of the judge's table. She was told to sit down and showed no sign that she had heard. Then the judge courteously asked her to take the chair. She refused. Stone nodded his head as if he had experienced that sort of thing before. He stroked his chin wearily, and Shefford conceived an idea that he was a kind man if he was a relentless judge.

"Please remove your veil," requested the prosecutor.

The woman did so, and proved to be young and handsome. Shefford had a thrill as he recognized her. She was Ruth, who had been one of his best-known acquaintances in the hidden village. She was pale, angry, almost sullen, and her breast heaved. She had no shame, but she seemed to be outraged. Her dark eyes, scornful and blazing, passed over the judge and his assistants, and on to the crowd behind the railing. Shefford, keen as a blade, with all his faculties absorbed, fancied he saw Ruth stiffen and change slightly as her glance encountered someone in that crowd. Then the prosecutor in deliberate and chosen words enjoined her to kiss the Bible handed to her and swear to tell the truth. How strange for Shefford to see her kiss that book he had studied for so many years, stranger still to hear the low murmur from the listening audience as she took the oath.

"What is your name?" asked Judge Stone, leaning back and fixing the cavernous eyes upon her.

"Ruth Jones," was the cool reply.

"How old are you?"

"Twenty."

"Where were you born?" went on the judge. He allowed time for the clerk to record his answers.

"Panquitch, Utah."

"Were your parents Mormons?"

"Yes."

"Are you a Mormon?"

"Yes."

"Are you a married woman?"

"No." The answer was instant, cold, final. It seemed to be the truth. Almost Shefford believed she spoke the truth.

The judge stroked his chin and waited a moment, and then hesitatingly he went on. "Have you . . . any children?"

"No." The blazing eyes met the cavernous ones.

That about the children was true enough, Shefford thought, and he could have testified to it.

"You live in the hidden village near this town?"

"Yes."

"What is the name of this village?"

"It has none."

"Did you ever hear of Fredonia, another village far west of here?"

"Yes."

"It is in Arizona near the Utah line. There are few men there. Is it the same kind of village as this one in which you live?"

"Yes."

"What does Fredonia mean? The name . . . has it any meaning?"

"It means Free Women."

The judge maintained silence for a moment, turned to whisper to his assistants, and then, without glancing up, said to the woman: "That will do."

Ruth was led back to the bench, and the woman next to her was brought forward. This was a heavier person, with the figure and step of a matured woman. Upon removing her bonnet, she showed the plain face of a woman of forty, and it was striking only in that strange, stony aloofness noted in the older men. Here, Shefford thought, was the real Mormon, different in a way he could not define from Ruth. This woman seated herself in the chair and calmly faced her prosecutors. She manifested no emotion whatever. Shefford remembered her and could not see any change in her deportment. This trial appeared to be of little moment to her, and she took the oath as if doing so had been a habit all her life.

"What is your name?" asked Judge Stone, glancing up from a paper he held.

"Mary Danton."

"Family or married name?"

"My husband's name was Danton."

"Was? Is he living?"

"No."

"Where did you live when you were married to him?"

"In Saint George, and later here in Stonebridge."

"You were both Mormons?"

"Yes."

"Did you have any children by him?"

"Yes."

"How many?"

"Two."

"Are they living?"

"One of them is living."

Judge Stone bent over his paper, and then slowly raised his eyes to her face.

"Are you married now?"

"No."

Again the judge consulted his notes, and held a whispered colloquy with the other two men at his table.

"Missus Danton, when you were arrested, there were five children found in your home. To whom do they belong?"

"Me."

"Are you their mother?"

"Yes."

"Your husband Danton is the father of only one, the eldest, according to your former statement. Is that correct?"

"Yes."

"Who then is the father . . . or who are the fathers of your other children?"

"I do not know."

She said it with the most stony-faced calmness, with utter disregard of what significance her words had. A strong, mystic wall of cold flint insulated her. Strangely it came to Shefford how impossible either to doubt or believe her. Yet he did both. Judge Stone showed a little heat.

"You don't know the father of even one of all of these four children?" he queried with sharply rising inflation of voice.

"I do not."

"Madam, I beg to remind you that you are under oath."

The woman did not reply.

"These children are nameless, then . . . illegitimate?"

"They are."

"You swear you are not the sealed wife of some Mormon?"

"I swear."

"How do you live . . . maintain yourself?"

"I work."

"What at?"

"I weave . . . sew . . . bake, and work in my garden."

"My men made note of your large and comfortable cabin, even luxurious, considering this country. How is that?"

"My husband left me comfortable."

Judge Stone shook a warning finger at the defendant.

"Suppose I were to sentence you to jail for perjury? For a year? Far from your home and children! Would you speak . . . tell the truth?"

"I am telling truth. I can't speak about what I don't know. Send me to jail."

Baffled, with despairing, angry impatience, Judge Stone waved the woman away.

"That will do for her. Fetch the next one," he said.

One after another he examined three more women, and arrived, by various questions and answers, different in tone and temper, at precisely the same point as had been made in the case of Mrs. Danton. Thereupon, the proceedings rested a few moments while the judge consulted with his assistants.

Shefford was grateful for this respite. He had been worked up to an unusual degree of interest, and now, as the next Mormon woman to be examined was she who he had loved, and believed he loved still, he felt rise in him emotion that threatened to make him conspicuous unless it could be hidden. The answers of these Mormon women had been not altogether unexpected by him, but once spoken in cold blood under oath how tragic — how appallingly significant of the shadow, the mystery, the yoke that bound them. He was amazed, saddened. He felt bewildered. He needed to think out the meaning of the falsehoods of women he knew to be good and noble. Surely religion, instead of fear, and loyalty were the foundation and the strength of this disgrace, this sacrifice. Absolutely shame was not in these women, although they swore to shameful facts. They had been coached to give these baffling answers, every one of which seemed to brand them, not the brazen mothers of illegitimate offspring, but faithful, unfortunate sealed wives. To Shefford the truth was not in their words, but it sat upon their somber brows.

Was it only his heightened imagination, or did the silence and the suspense grow more intense when a deputy led that dark-hooded, white-clad slender woman to the defendant's chair? She did not walk with the poise that had been manifest in the other women, and she sank into the chair as if she could no longer stand.

"Please remove your hood," requested the prosecutor.

How well Shefford remembered the strong shapely hands! He saw them tremble at the knot of ribbon, and that tremor was communicated to him in a sympathy that made his pulse beat. He held his breath while she removed the hood, and then there was revealed, he thought, the loveliest and most tragic face that ever was seen in a courtroom.

A low, whispering murmur that swelled like a wave ran through the hall, and by it Shefford divined, as clearly as if the fact had been blazoned on the walls, that Mary's face had been unknown to these villagers. But the name Sago Lily had not been unknown. Shefford heard it whispered on all sides.

The murmuring subsided. The judge and his assistants stared at Mary. As for Shefford, it needed not his powerful feeling to make the situation so suddenly dramatic. Not improbably Judge Stone had tried many Mormon women, but manifestly this one was different. Unhooded, Mary appeared to be only a young girl, and a court, confronted suddenly with her youth and the suspicion attached to her, could not but have been shocked. Then her beauty made her seem in that somber company, indeed, the white flower for which she had been named. But, more likely, it was her agony that bound the court into a silence that grew painful. Perhaps the thought that flashed into Shefford's mind was telepathic; it seemed to him that every watcher there realized that in this defendant the judge had a girl of softer mold, of different spirit, and from her the bitter truth could be wrung.

Mary faced the court and the crowd on that side of the platform. Unlike the other women, she did not look at or seem to see anyone behind the railing. Shefford was absolutely sure there was not a man or a woman who caught her glance. She gazed afar, with eyes strained, humid, fearful.

When the prosecutor swore her to the oath, her lips were seen to move, but no one heard her speak.

"What is your name?" asked the judge.

"Mary." Her voice was low with a slight tremor.

"What's your other name?"

"I won't tell."

Her singular reply, the tones of her voice, her manner before the judge marked her with strange simplicity. It was evident that she was not accustomed to questions.

"What were your parents' names?"

"I won't tell," she replied, very low.

Judge Stone did not press the point. Perhaps he wanted to make the examination as easy as possible for her or to wait till she showed more composure.

"Were your parents Mormons?" he went on.

"No, sir." She added the "sir" with a quaint respect contrasting markedly with the short replies of the women before her.

"Then you were not born a Mormon?"

"No, sir."

"How old are you?"

"Seventeen or eighteen. I'm not sure."

"You don't know your exact age?"

"No."

"Where were you born?"

"I won't tell."

"Was it in Utah?"

"Yes, sir."

"How long have you lived in Utah?"

"Always . . . except the last year."

"And that's been over here in the hidden village where you were arrested?"

"Yes."

"But you often visited here . . . this town of Stonebridge?"

"I never was here . . . till yesterday."

Judge Stone regarded her as if his interest as a man was running counter to his duty as an officer. Suddenly he leaned forward.

"Are you a Mormon *now?*" he queried forcibly.

"No, sir," she replied, and here her voice rose a little clearer.

It was an unexpected reply. Judge Stone stared at her. The low buzz ran through the listening crowd. As for Shefford, he was astounded. When his wits flashed back and he weighed her words and saw in her face truth as clear as light, he had the strangest sensation of joy. Almost it flooded away the gloom and pain that attended this ordeal.

The judge bent his head to his assistants as if for counsel. All of them were eager where formerly they had been weary. Shefford glanced around at the dark and somber faces, and a slow wrath grew within him. Then he caught a glimpse of Waggoner. The steel-blue, piercing intensity of the Mormon's gaze impressed him at a moment when all that older generation of Mormons looked as hard and immutable as iron. Either Shefford was overexcited and mistaken, or the hour had become fraught with greater suspense. The secret, the mystery, the power, the hate, the religion of a strange people was thick and tangible in that hall. For Shefford the feeling of the presence of Withers on his left was entirely different from that of the Mormon on his other side. If there was not a shadow there, then the sun did not shine as brightly as it had shone when he entered. The air seemed clogged with nameless passion.

"I gather that you've lived mostly in the country . . . away from people?" the judge began.

"Yes, sir," replied the girl.

"Do you know anything about the government of the United States?"

"No, sir."

He pondered again, evidently weighing his queries, leading up to the fatal and inevitable question. Still, his interest in this particular defendant had become visible.

"Have you any idea of the consequences of perjury?"

"No, sir."

"Do you understand what perjury is?"

"It's to lie."

"Do you tell lies?"

"No, sir."

"Have you never told a single lie?"

"Not . . . yet," she replied, almost whispering. It was the answer of a child and affected the judge. He fussed with his papers. Perhaps his task was not easy; certainly it was not pleasant. Then he leaned forward again, and fixed those deep, cavernous eyes upon the sad face.

"Do you understand what a sealed wife is?"

"I've never been told."

"But you know there *are* sealed wives in Utah?"

"Yes, sir. I've been told that."

Judge Stone halted there, watching her. The hall was silent except for faint rustlings, and here and there deep breaths drawn gradually. The vital question hung like a sword over the white-faced girl. Perhaps she divined its impending stroke, for she sat like a stone with dilating, appealing eyes upon her executioner.

"Are *you* a sealed wife?" he flung at her.

She could not answer at once. She made effort, but the words would not come. He flung the question again, sternly.

"*No!*" she cried.

Then there was silence. That poignant word quivered in Shefford's heart. It was a lie, and he knew it. He would have known it if this hour was the first in which he had ever seen the girl. He heard, he felt, he sensed the fatal thing. The beautiful voice had lacked some quality before present, and the thing wanting was something subtle, an essence, a beautiful ring — the truth. What a hellish thing to make that pure girl a liar, a perjurer! The heat deep within Shefford kindled to fire.

"You are not married?" went on Judge Stone.

"No, sir," she answered faintly.

"You have never been married?"

"No, sir."

237

"Do you expect ever to be married?"

"Oh! . . . no, sir."

She was ashen pale, now, quivering all over, with her strong hands clasping the black hood, and she could no longer meet the judge's glance. Plain to all it was that she lied, yet it was not guilt which agitated her. There was something else, and these keen men of the law detected it.

"Have you . . . any . . . any children?" the judge asked haltingly. It was a hard question to get out.

"Not . . . now."

"Had you any?"

"A baby boy. He . . . he died . . . last summer," she faltered. Again truth, now mingled with agony, spoke in her voice and shone upon her lips.

For a moment the hall and its somber inmates faded from Shefford's sight. He was in the dark. He was stealing under the piñons to Mary's porch, peering for the dim white shape in the shadows, and his heart was full. Then a tiny, pinpointed, exquisitely sweet wail pierced him, transfixed him. The wail of a baby — Mary's baby. He rushed away into the darkness . . . and he saw again the silent hall, with its listening crowd, its stern portent. Mary bowed her head there — that bright, beautiful, golden head.

Her baby was dead. He felt an inward voice crying out: "Thank God for that, oh, you poor child . . . oh, you poor doomed girl!" Then his pity was consumed in fury, and he cursed under his breath and deemed himself unsafe and dangerous in that moment. Wild projects tried to find lodging in his mind. If this unfortunate girl cared for him. . . .

Judge Stone leaned far over the table, and that his face was purple showed Shefford he was a man. His big fist clenched.

"Girl, your baby had to have a father," he said huskily.

She only quivered.

"You're not going to swear you, too, were not visited . . . over there by men . . . you're not going to swear that?"

"Oh . . . no, sir."

Judge Stone settled back in his chair, and, while he wiped his moist face, that same foreboding murmur, almost a menace, moaned through the hall.

Shefford was sick in his soul and afraid of himself. He did not know this spirit that flamed up in him. His helplessness was a most hateful fact.

"Come . . . confess you are a sealed wife," called her interrogator.

She maintained silence, but shook her head.

Suddenly the prosecutor seemed to leap forward. "Unfortunate child! Confess!"

That forced her to lift her head and face him, yet still she did not speak. It was the strength of despair. She could not endure much more.

"Who is your husband?" he thundered at her.

She rose wildly, terror-stricken. It was terror that dominated her, not of the stern judge, for she took a faltering step toward him, lifting a shaking hand, but of someone or something far more terrible than any punishment she could have received in the sentence of a court. Still she was not proof against the judge's will. She had weakened, and the terror must have been because of that weakening.

"Then who was the father of your baby?" he thundered relentlessly.

"I . . . never . . . knew . . . his . . . name."

"But you'd known his face. I'll arrest every Mormon in this country and bring him before you. You'd know his face?"

"Oh, thank God, I wouldn't . . . I couldn't tell! I . . . never . . . saw his face in the light!"

The tragic beauty of her, the certainty of some monstrous crime to youth and innocence, the presence of an agony and terror

that unfathomably seemed not to be for herself, these transfixed the court and the audience, and held them silenced, till she
reached out blindly, and then sank in a heap
to the floor.

Chapter Eleven

Shefford might have leaped over the railing but for Withers's restraining hand, and, when there appeared to be some sign of kindness in those other women for the unconscious girl, Shefford squeezed through the crowd and got out of the hall.

The gang outside that had been denied admittance pressed upon Shefford with jest and curious query and a good nature that jarred upon him. He was far from gentle as he jostled off the first importunities, and the others, gaping at him, opened a lane for him to pass through.

Then there was a hand laid on his shoulder that he did not take off. Nas-Ta-Bega loomed dark and tall beside him. Neither the trader nor Joe Lake or any white man Shefford had met influenced him as this Navajo.

"Nas-Ta-Bega! You here, too. I guess the whole country is here. We waited at

Kayenta. What kept you so long?"

The Indian, always slow to answer, did not open his lips till he drew Shefford apart from the noisy crowd.

"*Bi-nai*, there is sorrow in the hogan of Hosteen Doetin," he said.

"Glen-Nas-Pa!" exclaimed Shefford.

"My sister is gone from the home of her brother. She went away alone in the summer."

"Blue Cañon! She went to the missionary. Nas-Ta-Bega, I thought I saw her there. But I wasn't sure. I didn't want to make sure. I was afraid it might be true."

"A brave who loved my sister trailed her there."

"Nas-Ta-Bega, will you . . . will we go find her, take her home?"

"No. She will come home someday." What bitter sadness and wisdom there were in his words.

"But, my friend, that damned missionary . . . ," began Shefford passionately. The Indian had met him at a bad time.

"Willetts is here. I saw him go in there," interrupted Nas-Ta-Bega, and he pointed to the hall.

"Here! He gets around a good deal," declared Shefford. "Nas-Ta-Bega, what are you going to do to him?"

The Indian held his peace, and there was no telling from his inscrutable face what might be in his mind. He was dark, impassive. He seemed beyond any savagery, and the suffering Shefford divined was deep.

"He'd better keep out of my sight," muttered Shefford, more to himself than to his companion.

"The half-breed is here," said Nas-Ta-Bega.

"Shadd? Yes, we saw him. There! He's still with his gang. Nas-Ta-Bega, what are they up to?"

"They will steal what they can."

"Withers says Shadd is friendly with the Mormons."

"Yes, and with the missionary, too."

"With Willetts?"

"I saw them talk together . . . strong talk."

"Strange. But maybe it's not so strange. Shadd is known well in Monticello and Bluff. He spends money there. They are afraid of him, but he's welcomed just the same. Perhaps everybody knows him. It'd be like him to ride into Kayenta. But, Nas-Ta-Bega, I've got to look out for him, because Withers says he's after me."

"*Bi-nai* wears a scar that is proof," said the Indian.

"Then it must be he who found not long

ago I had a little money."

"It might be. But, *bi-nai,* the half-breed has a strange step on your trail."

"What do you mean?" demanded Shefford.

"Nas-Ta-Bega cannot tell what he does not know," replied the Navajo. "Let that be. We shall know someday. *Bi-nai,* there is sorrow to tell that is not the Indian's . . . sorrow for my brother."

Shefford lifted his eyes to the Indian's, and, if he did not see a dusky sadness there, it was his strange fancy.

"*Bi-nai,* long ago you told a story to the trader. Nas-Ta-Bega sat before the fire that night. You did not know he could understand your language. He listened and he learned what brought you to the country of the Indian. That night he made you his brother. All your lonely rides into the cañons have been to find the little golden-haired child, the lost girl . . . Fay Larkin. *Bi-nai,* I have found the girl you wanted for your sweetheart."

Shefford was bereft of speech. He could not see steadily, and the last solemn words of the Indian seemed far away.

"*Bi-nai,* I have found Fay Larkin," repeated Nas-Ta-Bega.

"Fay Larkin," gasped Shefford, shaking

his head. "But . . . she's dead."

"It would be less sorrow for *bi-nai* if she were dead."

Shefford clutched at the Indian. There was something terrible to be revealed. Like an aspen leaf in the wind he shook all over. He divined the revelation — divined the coming blow — but that was as far as his mind got.

"She's in there," said the Indian, pointing toward the hall.

"Fay Larkin?" whispered Shefford.

"Yes, *bi-nai*."

"My God! *How* do you know? Oh, I could have seen. I've been blind. Tell me, friend. Which one?"

"Fay Larkin is Sago Lily."

Shefford strode away into a secluded corner of the square where, in the shade and quiet of the trees, he suffered a storm of heart and mind. During that short or long time — he had no idea how long — the Indian remained with him. He never lost the feeling of Nas-Ta-Bega close beside him. When the period of acute pain left him and some order began to replace the tumult in his mind, he felt in Nas-Ta-Bega the same quality — silence or strength or help — that he had learned to feel in the deep cañons and the lofty crags. He realized then that the Indian was, indeed, a brother, and Shefford needed him. What he had to fight was more fatal than suffering and love — it was hate rising out of the unsuspected dark gulf of his hurt — the instinct to kill — the murder in his soul. Only now did he come to understand Jane Withersteen's tragic story and the passion of Venters and what had made Lassiter a gunman.

The desert had transformed Shefford. The elements had entered into his muscle and bone, into the very fiber of his heart. Sun, wind, sand, cold, storm, space, stone, loneliness — the iron of the desert man, the cruelty of the desert savage, the wildness of the mustang, the ferocity of hawk and wolf, the bitter struggle of every surviving thing — these were as if they had been melted and merged together and now made the dark and passionate stream that was his throbbing blood. He realized what he had become and gloried in it, yet there, looking on with grave and earnest eyes, was his old self, the man of reason, of intellect, of culture, who had been a good man despite the failure and shame of his life, and he gave heed to the voice of warning, of conscience. Not by revengefully seeking the Mormon who had ruined Fay Larkin and blindly dealing a wild justice could he help this unfortunate girl. His fierce, newborn strength and passion must be tempered by reason, but he became merely elemental, a man answering wholly to primitive impulses. In the darkness of that hour he mined deeply into his heart, understood himself, trembled at the thing he faced, and won his victory. He would go forth from that hour a man. He might fight, and perhaps there was death in the balance, but hate would never overthrow him.

Then, when he looked at future action, he found strangely in him an unalterable purpose to save Fay Larkin. She was very young — seventeen or eighteen, she had said — and there could be, there must be, some happiness before her. It had been his dream to chase a rainbow — it had been his determination to find her in the lost Surprise Valley. How sad the reality! He had found her. It never occurred to him to ask Nas-Ta-Bega how he had discovered that Sago Lily was Fay Larkin. The wonder was, Shefford thought, that he had so long been blind himself. How simply everything worked out now! Every thought, every recollection of her was proof. Her strange beauty, like that of the sweet and rare lily, her low voice that showed the habit of silence, her shapely hands with the clasp strong as a man's, her lithe form, her swift step, her wonderful agility upon the smooth, steep walls, the wildness of her upon the heights, and the haunting, brooding shadow of her eyes while she gazed across the cañons — all these fitted so harmoniously the conception of a child lost in beautiful Surprise Valley and growing up in its wildness and silence, tutored by the sad love of broken Jane and Lassiter. Yes, to save her had been Shefford's dream, and he had loved that dream. He had loved the dream and he had loved the child. The secret of her hiding place as revealed by the story told him and his slow growth from dream to action — these had strangely given Fay Larkin to him. He had loved her. Then had come the bitter knowledge that she was dead. In the light of this subsequent revelation, how easy to account for his loving Mary, too. Never would she be Mary again to him! Fay Larkin and Sago Lily were one and the same. She was here, near him, and he was powerless for the present to help her or to reveal himself. She was held back there in that somber hall among those somber Mormons, alien to the women, bound in some fatal way to one of the men, and now by reason of her weakness in the trial surely to be hated. Thinking of her past and her present, of the poor little dead baby, of the future, and that secret Mormon whose face she had never seen, Shefford felt a sinking of his heart, a terrible cold pang in his breast, a fainting of his spirit. She had sworn she was no sealed wife. But she had lied. That was the one lie on her lips. So then how utterly powerless he was!

But here to save him, to uplift him, came that strange mystic insight which had been the gift of the desert to him. She was not dead. He had found her. What mattered obstacles, even that implacable creed to which she had been sacrificed, in the face of this dilemma and overwhelming truth? It was as mighty as the love suddenly dawning upon him. A strong and terrible and deathly sweet wind seemed to fill his soul with the love of her. It was her fate that had drawn him, and now it was her agony, her innocence, her beauty that bound him for all time. Patience and cunning and toil, passion and blood, the unquenchable spirit of a man to save — these were nothing to give — life itself were little could he but free her.

Patience and cunning! His sharpening mind cut these out as his greatest assets for the present. His thoughts flashed like light through his brain. Judge Stone and his court would fail to convict any Mormon in

Stonebridge, just the same as they had failed in the northern towns. They would go away, and Stonebridge would fall to the slow, sleepy tenor of its former way. The hidden village must become known to all men, honest and outlawed, in that country, but this fact would hardly make any quick change in the plans of the Mormons. They did not soon change. They would send the sealed wives back to the cañon and, after the excitement had died down, visit them as usual. Nothing, perhaps, would ever change these old Mormons but death.

Shefford resolved to remain in Stonebridge and ingratiate himself deeper into the regard of the Mormons. He would find work there, if the sealed wives were not returned to the hidden village. He felt instinctively that he would know Fay Larkin's husband if he ever met him, and he hated, feared the conviction. In case the women went back to the valley, Shefford meant to resume his old duty of driving Withers's pack trains. Wanting that opportunity, he would find some other work, some excuse to take him there.

In due time he would reveal to Fay Larkin that he knew her. How the thought thrilled him! She might deny, might persist in her fear, might fight to keep her secret. But he would learn it — hear her story — hear what had become of Jane Withersteen and Lassiter — and, if they were alive, which now he believed, he would find them — and he would take them and Fay out of the country.

The duty, the great task held a grim fascination for him. He had a foreboding of the cost; he had a dark realization of the force he meant to oppose. There was duty here and pity and unselfish love, but these alone did not actuate Shefford. Mystically fate seemed again to come like a gleam and bade him follow.

When Shefford and Nas-Ta-Bega returned to the town hall, the trial had ended, the hall was closed, and only a few Indians and cowboys remained in the square, and they were about to depart. On the street, however, and the paths and in the doorways of stores were knots of people talking earnestly. Shefford walked up and down, hoping to meet Withers or Joe Lake. Nas-Ta-Bega said he would take the horses to water and feed, and then return.

There were indications that Stonebridge might experience some of the excitement and perhaps violence common to towns like Monticello or Durango. There was only one saloon in Stonebridge, and it was full of roistering cowboys and horse wranglers. Shefford saw the bunch of mustangs, in charge of the same Indian, that belonged to Shadd and his gang. The men were inside drinking in a tavern called Hopewell House, and it was a stone structure of some pretensions. There were Indians lounging outside. Shefford entered through a wide door and found himself in a large bare room, boarded like a loft, with no ceiling except the roof. The place was full of men and noise. Here he encountered Joe Lake, talking to Bishop Kane and other Mormons. Shefford got a friendly greeting from the bishop, and then was well received by the strangers, to whom Joe introduced him.

"Have you seen Withers?" asked Shefford.

"Reckon he's around somewhere," replied Joe. "Better hang up here, for he'll drop in sooner or later."

"When are you going back to Kayenta?" went on Shefford.

"Hard to say. We'll have to call off our hunt. Nas-Ta-Bega is here, too."

"Yes, I've been with him."

The older Mormons drew aside, and then Joe mentioned the fact that he was half starved. Shefford went with him into another clapboard room, which was evidently a dining room. There were half a dozen men at the long table. The seat at the end was a box and scarcely large enough or safe enough for Joe and Shefford, but they risked it.

"Saw you in the hall," said Joe. "Hell . . . wasn't it?"

"Joe, I never knew how much I dared say to you, so I don't talk much. But, it *was* hell," replied Shefford.

"You needn't be so damn' scared of me," spoke up Joe testily. That was the first time Shefford had heard the Mormon speak that way.

"I'm not scared, Joe. But I like you . . . respect you. I can't say so much of . . . of your people."

"Did you stick out the whole mix?" asked Joe.

"No. I had enough when . . . when they got through with Mary." Shefford spoke low and dropped his head. There was silence for a little space, in which time neither man looked at the other.

"Reckon the judge was pretty decent," Joe said finally.

"Yes, I thought so. He might have. . . ." But Shefford did not finish that sentence. "How'd the thing end?"

"It ended all right."

"Was there no conviction . . . no sentence?" Shefford felt a curious eagerness.

"Naw," he snorted, "that court might have saved its breath."

"I suppose. Well, Joe, between you and me, as old friends now, that trial established one fact, even if it couldn't be proved . . . those women *are* sealed wives."

Joe had no reply to that. He looked gloomy, and there was a stern line in his lips. Today he seemed more like a Mormon.

"Judge Stone knew that, as well as I knew," went on Shefford. "Any man of penetration could have seen it. What an ordeal that was for good women to go through! I know they're good. And there they were swearing to. . . ."

"Didn't it make me sick?" interrupted Joe in a kind of growl. "Reckon it made Judge Stone sick, too. After Mary went under, he conducted that trial like a man cuttin' out steers at a roundup. He wanted to get it over. He never forced any question. Bad job to ride down Stonebridge way! It's out of creation. There's only six men in the party, with a poor lot of horses. Really, government officers or not, they're not safe. And they've taken a hunch."

"Have they left already?" inquired Shefford.

"Were packed an hour ago. I didn't see them go, but somebody said they went. On the trail to Bluff, which sure is the only trail they could take, unless they wanted to go to Colorado by way of Kayenta. That might have been the safest trail."

"Joe, what might happen to them?" asked Shefford quietly, with eyes on the Mormon.

"Aw, you know that rough trail. Bad on horses. Weathered slopes . . . slipping ledges . . . a rock might fall on you anytime. Then Shadd's here, with his gang. And bad Paiutes."

"What became of the women?" Shefford asked.

"They're around among friends."

"Where are their children?"

"Left over there with the old women. Couldn't be fetched over. But there are some pretty young babies in that bunch . . . need their mothers."

"I should . . . think so," replied Shefford constrainedly. "When will their mothers get back to them?"

"Tonight, maybe, if this mob of cowpunchers and wranglers gets out of town. It's a bad mix. Shefford, here's a hunch on that. These fellows will get full of whisky and trouble might come, if they approach the women."

"You mean they might get drunk enough to take the oaths of those poor women . . . take the meaning literally . . . pretend to believe the women are what they swore they were?"

"Reckon you've got the hunch," replied Joe gloomily.

"My God, man, that would be horrible!" exclaimed Shefford.

"Horrible or not, it's liable to happen. The women *can* be kept here yet a while. Reckon there won't be any trouble here. Shefford, getting the women over there safe is a job that's been put up to me. I've got a bunch of fellows already. Can I count on you? I'm glad to say you're well thought of. Bishop Kane liked you, and what he says goes."

"Yes, Joe, you can count on me," replied Shefford.

They finished their meal then, and repaired to the big office room of the house. Several groups of men were there, and loud talk was going on outside. Shefford saw Withers talking to Bishop Kane and two other Mormons, both strangers to Shefford. The trader appeared to be speaking with unwonted force, emphasizing his words with energetic movements of his hands.

"Reckon something's up," whispered Joe

hoarsely. "It's been in the air all day."

Withers must have been watching for Shefford. "Here's Shefford now," he said to the trio of Mormons, as Joe and Shefford reached the group. "I want you to hear him speak for himself."

"What's the matter?" asked Shefford.

"Give me a hunch and I'll put in my say-so," said Joe Lake.

"Shefford, it's the matter of a good name more than a job," replied the trader. "A little while back I told the bishop I meant to put you on the pack job over to the valley . . . same as when you first came to me. Well, the bishop was pleased and said he might put something in your way. Just now I ran in here and find you . . . not wanted. When I kicked, I got the straight hunch. Willetts has said things about you. One of them . . . the one that sticks in my craw . . . was that you'd do anything, even pretend to be inclined toward Mormonism, just to be among those Mormon women over there. Willetts is your enemy, and he's worse than I thought. Now I want you to tell Bishop Kane *why* this missionary is bitter toward you."

"Gentlemen, I knocked him down," replied Shefford simply.

"What for?" inquired the bishop in surprise and curiosity.

Shefford related the incident that had occurred at Red Lake and that now seemed again to come forward fatefully.

"You insinuate he had evil intent toward the Indian girl?" queried Kane.

"I insinuate nothing. I merely state what led to my acting as I did."

"Principles of religion, sir?"

"No. A man's principles."

Withers interposed in his blunt way: "Bishop, did you ever see Glen-Nas-Pa?"

"No."

"She's the prettiest Navajo in the country. Willetts was after her, that's all."

"My dear man, I can't believe that of a Christian missionary. We've known Willetts for years. He's a man of influence. He has money back of him. He's doing good works. You hint a love relation."

"No, I didn't hint," replied Withers impatiently. "I *know*. It's not the first time I've known a missionary to do this sort of thing, nor is it the first time for Willetts. Bishop Kane, I live among the Indians. I see a lot I never speak of. My work is to trade with the Indians, that's all. But I'll not have Willetts or any other damned hypocrite run down my friend here. John Shefford is the finest young man that ever came to me in the desert. He's got to be put right before you all, or I'll not set foot in Stonebridge again. Willetts was after Glen-Nas-Pa. Shefford punched him, and later threw him out of the old Indian's hogan up in the mountain. That explains Willett's enmity. He was after the girl."

"What's more, gentlemen, he *got* her," added Shefford. "Glen-Nas-Pa has not been home for six months. I saw her at Blue Cañon. I would like to face this Willetts before you all."

"Easy enough," replied Withers with a grim chuckle. "He's just outside."

The trader went out. Joe Lake followed at his heels, and the three Mormons were next. Shefford brought up the rear and lingered in the door while his eye swept the crowd of men and Indians. His feeling was in direct contrast to his movements. Like the blood leaping in him, he wanted to be swift and fierce, but it seemed a face came between him and his passion — a sweet and tragic face that would have had power to check him in a vastly more critical moment than this. In an instant he had himself in hand and strangely, suddenly, felt the strength that had come to him.

Willetts stood in earnest colloquy with a short, squat Indian — the half-breed Shadd. They leaned against a hitching rail.

Other Indians were there and outlaws. It was a mixed group, rough and hard-looking.

"Hey, Willetts!" called the trader, and his loud, ringing voice, not pleasant, stilled the movement and sound.

When Willetts turned, Shefford was halfway across the wide walk. The missionary not only saw him but also Nas-Ta-Bega, who was standing forward. Joe Lake was ahead of the trader, the Mormons followed with decision, and they all confronted Willetts. He turned pale. Shadd had cautiously moved along the rail, nearer to his gang, and then they, with the others of the curious crowd, drew closer.

"Willetts, here's Shefford. Now say it to his face!" declared the trader. He was angry and evidently wanted the fact known as well as the situation.

Willetts had paled, but he showed boldness.

For an instant Shefford studied the smooth face, with its sloping lines, the dark, wine-colored eyes. "Willetts, I understand you've maligned me to Bishop Kane and others," began Shefford curtly.

"I called you an atheist," returned the missionary harshly.

"Yes, and more than that. And I told these men *why* you vented your spite on me."

Willetts uttered a half laugh, an uneasy, contemptuous expression of scorn and repudiation. "The charges of such a man as you are can't hurt me," he said.

The man did not exactly show fear as he showed disgust at the meeting. He seemed to be absorbed in thought, yet no serious consideration of the situation made itself manifest. Shefford felt puzzled. Perhaps there was no fire to strike from this man. The desert had certainly not made him flint. He had not toiled or suffered or fought.

"But *I* can hurt you," thundered Shefford with startling suddenness. "Here. Look at this Indian. Do you know him? Glen-Nas-Pa's brother. Look at him. Let us see you face him while I accuse you. You made love to Glen-Nas-Pa . . . took her from her home!"

"Harping infidel!" replied Willetts hoarsely. "So that's your game. Well, Glen-Nas-Pa came to my school of her own accord, and she will say so."

"Why will she? Because you blinded the simple Indian girl. Willetts, I'll waste little more time on you!"

Swift and light as a panther, Shefford leaped upon the man, and, fastening powerful hands around the thick neck, bore him to his knees and bent back his head over the rail. There was a convulsive struggle, a hard flinging of arms, a straining wrestle, and then Willetts was in a dreadful position. Shefford held him in iron grasp.

"You damned white-livered hypocrite . . . I'm liable to kill you!" cried Shefford. "I watched you and Glen-Nas-Pa that day up in the mountain. I saw you embrace her. I saw that she loved you. Tell *that*, you liar! That'll be enough."

The face of the missionary turned purple as Shefford forced his head back over the rail.

"I'll kill you, man," repeated Shefford piercingly. "Do you want to go to your God unprepared? Say you made love to Glen-Nas-Pa . . . tell that you persuaded her to leave her home. Quick!"

Willetts raised a shaking hand, and then Shefford relaxed the paralyzing grip and let his head come forward. The half-strangled man gasped out a few incoherent words that his livid guilty face made unnecessary.

Shefford gave him a shove, and he fell into the dust at the feet of the Navajo.

"Gentlemen, I leave him to Nas-Ta-Bega," said Shefford with a strange change from passion to calmness.

Late that night, when the roistering visitors had gone or were deep in drunken slumber, a melancholy and strange procession filed out of Stonebridge. Joe Lake and his armed comrades were escorting the Mormon women back to the hidden valley. They were mounted on burros and mustangs, and in all that dark and somber line there was only one figure that shone while under the pale moon.

At the starting, till that white-clad figure had appeared, Shefford's heart had seemed to be in his throat, and thereafter it beat, muffled and painful, in his breast. Yet there was some sad sweetness in the knowledge that he could see her now, be near her, watch over her.

By and by the overcast of clouds drifted and the moon shone bright. The night was still; the great dark mountain loomed to the stars; the numberless waves of rounded rock that must be crossed and circled lay deeply in shadow. There was only a steady pattering of light hoofs.

Shefford's place was near the head of the line, and he kept well back, riding close to one woman, and then another. No word was spoken. Those sealed wives rode, where their movements were led or driven, as blind in their hoods as veiled Arab women in palanquins, their heads drooped wearily and their shoulders bent, as if under a burden. It took an hour of steady riding to reach the ascent of the plateau and here, with the beginning of rough and smooth and shadowed trail, the work of the escort began. The line lengthened out, and each man kept to the several women assigned to him. Shefford had three and one of them was the girl he loved. She rode as if the world and life and time were naught to her. As soon as he dared trust his voice and his control, he meant to let her know the man who perhaps she had not forgotten was there, with her, a friend. Six months! It had been a lifetime to him. Surely eternity to her! Had she forgotten? He felt like a coward who had basely deserted her. Oh — had he only known!

She rode a burro that was slow, continually blocking the passage for those behind, and eventually grew lame. Thus the other women forged ahead. Shefford dismounted, and stopped her burro. It was a moment before she noted the halt and twice in that time Shefford tried to speak and failed. What poignant pain, regret, love made his utterance fail!

"Ride my horse," he finally said, and his voice was not like his own.

Obediently and wearily she dismounted from the burro and got up on Nack-Yal. The stirrups were long for her, and he had to change them. His fingers were all thumbs as he fumbled with the buckles.

Suddenly he became aware that there had been a subtle change in her. He knew it without looking up, and he seemed to be unable to go on with his task. If his life had depended upon keeping his head lowered, he could not have done it. The listlessness of her drooping form was no longer manifest. The peak of that dark hood pointed toward him. He knew then that she was gazing at him.

Never so long as he lived would that moment be forgotten. They were alone. The others had gotten so far ahead that no sound came back. The stillness was so deep it could be felt. The moon shone with white cold radiance and the shining slopes of smooth stone fell away in immovable waves, crossed by shadows of piñons.

Then she leaned a little toward him. One swift hand felt up to tear the black hood back, so that she could see. In its place flashed her white face, and her eyes were like the night.

"*You,*" she whispered.

His blood came leaping to sting neck and cheek and temple. What dared he interpret from that single word? Could any other word have meant so much?

"No . . . one . . . else," he replied unsteadily.

Her white hand flashed again, to him, and he met it with his own. He felt himself standing cold and motionless in the moonlight. He saw her, wonderful, with the deep shadowy eyes, and a silver sheen on her hair. As he looked, she released her hand, and lifted it, with the other, to her hood. He saw the shining hair darken and disappear, and then the lovely face with its sad eyes and tragic lips.

He drew Nack-Yal's bridle forward, and led him up the moonlit trail.

Chapter Twelve

The following afternoon cowboys and horse wranglers, keen-eyed as Indians for tracks and trails, began to arrive in the quiet valley to which the Mormon women had been returned. Under every cedar clump there were hobbled horses, packs, and rolled bedding in tarpaulins. Shefford and Joe Lake had pitched camp in the old site near the spring. The other men of Joe's escort went to the homes of the women. That afternoon, as the curious visitors began to arrive, these homes became as barred and dark and quiet as if they had been closed and deserted for the winter. Not a woman showed herself.

Shefford and Joe, by reason of the location of their camp and their alertness, met all the newcomers. The ride from Stonebridge was a long and hard one, calculated to wear off the effects of the whisky imbibed by the adventure seekers. This fact alone saved the situation. Nevertheless, Joe expected trouble. Most of the visitors were decent, good-natured fellows, merely curious, and simple-minded enough to believe that this really was what the Mormons had claimed — a village of free women. But there were those among them who were coarse, evil-minded, and dangerous.

By suppertime there were two dozen or more of these men in the valley, camped along the west wall. Fires were lighted, smoke curled up over the cedars, gay songs disturbed the usual serenity of the place. Later in the early twilight these curious visitors, by twos and threes, walked about the village, peering at the dark cabins and jesting among themselves. Joe had informed Shefford that all the women had been put in a limited number of cabins, so that they could be protected. So far as Shefford saw or heard there was no unpleasant incident in the village. However, as the sauntering visitors returned toward their camps, they loitered at the spring, and here developments threatened.

In spite of the fact that the majority of these cowboys and their comrades were decent-minded and beginning to see the real relation of things, they were not disposed to be civil to Shefford. They were certainly not Mormons, and his position, apparently, as a

269

Gentile among these Mormons was one open to criticism. They might have been jealous, too. At any rate remarks were passed in his hearing, meant for his ears, that made it exceedingly trying for him not to resent them. Moreover, Joe Lake's increasing impatience rendered the situation more difficult. Shefford welcomed the arrival of Nas-Ta-Bega. The Indian listened to the loud talk of several loungers around the campfire, and, thereafter, he was like Shefford's shadow, silent, somber, watchful.

Nevertheless, it did not happen to be one of the friendly and sarcastic cowboys that precipitated the crisis. A horse wrangler named Beale, a man of bad repute, as much outlaw as anything, took up the bantering.

"Say, Shefford, what in the hell's your job here, anyway?" he queried, as he kicked a cedar branch into the campfire. The brightening blaze showed him swarthy, unshaven, a large-featured, ugly man.

"I've been doing odd jobs for Withers," replied Shefford. "Expect to drive back trains in here for a while."

"You must stand strong with these Mormons. Must be a Mormon yerself?"

"No," said Shefford briefly.

"Wal, I'm stuck at your job. Do you need a packer? I can throw a diamond-hitch better'n any feller in this country."

"I don't need help."

"Mebbe you'll take me over to see the la-dies," he went on with a coarse laugh.

Shefford did not show that he had heard.

Beale waited, leering as he looked from the keen listeners to Shefford. "Want to hawg them all yerself, eh?" he jeered.

Shefford struck him — sent him tum-bling heavily, like a log. Beale, cursing as he half rose, jerked out his gun. Nas-Ta-Bega, swift as light, kicked the gun out of his hand. Joe Lake picked it up. Deliberately the Mormon cocked the weapon and stood over Beale.

"Get up!" he ordered, and Shefford heard the ruthless Mormon cuff him then.

Beale rose slowly. Then Joe prodded him in the middle with the cocked gun. Shefford, startled, expected the gun to go off. So did the others, especially Beale, who cringed in panic from the dark Mormon.

"Rustle!" said Joe, and gave the man a harder prod. Assuredly the gun did not have a hair-trigger.

"Joe, mebbe it's loaded!" protested one of the cowboys.

Beale shrank back, and turned to hurry away with Joe close after him. They disap-peared in the darkness. A constrained silence was maintained around the campfire for a while. Soon some of the men walked off, and others began to converse. Everybody heard the sound of hoofs passing down the trail. The patter ceased, and in a few moments Lake returned. He still carried Beale's gun.

The crowd dispersed completely then. There was no indication of further trouble. However, Shefford and Joe and Nas-Ta-Bega divided the night into watches, so that someone would be wide-awake.

Early next morning there was an exodus from the village of the better element among these visitors. "No fun hangin' around hyar," one of them expressed it, and, as good-naturedly as they had come, they rode away. Six or seven of the desperado class remained behind, bent on mischief, and they were reinforced by more arrivals from Stonebridge. They avoided the camp by the spring, and, when Shefford and Lake attempted to approach them, they gave them a wide berth. This caused Joe to assert that they were up to some dirty work. All morning they lounged around under the cedars, keeping out of sight, and evidently the reinforcement from Stonebridge had brought liquor. When they gathered together at their camp, half drunk, all noisy, some wanting to rant in the village and others trying to hold them back, Joe Lake said grimly that somebody was going to get shot. Indeed, Shefford saw that there was every likelihood of bloodshed.

"Reckon we'd both better take to one of the cabins," said Joe.

Thereupon the three repaired to the nearest cabin and, entering, kept watch from the windows. During a couple of hours, however, they did not see or hear anything of the ruffians. Then came a shot from over in the village, a single yell, and after that a scattering volley. The silence and suspense following were finally broken by hoof beats. Nas-Ta-Bega called Joe and Shefford to the window he had been stationed at. From here they saw the unwelcome visitors ride down the trail to disappear in the cedars toward the outlet of the valley. Joe, who had numbered them, said that all but one of them had gone.

"Reckon he got it," added Joe.

So, indeed, it turned out. One of the men, a well-known rustler named Harker, had been killed, but by whom did not come out. He had brazenly tried to force his way into one of the houses, and the act had cost him his life. Naturally Shefford, never free from his civilized habit of thought, remarked apprehensively that he hoped this affair would not cause the poor women to be arrested again and hailed before some rude court.

"Law!" Joe grunted. "There isn't any. The nearest sheriff is in Durango. That's Colorado. And he'd give us a medal for killing Harker. It was a good job, for it'll teach these rowdies a lesson."

The Mormons, despite their indifference to the killing of the desperado, gave him decent burial, and prayed for his soul.

Next day the old order of life was resumed in the village, and the arrival of a heavily laden pack train, under the guidance of Withers, attested to the fact that the Mormons meant not only to continue inhabiting the valley, but also to build and plant and enlarge. This was good news to Shefford. At least, the village could be made less lonely, and there was plenty of work to give him excuse for staying there. Furthermore, Withers brought a message from Bishop Kane to the effect that the young man was offered a place as teacher in the school, in co-operation with the Mormon teachers. Shefford experienced no twinge of conscience when he accepted.

It was the fourth evening after the never to be forgotten moonlight ride to the valley that Shefford passed under the dark piñon trees on his way to Fay Larkin's cottage. He paused in the gloom, and memory beset him. The six months were annihilated, and it was the night he had fled from a tiny, soul-piercing wail. But now all was silent. He seemed to be trying to drag himself back. A beginning must be made. Only how to meet her — what to say — what to conceal!

He tapped on the door, and she came out. After all, it was a meeting vastly different from what his feeling made him imagine it might have been. She was nervous, frightened, as were all the other women for that matter. She was alone in the cottage. He made haste to reassure her about the improbability of any further trouble such as had befallen the last week. As he had always done on those former visits to her, he talked rapidly, using all his wit, and here his emotion made him eloquent. He avoided personalities, except to tell about his prospect of work in the village, and he sought above all to lead her mind from thought of herself and her condition. Before he left he had the gladness of knowing he had succeeded.

When he said good night, he felt the strange falsity of his position. He did not expect to be able to keep up the deception for long. That roused him, and half the night he lay awake thinking. Next day he was the life of the work and study and play in that village. Kindness and goodwill did not need inspiration, but it was keen deep passion that made him a plotter for influence and friendship. Was there a woman in the village who he might trust, in case he needed one? His instinct guided him to her who he had liked well — Ruth. Ruth Jones she had called herself at the trial, and, when Shefford used the name, she laughed mockingly. Ruth was not very religious, and sometimes she was bitter and hard. She wanted life, and here she was a prisoner in a lonely valley. She welcomed Shefford's visits. He imagined that she had slightly changed, and whether it was the added six months with its trouble and pain, or a growing revolt, he could not tell. After a time he divined that the inevitable retrogression had set in: she had not enough faith to uphold the burden she had accepted, or the courage to cast it off. She was ready to love him. That did not frighten Shefford, and, if she did love him, he was not so sure it would not be an anchor for him. He saw her danger, and then he became what he had never really been in all the days of his ministry — the real helper. Unselfishly, for her sake, he found power to influence her, and selfishly, for the sake of Fay Larkin, he began slowly to win her to a possible need.

The days passed swiftly. Mormons came and went, although in the open day as laborers. New cabins went up, and a store, and other improvements. Some part of every evening Shefford spent with Fay, and these visits were no longer unknown to the village. Women gossiped in a friendly way about Shefford, but with jealous tongues about the girl. Joe Lake told Shefford the run of the village talk. Anything concerning Sago Lily the droll Mormon took to heart. He had been hard hit and admitted it. Sometimes he went with Shefford to call upon her, but he talked little and never remained long. Shefford had anticipated antagonism on the part of Joe. However, he did not find it.

Shefford really lived the busy day for that hour with Fay in the twilight. Yet every evening seemed the same. He would find her in the dark, alone, silent, brooding, hopeless. Her mood did not puzzle him, but how to keep from plunging her deeper into despair baffled him. He exhausted all his powers trying to do for her what he had been able to do for Ruth, but he failed. Something had blunted her. Had she loved the baby? He dared not ask. The shadow of that baneful trial hovered over her, and he came to sense a strange terror in her. It was mostly always present. Was she thinking of Jane Withersteen and Lassiter, left dead or imprisoned in the valley from which she had been brought so mysteriously? Shefford wearied his brain revolving these questions. Her baby, the fate of her friends, and the cross she bore — of these was tragedy born, but the terror — that Shefford divined came of waiting for the visit of the Mormon whose face she had never seen. Shefford prayed that he might never meet this man. Finally he grew desperate. When he first arrived at the girl's home, she would speak, she showed gladness, relief, and then straightaway she dropped back into the shadows of her gloom. When he got up to go, then there was a wistfulness, an unspoken need, an unconscious reliance, in her reluctant good night.

The hour finally came when he had reached his limit. He must begin his revelation.

"You never ask me anything . . . let alone about myself," he said.

"I'd like to hear," she replied timidly.

"Do I strike you as an unhappy man?"

"No, indeed."

"Well, how *do* I strike you?"

This was an entirely new tack he had veered to.

"Very good and kind to us women," she said.

"I don't know about that. If I am so, it doesn't bring me happiness. Do you remember what I told you once, about my being a preacher . . . disgrace, ruin, and all that . . . and my rainbow-chasing dream out here after a . . . a lost girl?"

"I . . . remember all . . . you said," she replied, very low.

"Listen." His voice was a little husky, but behind it there seemed a tide of resistless utterance. "Loss of faith and name did send me to this wilderness. But I had love . . . love for that lost girl, Fay Larkin. I dreamed about her till I loved her. I dreamed that I would find her . . . my treasure . . . at the foot of a rainbow. Dreams! When you told me she was dead, I accepted that. There was truth in your voice. I respected your reticence. But something died in me, then. I lost myself, the good that might have uplifted me. I went away, down upon the barren desert, and there I rode and slept and grew into another and a harder man. Yet strange to say, I never forgot her, though my dreams were done. As I toiled and suffered and changed, I loved her . . . if not her, the thought of her . . . more and more. Now I have come back to these walled valleys . . . to

279

the smell of piñon, to the flowers in the nooks, to the wind in the heights, to the silence and loneliness and beauty. Here the dreams came back, and *she* is with me always. Her spirit is all that keeps me kind and good, as you say I am. But I suffer, I long for her alive. If I love her dead, how could I love her living! Always I torture myself with the vain dream that . . . that she *might* not be dead. I have never been anything but a dreamer. And here I go about my work by day and lie awake at night with that lost girl in my mind. I love her. Does that seem strange to you? But it would not if you understood. Think. I had lost faith, hope. I set myself a great work . . . to find Fay Larkin. And by the fire and the iron and the blood, that I felt it would cost to save her, some faith must come to me again. My work is undone . . . I've never saved her. But, listen, how strange it is to feel . . . now . . . as I let myself go . . . that just loving her and the living here in the wildness that holds her somewhere have brought me hope again. Some faith must come, too. It was through her that I met this Indian, Nas-Ta-Bega. He has saved my life . . . taught me much. What would I ever have learned if the naked and vast earth, if the sublimity of the wild uplands, of the storm and night and sun, if I had not followed a gleam she inspired? In my hunt for a lost girl perhaps I wandered into a place where I shall find God, and my salvation. Do you marvel that I love Fay Larkin . . . that she is not dead to me? Do you marvel that I love her, when I *know*, were she alive, chained in a cañon, or bound, or lost in any way, my destiny would lead me to her, and she should be saved?"

Shefford ended, overcome with emotion. In the dusk he could not see the girl's face, but the white form that had drooped so listlessly seemed now charged by some vitalizing current. He knew he had spoken irrationally; still, he held it no dishonor to have told her he loved her as one dead. If she took that love to the secret heart of the living Fay Larkin, then perhaps a spirit might light in her darkened soul. He had no thought yet that Fay Larkin might ever belong to him. He divined a crime. He had seen her agony. He knew she was a sealed wife, yet not a wife. This avowal of his was only one step toward her deliverance.

Softly she rose, retreating into the shadow.

"Forgive me if I . . . I disturbed you, distressed you," he said. "I wanted to tell you. She was . . . somehow known to you. I am not happy. And are *you* happy? Let her memory be a bond between us. Good night."

"Good night."

Faintly as the faintest whisper, a breathless reply, and it came from a child forced into womanhood, who had known motherhood, and that dark burden weighing on a sealed wife, it whispered of girlhood not dead, of sweet incredulity, of amazed tumult, of a wondering, frantic desire to run and hide, of the bewilderment incident to a first hint of love.

Shefford walked away into the darkness. The whisper filled his soul. Had a word of love ever been spoken to that girl? Never — not the love that had been in his life. Fay Larkin's lonely life spoke clearly only in her whisper.

Next morning, as the sun gilded the looming peaks and shafts of gold slanted into the valley, she came swiftly down the path to the spring. Shefford paused in his task of chopping wood. Joe Lake, on his knees, with his big hands in a pan of dough, lifted his head to stare. She had left off the somber black hood, and, although that made a vast difference in her, still it was not enough to account for what struck both men.

"Good morning," she called brightly.

They both answered, but not spontaneously. She stooped at the spring, and with one sweep of her strong arm filled the bucket, and lifted it. Then she started back down the path and, pausing opposite the camp, set the bucket down.

"Joe, do you still pride yourself on your sourdough?" she asked.

"Reckon I do," replied Joe with a grin.

"I've heard about your boasts, but never tasted your bread," she went on.

"I'll ask you to eat with us someday."

"Don't forget," she replied.

Then shyly she looked at Shefford. She was like the fresh dawn, and the gold of the sun shone on her head.

"Have you chopped all that wood . . . so early?" she asked.

"Sure," replied Shefford, laughing. "I have to get up early to keep Joe from doing all the camp chores."

She smiled, and then to Shefford she seemed to gleam, to be radiant.

"It'd be a lovely morning to climb . . . 'way high."

"Why . . . yes . . . it would," replied Shefford awkwardly. "I wish I didn't have my work."

"Joe, will *you* climb with me someday?"

"I should smile I will," declared Joe.

"But I can run right up the walls."

"I reckon. Mary, it wouldn't surprise me to see you fly."

"Do you mean I'm like a cañon swallow or an angel?"

Then, as Joe stared speechlessly, she said good bye and, taking up the bucket, went on with her swift, graceful step.

"She's perked up," said the Mormon, staring after her. "Never heard her say more'n yes or no till now."

"She did seem . . . bright," replied Shefford. He was stunned. What had happened to her? Today, this girl had not been Mary, the sealed wife, or Sago Lily, alien among Mormon women. Then it flashed upon him — she was Fay Larkin. She who had regarded herself as dead had come back to life. In one short night what had transformed her, what had taken place in her heart? Shefford dared not accept, or allow to lodge in his mind, a thrilling idea that he had made her forget her misery.

"Shefford, did you ever see her like that?" asked Joe.

"Never."

"Haven't you . . . something to do with it?"

"Maybe I have. I . . . I hope so."

"Reckon you've seen how she's faded . . . since the trial?"

"No," replied Shefford swiftly. "But I've not seen her face in daylight since then."

"Well, take my hunch," said Joe soberly. "She's begun to fade like the cañon lily when it's broken. And she's going to die unless. . . ."

"Why, man!" ejaculated Shefford. "Didn't you see . . . ?"

"Sure I see," interrupted the Mormon. "I see a lot you don't. She's so white you can look through her. She's grown thin, all in a week. She doesn't eat. Oh, I know, because I've made it my business to find out. It's no news to the women. But they'd like to see her die. And she will die unless. . . ."

"My God!" exclaimed Shefford huskily. "I never noticed . . . I never thought . . . Joe, hasn't she any friends?"

"Sure. You, and Ruth . . . and me. Maybe Nas-Ta-Bega, too. He watched her a good deal."

"We can do so little, when she needs so much."

"Nobody can help her, unless it's you," went on the Mormon. "That's plain talk. She seemed different this morning. Why she was alive . . . she talked . . . she smiled. Shefford, if you cheer her up, I'll . . . I'll go to hell for you!"

The big Mormon, on his knees, with his

hands in a pan of dough and his shirt all covered with flour, presented an incongruous figure of a man activated by pathos and passion. Yet the contrast made his emotion all the simpler and stronger. Shefford grew closer to Joe in that moment.

"Why do you think *I* can cheer her . . . help her?" queried Shefford.

"I don't know. But she's different with you. It's not that you're a Gentile, though, for all the women are crazy about you. You talk to her. You have power over her, Shefford. I feel that. She's only a kid."

"Who is she, Joe? Where did she come from?" asked Shefford, very low, with his eyes cast down.

"I don't know. I can't find out. Nobody knows. It's a mystery . . . to all the younger Mormons, anyway."

Shefford burned to ask questions about the Mormon whose sealed wife the girl was, but he respected Joe too much to take advantage of him in a poignant moment like this. Besides, it was only jealousy that made him burn to know the Mormon's identity, and jealousy had become a creeping, insidious, growing fire. He would be wise not to add fuel to it. He rejected many things before he thought of one that he could voice to his friend. "Joe, it's only her body that belongs to . . . to . . . her soul isn't lost to. . . ."

"John Shefford, let that go. My mind's tired. I've been taught so and so, and I'm not bright. But, after all, men are much alike. The thing with you and me is this . . . we don't want to see *her* grave."

Love spoke there. The Mormon had seized upon the single elemental point that concerned him and his friend in their relation to this unfortunate girl. His simple powerful statement united them. It gave the lie to his limit of denseness. It stripped the truth naked. It was such a wonderful, thought-provoking statement that Shefford needed time to ponder how deep the Mormon was. To what limit would he go? Did he mean that here, between two men who loved the same girl, class, duty, honor, creed were nothing if they stood in the way of her deliverance and her life?

"Joe Lake, you Mormons are impossible," said Shefford deliberately. "You don't want to see her grave. So long as she lives . . . remains on the earth . . . white and gold like the flower you call her, that's enough for you. It's her body you think of. And that's the great and horrible error in your religion. But death of the soul is infinitely worse than death of the body. I have been thinking of her soul. So here we stand, you and I. You to save her life . . . I to save her soul. What will you do?"

"Why, John, I'd turn Gentile," he said with terrible softness. It was a softness that scorned Shefford for asking, and likewise it flung defiance at his creed and into the face of hell.

Shefford felt the sting and the exaltation. "And I'd be a Mormon," he said.

"All right. We understand each other. Reckon there won't be any call for such extremes. I haven't an idea what you mean . . . what can be done. But I say, go slow, so we won't all find graves. First cheer her up somehow. Make her want to live. But go slow, John. And don't be with her late!"

That night Shefford found her waiting for him in the moonlight — a girl who was as transparent as crystal clear water — who had left off the somber gloom with the black hood — who was at one moment timid and wild, like a half-frightened fawn, and the next exquisitely half conscious of what it meant to be thought dead but to be alive, to be awakening, wondering, palpitating, and to be loved.

Shefford lived the hour as a dream, and went back to the quiet darkness under the cedars, to lie wide-eyed, trying to recall all that she had said. For she had talked as if utterance had long been dammed behind a barrier of silence.

There followed other hours like that one, indescribable hours, so sweet they stung, and in which, keeping pace with his love, was the nobler stride of a spirit that more every day lightened her burden. The thing he had to do, sooner or later, was to tell her he knew she was Fay Larkin, not dead but alive, and that not love but sacrifice nailed her down to her martyrdom. Many and many a time he had tried to force himself to tell her, only to fail. He hated to risk ending this sweet, strange, thoughtless, girlish mood of hers. It might not be soon won back — perhaps never. How could he tell what chains bound her? He vacillated between Joe's cautious advice to go slow and his own pity. The days and weeks slipped by.

One haunting fear kept him sleepless half the night and sick even in his dreams, and it was that the Mormon whose sealed wife she was might come, surely would come some night. Shefford could bear it, but what would that visit do to Fay Larkin? Shefford instinctively feared the awakening in the girl of womanhood, of deeper insight, of a spiritual realization of what she was, of a physical dawn.

He might have spared himself needless torture. One day Joe Lake eyed him with a penetrating glance. "Reckon you don't have to sleep right on that Stonebridge trail," said the Mormon significantly.

Shefford felt the blood burn his neck and face. He had pulled his tarpaulin closer to the trail, and his motive was as an open page to the keen Mormon.

"Why?" asked Shefford.

"There won't be any Mormons riding in here soon . . . by night . . . to visit the women," replied Joe bluntly. "Haven't you figured there might be government spies watching the trail?"

"No, I haven't."

"Well, take a hunch, then," added the Mormon gruffly, and Shefford divined, as well as if he had been told, that warning word had gone to Stonebridge, gone despite the fact that Nas-Ta-Bega had reported every trail free of watchers. There was no sign of any spies, cowboys, outlaws, or Indians in the vicinity of the valley. A passionate gratitude to the Mormon overcame Shefford, and the unreasonableness of it, the nature of it, perturbed him greatly. But something hammered into his brain, if he loved one of these sealed wives, how could he help being jealous?

The result of Joe's hint was that Shefford put off the hour of revelation, lived in his dream, helped the girl grow further and further away from her trouble, till that inevitable hour arrived when he was driven by accumulated emotion as much as the exigency of the case.

He had not often walked with her beyond the dark shade of the piñons around her cottage, but this night, when he knew he must tell her, he led her away from the path, through the cedar grove to the west end of the valley where it was wild and lonely and sad and silent.

The moon was full, and the great peaks were crowned as with snow. A coyote let out his cutting cry. There were a few melancholy notes from a night bird near the stone walls. The air was clear and cold, with a tang of frost in it. Shefford gazed about him at the vast, uplifted, insulating walls, and that feeling of his which was more than a sense told him how walls like these, and the silence and shadow and mystery, had been nearly all of Fay Larkin's life. He felt them all in her.

He stepped out in the open, near the line where the dark shadow of the wall met the silver moonlight on the grass, and here, by a huge flat stone where he had come often alone and sometimes with Ruth, he faced Fay Larkin in the spirit to tell her gently that he knew her, and sternly to force her secret from her.

"Am I your friend?" he began.

"Ah! . . . my only friend," she said.

"Do you trust me, believe I mean well by you, want to help you?"

"Yes, indeed."

"Well, then, let me speak of you. You know one topic we've never touched upon. You!"

She was silent, and looked wonderingly, a little fearfully, at him, as if vague, disturbing thoughts were entering the fringe of her mind.

"Our friendship is a strange one, is it not?" he went on.

"How do I know? I never had any other friendship. What do you mean by strange?"

"Well, I'm a young man. You're a . . . a married woman. We are together a good deal . . . and like to be."

"Why is that strange?" she asked.

Suddenly Shefford realized that there was nothing strange in what was natural. A remnant of sophistication clung to him and that had spoken. He needed to speak to her in a way that in her simplicity she would understand.

"Never mind strange. Say that I am interested in you, and, as you're not happy, I want to help you. And say that your neighbors are curious, and oppose my idea. Why do they?"

"They're jealous and want you themselves," she replied with sweet directness. "They've said things I don't understand. But I felt they . . . they hated in me what would be all right in themselves."

Here to simplicity she added truth and wisdom, as an Indian might have expressed them. But shame was unknown to her, and she had as yet only vague perceptions of love and passion. Shefford began to realize through the quickness of her mind that she was, indeed, awakening.

"They are jealous . . . were jealous before I ever came here. That's only human nature. I was trying to get to a point. Your neighbors are curious. They oppose me. They hate you. It's all bound up in the . . . the fact of your difference from them, your youth, beauty . . . that you're not a Mormon . . . that you nearly betrayed their secret at the trial in Stonebridge."

"Please . . . please don't . . . speak of that," she faltered.

"But I must," he replied swiftly. "That trial was a torture to you. It revealed so

293

much to me. I know you are a sealed wife. I know there has been a crime. I know you've sacrificed yourself. I know that love and religion have nothing to do with . . . what you are . . . now, is not all that true?"

"I must not tell," she whispered.

"But I shall *make* you tell," he replied, and his voice rang.

"Oh, no, you cannot," she said.

"I can . . . with just one word."

Her eyes were great, starry, shadowy gulfs, dark in the white beauty of her face. She was calm now. She had strength. She invited him to speak the word, and the wistful, tremulous quiver of her lips was for his earnest thought of her.

"Wait . . . a . . . little," said Shefford unsteadily. "I'll come to that presently. Tell me this. Have you ever thought of being free?"

"Free!" she echoed, and there was singular depth and richness in her voice. That was the first spark of fire he had struck from her. "Long ago, the minute I was unwatched, I'd have leaped from a wall had I dared. Oh, I wasn't afraid. I'd love to die that way. But I never dared!"

She was silent then.

"Suppose I offered to give you freedom . . . that meant life?"

"I couldn't . . . take it."

"Why?"

"Oh, my friend, don't ask me any more."

"I know. I can see . . . you want to tell me . . . you *need* to tell."

"But I daren't."

"Don't you trust me?"

"I do. I do."

"Then tell me."

"No . . . no . . . oh, no!"

The moment had come. How sad, tragic, yet glorious for him! It would be like a magic touch upon this lovely, cold, white ghost of Fay Larkin, transforming her into a living, breathing girl. He had held his love as a thing aloof and, as such, intangible. Because of the living death she believed she lived, it had no warmth and intimacy for them. What might it not become with a lightning flash of revelation? He dreaded, yet he was driven to speak. He waited, swallowing hard, fighting the tumultuous storm of emotion, and his eyes dimmed.

"What did I come to this country for?" he asked suddenly in a ringing, powerful voice.

"To find a girl," she whispered.

"I've found her!"

She began to shake. He saw a white hand go to her breast.

"Where is Surprise Valley? How were you

taken from Jane Withersteen and Lassiter? I
know they're alive. But where?"

She seemed to turn to stone.

"Fay! *Fay Larkin! I know you!*" he cried
brokenly.

She slipped off the stone to her knees,
swayed forward blindly with her hands
reaching out, her head falling back to let the
moon fall fully upon the beautiful, snow-
white, tragically convulsed face.

Chapter Thirteen

". . . Oh, I remember so well! Even now I dream of it sometimes. I hear the roll and crash of falling rock . . . like thunder. We rode and rode. Then the horses fell. Uncle Jim took me in his arms and started up the cliff. Mother Jane climbed close after us. They kept looking back. Down there in the gray valley came the Mormons. I see the first one now. He rode a white horse. That was Tull. Oh, I remember so well! And I was five or six years old.

"We climbed up and up, into dark cañons, and wound in and out. Then there was the narrow white trail, straight up, with the little cut steps and the great, red, ruined walls. I looked down over Uncle Jim's shoulder. I saw Mother Jane dragging herself up. Uncle Jim's blood spotted the trail. He reached a flat place at the top and fell with me. Mother Jane crawled up to us.

"Then she cried out, and pointed. Tull

was 'way below, climbing the trail. His men came behind him. Uncle Jim went to a great tall rock, and leaned against it. There was a bloody hole in his hand. He pushed the rock. It rolled down, banging the loose walls. They crashed and crashed . . . then all was terrible thunder and red smoke. I couldn't hear . . . I couldn't see.

"Uncle Jim carried me down and down out of the dark and dust into a beautiful valley all red and gold, with a wonderful arch of stone over the entrance. I don't remember well what happened then for what seemed a long, long time. I can feel how the place looked, but not so clear as it is now in my dreams. I seem to see myself with the dogs, and with Mother Jane.

"But I remember now how I felt when I first understood we were shut in forever. Shut in Surprise Valley where Venters had lived so long. I was glad. The Mormons would never get me. I was seven or eight years old then. From that time all is clear in my mind.

"Venters had left supplies and tools and grain and cattle and burros, so we had a good start to begin life there. He had killed off the wildcats and kept the coyotes out, so the rabbits and quail multiplied till there were thousands of them. We raised corn and fruit, and stored what we didn't use. Mother Jane taught me to read and write with the soft red stone that marked so well on the walls.

"The years passed. We kept track of time pretty well. Uncle Jim's hair turned white, and Mother Jane grew gray. Every day was like the one before. Mother Jane cried sometimes, and Uncle Jim was sad because they could never be able to get me out of the valley. It was long before they stopped looking and listening for someone. Venters would come back, Uncle Jim always said. But Mother Jane did not think so.

"I loved Surprise Valley. I wanted to stay there always. I remembered Cottonwoods, how the children there hated me, and I didn't want to go back. The only unhappy times I ever had in the valley were when Ring and Whitie, my dogs, grew old and died. I roamed the valley. I climbed to every rock up on the mossy ledges. I learned to run up the steep cliffs. I could almost stick on the straight walls. Mother Jane called me a wild girl. We had put away the clothes we wore when we got there, to save them, and we made clothes of skins. I always laughed when I thought of my little dress . . . how I grew out of it. I think Uncle Jim and Mother Jane talked less as the years went by. And after I'd learned all she could teach me, we didn't talk much. I used to scream in the caves just to hear my voice, and the echoes would frighten me.

"The older I grew the more I was alone. I was always running around the valley. I would climb to a high place and sit there for hours, doing nothing. I just watched and listened. I used to stay in the cliff-dwellers caves and wonder about them. I loved to be out in the wind. My happiest time was in the summer storms with the thunder echoes under the walls. At evening it was such a quiet place . . . after the night birds' cry, no sound. The quiet made me sad, but I loved it. I loved to watch the stars as I lay awake. So it was beautiful and happy for me there till . . . till. . . .

"Two years or more ago there was a bad storm, and one of the great walls caved. The walls were always weathering, slipping. Many and many a time have I heard the rumble of an avalanche, but most of them were in other cañons. This slide in the valley made it possible, Uncle Jim said, for men to get down into the valley. But we could not climb out unless helped from above. Uncle Jim never rested well after that. But it never worried me.

"One day, while I was across the valley, I

heard strange shouts, and then screams. I ran to our camp. I came upon men with ropes and guns. Uncle Jim was tied, and a rope was around his neck. Mother Jane was lying on the ground. I thought she was dead till I heard her moan. I was not afraid. I screamed and flew at Uncle Jim to tear the ropes off him. The men held me back. They called me a pretty cat. Then they talked together, and some were for hanging Lassiter . . . that was the first time I ever knew any name for him but Uncle Jim . . . and some were for leaving him in the valley. Finally they decided to hang him. But Mother Jane pleaded so, and I screamed and fought so, that they left off. Then they went away, and we saw them climb out of the valley.

"Uncle Jim said they were Mormons and some among them had been born in Cottonwoods. I was not told why they had terrible hate for him. He said they would come back and kill him. Uncle Jim had no guns to fight with.

"We watched and watched. In five days they did come back, with more men, and some of them wore black masks. They came to our cave with ropes and guns. One was tall. He had a cruel voice. The others ran to obey him. I could see white hair and sharp eyes behind the mask. The men caught me and brought me before him.

"He said Lassiter had killed many Mormons. He said Lassiter had killed his father and should be hanged. But he, Lassiter, could be let live and Mother Jane could stay with him, both prisoners there in the valley, if I would marry the Mormon. I must marry him, accept the Mormon faith, and bring up my children as Mormons. If I refused, they would hang Lassiter, leave the heretic Jane Withersteen alone in the valley, and take me and break me to their rule. To save Lassiter and Jane Withersteen I must become a Mormon wife and take an awful oath to be true to my duty. If I failed, if I betrayed the secret of Surprise Valley, they would return to take vengeance upon Lassiter and leave Mother Jane alone.

"I agreed, and right then they married me to the Mormon with the cruel voice. It nearly killed me to leave Uncle Jim and Mother Jane. I was carried and lifted out of the valley, and rode a long way on a horse. They brought me here to the cabin where I live, and I have never been away except that . . . that time . . . to . . . Stonebridge. Only little by little did I learn my position. Bishop Kane was kind, but stern, because I was not quick to learn the faith.

"I am a sealed wife. I don't know what

that is. My . . . my husband has other wives. He visited me often . . . at night . . . till lately. He never told me a name . . . except Saint George. I don't . . . know my married name. I don't . . . know him . . . except his voice. I never . . . saw his face . . . in the light!"

Fay Larkin ended her story. Toward its close, Shefford had grown involuntarily restless, and, when her last tragic whisper ceased, all his body seemed shaken with a terrible violence that corresponded with the state of his mind. He strode to and fro in the dark shadow of the stone. The receding blood left his exterior cold, with a pricking, sickening sensation, and there seemed to be an overwhelming tide accumulating deep in his breast — a tide of passion and pain. He dominated the passion, but the ache remained.

He returned to the quiet figure on the stone. "Fay Larkin," he ejaculated with a deep breath of relief that the secret was disclosed. "I felt it was sacrifice. I knew there had been a crime. For crime it is. You child! You can't understand what crime. My God . . . oh, almost I wish you and Jane and Lassiter had never been found. But that's vile of me. This time of agony . . . it shall not ruin your entire life. Fay, I will take you away."

"Where?" she whispered.

"Away from this Mormon country . . . to the East," he replied, and he spoke of what he had known, of travel, of cities, of people, of the happiness possible for a young girl who had spent all her life hidden between the narrow walls of a silent lonely valley — he spoke swiftly and eloquently till he lost his breath.

There was an instant of flashing wonder and joy on her white face, and then the radiance paled, the glow died. Her soul was the darker for that one strange, leaping glimpse of a glory not for such as she. "I must stay here," she said, shuddering.

"Fay! How strange to *say* Fay aloud, to *you!* Fay, do you know the way to Surprise Valley?"

"I don't know where it is, but I could go straight to it," she replied.

"Take me there. Show me your beautiful valley. Let me see where you ran and climbed, and spent so many lonely years."

"Ah! how I'd love to. But I dare not. And why should you want me to take you? We can run and climb here."

"I want to . . . I mean to save Jane Withersteen and Lassiter," he declared.

She uttered a little cry of pain. "Save them?"

"Yes. Save them. Get them out of the valley, take them out of the country, far away, where they and *you*. . . ."

"But I can't go," she wailed.

"Why?" he demanded.

"I'm his . . . sealed wife. I'm bound. That awful oath! It *can't* be broken. If I dared . . . if I tried to go . . . they would catch me. They would hang Uncle Jim and leave Mother Jane alone there to starve."

"Fay, Lassiter and Jane both will starve . . . at least, they will die there, if we do not save them. As for your being a sealed wife . . . that's a crime. You have been terribly wronged. You're a slave. You're not a wife. Why, even if you had desired this marriage, you couldn't be a wife . . . not *his* wife. A man *can't* have two wives. The sealed wife is . . . is nothing. Once out of this country you can be freed . . . you can get a divorce."

"Divorce? What's that?"

"Your marriage tie will be broken by law."

"Law? Oh, I don't understand law. Was that terrible trial law? Besides, whatever may be broken, my oath cannot."

"Why not? It wasn't fair. It was your sacrifice. Any honest man would uphold you."

"They . . . they said my oath was made to God. I'd be burned in hell if I broke it. Mother Jane never taught me about God. I don't know. But *he* . . . who said I was to call him Saint . . . he said God was there. I dare not break it."

"Fay, you have been deceived by old men . . . Mormons . . . religious fanatics . . . crazy on the subject of bibles found in the ground and saints and prophets on earth, and God appearing to chosen individuals. Let them have their creed. But *you* mustn't accept it. You are a Gentile."

"John, what is God to you?"

"Dear child, I . . . I am not sure of that myself," he replied huskily. "When all this trouble is behind us, surely I can help you to understand, and you can help me. The fact that you are alive . . . that Lassiter and Jane are alive . . . that I shall save you all . . . that lifts me up. I tell you . . . Fay Larkin will be my salvation."

"Your words trouble me. Oh, I shall be torn one way and another. But, John, I daren't break that oath. I will not tell you where to find Lassiter and Mother Jane."

"I shall find them. I have the Indian. He found you for me. Nas-Ta-Bega will find Surprise Valley."

"Nas-Ta-Bega! Ah, I remember. There was an Indian with the Mormons who found us. But he was a Paiute."

"Nas-Ta-Bega never told me how he

learned about you. That he learned was enough. And Fay, he will find Surprise Valley. He will save Uncle Jim and Mother Jane."

Fay's hands clasped Shefford's in strong, trembling pressure; the tears streamed down her white cheeks; a tragic and eloquent joy convulsed her face.

"Oh, my friend, save them! But I can't go. Let them keep me! Let him kill me."

"*Him?* You mean your husband? Fay . . . he shall not harm you," replied Shefford in passionate earnestness.

She caught the hand he had struck out with. "You talk . . . you look like Uncle Jim when he spoke of Mormons," she said. "Then I used to be afraid of him. He was so different. John, you must not do anything about me. Let me be. It's too late. He . . . and his men . . . they would hang you. And I couldn't bear that. I've enough to bear without losing my friend. Say, you won't watch and wait for . . . for my husband!"

Shefford had to promise her. Like the Indian, she gave expression to primitive feeling, for it certainly never occurred to her that whatever Shefford might do, he was not the kind of man to wait in hiding for an enemy. Fay had faltered through her last speech and was now weak and nervous and frightened. Shefford took her back to the cabin.

"Fay, don't be distressed," he said. "I can't do anything right away. You can trust me. I won't be rash. I'll consult you before I make a move. I haven't an idea what I could do, anyway. You must bear up. Why, it looks as if you're sorry I found you."

"Oh . . . I'm glad," she whispered.

"Then, if you're glad, you must not break down this way again. Suppose some of the women happened to run into me."

"I won't again. It's only you . . . you surprised me so. I used to think how I'd like you to know . . . I wasn't really dead. But now . . . it's different. It hurts me . . . here. Yet I'm glad . . . if my being alive makes you . . . a little happier."

Shefford felt that he had to go then. He could not trust himself any further.

"Good night, Fay," he said.

"Good night, John," she replied. "I promise . . . to be good tomorrow."

She was crying softly when he left her. Twice he turned to see the dim, white, slender form against the gloom of the cabin. Then he went on under the piñons, blindly down the path, with his heart as heavy as lead. That night, as he rolled in his blanket and stretched wearily, he felt that he would never be able to sleep. The wind in the cedars made him shiver. The great stars seemed relentless, passionless white eyes, mocking his little destiny and his pain. The huge shadow of the mountain resembled the shadow of the insurmountable barrier between Fay and him.

Her pitiful, childish promise to be good was in his mind when he went to her home on the next night. He wondered how she would be, and he realized a desperate need of self-control.

But that night Fay Larkin was a different girl. In the dark, before she spoke, he felt a difference that afforded him surprise and relief. He greeted her as usual, and then it seemed, although not at all clearly, that he was listening to a girl, strangely and unconsciously glad to see him, who spoke with deeper note in her voice, who talked where always she had listened, whose sadness was there under an eagerness, a subdued gaiety new to her, as sweet as it was bewildering. He responded with emotion, so that the hour passed swiftly, and he found himself back in camp in a kind of dream, unable to remember much of what she had said, sure only of this strange sweetness suddenly come to her.

Upon the following night, however, he discovered what had wrought this singular change in Fay Larkin. She loved him, and she did not know it. How passionately sweet and sad and painful was that realization for Shefford! The hour spent with her there was only a moment.

He walked under the stars that night, and they shed a glorious light upon him. He tried to think, to plan, but the sweetness of remembered word or look made mental effort almost impossible. He got as far as the thought that he would do well to drift, to wait till she learned she loved him, and then perhaps she could be persuaded to let him take her and Lassiter and Jane away together. From that night, he went at his work and the part he played in the village with a zeal and a cunning that left him free to seek Fay when he chose.

Sometimes in the afternoon, always for a while in the evening he was with her. They climbed the walls, and sat upon a lonely height to look afar; they walked under the stars, and the cedars, and the shadows of the great cliffs. She had a beautiful mind. Listening to her, he imagined he saw down into beautiful Surprise Valley with all its weird shadows, its colored walls, and painted caves, its golden shafts of morning light and

310

the red haze at sunset, and he felt the silence that must have been there, the singing of the wind in the cliffs, and the sweetness and fragrance of the flowers, the wildness of it all. Love had worked a marvelous transformation in this girl who had lived her life in a cañon. The burden upon her did not weigh heavily. She could not have an unhappy thought. She forgot her husband. She spoke of the village, of her Mormon companions, of daily happenings, of Stonebridge, of many things in a matter-of-fact way that showed how little they occupied her mind. She even spoke of sealed wives in a kind of dreamy abstraction. Something had possession of her, something as strong as the nature which had developed her, and in its power she, in her simplicity, was utterly unconscious, just a watching and feeling girl. A strange, bewitching radiant beauty lurked in her smile. Shefford heard her laugh in his dreams.

The weeks slipped by. The black mountain took on a white cap of snow. In the early mornings there was ice in the crevices on the heights and frost in the valley. In the sheltered cañons, where the sunshine seemed to linger, it was warm and pleasant, so that winter did not kill the flowers.

Shefford waited so long for Fay's awakening that he believed it would never come and, believing, had not the heart to force it upon her. Then there was a growing fear within him. What would Fay Larkin do when she awakened to the truth so horrible to a good woman — that she was bound to one man and loved another? Fay was, indeed, like that white and fragile lily that bloomed in the silent lonely cañons, but the same nature that had created it had created her. Would she droop as the lily would in a furnace blast? More than that he feared a sudden flashing into life of strength, power, passion, hate. She did not hate yet because she did not yet realize love. She was utterly innocent of what wrong had been done her. When she realized it, would she not run straight for a cañon rim? More and more he began to fear, and a foreboding grew upon him. He made up his mind to broach the subject of Surprise Valley and of escaping with Lassiter and Jane. Still, every time he was with Fay, the girl and her beauty and her love were so wonderful that he put off the ordeal till the next night. As time flew by, he excused his vacillation on the score that winter was not a good time to try to cross the desert. There was no grass for the mustangs, except in well-known valleys, and these he must shun. Spring would soon come. So the days passed, and he loved Fay more all the time, desperately living out to its limit the sweetness of every moment with her, and paying for his bliss in the increasing trouble that beset him when once away from her charm.

One starry night, about ten o'clock, he went, as was his custom, to drink at the spring. Upon his return to the cedars, Nas-Ta-Bega, who slept under the same tree with him, had arisen, with his blanket hanging half off his shoulder.

"Listen," said the Indian.

Shefford took one glance at the dark, somber face with its inscrutable eyes, now so strange and piercing, and then, with a kind of cold excitement, he faced the way the Indian looked and listened. He heard only the soft moan of the night wind in the cedars.

Nas-Ta-Bega kept the rigidity of his position for a moment, and then he relaxed and stood at ease. Shefford knew the Indian had made a certainty of what must have been a doubtful sound. Shefford leaned his ear to the wind and strained his hearing. The soft night breeze brought a faint patter — the slow trot of horses on a hard trail. Someone was coming into the village at a late hour.

Shefford thought of Joe Lake. But Joe lay right behind him asleep in his blankets. It could not be Withers, for the trader was in Durango at that time. Shefford thought of Willetts and Shadd.

"Who's coming?" he asked in a low voice.

Nas-Ta-Bega pointed down the trail without speaking. Shefford peered through the white dim haze of starlight, and presently he made out moving figures. Horses with riders — a string of them — one, two, three, four, five — he counted up to eleven. Eleven horsemen riding into the village! He was amazed, and suddenly keenly anxious. This visit might be one of Shadd's raids.

"Shadd's gang?" he whispered.

"No, *bi-nai*," replied Nas-Ta-Bega, and he drew Shefford farther into the shade of the cedars. His voice, his action, the way he kept a hand on Shefford's shoulder — these were revealing to the young man.

Mormons were coming on a night visit to sealed wives! Shefford realized it with a slight shock, merely a tremor. Then swift as a lightning flash he was rent by another shock — one that left him with cold sweat, a horrible sickness at the pit of his stomach and in his heart a flame of hell.

He was shaking when he found the support of a log under him. Like a shadow the

Indian silently moved away. Shefford watched the eleven horses pass the camp, go down the road, to disappear in the village. They vanished, and the soft *clip-clops* of hoofs died away. There was nothing left to prove he had not dreamed he had seen them. Nothing to prove it except this sudden terrible demoralization of his physical and spiritual being! While he peered out into the valley, toward the black patch of cedars and piñons that hid the cabins, moments and moments passed, and in them he was gripped with cold and fire, with a violent, convulsive muscular disturbance — while they racked him, his mind seemed to explode in a fiery burst of thought. Was he — the husband of Fay — the Mormon who owned her — the man with the cruel voice — was *he* among those eleven horsemen? He might not have been. What a torturing hope! But vain — vain, for inevitably he must be among them. He was there at the cabin already. He had dismounted, tied his horse, had knocked on her door. Did he need to knock? No — he would go in — he would call her in that cruel voice — and then . . . poor unfortunate innocent girl who was a sealed wife!

Shefford pulled a blanket from his bed, and covered his cold and trembling body.

He had sunk down off the log, was leaning with his back upon it. The stars were pale, far off, and the valley seemed unreal. He found himself listening — listening with sick and terrible earnestness, trying to hear against the thrum and beat of his heart, straining to catch a sound in all that cold, star-blanched, silent valley. But he could hear no sound. It was as if death held the valley in its perfect silence. How he hated that silence! There ought to have been a million horrible bellowing demons making the night hideous. Did the stars serenely look down upon the lonely cabins of these exiles, these sealed wives? Was there no thunder-bolt to drop down from that dark and looming mountain upon the silent cabin where tragedy had entered? In all the world, under the sea, in the abysmal caves, in the vast spaces of the air there was no such terrible silence as this. A screaming, long cry, a moan — those were natural to a woman, and why did not one of these sealed wives, why did not Fay Larkin, damn this ever-lasting acquiescent silence? Perhaps she would fly out of her cabin, come running along the path. Shefford peered into the bright patches of starlight and into the shadows of the cedars, but he saw no moving form in the open, no dim white shape against the gloom, and he heard no sound — not a whisper of wind in the branches overhead.

Nas-Ta-Bega returned to the shade of the cedar and, lying down on his blankets covered himself and went to sleep. The fact seemed to bring bitter reality to Shefford. Nothing was going to happen. The valley was to be the same this night as any other night. The Mormons had come, and they were now with their sealed wives. Shefford accepted the truth. He experienced a kind of self-pity. The night he had thought so much about, prepared for, and had forgotten, had now arrived. Then he threw another blanket around him, and coldly, darkly, grimly he faced that lonely night, meaning to sit there wide-eyed, to endure and to wait.

Jealousy and pain, following his frenzy, abided with him long hours, and, when they passed, he divined that selfishness passed with them. What he suffered then was for Fay Larkin and for her sisters in misfortune, and, as that hour of revelation wore on, he suffered in a larger way, for all mortal pain and blindness, even for these Mormon husbands, cold, slight-natured, narrow men.

He grew big enough to pity these fanatics. The fiery, hot-pressed, racing tide of blood that had made of him only an animal had cooled with thought of others. Still, he feared that stultifying thing which must have been hate. What a tempest had raged within him! This blood of his, that had received a stronger strain from his desert life, might in a single moment flood out reason and intellect, and make him a vengeful man. So in those starlit hours that dragged interminably he looked deeply into his heart and tried to fortify himself against a dark and evil moment to come.

Midnight — and the valley seemed a tomb! Did he alone keep wakeful? The sky was a darker blue, the stars burned a whiter fire, the peaks stood looming and vast, tranquil sentinels of that valley, and the wind rose to sigh, to breathe, to mourn through the cedars. It was a sad music. The Indian lay prone, dark face to the stars. Joe Lake lay prone, sleeping as quietly, with his dark face exposed to the starlight. The gentle movement of the cedar branches changed the shape of the bright patches on the grass where shadow and light met. The walls of the valley waved upward, dark below and growing paler, to shine faintly at the rounded rims. There was a tiny silvery tinkle of running water over stones.

Here was a little nook of the vast world.

Here was tranquility, beauty, music, loneliness, life. Shefford wondered — did he alone keep wakeful? Did he feel that he could see dark, wide eyes peering up into the gloom? It came to him after a time that he was not alone in his vigil, nor was Fay Larkin alone in her agony. There was someone else in the valley, a great and breathing and watchful spirit. It entered into Shefford's soul, and he trembled. What had come to him? And he answered — only added pain and new love, and a strange strength from the firmament and the peaks and the silence and the shadows.

The bright belt with its three radiant stars sank behind the western wall, and there was a paler gloom upon the valley. A cock crowed mournfully.

Then a few lights twinkled in the darkness that enveloped the cabins. A woman's laugh strangely broke the silence, profaning it, giving the lie to that somber yoke which seemed to consist of the very shadows. The voices of men were heard, and then the slow *clip-clop* of trotting horses on the hard trail.

Shefford saw the Mormons file out into the paling starlight, ride down the valley, and vanish in the gray gloom. He was aware that the Indian sat up to watch the proces-

319

sion ride by, and that Joe turned over, as if disturbed.

One by one the stars went out. The valley became a place of gray shadows. In the east a light glowed. Shefford sat there, haggard and worn, watching the coming of the dawn, the kindling of the light, and had the power been his the dawn would never have broken and the rose and gold never have tipped the lofty peaks.

Shefford attended to his camp chores as usual. Several times he was aware of Joe's close scrutiny, and finally without looking at him Shefford told of the visit of the Mormons. A violent expulsion of breath was Joe's answer, and it might have been a curse. Straightway Joe ceased his cheery whistling and became as somber as the Indian. The camp was silent; the men did not look at each other. While they sat at breakfast, Shefford's back was toward the village; he had not looked in that direction since dawn.

"Ugh!" suddenly exclaimed Nas-Ta-Bega.

Joe Lake muttered, low and deep, and this time there was no mistake about the nature of his speech. Shefford did not have the courage to turn to see what had caused these exclamations. He knew since the day had dawned that there was calamity in the air.

"Shefford, I reckon if I know women, there's a little hell coming to you," said the Mormon significantly.

Shefford wheeled as if a powerful force had turned him as a pivot. He saw Fay Larkin. She seemed to be almost running. She was unhooded and her bright hair streamed down. Her swift, lithe action was without its usual grace. She looked wild, and she almost fell crossing the stepping-stones of the brook.

Joe hurried to meet her, took hold of her arm, and spoke, but she did not seem to hear him. She drew him along with her, up to the little bench under the cedars straight toward Shefford. For her sake, Shefford was trying to find the manhood to face her, to conceal how desperately hard it was to look at her. But he might have spared himself that pain. She who had never known shame was above it now. Her face held a white, mute agony as if in the hour of strife it had hardened into marble, but her eyes were dark purple fire — windows of an extraordinarily intense and vital life. In one night the girl had become a woman. Yet, the blight Shefford had dreaded to see — this withering of the exquisite soul and spirit and purity he had considered inevitable, just as inevitable as the death of something similar in the flower she resembled, when it was broken and defiled, — nothing of this was manifest in her. Straight and swiftly she came to him, back in the shade of the cedars, and took hold of his hands.

"Last night . . . *he came*," she said.

"Yes . . . Fay . . . I . . . I know," replied Shefford haltingly. He was tremblingly conscious of amaze at her — of something wonderful in her. She did not heed Joe, who stepped aside a little. She did not see Nas-Ta-Bega, who sat motionless on a log, apparently oblivious to her presence.

"You knew he came?"

"Yes, Fay. I was awake when they rode in. I watched them. I sat up all night. I saw them ride away."

"If you knew when he came, why didn't you run to me . . . to get to me before he did?"

Her question was unanswerable. It had the force of a blow. It stunned him. No sharp, frank directness sprang from the simplicity and a strength that had not been nurtured in the life he had lived. So far men had wandered from truth and nature!

"I came to you as soon as I was able," she

went on. "I must have fainted. It wasn't easy to dress. I just had to drag myself around . . . and now I can tell you."

He was as powerless to reply as if she had put another unanswerable question. What did she mean to tell him? What might she not tell him? She loosed her hands from his, and lifted them to his shoulders, and that was the first conscious action of feeling, of intimacy that she had ever shown. It quite robbed Shefford of strength, and in spite of his sorrow there was an indefinable thrill in her touch. He looked at her, saw the white and gold beauty that was hers yesterday and seemed changed today, and he recognized Fay Larkin in a woman he did not know.

"Listen. He came. . . ."

"Fay, don't tell me," interrupted Shefford.

"I *will* tell you," she said. Did the instinct of love teach her how to mitigate his pain? Shefford felt that, as he felt the newborn strength in her. "Listen," she went on. "He came when I was undressing for bed. I heard the horse. He knocked on the door. Something terrible happened to me then. I felt sick and my head wasn't clear. I remember next . . . his being in the room . . . the lamp was out. I couldn't see very well. He thought I was sick, and he gave me a drink and let the air blow in on me through the window. I remember I lay back in the chair and I thought. And I listened. When would you come? I didn't feel that you could leave me there alone with him. For his coming was different this time. That pain like a blade in my side! When it came, I was not the same. I loved you. I understood then. I belonged to you. I couldn't let him touch me. I had never been his wife. When I realized this . . . he was there . . . that you might suffer for it. I cried right out.

"He thought I was sick. He worked over me. He gave me medicine. And then he prayed. I saw him, in the dark, on his knees, praying for me. That seemed strange. Yet he was kind, so kind that I begged him to let me go. I said I had found out I didn't love him. I was not a Mormon. I couldn't keep my vows. I begged him to let me go. Then he thought I had been deceiving him. He fell into a fury. He talked for a long time. He called upon God to visit my sins upon me. He tried to make me pray. But I wouldn't. I was his wife, sealed to him, he said . . . and then . . . I fought him. I'd have screamed for you had he not smothered me. I got weak . . . and you never came. I know I thought you would come. But you didn't. Then I . . . I gave in. And after . . .

sometime . . . I must have fainted."

"Fay! For heaven's sake, how could I come to you?" burst out Shefford, hoarse and white with remorse, passion, pain. "You're his sealed wife."

"If I'm any man's wife, I'm yours. It's a thing you *feel*, isn't it? I know that now . . . but I want to know if I should go on living. Do you want me to live?"

"Fay!" he cried huskily.

"If it weren't for you, I'd climb the wall and throw myself off. That would be easy for me. I'd love to die that way. All my life I've been high up on the walls. To fall would be nothing! Do you want me to live?"

"Yes, yes. Oh, you mustn't talk like that."

"Do you love me . . . *now*, after last night?" she asked, with a low and deathless sweetness.

"Love you! . . . with all my heart and soul! Nothing can change that!"

"Do you want me . . . as you used to want the Fay Larkin lost in Surprise Valley? Do you love me that way? I understand things better than before, but still . . . not all. I *am* Fay Larkin. I think I must have dreamed of you all my life. I was glad when you came here. I've been happy lately. I forgot . . . till last night. Maybe it needed that to make me see I've loved you all the time . . . and I fought him like a wildcat! Tell me the truth. I *feel* I'm yours. Is that true? If I'm not . . . I'll not live another hour. Something holds me up. I am the same . . . do you want me?"

"Yes, Fay Larkin, I want you," replied Shefford steadily, with his grip on her arms.

"Then take me away. I don't want to live here another hour."

"Fay, I will take you. But it can't be done at once. We must plan. I need help. There are Lassiter and Jane to get out of Surprise Valley. Give me time, dear . . . give me time. It'll be a hard job, and we must plan so we can positively get away. Give me time, Fay."

"Suppose *he* comes back?" she queried with a singular depth of voice.

"We'll have to risk that," replied Shefford miserably. "But . . . he won't come soon."

"He said he would," she flashed.

Shefford seemed to freeze inwardly with her words. Love had made her a woman, and now the woman in her was speaking. She saw the truth as he could not see it, and the truth was nature. She had been hidden all her life from the world, from knowledge as he had it, yet when her love betrayed her womanhood to her she acquired all its subtlety.

"If I wait and he *does* come, will you keep me from him?" she asked.

"How can I? I'm staking all on the chance of his not coming soon . . . but Fay, if he does come and I don't give up our secret . . . how on earth can I keep you from him?" demanded Shefford.

"If you love me, you will do it," she said, as simply as if she were fate.

"But how?" cried Shefford, almost beside himself.

"You are a man. Any man would save the woman who loves him from . . . from . . . oh! . . . from a beast. How would Lassiter do it?"

"Lassiter!"

"You can kill him!"

It was there, deep and full in her voice, the strength of the elemental forces that had surrounded her, primitive passion and hate and love, as they were in woman in the beginning.

"My God!" Shefford cried aloud with his spirit when all that was red in him sprang again into a flame of hell. That was what had been wrong with him last night. He could kill this stealthy night-riding husband, and now, face to face with the wife, who had never been so beautiful and wonderful as in this hour when she made love the only and the sacred thing of life, now he had it in him to kill. Yet murder — even to kill a brute — that was not for John Shefford, not the way for him to save a woman. Reason and wisdom still fought the passion in him. If he could but cling to them — have them with him in the dark and contending hour!

She leaned against him now, exhausted, her soul in her eyes, and they saw only him. Shefford was all but powerless to resist the longing to take her into his arms, to hold her to his heart, to let himself go. Did not her love give her to him? What were a few words over an outlaw bible — what was an oath exacted through fear — what was the bond of a sealed wife? Shefford gazed helplessly at the stricken Joe Lake, at the somber Indian, as if from them he expected help.

"I know him now," said Fay, breaking the silence with startling suddenness.

"What!"

"I've seen him in the light. I flashed a candle in his face. I saw it. I know him now. He was there at Stonebridge with us, and I never knew him. But I know him now. His name is. . . ."

"For God's sake, don't tell me who he is!" implored Shefford. Ignorance was Shefford's safeguard against himself. To make a name of this heretofore intangible husband, to give him an identity apart from the crowd, to be able to recognize him — that for Shefford would be fatal. "Fay . . . tell me no more," he said brokenly. "I love you, and I will give you my life. Trust me. I swear I'll save you."

"Will you take me away soon?"

"Yes."

She appeared satisfied with that and dropped her hands and moved back from him. A light flitted over her white face, and her eyes grew dark and humid, losing their fire in changing shadowy thought of submission, of trust, of hope.

"I can lead you to Surprise Valley," she said. "I feel the way. It's there!"

She pointed to the west.

"Fay, we'll go . . . soon. I must plan. I'll see you tonight. Then we'll talk. Run home now, before some of the women see you here."

She said good bye and started away under the cedars, and into the open where her hair shone like gold in the sunlight. She took the steppingstones with her old free grace, and strode down the path, swift and lithe as an Indian. Once she turned to wave a hand.

Shefford watched her with a torture of pride, love, hope, and fear contending within him.

Chapter Fourteen

That morning a Paiute rode into the valley. Shefford recognized him as the brave who had been in love with Glen-Nas-Pa. The moment Nas-Ta-Bega saw this visitor, he made a singular motion with his hands — a motion that somehow to Shefford suggested despair — and then he waited, somber and statuesque, for the messenger to come to him. It was the Paiute who did all the talking, and that was brief. Then the Navajo stood motionless with his hands crossed over his breast. Shefford drew near and waited.

"*Bi-nai*," said the Navajo, "Nas-Ta-Bega said his sister would come home some day. Glen-Nas-Pa is in the hogan of her grandfather."

He spoke in his usual slow, guttural voice, and he might have been bronze for all the emotion he expressed, yet Shefford instinctively felt the despair that had been hinted to him, and he put his hand on the Indian's shoulder.

"If I am the Navajo's brother, then I am brother to Glen-Nas-Pa," he said. "I will go with you to the hogan of Hosteen Doetin."

Nas-Ta-Bega went away into the valley for the horses. Shefford hurried into the village, made his excuses to Fay that trouble of some kind had come to the Indian.

Soon afterward he was riding Nack-Yal on the rough and winding trail up through the broken country of cliffs and cañons to the great league-long sage and cedar slope of the mountain. It had been weeks since he had ridden the mustang. Nack-Yal was fat and lazy. He loved his master, but he did not like the climb, and so fell far behind the lean and wiry pony that carried Nas-Ta-Bega. The sage levels were as purple as the haze of distance, and there was a bitter-sweet tang on the strong, cool wind. The sun was gold behind the dark line of fringe on the mountaintop. A flock of sheep swept down one of the sage levels, looking like a narrow stream of white and black and brown. It was always amazing for Shefford to see how swiftly these Navajo sheep grazed along. Wild mustangs plunged out of the cedar clumps, and stood upon the ridges whistling defiance or curiosity, and their manes and tails waved in the wind.

Shefford mounted slowly to the cedar bench, in the midst of which were hidden the few hogans. He halted at the edge to dismount and take a look at that downward sweeping world of color, of wide space, at the wild desert upland that from there unrolled its magnificent panorama. Then he passed on into the cedars. How strange to hear the lambs bleating again! Lambing time had come early, but still spring was there in the new green of grass, in the bright upland flowers. He led his mustang out of the cedars into the cleared circle. It was full of colts and lambs, and there were the shepherd dogs and a few old rams and ewes. But the circle was a quiet place this day. There were no Indians in sight. Shefford loosened the saddle girths on Nack-Yal and, leaving him to graze, went toward the hogan of Hosteen Doetin. A blanket was hung across the door. Shefford heard a low chanting. He waited beside the door till the covering was pulled in, then he entered.

Hosteen Doetin met him, clasped his hand. The old Navajo could not speak; his fine face was working in grief; tears streamed from his dim old eyes and rolled down his wrinkled cheeks. His sorrow was no different from a white man's sorrow. Beyond him, Shefford saw Nas-Ta-Bega standing with folded arms, somehow terrible in his somber impassiveness. At his feet crouched the old woman, Hosteen Doetin's wife, and beside her, prone and quiet, half covered with a blanket, lay Glen-Nas-Pa.

She was dead. To Shefford she seemed older than when he had last seen her. And she was beautiful. Calm, cold, dark with only bitter lips to give the lie to peace! There was a story in those lips.

At her side, half hidden under the fold of blanket, lay a tiny bundle. Its human shape startled Shefford. Then he did not need to be told of the tragedy. When he looked again at Glen-Nas-Pa's face, he seemed to understand all that had made her older, to feel the pain that had lined and set her lips.

She was dead, and she was the last of Nas-Ta-Bega's family. In the old grandfather's agony, in the wild chant of the stricken grandmother, in the brother's stern and terrible calmness Shefford felt more than the death of a loved one. The shadow of ruin, of doom, of death hovered over the girl and her family and her tribe and her race. There was no consolation to offer these relatives of Glen-Nas-Pa. Shefford took one more fascinated gaze at her dark, eloquent, prophetic face, at the tragic tiny shape by her side, and then with bowed head he left the hogan.

Outside he paced to and fro, with an aching heart for Nas-Ta-Bega, with something of the white man's burden of crime toward the Indian weighing upon his soul. Old Hosteen Doetin came to him with shaking hands and words memorable of the time Glen-Nas-Pa had left his hogan.

"Me no savvy Jesus Christ. Me hungry. Me no eat Jesus Christ!"

That seemed to be all of his trouble that he could express to Shefford. He could not understand the religion of the missionary, this Jesus Christ who had called his granddaughter away. The great fear of an old Indian was not death, but hunger. Shefford remembered a custom of the Navajos, a thing barbarous when looked at with a white man's mind. If an old Indian failed on a long march, he was enclosed by a wall of stones, given plenty to eat and drink, and left there to die in the desert. Not death did he fear, but hunger! Old Hosteen Doetin expected to starve now that the young and strong squaw of his family was gone.

Shefford spoke in his halting Navajo, and he assured the old Indian that Nas-Ta-Bega would never let him starve.

At sunset Shefford stood with Nas-Ta-

Bega, facing the west. The Indian was magnificent in repose. He watched the sun go down upon the day that had seen the burial of the last of his family. He resembled an impassive destiny, upon which no shocks fell. He had the light of that flaring golden sky in his face, the majesty of the mountain in his mien, the silence of the great gulf below on his lips. This educated Navajo, who had reverted to the life of his ancestors, found in the wildness and loneliness of his environment a strength no white teaching could ever have given him. Shefford sensed in him a measureless grief, an impenetrable gloom, a tragic acceptance of the meaning of Glen-Nas-Pa's ruin and death — the vanishing of his race from the earth. Death had written the law of such bitter truth around Glen-Nas-Pa's life, and the same truth was here in the grandfather and the gloom of the Navajo.

"*Bi-nai,*" he said, with the beautiful sonorous roll in his voice, "Glen-Nas-Pa is in her grave, and there are no paths to the place of her sleep. Glen-Nas-Pa is gone."

"Gone! Where? Nas-Ta-Bega, remember I lost my own faith and I have not yet learned yours."

"The Navajo has one mother . . . the earth. Her body has gone to the earth, and it will become dust. But her spirit is in the air. It shall whisper to me from the wind. I shall hear it on running waters. It will hide in the morning music of a mockingbird and in the lonely night cry of the cañon hawk. Her blood will go to make the red of the Indian flowers, and her soul will rest at midnight in the lily that opens only to the moon. She will wait in the shadow for me and live in the great mountain that is my home, and forever step behind me on the trail."

"You will kill Willetts?" demanded Shefford.

"The Navajo will not seek the missionary."

"But if you meet him, you'll kill him?"

"*Bi-nai,* would Nas-Ta-Bega kill after it is too late? What good could come? The Navajo is above revenge."

"If he crosses my trail, I think I couldn't help but kill him," muttered Shefford in a passion that wrung the threat from him.

The Indian put his arm around the white man's shoulders. "*Bi-nai,* long ago I made you my brother. And now you make me your brother. Is it not so? Glen-Nas-Pa's spirit calls for wisdom, not revenge. Willetts must be a bad man. But we'll let him live. Life will punish him. Who knows if he was all to blame. Glen-Nas-Pa was only one pretty Indian girl. There are many white men in the desert. She loved a white man when she was a baby. The thing was a curse . . . listen, *bi-nai,* and the Navajo will talk.

"Many years ago the Spanish *padres,* the first white men, came into the land of the Indian. Their search was for gold. But they were not wicked men. They did not steal and kill. They taught the Indian many useful things. They brought him horses. But when they went away, they left him unsatisfied with his life and his God.

"Then came the pioneers. They crossed the great river and took the pasture lands and the hunting grounds of the Indian. They drove him backward, and the Indian grew sullen. He began to fight. The white man's government made treaties with the Indian, and these were broken. Then war came, fierce and bloody war. The Indian was driven to the waste places. The stream of pioneers, like a march of ants, spread on into the desert. Every valley where grass grew, every river became a place for farms and towns. Cattle choked the water holes where the buffalo and deer had once gone to drink. The forests in the hills were cut, and the springs dried up. And the pioneer followed to the edge of the desert.

"Then came the prospectors, mad like the

padres, for the gleam of gold. The day was not long enough for them to dig in the creeks and the cañons . . . they worked in the night. And they brought weapons and rum to the Indian, to buy from him the secret of the places where the shining gold lay hidden.

"Then came the traders, and they traded with the Indian. They gave him little for much, and that little changed his life. He learned a taste for the sweet foods of the white man. Because he could trade for a sack of flour, he worked less in the field. And the very fiber of his bones softened.

"Then came the missionaries. They were proselytizers for converts to their religion, as the Mormons are proselytizers for more wives. The missionaries are good men. There may be a bad missionary, like Willetts, the same as there are bad men in other callings, or bad Indians. They say Shadd is a half-breed. But the Paiutes can tell you he is a full-blood, and he, like me, was sent to a white man's school. In the beginning the missionaries did well for the Indian. They taught him cleaner ways of living, better farming, useful work with tools . . . many good things. But the wrong to the Indian was the undermining of his faith. It was not humanity that sent the missionary to the Indian. Humanity would have helped the Indian in his ignorance of sickness and work, and left him his God. For to trouble the Indian about his God worked at the roots of his nature.

"The beauty of the Indian's life is in his love of the open, of all that is nature, of silence, freedom, wildness. It is a beauty of mind and soul. The Indian would have been content to watch and feel. To a white man he might be dirty and lazy . . . content to dream life away without trouble or what the white man calls evolution. The Indian might seem cruel because he leaves his old father out in the desert to die. But the old man wants to die that way, alone with his spirits and the sunset. And the white man's medicine keeps his old father alive days and days after he might be dead. Which is more cruel? The Navajos used to fight with other tribes, and then they were stronger men than they are today.

"But leaving religion, greed, and war out of the question, contact with the white man would alone have ruined the Indian. The Indian and the white man cannot mix. The Indian brave learns the habits of the white man, acquires his diseases, and has not the mind or body to withstand them. The Indian girl learns to love the white man . . .

and that is death of her Indian soul, if not of life.

"So the red man is passing. Tribes once powerful have died in the life of Nas-Ta-Bega. The curse of the white man is already heavy upon my race in the south. Here in the north, in the wildest corner of the desert, chased here by the great soldier, Carson, the Navajo has made his last stand.

"*Bi-nai,* you have seen the shadow in the hogan of Hosteen Doetin. Glen-Nas-Pa has gone to her grave, and no sisters, no children will make paths to the place of her sleep. Nas-Ta-Bega will never know a wife . . . have a child. He sees the end. It is the sunset of the Navajo. *Bi-nai,* the Navajo is dying . . . dying . . . dying. . . ."

Chapter Fifteen

A crescent moon hung above the lofty peak over the valley and a train of white stars ran along the bold rim of the western wall. A few young frogs peeped plaintively. The night was cool, yet had a touch of balmy spring and a sweeter fragrance, as if the cedars and piñons had freshened in the warm sun of that day.

Shefford and Fay were walking in the aisles of moonlight and the patches of shade, and Nas-Ta-Bega, more than ever a shadow of his white brother, followed them silently.

"Fay, it is growing late. Feel the dew," said Shefford. "Come. I must take you back."

"But the time's so short. I have said nothing that I wanted to say," she replied.

"Say it quickly then as we go."

"After all, it's only . . . will you take me away soon?"

"Yes, very soon. The Indian and I have

talked. But we've made no plan yet. There are only three ways to get out of this country. By Stonebridge, by Kayenta and Durango, and by Red Lake. We must choose one. All are dangerous. We must lose time finding Surprise Valley. I hoped the Indian could find it. Then we'd bring Lassiter and Jane here and hide them near till dark, then take you and go. That would give us a night's start. But you must help us to Surprise Valley."

"I can go right to it, blindfolded, or in the dark . . . oh, John, hurry! I dread the wait. *He* might come very soon."

"Is it far . . . where we're going . . . out of the country?"

"Ten days' hard riding. Oh, that night ride to and from Stonebridge nearly killed me. You know I'd never ridden a horse. But I could walk very far and climb forever."

"Fay, we'll get out of the country if I have to carry you."

When they arrived at the cabin, Fay turned on the porch step and with her face nearer a level with his, white and sweet in the moonlight, with her eyes shining and unfathomable, she was more than beautiful.

"You've never been inside my house," she said. "Come in. I've something for you."

"But it's late," he remonstrated. "I suppose you've got me cake or pie . . . something to eat. You women all think Joe and I have to be fed."

"No. You'd never guess. Come in," she said, and the rare smile on her face was something Shefford would have gone far to see.

"Well, then, for a minute."

He crossed the porch, the threshold, and entered her home. Her dim, white shape moved in the darkness, and he followed into a room where the moon shone through the open window, giving soft, mellow, shadowy light. He discerned objects, but not clearly, for his senses seemed absorbed in the strange warmth and intimacy of being for the first time with her in her home.

"No, it's not good to eat," she said, and her laugh was happy. "Here. . . ."

Suddenly she abruptly ceased speaking. Shefford saw her plainly, and the slender form had stiffened, alert and strained. She was listening.

"What was that?" she whispered.

"I didn't hear anything," he whispered back.

He stepped softly nearer the open window, and listened.

Clip-clop. Clip-clop. Clip-clop. Hard hoofs on the hard path outside. A strong and rippling thrill went over Shefford. In the soft light her eyes seemed unnaturally large and black and fearful.

Clip-clop. Clip-clop.

The horse stopped outside. Then followed a metallic clink of spur against stirrup — thud of boots on hard ground — heavy footsteps upon the porch.

A swift cold contraction of throat, of breast, convulsed Shefford. His only thought was that he could not think.

"Ho . . . wife!"

A voice liberated both Shefford's muscle and mind — a voice of strange, vibrant power. Authority of religion and cruelty of will — these Mormon attributes constituted that power — and Shefford suffered a transformation that must have been ordered by demons of hell. That sudden flame seemed to curl and twine and shoot along his veins with blasting force. A rancorous and terrible cry leaped to his lips.

"Ho . . . wife!" Then came a heavy tread across the threshold of the outer room.

Shefford dared not look at Fay. Yet, dimly, from the corner of his eye, he saw her, a pale shadow, turned to stone, with her arms out. If he looked — if he made sure of that — he was lost. When had he drawn his gun? It was there, a dark and glinting thing in his hand. He must fly — not through cowardice and fear, but because in one more moment he would kill her husband. Swift as the thought, he dived through the open window. Leaping up, he ran under the dark piñons toward the camp.

Joe Lake had been out late himself. He sat by the fire smoking his pipe. He must have seen or heard Shefford's coming, for he rose with unwonted alacrity. He kicked the smoldering logs into a flickering blaze.

Shefford, realizing only his deliverance, came panting, staggering into the light. The Mormon uttered an exclamation. Then he spoke anxiously, but what he said was not clear in Shefford's thick and throbbing ears. Joe Lake dropped his pipe, a sign of perturbation, and he stared. But Shefford, without a word, lunged swiftly away into the shadow of the cedars. He found relief in action. He began a steep ascent of the east wall, a dangerous slant he had never dared even in daylight, and he climbed it without a slip. Danger, steep walls, perilous heights, night, and black cañon the same — these he never thought of. But something drove him to desperate effort, that the hours might seem short.

The red sun was tipping the eastern wall

when he returned to camp, and he was neither calm nor sure of himself, or ready for sleep or food. Only he had put the night behind him.

The Indian showed no surprise, but Joe Lake's jaw dropped and his eyes rolled. Moreover, Joe bore a singular aspect, the exact nature of which did not at once dawn upon Shefford.

"By God, you've got nerve . . . or you're crazy!" he ejaculated hoarsely.

Then it was Shefford's turn to stare. The Mormon was haggard, grieved, frightened, and utterly amazed. He appeared to be trying to make certain of Shefford's being there in the flesh and then to find reason for it.

"I've no nerve and I am crazy," replied Shefford. "But Joe . . . what do you mean? Why do you look at me like that?"

"I reckon, if I get your horse, that'll square us. Did you come back for him? You'd better hit the trail quick."

"It's you now who're crazy," burst out Shefford.

"Wish to God I was," replied Joe.

It was then Shefford realized catastrophe, and cold fear gnawed at his vitals, so that he was sick. "Joe, what's happened?" he asked, with the blood thick at his breast.

"Hadn't you better tell me?" demanded the Mormon, and a red wave blotted out the haggard shade of his face.

"You talk like a fool," said Shefford sharply, and he strode straight up to Joe.

"See here, Shefford. We've been pards. You're making it hard for me. Reckon you ain't square."

Shefford shot out a long arm, and his hand clutched the Mormon's burly shoulder. "Why am I not square? What do you mean?"

Joe swallowed hard, and gave himself a shake. Then he eyed his comrade steadily. "I was afraid you'd kill him. I reckon I can't blame you. I'll help you get away . . . and I'm a Mormon! Do you take the hunch? . . . but don't deny you killed him."

"Killed who?" gasped Shefford.

"Her husband!"

Shefford seemed stricken by a slow, paralyzing horror. The Mormon's changing face grew huge and indistinct and awful in his sight. He was clutched and shaken in Joe's rude hands, yet scarcely felt them. Joe seemed to be bellowing at him, but the voice was far off. Then Shefford began to see, to hear through some cold and terrible deadness that had come between him and everything.

"Say *you* killed him!" hoarsely suppli-
cated the Mormon.

Shefford had not yet control of speech.
Something in his gaze appeared to drive Joe
frantic.

"Damn you! Tell me quick. Say *you* killed
him! If you want to know my stand, why, by
God, I'm glad! Shefford, don't look so
stony! For Christ's sake, for *her* sake, say you
killed him!"

Shefford stood with a face as gray and still
as stone. With a groan, the Mormon drew
away from him and sank upon a log. He
bowed his head; his broad shoulders heaved;
husky sounds came from him. Then with a
violent wrench he plunged to his feet, and
shook himself like a huge savage dog.

"Reckon it's no time to weaken," he said
huskily, and with the words a dark, hard,
and somber bitterness came to his face.

"Where . . . is . . . *she?*" whispered
Shefford.

"Shut up in the schoolhouse," he replied.

"Did she . . . did she . . . ?"

"She neither denied nor confessed."

"Have you . . . seen her?"

"Yes."

"How did . . . she look?"

"Cool and quiet as the Indian there.
Game as hell! She always had stuff in her."

348

"Oh, Joe! It's unbelievable!" cried Shefford. "That lovely, innocent girl! She couldn't . . . she couldn't. . . ."

"She's fixed him. Don't think of that. It's too late. We ought to have saved her."

"God! She begged me to hurry to take her away."

"Think what we can do *now* to save her," cut in the Mormon.

Shefford sustained a vivifying shock. "To save her?" he echoed.

"Think, man!"

"Joe, I can hit the trail and let you tell them I killed him," burst out Shefford in panting excitement.

"Reckon you can."

"So help me God I'll do it!"

"You mustn't leave her. She killed him for your sake. You must fight for her now . . . save her . . . take her away."

"But the law!"

"Law!" scoffed Joe. "In these wilds men get killed, and there's no law. But if she's taken back to Stonebridge, those iron-jawed old Mormons will make law enough to . . . to. . . . Shefford, the thing is . . . get her away. Once out of the country she's safe. Mormons keep their secrets."

"I'll take her. Joe, will you help me?"

Shefford, even in his agitation, felt the

Mormon's silence to be a consent that need not have been asked, and Shefford felt a passionate gratefulness toward his comrade. That stultifying and blinding prejudice, which had always seemed to remove a Mormon outside the pale of certain virtue, suffered final eclipse, and Joe Lake stood out a man, strange and crude, but with a heart and a soul.

"Joe, tell me what to do," said Shefford with a simplicity that meant he needed only to be directed.

"Pull yourself together. Get your nerve back," replied Joe. "Reckon you'd better show yourself over there. No one saw you come in this morning . . . your absence from camp isn't known. It's better you seem curious and shocked like the rest of us. Come on. We'll go over. And, afterward, we'll get the Indian, and plan."

They left camp and, crossing the brook, took the shaded path toward the village. Hope of saving Fay, the need of all his strength and nerve and cunning to effect that end, gave Shefford the supreme courage to overcome his horror and fear. On that short walk under the piñons to Fay's cabin, he had suffered many changes of emotion, but never anything like this change which made him fierce and strong to fight, deep and crafty to plan, hard as iron to endure.

The village appeared very quiet, although groups of women stood at the doors of cabins. If they talked, it was very low. Henniger and Smith, two of the three Mormon men living in the village, were standing before the closed door of the schoolhouse. Something tigerish had birth in Shefford when he saw them on guard there. Shefford purposely avoided looking at Fay's cabin as long as he could keep from it. When he had to look, he saw several hooded, whispering women in the yard, and Beal, the other Mormon man, standing in the cabin door. Upon the porch lay the long shape of a man, covered with blankets.

Shefford experienced a horrible curiosity.

"Say, Beal, I've fetched Shefford over," said Lake. "He's pretty much cut up."

Beal wagged a solemn head, but said nothing. His mind seemed absent or steeped in gloom, and he looked up as one silently praying.

Joe Lake strode upon the little porch, and, reaching down, he stripped the blanket from the shrouded form.

Shefford saw a sharp, cold, ghastly face.

"Waggoner," he whispered.

"Yes," replied Lake.

Waggoner, the known husband of five wives and father of fifty-five children! Fay Larkin had been this man's sealed wife. Shefford remembered the strange power in his face, and now that life had gone, that power was stripped of all disguise. Death, in Shefford's years of ministry, had laid under his gaze many times and in a multiplicity of aspects, but never before had he seen it stamped so strangely. Shefford did not need to be told that here was a man who had believed he had conversed with God on earth — who believed he had a divine right to rule women — who had a will that would not yield itself to death utterly. Waggoner, then, was the devil who had come masked to Surprise Valley — had imposed a martyrdom upon Fay Larkin. He was the Mormon who had made her a sealed wife. This was the husband who had made Fay Larkin a murderer. Shefford had hated him living, and now he hated him dead. Death here was robbed of all nobility, of pathos, of majesty. It was only retribution. Wild justice! But, alas, that it had to be meted out by a white-souled girl, whose innocence was as great as the unconscious savagery which she had assimilated from her lonely and wild environment. Shefford laid a despairing curse upon his own head, and a terrible remorse knocked at his heart. He had left her alone, this girl in whom love had made the great change — like a coward he had left her alone. That curse he visited upon himself because he had been the spirit and the motive of this wild justice and his should have been the deed.

Joe Lake touched Shefford's arm, and pointed at the haft of a knife protruding from Waggoner's breast. It had a wooden haft. Shefford had seen it before somewhere. Then Shefford was struck with what perhaps Joe had meant him to see — the singular impression the haft gave of one sweeping, accurate, powerful stroke. A strong arm had driven that blade home. The haft was sunk deeply. There was a little depression in the cloth. No blood showed, and the weapon looked as if it could not be pulled out. Shefford's thought went fatally and irresistibly to Fay Larkin's strong arm. He saw her flash that white arm, and lift the heavy bucket from the spring with an ease he wondered at. He felt the strong clasp of her hand, as she had given it to him in a flying leap across a crevice up on the walls. Yes, her fine hand and the round, strong arm possessed the strength to have given that blade its singular directness and force. The marvel was not in the physical action. It was hidden inscrutably in the mystery of deadly passion rising out of a gentle and sad heart.

Joe Lake drew up the blanket and shut from Shefford's fascinated gaze that spare form, that accusing knife, that face of strange, cruel power. Shefford felt uplifted as from a dark and drawing gulf.

"Anybody been sent for?" asked Lake of Beal.

"Yes. An Indian boy went for the Paiute. We'll send him to Stonebridge," replied the Mormon.

"How soon do you expect anyone here from Stonebridge?"

"Tomorrow, mebbe by noon."

"Meantime, what's to be done with . . . this?"

"Elder Smith thinks the body should stay right where it fell till they come from Stonebridge."

"Waggoner was found here, then?"

"Right here."

"Who found him?"

"Mother Smith. She came over early. An' the sight made her scream. The women all came runnin'. Mother Smith had to be put to bed."

"Who found . . . Mary?"

"See here, Joe, I told you all I knowed once before," replied the Mormon testily.

"I've forgotten. Was sort of bewildered. Tell me again . . . who found . . . her?"

"The womenfolks. She laid right inside the door, in a dead faint. She hadn't undressed. There was blood on her hands an' a cut or scratch. The women fetched her to. But she wouldn't talk. Then Elder Smith came an' took her. They've got her locked up."

Joe led Shefford away from the cabin and farther on into the village. When they were halted by the somber, grieving women, it was Joe who did the talking. They passed the schoolhouse, and here Shefford quickened his step. He could scarcely bear the feeling that rushed over him, and the Mormon gripped his arm as if he understood.

"Shefford, which one of these younger women do you reckon is your best friend? . . . Ruth?" asked Lake earnestly.

"Ruth, by all means. Just lately I haven't seen her often. But we were close friends. I think she'd do much for me."

"Maybe there'll be a chance to find out. Maybe we'll need Ruth. Let's have a word with her. I haven't seen her out among the women."

They stopped at the door of Ruth's cabin. It was closed. When Joe knocked, there came a sound of footsteps inside, a hand drew aside the window blind, and the door opened. Ruth stood there, dressed in somber hue. She was a pretty, slender, blue-eyed, brown-haired young woman. Shefford imagined from her pallor and the set look of shock upon her face that the tragedy had affected her more powerfully than it had the other women. When he remembered that she had been friendlier with Fay Larkin than any other neighbor, he became sure he was right in his conjecture.

"Come in," was Ruth's greeting.

"No. We just wanted to say a word. I noticed you've not been out. Do you know . . . all about it?"

She gave them a strange glance.

"Any of the womenfolks been in?" added Joe.

"Hester ran over. She told me through the window. Then I barred my door to keep the other women out."

"What for?" asked Joe curiously.

"Please come in," she said in reply.

They entered, and she closed the door after them. The change that came over her then was the loosing of restraint.

"Joe . . . what will they do with Mary?" she queried tensely.

The Mormon studied her with dark, speculative eyes. "Hang her," he rejoined in brutal hardness.

"Oh, Mother of Saints!" she cried, and her hands went up.

"You're sorry for Mary, then?" asked Joe bluntly.

"My heart is breaking for her."

"Well, so's Shefford's," said the Mormon huskily. "And mine's kind of damn' shaky."

Ruth eyes glided to Shefford with a woman's swift softness. "You've been very good . . . my best friend. You were hers, too. Oh, I know! Can't you do something for her?"

"I hope to God I can," replied Shefford.

Then the three stood drawn together, looking from one to the other in a strong and subtly realizing moment.

"Ruth," whispered Joe hoarsely, and then he glanced fearfully around at the window and door, as if listeners were there. It was certain that his dark face had paled. He tired to whisper more, only to fail. Shefford divined the weight of Mormonism that burdened Joe Lake then. Joe was faithful to a love for Fay Larkin, noble in friendship to Shefford, desperate in a bitter strait with his own manliness, but the power of that creed by which he had been raised struck his lips mute, for to speak further meant to be false to that creed. Already in his heart he had decided, yet he could not voice the thing.

"Ruth," Shefford took up the Mormon's unfinished whisper. "If we plan to save her . . . if we need you . . . will you help?"

Ruth turned white, but in an instant a splendid fire shone in her eyes. "Try me," she whispered back. "I'll change places with her . . . so you can get her away. They can't do much to me."

Shefford wrung her hands.

Joe licked his lips and found his voice. "We'll come back later." Then he led the way out, and Shefford followed. They were silent all the way to the camp.

Nas-Ta-Bega sat in repose where they had left him, a thoughtful, somber figure. Shefford went directly to the Indian, and Joe tarried at the campfire where he raked out some red embers and put one upon the bowl of his pipe. He puffed clouds of white smoke, then found a seat beside the others.

"Shefford, go ahead. Talk. It'll take a deal of talk. I'll listen. Then I'll talk. It'll be Nas-Ta-Bega who makes the plan out of it all."

Shefford launched himself so swiftly that he scarcely talked coherently. But he made clear the points that he must accomplish to save Fay — get her away from the village — let her lead him to Surprise Valley — rescue Lassiter and Jane Withersteen —

and take them all out of the country.

Joe Lake dubiously shook his head. Manifestly the Surprise Valley part of the situation presented a new and serious obstacle. It changed the whole thing. To try to take the three out by way of Kayenta and Durango was not to be thought of for reasons he briefly stated. The Red Lake trail was the only one left, and, if that were taken, the chances were against Shefford. It was five days over sand to Red Lake — impossible to hide a trail — and even with a day's start Shefford could not escape the hard-riding men who would come from Stonebridge. Besides, after reaching Red Lake, there were days and days of desert travel needful to avoid places like Blue Cañon, Inba, Moencopie, and the Indian villages.

"We'll have to risk all that," declared Shefford desperately.

"It's a fool risk," retorted Joe. "Listen. By tomorrow noon all of Stonebridge, more or less, will be riding in here. You've got to get away tonight with the girl . . . or never! And tomorrow you've got to find that Lassiter and the woman in Surprise Valley. This valley must be back, deep in the cañon country. Well, you have got to come out this way again. No trail through here would be safe. Why, you'd put all your heads in a rope!

359

You mustn't come through this way. It'll have to be tried across country, off the trails, and that means hell . . . day and night travel, no camp, no feed for horses . . . maybe no water. Then you'll have the best trackers in Utah like hounds on your trail."

When the Mormon ceased his forceful speech, there was a silence fraught with hopeless meaning. He bowed his head in gloom. Shefford, growing sick again to his marrow, fought a cold sense of despair.

"Bi-nai!" In his extremity he called to the Indian.

"The Navajo has heard," replied Nas-Ta-Bega, strangely speaking in his own language.

With a long, slow heave of breast Shefford felt his despair leave him. In the Indian lay his salvation. He knew it. Joe Lake caught the subtle spirit of the moment, and looked up eagerly.

Nas-Ta-Bega stretched an arm toward the east and spoke in Navajo. But Shefford, owing to the hurry and excitement of his mind, could not translate. Joe Lake listened, gave a violent start, leaped up with all his big frame quivering, and then he fired question after question at the Indian. When the Indian had replied to all, Joe drew himself up as if facing an irrevocable decision that must needs wring his very soul. What did he cast off in that moment? What did he grapple with? Shefford had no means to tell, except by that instinct which baffled him. But whether the Mormon's trial was one of spiritual rending or the natural physical fear of a perilous, virtually impossible venture, the fact was he was magnificent in his acceptance of it. He turned to Shefford, white, cold, yet glowing.

"Nas-Ta-Bega believes he can take you down a cañon to the big river . . . the Colorado. He knows the head of this cañon. Nonnezoshe Boco it's called . . . cañon of the rainbow bridge. He has never been down it. Only two or three living Indians have ever seen the great stone bridge. But all have heard of it. They worship it as a god. There's water runs down this cañon, and water runs to the river. Nas-Ta-Bega thinks he can take you down to the river."

"Go on," cried Shefford breathlessly, as Joe paused.

"The Indian plans this way. God, it's great! If only I can do my end! He plans to take mustangs today, and wait with them for you tonight or tomorrow till you come with the girl. You'll go get Lassiter and the woman out of Surprise Valley. Then you'll strike east for Nonnezoshe Boco. If possible, you must take a pack of grub. You may be days going down and waiting for me at the mouth of the cañon, at the river."

"Joe, where will you be?"

"I'll ride like hell for Kayenta, get another horse there, and ride like hell for the San Juan River. There's a big flat boat at the Durango crossing. I'll go down the San Juan in that . . . into the big river. I'll drift down by day, tie up by night, and watch for you at the mouth of every cañon till I come to Nonnezoshe Boco."

Shefford could not believe the evidence of his ears. He knew the treacherous San Juan River. He had heard of the great, sweeping, terrible red Colorado and its roaring rapids.

"Oh, it seems impossible," he gasped. "You'll just lose your life for nothing."

"The Indian will turn the trick, I tell you. Take my hunch. It's nothing for me to drift down a swift river. I worked a ferry boat once."

Shefford, to whom flying straws would have seemed more stable, caught the inflection of defiance and daring and hope in the Mormon's spirit.

"What then . . . after you meet us at the mouth of Nonnezoshe Boco?" he queried.

"We'll all drift down to Lee's Ferry. That's at the head of Marble Cañon. We'll get out on the south side of the river there, avoiding any Mormons at the ferry. Nas-Ta-Bega knows the country. It's open desert . . . on the other side of these plateaus. He can get horses from Navajos. Then you'll strike south for Willow Springs."

"Willow Springs? That's Presbrey's trading post," said Shefford.

"Never met him. But he'll see you safe out of the Painted Desert. The thing that worries me most is how not to miss you all at the mouth of Nonnezoshe. You must have sharp eyes. But I forget the Indian. A bird couldn't pass him. And suppose Nonnezoshe Boco has a steep-walled, narrow mouth opening into a rapids . . . whew! Well, the Indian will figure that, too. Now, let's put our heads together and plan how to turn this end of the trail here. Getting the girl."

After a short colloquy it was arranged that Shefford would go to Ruth and talk to her of the aid she had promised. Joe averred that this aid could be best given by Ruth going in her somber gown and hood to the schoolhouse, and there, while Joe and Shefford engaged the guards outside, she would change apparel and places with Fay and let her come forth.

"What'll they do to Ruth?" demanded Shefford. "We can't accept her sacrifice if she's to suffer . . . or be punished."

"Reckon Ruth has a strong hunch that she can get away with it. Did you notice how strange she said that? Well, they can't do much to her. The bishop may damn her soul. But Ruth. . . ." Here Lake hesitated, and broke off. Not improbably he had meant to say that of all the Mormon women in the valley Ruth was the least likely to suffer from punishment inflicted upon her soul. "Anyway, it's our only chance," he went on, "unless we kill a couple of men. Ruth will gladly take what comes to help you."

"All right, I consent," replied Shefford with emotion. "And now after she comes out . . . the supposed Ruth . . . what then?"

"You can be natural-like. Go with her back to Ruth's cabin. Then stroll off into the cedars. Then climb the west wall. Meanwhile, Nas-Ta-Bega will ride off with a pack of grub and Nack-Yal and several other mustangs. He'll wait for you, or you'll wait for him, as the case may be, at some appointed place. When you're gone, I'll jump my horse and hit the trail for Kayenta and the San Juan."

"Very well, that's settled," said Shefford soberly. "I'll go at once to see Ruth. You and Nas-Ta-Bega decide on where I'm to meet him."

"Reckon you'd do just as well to walk

around and come up to Ruth's from the other side . . . instead of going through the village," suggested Lake.

Shefford approached Ruth's cabin in a roundabout way. Nevertheless, she saw him coming before he got there and, opening the door, stood pale, composed, quietly bidding him enter. Briefly, in low and earnest voice, Shefford acquainted her with the plan.

"You love her so much," she said wistfully, wonderingly.

"Indeed, I do. Is it too much to ask of you to do this thing?" he replied.

"Do it?" she queried with a flash of spirit. "Of course, I'll do it."

"Ruth, I can't thank you. I can't. I've only a faint idea what you're risking. That distresses me. I'm afraid of what may happen to you."

She gave him another of the strange glances. "I don't risk as much as you think," she said significantly.

"Why?"

She came close to him, her hands clasped his arms, and she looked up at him, her eyes darkening and her face growing paler. "Will you swear to keep my secret?" she asked, very low.

"Yes, I swear."

"I was one of Waggoner's sealed wives!"

"God Almighty!" broke out Shefford, utterly overwhelmed.

"Yes. That's why I say I don't risk so much. I will make up a story to tell the bishop and everybody. I'll tell that Waggoner was jealous . . . that he was brutal to Mary . . . that I believed she was goaded to her mad deed . . . that I thought she ought to be free. There'll be trouble. But what can they do to me? My husband is dead . . . and, if I have to go to hell to keep from marrying another married Mormon, I'll go!"

In that low, passionate utterance Shefford read the death blow to the old Mormon polygamous creed. In the uplift of his spirit, in his joy at this revelation, he almost forgot the stern matter at hand. Ruth and Joe Lake belonged to a young generation of Mormons. Their nobility in this instance was in part a revolt at the conditions of their lives. Doubt was knocking at Joe Lake's heart, and conviction had come to this young sealed wife, bitter and hopeless while she had been fettered, strong and mounting now that she was free. In a flash of inspiration Shefford saw the old order changing. The Mormon creed might survive, but that part of it which was an affront to nature, a horrible yoke on women's necks, was doomed. It could not live. It never could have survived more than a generation or two of religious fanatics. Shefford had marked a different force and religious fervor in the younger Mormons, and now he understood them.

"Ruth, you talk wildly," he said. "But I understand. I see. You are free, and you're going to stay free. . . . It stuns me to think of that man of many wives. What did you feel when you were told he was dead?"

"I dare not think of that. It makes me wicked. And he was good to me. Listen . . . last night about midnight he came to my window and woke me. I got up and let him in. He was in a terrible state. I thought he was crazy. He walked the floor, and called on his saints and prayed. When I wanted to light a lamp, he wouldn't let me. He was afraid I'd see his face. But I saw well enough in the moonlight. And I knew something had happened. So I soothed and coaxed him. He had been a man as close-mouthed as a stone. Yet, I got him to talk . . . he had gone to Mary's and, upon entering, thought he heard someone with her. She didn't answer him at first. When he found her in her bedroom, she was like a ghost. He accused her. Her silence made him furious. Then he berated her, brought down the wrath of God upon her, threatened her with damnation. All of which she never seemed to hear. But when he tried to touch her, she flew at him like a she-panther. That's what he called her. She said she'd kill him! And she drove him out of her house. He was all weak and unstrung, and, I believe, scared, too, when he came to me. She must have been a fury. Those quiet, gentle women are furies when they're once roused. Well, I was hours up with him, and finally he got over it. He didn't pray any more. He paced the room. It was just daybreak when he said the wrath of God had come to him. I tried to keep him from going back to Mary. But he went. An hour later, the women ran to tell me he had been found dead at Mary's door."

"Ruth . . . she was mad . . . driven . . . she didn't know what she was doing," said Shefford brokenly.

"She was always a strange girl, more like an Indian than anyone I ever knew. We called her Sago Lily. I gave her the name. She was so sweet, lovely, white and gold, like those flowers. And to think . . . oh, it's horrible for her. You must save her. If you get her away, there never will be anything come of it. The Mormons will hush it up."

"Ruth, time is flying," rejoined Shefford hurriedly. "I must go back to Joe. You be ready for us when we come. Wear something loose, easily thrown off, and don't forget the long hood."

"I'll be ready and watching," she said. "The sooner the better, I'd say."

He left her, and returned toward camp in the same circling route by which he had come. The Indian had disappeared and so had his mustang. This significant fact augmented Shefford's hurried, thrilling excitement. But one glance at Joe's face changed all that to a sudden numbness, a sinking of his heart.

"What is it?" he queried.

"Look there!" exclaimed the Mormon.

Shefford's quick eye caught sight of horses and men down the valley. He saw several Indians and three or four white men. They were making camp.

"Who are they?" demanded Shefford.

"Shadd and some of his gang. Reckon that Paiute told the news. By tomorrow the valley will be full as a horse wrangler's corral. Lucky Nas-Ta-Bega got away before that gang rode in. Now things won't look as queer as they might have looked. The Indian took a pack of grub, six mustangs, and my guns. Then there was your rifle in your saddle sheath. So you'll be well heeled in case you come to close quarters. Reckon you can look for a running fight. For now, as soon as your flight is discovered, Shadd will hit your trail. He's in with the Mormons. You know him . . . what you'll have to deal with. But the advantage will all be yours. You can ambush the trail."

"We're in for it. And the sooner we're off, the better," replied Shefford grimly.

"Reckon that's gospel. Well . . . come on."

The Mormon strode off, and Shefford, catching up with him, kept at his side. Shefford's mind was full, but Joe's dark and gloomy face did not invite communication. They entered the piñon grove, and passed the cabin where the tragedy had been enacted. A tarpaulin had been stretched across the front of the porch. Beal was not in sight, nor were any of the women.

"I forgot," said Shefford suddenly. "Where am I to meet the Indian?"

"Climb the west wall, back of camp," replied Joe. "Nas-Ta-Bega took the Stonebridge trail. But he'll leave that, climb the rocks, then hide the outfit, and come to watch for you. Reckon he'll see you when you top the wall."

They passed on into the heart of the village. Joe tarried at the window of a cabin, and passed a few remarks to a woman there, and then he inquired for Mother Smith at her house. When they left her, the Mormon gave Shefford a nudge. Then they separated, Joe going toward the schoolhouse while Shefford bent his steps in the direction of Ruth's home.

Her door opened before he had a chance to knock. He entered. Ruth, white and resolute, greeted him with a wistful smile.

"All ready?" she asked.

"Yes. Are you?" he replied, low-voiced.

"I've only to put on my hood. I think luck favors you. Hester was here, and she said Elder Smith told someone that Mary hadn't been offered anything to eat yet. So I'm taking her a little. It'll be a good excuse to see her. I can throw off this dress, and she can put it on in a minute. Then the hood. I mustn't forget to hide her golden hair. You know how it flies. This is a big hood . . . well, I'm ready now. And . . . this's our last time together."

"Ruth, what can I say . . . how I can thank you?"

"I don't want any thanks. It'll be something to think of always . . . to make me happy . . . only I'd like to feel you . . . you cared a little."

The wistful smile was there, a tremor on the sad lips, and a shadow of soul hunger in her eyes. Shefford did not misunderstand her. She did not mean love, although it was a yearning for real love that she had mutely expressed.

"Care! I shall care all my life," he said with strong feeling. "I shall never forget you."

"It's not likely I'll forget you . . . good bye, John."

Shefford took her in his arms, and held her close.

"Ruth . . . good bye," he said huskily.

Then he released her. She adjusted the hood, and, taking up a little tray that contained food covered with a napkin, she turned to the door. He opened it, and they went out. They did not speak another word.

It was not a long walk from Ruth's home to the schoolhouse, yet, if it were to be measured by Shefford's emotion, the distance would have been unending. The sacrifices offered by Ruth and Joe would have been noble under any circumstances, had they been Gentiles or persons with no particular religion, but considering that they were Mormons, that Ruth had been a sealed wife, that Joe had been brought up under the strange, secret, and binding creed, their actions were no less than tremendous in their import. Shefford took it to mean vastly more than loyalty to him and pity for Fay Larkin. As Ruth and Joe had arisen to this height, so perhaps would any other young Mormons have arisen. It needed only the situation, the climax, to focus these long-insulated, slow-developing, and inquiring minds upon the truth — that one wife, one mother of children, for one man at one time was a law of nature, love, and righteousness. Shefford felt as if he were marching with the whole younger generation of Mormons, as if somehow he had been a humble instrument in the working out of their destiny, in the awakening that was to eliminate from the religion the only thing which kept it from being as good for man, and perhaps as true, as any other religion.

Then, suddenly, he turned the corner of the schoolhouse to encounter Joe talking with the Mormon Henniger. Elder Smith was not present.

"Why, hello, Ruth," greeted Joe. "You've fetched Mary some dinner. Now that's good of you."

"May I go in?" asked Ruth.

"Reckon so," replied Henniger, scratching his head. He appeared to be tractable, and probably was good-natured under pleasant conditions. "She ought to have somethin' to eat. An' nobody 'pears to have remembered that . . . we're so upset."

He unbarred the huge, clumsy door and

allowed Ruth to pass in.

"Joe, you can go in, if you want," he said. "But hurry out before Elder Smith comes back from his dinner."

Joe mumbled something, gave a husky cough, and then went in.

Shefford experienced great difficulty in presenting to this mild Mormon a natural and unagitated front. When all his internal structure seemed to be in a state of turmoil, he did not see how it was possible to keep the fact from showing in his face. So he turned away, and took aimless steps here and there.

" 'Pears like we'll hev rain," observed Henniger. "It's right warm, an' them clouds are unseasonable."

"Yes," replied Shefford. "Hope so. A little rain would be good for the grass."

"Joe tells me Shadd rode in, an' some of his fellers."

"So I see. About eight in the party."

Shefford was gritting his teeth and preparing to endure the ordeal of controlling his mind and expression when the door opened, and Joe stalked out. He had his sombrero pulled down so that it hid the upper half of his face. His lips were a shade off healthy color. He stood there with his back to the door.

"Say, what Mary needs is quiet . . . to be left alone," he said. "Ruth says, if she rests, sleeps a little, she won't get fever. Henninger, don't let anybody disturb her."

"All right, Joe," replied the Mormon. "An' I take it good of Ruth an' you to concern yourselves."

A slight tap on the inside of the door sent Shefford's pulses to throbbing. Joe opened it with a strong and vigorous sweep that meant more than the mere action.

"Ruth . . . reckon you didn't stay long," he said, and his voice rang clearly. "Sure you feel sick and weak. Why, seeing her flustered even me."

A slender, dark-garbed woman wearing a long black hood stepped out uncertainly. She appeared to be Ruth. Shefford's heart stood still because she looked so like Ruth. But she did not step steadily, she seemed dazed, she did not raise the hooded head.

"Go home," said Joe, and his voice rang a little louder. "Take her home, Shefford. Or better, walk her around some. She's faintish. And see here, Henniger. . . ."

Shefford led the girl away with a hand in apparent carelessness on her arm. After a few rods she walked with a freer step, and then a swifter. He found it necessary to make that hold on her arm a real one, so as to keep her from walking too fast. No one, however, appeared to observe them. When they passed Ruth's house, then Shefford began to lose his fear that this was not Fay Larkin. He was far from being calm or clear-sighted. He thought he recognized that free step; nevertheless, he could not make sure. When they passed under the trees, crossed the brook, and turned down along the west wall, then doubt ceased in Shefford's mind. He knew this was not Ruth. Still, so strange was his agitation, so keen was his suspense, that he needed confirmation of ear, of eye. He wanted to hear her voice, to see her face, yet just as strangely there was a twist of feeling, a reluctance, a sadness that kept off the moment.

They reached the low, slow-swelling slant of wall, and started to ascend. How impossible not to recognize Fay Larkin move in that swift grace and skill on the steep wall! Still, although he knew her, he perversely clung to the unreality of the moment. But when a long braid of gold hair tumbled from under the hood, then his heart leaped. That identified Fay Larkin. He had freed her. He was taking her away. Then a sadness embittered his joy.

As always before, she distanced him in the

ascent to the top. She went on without looking back. But Shefford had an irresistible desire to look again, and for the last time, at this valley where he had suffered and loved so much.

Chapter Sixteen

From the summit of the wall, the plateau waved away in red and yellow ridges with here and there little valleys green with cedar and piñon. Upon one of these ridges, silhouetted against the sky, appeared the stalking figure of the Indian. He had espied the fugitives. He disappeared in a niche, and came again into view around a corner of cliff. Here he waited, and soon Shefford and Fay joined him.

"*Bi-nai,* it is well," he said.

Shefford eagerly asked for the horses, and Nas-Ta-Bega silently pointed down the niche, which was evidently an opening into one of the shallow cañons. Then he led the way, walking swiftly. It was Shefford, and not Fay, who had difficulty in keeping close to him. His speed caused Shefford to become more alive to the business, instead of the feeling, of the flight. The Indian entered a crack between low cliffs — a very narrow cañon full of rocks and clumps of cedars. In half an hour or less they came to where the mustangs were haltered among some cedars. Three of the mustangs, including Nack-Yal, were saddled. One bore a small pack, and the remaining two had blankets strapped on their backs.

"Fay, can you ride in that long skirt?" asked Shefford. How strange it seemed that his first words to her were practical when all his impassioned thought had been only mute, but the instant he spoke, he experienced a relief, a relaxation.

"I'll take it off," replied Fay, just as practically. In a twinkling she slipped out of both waist and skirt. She had worn them over the short, white flannel dress with which Shefford had grown familiar.

As Nack-Yal appeared to be the safest mustang for her to ride, Shefford helped her up on him, and then attended to the stirrups. When he had adjusted them to the proper length, he drew the bridle over Nack-Yal's head and, upon handing it to her, found himself suddenly looking into her face. She had taken off the hood, too. The instant their eyes met, he realized that she was strangely afraid to meet his glance, as he was to meet hers. That seemed natural. But her face was flushed and there were unmistakable signs upon it of growing excitement, of mounting happiness. Save for that fugitive glance, she would have been the Fay Larkin of yesterday. How he expected her to look, he did not know, but it was not like this. Never had he felt her strange quality of simplicity so powerfully.

"Have you ever been here . . . through this little cañon?" he asked.

"Oh, yes, lots of times."

"You'll be able to lead us to Surprise Valley, you think?"

"I know it. I shall see Uncle Jim and Mother Jane before sunset."

"I hope you do," he replied a little shakily. "Perhaps we'd better not tell them of the . . . the . . . about what happened last night."

Her beautiful, grave, and troubled glance returned to meet his, and he received a shock that he considered was amaze. After more swift consideration he believed he was amazed because that look, instead of betraying fear or gloom or any haunting shadow of darkness, betrayed apprehension for him, grave, sweet, troubled love for him. She was not thinking of herself at all — of what he might think of her — of a possible gulf between them — of a vast and terrible change in the relation of soul to soul. He experienced a profound gladness. Although he could not understand her, he was happy that the horror of her husband's death had escaped her. He loved her, he meant to give his life to her, and right then and there he accepted the burden of her deed and meant to bear it without ever letting her know of the shadow between them.

"Fay, we'll forget . . . what's behind us," he said. "Now to find Surprise Valley. Lead on. Nack-Yal is gentle. Pull him the way you want to go. We'll follow."

Shefford mounted the other saddled mustang, and they set off, Fay in advance. They rode out of this cañon up to level, cedar-patched, solid rock, and here Fay turned straight west. Evidently she had been over the ground before. The heights to which he had climbed with her were up to the left, great slopes and looming promontories. The course she chose was as level and easy as any he could have picked out in that direction.

When a mile or more of this up and down travel had been traversed, Fay halted and appeared to be hesitant. The plateau was losing its rounded, smooth, wavy characteristics and to the west grew bolder, more rugged, more cut up into low crags and buttes. After a long, sweeping glance, Fay headed straight for this rougher country.

Thereafter, from time to time she repeated this action.

"Fay, how do you know you're going in the right direction?" asked Shefford anxiously.

"I never forget any ground I've been on. I keep my eyes close ahead. All that seems strange to me is the wrong way. What I've seen before must be the right way because I saw it when they brought me from Surprise Valley."

Shefford had to acknowledge that she was following an Indian's instinct for ground he had once covered. Still Shefford began to worry, and finally dropped back to question Nas-Ta-Bega.

"*Bi-nai*, she has the eye of a Navajo," replied the Indian. "Look! Iron-shod horses have passed here. See the marks in the stone."

Shefford, indeed, made out faintly cut tracks that would have escaped his own sight. They had been made long ago, but they were unmistakable.

"She's following the trail by memory. She must remember the stones, trees, sage, cactus," said Shefford in surprise.

"Pictures in her mind," replied the Indian.

Thereafter, the farther she progressed,

the less uncertain she appeared, and the faster she traveled. She made several miles an hour and about the middle of the afternoon entered upon the more broken region of the plateau where the view became somewhat restricted. Low walls, ruined cliffs of red rock with cedars at their base, and gullies growing into cañons and cañons opening into larger ones — these were passed and crossed and climbed and rimmed in travel that grew more difficult as the going became wilder. Then there was a steady ascent, up and up all the time, although not steep, till another level, green with cedar and piñon, was reached.

It reminded Shefford of the forest near the mouth of the Sagi. It was so dense he could not see far ahead of Fay, and often he lost sight of her entirely. Presently he rode out of the forest into a strip of purple sage. It ended abruptly, and above that abrupt line, seemingly far away, rose a long red wall. Instantly he recognized that to be the opposite wall of a cañon that as yet he could not see.

Fay was acting strangely, and he hurried forward. She slipped off Nack-Yal and fell, sprang up, and ran wildly, to stand upon a promontory, her arms uplifted, her hair a mass of moving gold in the wind, her attitude one of wild and eloquent significance.

Shefford ran, too, and, as he ran, the red wall in his eager sight seemed to enlarge downward, deeper and deeper, and then it merged into a strip of green. Suddenly beneath him yawned a red-walled gulf — a deceiving gulf seen through transparent haze — a softly shining green and white valley, strange, wild, beautiful, like a picture in his memory.

"Surprise Valley!" he cried in wondering recognition.

Fay Larkin waved her arms as if they were wings to carry her swiftly downward, and her plaintive cry fitted the wildness of her manner and the lonely height where she leaned.

Shefford drew her back from the rim. "Fay, we are here," he said. "I recognize the valley. I miss only one thing . . . the arch of stone."

His words seemed to recall her to reality.

"The arch? That fell when the wall slipped, in the great avalanche. See! Here is the place. We can get down here. Oh, let us hurry."

The Indian reached the ruin, and his falcon gaze swept the valley.

"Ugh!" he exclaimed. He, too, recognized the valley that he had vainly sought for half a year.

"Bring the lassoes," said Shefford.

With Fay leading, they followed the rim toward the head of the valley. Here the wall had caved in, and there was a slope of jumbled rock a thousand feet wide and more than that in depth. It was easy to descend because there were so many rocks waist-high that afforded a hand hold. Shefford marked, however, that Fay never took advantage of these. More than once he paused to watch her. Swiftly she went down; she stepped from rock to rock; lightly she crossed cracks and pits; she ran along the sharp and broken edge of a long ledge; she poised on a pointed stone, and, sure-footed as a mountain sheep, she sprang to another that had scarcely surface for a foot hold. Her moccasins flashed, seemed to hold wondrously on any angle, and, when a rock tipped or slipped with her, she leaped to a surer stand. Shefford watched her performance, so swift, agile, so perfectly balanced, showing such wonderful accord between eye and foot, and then, when he swept his gaze down upon that wild valley where she had roamed alone for twelve years, he marveled no more.

The farther down he got, the greater became the size of rocks, till he found himself amid huge pieces of cliff as large as houses.

He lost sight of Fay entirely, and he anxiously threaded a narrow, winding, descending way between the broken masses. Finally he came out upon flat rock again. Fay stood on another rim, looking down. He saw that the slide had moved far out into the valley, and the lower part of it consisted of great sections of wall. In fact, the base of the great wall had just moved out with the avalanche, and this much of it had held its vertical position. Looking upward, Shefford was astounded and thrilled to see how far he had descended, how the walls leaned like a great, wide, curving, continuous rim of mountain.

"Here! Here!" called Fay. "Here's where they got down . . . where they brought me up. Here are the sticks they used. They stuck them in this crack, down to that ledge."

Shefford ran to her side, and looked down. There was a narrow split in this section of wall, and it was perhaps sixty feet in depth. The floor of rock below led out in a ledge, with a sheer drop to the valley level.

As Shefford gazed, pondering a way to descend lower, the Indian reached his side. He had no sooner looked than he proceeded to act. Selecting one of the sticks, which were strong pieces of cedar, well-hewn and trimmed, he jammed it between the walls of the crack till it stuck fast. Then, sitting astride this one, he jammed in another some three feet below. When he got down upon that one, it was necessary for Shefford to drop him a third stick. In a comparatively short time the Indian reached the ledge below. Then he called for the lassoes. Shefford threw them down. His next move was an attempt to assist Fay, but she slipped out of his grasp and descended the ladder with a swiftness that made him hold his breath. Still, when his turn came, her spirit so governed him that he went down as swiftly, and even leaped sheer the last ten feet.

Nas-Ta-Bega and Fay were leaning over the ledge.

"Here's the place," she said excitedly. "Let me down on the rope."

It took two thirty-foot lassoes tied together to reach the floor of the valley. Shefford folded his vest, put it around Fay, and slipped a loop of the lasso under her arms. Then he and Nas-Ta-Bega lowered her to the grass below. Fay, throwing off the loop, bounded away like a wild creature, uttering the strangest cries he had ever heard, and she disappeared along the wall.

"I'll go down," said Shefford to the Indian. "You stay here to help pull us up."

Hand over hand, Shefford descended, and, when his feet touched the grass, he experienced a shock of the most singular exultation.

"In Surprise Valley," he breathed softly. The dream that had come to him with his friend's story, the years of waiting, wondering, and then the long, fruitless, hopeless search in the desert uplands — these were in his mind as he turned along the wall where Fay had disappeared. He faced a wide terrace, green with grass and moss and starry with strange white flowers and dark-foliaged, spear-pointed spruce trees. Below the terrace sloped a bench covered with a thick copse, and this merged into a forest of dwarf oaks and beyond that was a beautiful strip of white aspens, thin leaves quivering in the stillness. The air was close, sweet, warm, fragrant, and remarkably dry. It reminded him of the air he had smelled in dry caves under cliffs. He reached a point from where he saw a meadow dotted with red and white-spotted cattle and little black burros. There were many of them, and he remembered with a start the agony of toil and peril Venters had endured bringing the progenitors of this stock into the valley. What a strange, wild, beautiful story it all was! But a story connected with this valley could not have been otherwise.

Beyond the meadow, on the other side of the valley, extended the forest, and that ended in the rising bench of thicket, which gave place to green slope and mossy terrace of sharp-tipped spruces, and all this led the eye irresistibly up to the red wall where a vast, dark, wonderful cavern yawned with its rust-colored streaks of stain on the wall and the queer little houses of the cliff-dwellers, with their black, vacant, silent windows speaking so weirdly of the unknown past.

Shefford passed a place where the ground had been cultivated, but not as recently as the last six months. There was a scant shock of corn and many meager standing stalks. He became aware of a low, whining hum and a fragrance overpowering in its sweetness. There around another corner of wall he came upon an orchard all pink and white in blossom and melodious with the buzz and hum of innumerable bees.

He crossed a little stream that had been dammed, went along a pond, down beside an irrigation ditch that furnished water to orchard and vineyard, and from there he strode into a beautiful cove between two jutting corners of red wall. It was level and green and the spruces stood gracefully everywhere. Beyond their dark trunks he saw caves in the wall.

Suddenly the fragrance of blossom was overwhelmed by the stranger fragrance of smoke from a wood fire. Swiftly he strode under the spruces. Quail fluttered before him as tame as chickens. Big gray rabbits scarcely moved out of his way. The branches above were full of mockingbirds. And then — there before him stood three figures.

Fay Larkin was held close to the side of a magnificent woman, barbarously clad in garments made of skins and pieces of blanket. Her face worked in noble emotion. Shefford seemed to see the ghost of that fair beauty Venters had said was Jane Withersteen's. Her hair was gray at the temples. Near her stood a lean, stoop-shouldered man whose long hair was perfectly white. His gaunt face was bare of beard. It had strange sloping sad lines, and he was staring with mildly surprised eyes.

The moment was great for Shefford, and it held him mute till sight of Fay Larkin's tear-wet face broke his spell. He leaped forward, and his strong hands reached for the woman and the man.

"Jane Withersteen! Lassiter! I have found you!"

"Oh, sir, who are you?" Jane cried with rich and deep and quivering voice. "This child came running . . . screaming. She could not speak. We thought she had gone mad . . . and escaped to come back to us."

"I am John Shefford," replied Shefford swiftly. "I am a friend of Bern Venters . . . of his wife Bess. I learned your story. I came West. I've searched a year. I found Fay. And we've come back to take you away."

"You found Fay? But her husband! That masked Mormon who forced her to sacrifice herself to save me! What of him? It's not been so many long years . . . I remember what my father was . . . and Dyer and Tull . . . all those cruel churchmen."

"Waggoner, who made Fay his sealed wife, is dead," replied Shefford.

"Dead? She is free! Oh, what . . . how did he die?"

"He was killed."

"Who did it?"

"*I killed him!*" replied Shefford stonily, and he met her gaze with steady eyes. "He's out of the way. Fay's free. We've come to take you out of the country. We must hurry. We'll be tracked . . . pursued. But we've horses and an Indian guide. We'll get away . . . I think it better to leave here at once. There's no telling how soon we'll be hunted.

Get what things you want to take with you."

"Oh . . . yes . . . Mother Jane, let us hurry," cried Fay. "I'm so full. I can't talk . . . my heart hurts so!"

Jane Withersteen's face shone with an exceedingly radiant light, and a glory blended with a terrible fear in her eyes. "Fay, my little Fay."

Lassiter had stood there with his clear blue eyes upon Shefford.

"I shore am glad to see you-all," he drawled, and extended his hand as if the meeting were casual. "What'd you say your name was?"

Shefford repeated it as he met the proffered hand.

"How's Bern an' Bess?" Lassiter inquired.

"They were well, prosperous, happy when last I saw them. They had a baby."

"Now ain't thet fine. Jane, did you hear? Bess has a baby. An' Jane, didn't I always say Bern would come back to get us out? Shore it's just the same."

How cool, easy, slow, and mild this Lassiter seemed. Had the man grown old, Shefford wondered? The past to him manifestly was only yesterday, and the danger of the present was as nothing. Looking into Lassiter's face, Shefford was baffled. If he had not remembered the greatness of this old gunman, he might have believed that the lonely years in the valley had unbalanced his mind. In an hour like this, coolness seemed inexplicable — assuredly would have been impossible in an ordinary man. Yet what hid behind that drawling coolness — what was the meaning of those long, sloping, shadowy lines of the face — what spirit lay deeply in the mild clear eyes? Shefford experienced a sudden check to what had been his first growing impression of a drifting, broken old man.

"Lassiter, pack what little you can carry . . . it mustn't be much . . . and we'll get out of here," said Shefford.

"I shore will. Reckon I ain't a-goin' to need a pack train. We saved the clothes we wore in here. Jane never thought it no use, but I figgered we might need them someday. They won't be stylish, but I reckon they'll do better'n these skins. An' there's an' old coat that was Venters's." The wild, dreamy look became intensified in Lassiter's eyes. "Did Venters have any hosses when you knowed him?" he asked.

"He had a farm full of horses," replied Shefford with a smile. "And there were two blacks . . . the grandest horses I ever saw. Black Star and Night! You remember, Lassiter?"

"Shore. I was wonderin' if he got the blacks out. They must be growin' old by now. Grand hosses, they was. But Jane had another hoss, a big devil of a sorrel. His name was Wrangle. Did Venters ever tell you about him . . . an' thet race with Jerry Cord?"

"A hundred times," replied Shefford.

"Wrangle run the blacks off their legs. But Jane never would believe thet. An' I couldn't change her all these years. Reckon, mebbe we'll get to see them blacks?"

"Indeed, I hope . . . I believe you will," replied Shefford feelingly.

"Shore won't thet be fine. Jane, did you hear? Black Star an' Night are livin'? An' we'll get to see them."

But Jane Withersteen only clasped Fay in her arms and looked at Lassiter with wet and glistening eyes.

Shefford told them to hurry and come to the cliff where the ascent from the valley was to be made. He thought best to leave them alone to make their preparations and bid farewell to the cavern home they had known for so long.

Then he strolled back along the wall, loitering here to gaze into a cave, and there to study crude red paintings in the nooks. Sometimes he halted thoughtfully, and he'd not see anything. At length he rounded a corner of cliff to espy Nas-Ta-Bega sitting upon the ledge, reposeful and watchful as usual. Shefford told the Indian they would be climbing out soon, and then he sat down to wait, and let his gaze rove over the valley.

He might have sat there a long while, so sad and reflective and wandering was his thought, but it seemed a very short time till Fay came in sight with her free, swift grace, and Lassiter and Jane some distance behind. Jane carried a small bundle, and Lassiter had a sack over his shoulder that appeared no inconsiderable burden.

"Them beans shore is heavy," he drawled as he deposited the sack upon the ground.

Shefford curiously took hold of the sack and was amazed to find that a second and hard muscular effort was required to lift it.

"Beans?" he queried.

"Shore," replied Lassiter.

"That's the heaviest sack of beans I ever saw. Why, it's not possible it can be. . . . Lassiter, we've a long rough trail. We've got to pack light."

"Wal, I ain't a-goin' to leave this here sack behind. Reckon I've been all of twelve years in fillin' it," he declared mildly.

Shefford could only stare at him.

"Fay may need them beans," went on Lassiter.

"Why?"

"Because they're gold."

"Gold!" ejaculated Shefford.

"Shore. An' they represent some work. Twelve years of diggin' an' washin'."

Shefford laughed constrainedly. "Well, Lassiter, that alters the case considerably. A sack of gold nuggets and grains, or beans, as you call them, certainly must not be left behind. Come now, we'll tackle this climbing job."

He called up to the Indian and, grasping the rope, began to walk up the first slant, and then by dint of hand over hand effort and climbing with knees and feet he succeeded, with Nas-Ta-Bega's help, in making the ledge. Then he let down the rope to hand up the sack and bundle. That done, he directed Fay to fasten the noose around her, as he had fixed it before. When she had complied, he called to her to hold herself out from the wall while he and Nas-Ta-Bega hauled her up.

"Hold the rope tight," replied Fay. "I'll walk up."

To Shefford's amaze and admiration, she virtually walked up that almost perpendicular wall, by slipping her hands along the rope and stepping as she pulled herself up. There, if never before, he saw the fruit of her years of experience on steep slopes. Only much experience could have made the feat possible.

Jane had to be hauled up, and the task was a painful one for her. Lassiter's turn came then, and he showed more strength and agility than Shefford had supposed him capable of. From the ledge they turned their attention to the narrow crack with its ladder of sticks. Fay had already ascended and now hung over the rim, her white face and golden hair framed vividly in the narrow stream of blue sky above.

"Mother Jane! Uncle Jim! You are so slow!" she called.

"Wal, Fay, we haven't been second cousins to a cañon squirrel all these years," replied Lassiter.

This upper half of the climb bid fair to be as difficult for Jane, if not so painful, as the lower. It was necessary for the Indian to go up and drop the rope, which was looped around her, and then, with him pulling from above, and Shefford assisting Jane as she climbed, she was finally gotten up without mishap.

When Lassiter reached the level, they rested a little while, and then faced the great slide of jumbled rocks. Fay led the way, light, supple, tireless, and Shefford never ceased looking at her. At last they surmounted the long slope and, winding along the rim, reached the point where they had led out of the cedars.

Nas-Ta-Bega then was the one to whom Shefford looked for every decision or action of the immediate future. The Indian said he had seen a pool of water near in a rocky hole, that the day was spent, that here was a little grass for the mustangs, and it would be well to camp right there. So, while Nas-Ta-Bega attended to the mustangs, Shefford set about such preparations for camp and supper as their light pack afforded. The question of beds was easily answered, for the mats of soft needles under piñons and cedar would be comfortable places to sleep.

When Shefford felt free again, the sun was settling. Lassiter and Jane were walking under the trees. The Indian had returned to camp. But Fay was missing. Shefford imagined he knew where to find her, and, upon going to the edge of the forest, he saw her sitting on the promontory. He approached her, drawn in spite of a feeling that perhaps he ought to stay away.

"Fay, would you rather be alone?" he asked.

His voice startled her.

"I want you," she replied, and held out her hand. Taking it in his own, he sat beside her.

The red sun was at their backs. Surprise Valley lay hazy, dusky, shadowy beneath them. The opposite wall seemed fired by crimson flame, save far down at its base where the sun no longer touched. The dark line of red slowly rose, encroaching upon the bright crimson. Changing, transparent, yet dusty veils seemed to float between the walls. Long red rays, where the sun shone through notch or crack in the rim, split the darker spaces. Deep down at the floor the forest darkened, the strip of aspens paled, the meadow turned gray, and under the shelves and in the great caverns a jungle gloom deepened. Then the sun set. Swiftly twilight was there below, while day lingered above. On the opposite wall the fire died, and the stone grew cold.

A cañon nighthawk voiced his lonely, wild, and melancholy cry, and it seemed to pierce and mark the silence. A pale star, peering out of a sky that had begun to turn blue, marked the end of twilight. All the purple shadows moved and hovered and changed till, softly and mysteriously, they embraced black night.

Beautiful, wild, strange, silent Surprise

Valley! Shefford saw it before and beneath him, a dark abyss now, the abode of loneliness. He imagined faintly what was in Fay Larkin's heart. For the last time she had seen the sun set there and night come with its dead silence and sweet mystery and phantom shadows, its velvet blue of sky and white trains of stars. He, who had dreamed and longed and searched, found that the hour had been incalculable for him in its import.

Chapter Seventeen

When Shefford awoke next morning and sat up on his bed of piñon boughs, the dawn had broken cold with a ruddy gold brightness under the trees. Nas-Ta-Bega and Lassiter were busy around a campfire; the mustangs were haltered nearby; Jane Withersteen combed out her long, tangled tresses with a crude wooden comb. Fay Larkin was not in sight. As she had been missing from the group at sunset, so she was now at sunrise. Shefford went out to take his last look at Surprise Valley.

On the evening before the valley had been a place of dusky red veils and purple shadows, and now it was pink-walled, clear and rosy and green and white, with wonderful shafts of gold slanting down from the notched eastern rim. Fay stood on the promontory, and Shefford did not break the spell of her silent farewell to her wild home. A strange emotion abided with him, and he knew he would always, all his life, regret leaving Surprise Valley.

Then the Indian called.

"Come, Fay," said Shefford gently.

She turned away with dark, haunted eyes and a white, still face.

The somber Indian gave a silent gesture for Shefford to make haste. While they had breakfast, the mustangs were saddled and packed. Soon all was in readiness for the flight. Fay was given Nack-Yal, Jane the saddled horse Shefford had ridden, and Lassiter the Indian's roan. Shefford and Nas-Ta-Bega were to ride the blanketed mustangs and the sixth and last one bore the pack. Nas-Ta-Bega set off leading this horse; the others of the party lined behind, with Shefford at the rear.

Nas-Ta-Bega led at a brisk trot, sometimes on level pieces of ground at an easy canter. Shefford had a grim realization of what this plight was going to be for these three fugitives so unhardened to riding. Jane and Lassiter, however, needed no watching and showed they had never forgotten how to manage a horse. The Indian backtracked the trail of yesterday for an hour, then headed west to the left and entered a low pass. All parts of this plateau country looked alike, and Shefford was at some pains to tell the difference of this strange ground from that which he had been over. In another hour they got out of the rugged broken rock to the wind-worn and smooth, shallow cañons. Shefford calculated that they were coming to the end of the plateau. The low walls slanted lower. The cañon made a turn. Nas-Ta-Bega disappeared, and then the others of the party. When Shefford turned the corner of wall, he saw a short strip of bare rocky ground with only sky beyond. The Indian and his followers had halted in a group. Shefford rode to them, halted himself, and in one sweeping glance realized the meaning of their silent gaze. Immediately Nas-Ta-Bega started down, and the mustangs, without word or touch, followed him. Shefford, however, lingered on the promontory.

His gaze seemed impelled and held by things afar, the great yellow and purple corrugated world of distance, now on a level with his eyes. He was drawn by the beauty and the grandeur of that scene and transfixed by the realization that he had dared to venture to find a way through this vast, wild, and upflung fastness. He kept looking afar, sweeping the three-quarter circle of horizon till his judgment of distance was confounded and his sense of proportion dwarfed one moment and magnified the next. Then he withdrew his fascinated gaze to adopt the Indian method of studying unlimited spaces in the desert — to look with slow, contracted eyes from near to far.

His companions had begun to zigzag down a long slope, bare of rock, with yellow gravel patches showing between the scant strips of green and here and there a scrub cedar. Half a mile down, the slope merged into green level. But close keen gaze made out this level to be a rolling plain, growing darker green, with blue lines of ravines and thin, undefined spaces that might be mirage. Miles and miles it swept and rolled and heaved to lose its waves in apparent darker level. A round red rock stood isolated, marking the end of the barren plain, and farther on were other round rocks, all isolated, all of different shapes. They resembled huge, grazing cattle. As Shefford gazed and his sight gained strength from steadily holding it to separate features, these rocks were strangely magnified. They grew and grew into mounds, castles, domes, crags — great, red, wind-carved buttes. One by one they drew his gaze to the wall of rippling rock. He seemed to see a thousand domes of a thousand shapes and colors, and among them a thousand blue clefts, each one a little mark in his sight, yet which he knew was a cañon.

So far he gained some idea of what he saw, but beyond this wide area of curved lines rose another wall, dwarfing the lower, dark red, horizon-long, magnificent in frowning boldness, and because of its limitless deceiving surfaces, breaks, and lines, incomprehensible to the sight of man. Away to the eastward began a winding, ragged blue line, looping back upon itself, and then winding away again, growing wider and bluer. This line was the San Juan Cañon. Where was Joe Lake at that moment? Had he embarked yet on the river — did that blue line, so faint, so deceiving, hold him and the boat? Almost it was impossible to believe. Shefford followed the blue line all its long length, a hundred miles he fancied, down toward the west where it joined a dark purple shadowy cleft. This was the Grand Cañon of the Colorado. Shefford's eye swept along with that winding mark, farther and farther to the west, around to the left, till the cleft, growing larger and coming closer, losing its deception, was seen to be a wild and winding cañon. Still farther to the left, as he swung in fascinated gaze, it split the wonderful wall — a vast plateau now with great red peaks and yellow mesas. The cañon was full of purple smoke. It turned, it closed, it gaped, it lost itself and showed again in that chaos of a million cliffs. Then farther on it became again a cleft, a purple line, at last to fail entirely in deceiving distance.

Shefford imagined there was no scene in all the world to equal that. The tranquility of lesser space was not here manifest. Sound, movement, life seemed to have no fitness here. Ruin was here and desolation and decay. The meaning of the ages was flung at him and a man became nothing. When he had gazed at the San Juan Cañon, he had been appalled at the nature of Joe Lake's Herculean task. He had lost hope, faith. The thing was not possible. But when Shefford gazed at that sublime and majestic wilderness of earth's naked crust, in which the Grand Cañon was only a dim line, he strangely lost his terror and something else came to him from across the shining spaces. If Nas-Ta-Bega led them safely down to the river, if Joe Lake met them at the mouth of Nonnezoshe Boco, if they survived the rapids of that terrible gorge — then Shefford would have to face his soul and the meaning of this spirit that breathed on the wind.

He urged his mustang to the descent of the slope, and, as he went down, slowly drawing nearer to the other fugitives, his mind alternated between this strange intimation of faith, this subtle uplift of his spirit, and the growing gloom and shadow in his love for Fay Larkin. Not that he loved her less, but more. A possible God hovering near him, like the Indian's spirit step on the trail, made his soul the darker for Fay's crime, and he saw with clearer sight, with deeper sadness, with sterner truth.

More than once he saw the Indian turn on his mustang to look up the slope, and the light flashed from his dark, somber face. Shefford instinctively looked back himself, and then realized the unconscious motive of the action. Deep within him there had been a premonition of certain pursuit, and the Indian's reiterated backward glance had at length brought the feeling upward. Thereafter, as they descended, Shefford gradually added to his already wrought emotions a mounting anxiety.

No sign of a trail showed where the base of the slope rolled out to meet the green plain. The earth was gravelly, with dark patches of heavy silt, almost like cinders, and round black rocks, flinty and glassy, cracked away from the hoofs of the mustangs. There was a level bench a mile wide, then a ravine, and then an ascent, and after that rounded ridge and ravine, one after the other, like huge swells of a monstrous sea. Indian paintbrush vied in its scarlet hue with the deep magenta of cactus. There was no sage. Soapweed and meager grass and a bunch of cactus here and there lent the green to that barren, and it was green only at a distance. Nas-Ta-Bega climbed. The wind rose and whipped dust from under the mustangs.

Shefford looked back often, and the farther out in the plain he reached, the higher loomed the plateau they had descended; and, as he faced ahead again, the lower sank the red domed and castled horizon to the fore. The ravines became deeper, with dry rock bottoms, and the ridge tops sharper with outcropping of yellow, crumbling ledges. Once across the central depression of that wide plain a gradual ascent became evident, and the red round rocks grew clearer in sight, began to rise and shine and grow. Thereafter every slope brought them nearer.

The sun was straight overhead and hot when Nas-Ta-Bega halted the party under the first lonely scrub cedar. They all dismounted to stretch their limbs and rest the horses. It was not a talkative group. Lassiter's comments on the never-ending green plain elicited no response. Jane Withersteen looked afar with the past in her eyes. Shefford felt Fay's wistful glance and could not meet it. Indeed, he seemed to want to hide something from her. The Indian bent a falcon gaze on the distant slope, and Shefford did not like that intent, searching, steadfast watchfulness. Suddenly Nas-Ta-Bega stiffened, and whipped the halter he held.

"Ugh!" he exclaimed.

All eyes followed the direction of his dark hand. Puffs of dust rose from the base of the long slope they had descended. Tiny, dark specks moved with the pace of snails.

"Shadd," added the Indian.

"I expected it," said Shefford darkly, as he rose.

"An' who's Shadd?" drawled Lassiter in his cool, slow speech.

Briefly Shefford explained, and then, looking at Nas-Ta-Bega, he added: "The hardest-riding outfit in the country. We can't get away from them."

Jane Withersteen was silent, but Fay uttered a low cry. Shefford did not look at either of them. The Indian began swiftly to tighten the saddle cinches of his roan, and Shefford did likewise for Nack-Yal. Then Shefford drew his rifle out of the saddle sheath, and Joe Lake's big guns from the saddlebag.

"Here, Lassiter, maybe you haven't forgotten how to use these," he said.

The old gunman started as if he had seen ghosts. His hands grew claw-like as he reached for the guns. He threw open the cylinders, spilled out the shells, snapped back the cylinders. Then he went through motions too swift for Shefford to follow, but Shefford heard the hammers falling so swiftly they blended their *clicks* almost in one sound. Lassiter reloaded the guns with a speed comparable with the other actions. A remarkable transformation had come over him. He did not seem the same man. The mild eye had changed, the long, shadowy, sloping lines were tense cords, and there was a cold, ashy shade on his face.

"Twelve years," he muttered to himself. "I dropped them old guns back there where I rolled the rock. Twelve years."

Shefford realized the twelve years were as if they had never been, and he would rather have had this old gunman with him than a dozen ordinary men.

The Indian spoke rapidly in Navajo, saying that once in the rocks they were safe. Then, after another look at the distant dust puffs, he wheeled his mustang.

It was doubtful if the party could have kept near him had they been responsible for the gait of their mounts. The fact was that the way the Indian called to his mustangs or some leadership in the one he rode drew the others to a like trot or climb or canter. For a long time Shefford did not turn around; he knew what to expect. When he did turn, he was startled at the gain made by the pursuers. But he was encouraged as well by the looming red rounded peaks seemingly now so close. He could see the dark splits between the sloping curved walls, the piñon patches in the amphitheaters under the circled walls. That was a wild place they were approaching, and once in there he believed pursuit would be useless. However, there were miles to go still, and those hard-riding devils behind made alarming decrease in the intervening distance. Shefford could see the horses plainly now. How they made the dust fly! He counted up to six, and then the dust and moving line caused the others to be indistinguishable.

At last only a long, gently rising slope separated the fugitives from that labyrinthine network of wildly carved rock. But it was the clear air that made the distance seem short. Mile after mile the mustangs climbed, and, when they were perhaps halfway across that last slope to the rocks, the first horse of the pursuers mounted to the level behind. In a few moments the whole band was strung out in sight. Nas-Ta-Bega kept his mustang at a steady walk, in spite of the gaining pursuers. There came a point, however, when the Indian, reaching comparatively level ground, put his roan to a swinging canter. The other mustangs broke into the same gait.

It became a race then with the couple of miles between fugitives and pursuers only imperceptibly lessened. Nas-Ta-Bega had saved his mustangs and Shadd had ridden his to the limit. Shefford kept looking back, gripping his rifle, hoping it would not come to a fight, yet slowly losing that reluctance.

Sage began to show on the slope and other kinds of brush and cedars straggled everywhere. The great rocks loomed closer, the red color mixed with yellow, and the slopes lengthening out, not so steep, yet infinitely longer than they had seemed at a distance.

Shefford ceased to feel the dry wind in his face. They were already in the lea of the wall. He could see the rock squirrels scampering to their holes. The mustangs valiantly held to the gait, and at last the Indian disappeared between two rounded corners of cliff. The others were close behind. Shefford wheeled once more. Shadd and his gang were a mile in the rear, but coming fast despite winded horses.

Shefford rode around the wall into a widening space thick with cedars. It ended in a bare slope of smooth rock. Here the Indian dismounted. When the others came up with him, he told them to lead their horses and follow. Then he began the ascent of the rock.

It was smooth and hard, although not slippery. There was not a crack. Shefford did not see a broken piece of stone. Nas-Ta-Bega climbed straight up for a while, and then wound around a swell, to turn this way and that, always going up. Shefford began to see similar mounds of rock all around him, of every shape that could be called a curve. There were yellow domes far above and small red domes far below. Ridges ran from one hill of rock to another. There were no abrupt breaks, but holes and pits and caves were everywhere, and occasionally deep down an amphitheater green with cedars and piñon. The Indian appeared to have a clear idea of where he wanted to go, although there was no vestige of a trail on those bare slopes. At length Shefford was high enough to see back upon the plain, but the pursuers were no longer in sight.

Nas-Ta-Bega led to the top of that wall, only to disclose to his followers another and a higher wall behind, with a ridged, bare, wild, and scalloped depression between. Here footing began to be precarious for both man and beast. When the ascent of the second wall began, it was necessary to zigzag up, slowly and carefully, taking advantage of every bulge or depression. They must have consumed half an hour mounting this slope to the summit. Once there, Shefford drew sharp breaths with both backward and forward glances. Shadd and his gang in single file showed darkly upon the bare stone ridge behind, and to the fore there twisted and dropped and curved the most dangerous slopes Shefford had ever seen. The fugitives had reached the height of stone wall of the divide, and many of the drops upon this side were perpendicular and too deep to see the bottom.

Nas-Ta-Bega led along the ridge top, and then started down following the waves in the rock. He came out upon a round promontory from which there could not have been any turning of a horse. The long slant leading down was at an angle Shefford declared impossible for the animals. Yet the Indian started down. His mustang needed urging, but at last edged upon the steep descent. Shefford and the others had to hold back and wait. It was thrilling to see the intelligent mustang. He did not step. He slid his fore hoofs a few inches at a time and kept directly behind the Indian. If he fell, he would knock Nas-Ta-Bega off his feet and they would both roll down together. There was no doubt in Shefford's mind that the mustang knew this as well as the Indian. Foot by foot they worked down to a swelling bulge, and here Nas-Ta-Bega left his mustang and came back for the pack horse. It was even more difficult to get this beast down. Then the Indian called for Lassiter and Jane and Fay to come down. Shefford began to keep a sharp look-out behind and above, and did not see how the three fared on the slope, but evidently there was no mishap. Nas-Ta-Bega mounted the slope again, and at that moment sight of Shadd's dark bays, silhouetted against the sky, caused Shefford to call out: "We've got to hurry!"

The Indian led one mustang and called to the others. Shefford stepped close behind. They went down in single file, inch by inch, foot by foot, and safely reached the comparative level below.

"Shadd's gang are riding their horses up

and down these walls!" exclaimed Shefford.

"Shore," replied Lassiter.

Both the women were silent.

Nas-Ta-Bega led the way swiftly to the right. He rounded a huge dome, climbed a low, rolling ridge, descended and ascended, and came out upon the rim of a steep-walled amphitheater. Along the rim was a yard-wide level, with the chasm to the left and steep slope to the right. There was no time to flinch at the danger, when an even greater danger menaced from the rear. Nas-Ta-Bega led and his mustang kept at his heels. One misstep would have plunged the animal to his death. But he was sure-footed, and his confidence helped the others. At the apex of the curve the only course led away from the rim, and here there was no level. Four of the mustangs slipped and slid down the smooth rock till they stopped in a shallow depression. It cost time to get them out, to straighten pack and saddles. Shefford thought he heard a yell in the rear, but he could not see anything of the gang.

They rounded this precipice only to face a worse one. Shefford's nerve was sorely tried when he saw steep slants everywhere, all apparently leading down into chasms, and no place a man, let alone a horse, could put a foot with safety. Nevertheless, the imperturbable Indian never slacked his pace. Always he appeared to find a way, and he never had to turn back. His winding course, however, did not now cover much distance in a straight line, and herein lay the greatest peril. Any moment Shadd and his men might come within range.

Upon a particularly tedious and dangerous side of rocky hill the fugitives lost so much time that Shefford grew exceedingly alarmed. Still, they accomplished it without accident, and their pursuers did not heave in sight. Perhaps they were having trouble in a bad place.

The afternoon was waning. The red sun hung low above the yellow mesa to the left, and there was a perceptible shading of light.

At last Nas-Ta-Bega came to a place that halted him. It did not look so bad as places they had successfully passed. Yet upon closer study Shefford did not see how they were to get around the neck of the gully at their feet. Presently the Indian put the bridle over the head of his mustang and left him free. He did likewise for two more mustangs, while Lassiter and Shefford rendered a like service to theirs. Then the Indian started down with his mustang following him. The pack animal came next, then Fay and Nack-Yal, then Lassiter and his mount, with Jane and hers next, and Shefford last. They followed the Indian, picking their steps swiftly, looking nowhere except at the stone under their feet. The right side of the chasm was rimmed, the curve at the head crossed, and then the real peril of this trap had to be faced. It was a narrow slant of ledge, doubling back parallel with the course already traversed.

A sharp warning cry from Nas-Ta-Bega scarcely prepared Shefford for hoarse yells, and then a rattling rifle volley from the top of the slope opposite. Bullets thudded on the cliff, whipped up red dust, and *spanged* and droned away.

Fay Larkin screamed and staggered back against the wall. Nack-Yal was grazed, and with frightened snort he reared, pawed the air, and came down pounding the stone. The mustang behind him went to his knees, sank with his head over the rim, and, slipping off, plunged into the depths. In an instant a dull crash came up.

For a moment there was imminent peril for the horses, more in the yawning hole than in the *spanging* of badly aimed bullets. Lassiter drew Jane up the little slope out of the way of the frightened mustangs, and Shefford, risking his neck, rushed to Fay. She was holding her arm, which was bleeding. Unheeding the rain of bullets, he half carried, half dragged her along the slope of the low bluff where he hid behind a corner till the Indian drove the mustangs around it. Fay had sustained a wound to her arm. Shefford's swift fingers were wet and red with her blood when he had bound the wound with his scarf. Lassiter had got around to Jane and was calling Shefford to hurry.

It had been Shefford's idea to halt there and fight. But he did not want to send Fay on alone, so he hurried ahead with her. The Indian had the horses going fast on a long level, working by a bulging wall. Lassiter and Jane were looking back. Shefford, becoming aware of a steep slope to his left, looked down to see a tremendous narrow chasm, great crevices in split cliffs, and bunches of cedars — a wild and rugged place.

Nas-Ta-Bega disappeared with the mustangs. He had evidently turned off to go down behind the split cliffs. Shefford and Fay caught up with Lassiter and Jane, and panting, hurrying, looking backward and then forward, they kept, as best they could, to the Indian's course. Shefford was sure they had lost him when Nas-Ta-Bega appeared down to the left. Then they all ran to catch up with him. They went around the chasm, and then through one of the narrow cracks to come out upon the rim, among the cedars. Here the Indian waited for them. He pointed down another long swell of naked stone to a narrow green split, which was evidently different from all these curved pits and holes and abysses, for this one had straight walls and wound away out of sight. It was the head of a cañon.

"Nonnezoshe Boco!" said the Indian.

"Nas-Ta-Bega, go on," replied Shefford. "When Shadd comes out on that slope above, he can't see you . . . where you go down. Hurry on with the horses and women. Lassiter, you go with them. If Shadd passes me and comes up with you . . . do your best. . . . I'm going to ambush that Paiute and his gang!"

"Shore, you've picked out a good place," replied Lassiter.

In another moment Shefford was alone. He heard the light, soft pat and slide of the hoofs of the mustangs as they went down. Presently that sound ceased.

He looked at the red stain on his hands — from the blood of the girl he loved. He had to stifle a terrible wrath that shook his frame. In regard to Shadd's pursuit it had not been blood that he had feared, but capture for Fay. He and Nas-Ta-Bega might have expected a shot if they resisted, but to wound that unfortunate girl — it made a tiger out of him. When he had stilled the emotions that weakened and shook him and reached cold and implacable control of himself, he crawled under the cedars to the rim, and, well hidden, he watched and waited.

Shadd appeared to be slow for the first time since he had been sighted. With keen eyes Shefford watched the corner where he and the others had escaped from that murderous volley. But Shadd did not come.

The sun had lost its warmth and was tipping the lofty mesa to his right. Soon twilight would make travel on those walls more perilous, and darkness would make it impossible. Shadd must hurry or abandon the pursuit for that day. Shefford found himself grimly hopeful.

Suddenly he heard the *click* of hoofs. It came faintly yet clearly on the still air. He glued his sight upon that corner where he expected the pursuers to appear. More *clicks* of hoofs pierced his ear, clearer and sharper, this time. Presently he gathered that they could not possibly come from beyond the corner he was watching. So he looked far to the left of that place, seeing no one, then far to the right. Over a bridge of stone he caught sight of the bobbing head of a horse — then another — and still another.

He was astounded. Shadd had gone below that place where the attack had been made, and he had come up this steep slope. More horses appeared — to the number of eight. Shefford easily recognized a low, broad, squat rider to be Shadd. Assuredly the Paiute did not know this country. Possibly, however, he had feared an ambush, but Shefford grew convinced that Shadd had not really expected an ambush, or at least did not fear one, had only mistaken the Indian's course. Moreover, if he led his gang farther up that slope, he would do worse than make a mistake — he would be facing a double peril.

What fearless horsemen these Indians were! Shadd was mounted, as were three others of his gang. Evidently the white men, the outlaws, and a few Paiutes were the men on foot. Shefford thrilled and his veins stung when he saw these pursuers come passing what he considered the danger mark. Manifestly they could not see their danger. Assuredly they were aware of the chasm; however, the level upon which they were advancing narrowed gradually, and they could not tell that very soon they could not go any farther, nor could they turn back.

The alternative was to climb the slope and that was a desperate chance.

They came up, now about on a level with Shefford, and perhaps three hundred yards distant. He gripped his rifle with a fatal assurance that he could kill one of them now. Still he waited. Curiosity consumed him because every foot they advanced heightened their peril. Shefford wondered if Shadd would have chosen that course if he had not supposed the Navajo had chosen it first. It was plain that one of the walking Paiutes stooped now and then to examine the rock. He was looking for some faint sign of a horse track.

Shadd halted within two hundred yards of where Shefford lay hidden. His keen eye had caught the significance of the narrowing land before he had reached the end. He pointed and spoke. Shefford heard his voice. The others replied. They all looked up at the steep slope, down into the chasm right below them, and across into the cedars. The Paiute in the rear succeeded in turning his horse, went back, and began to circle up the slope. The others entered into an argument, and they became more closely grouped upon the narrow bench. Their mustangs were lean, wiry, vicious, and Shefford calculated grimly on what a stampede might mean in that position.

Then Shadd turned his mustang up the slope. Like a goat he climbed. Another Indian in the rear succeeded in pivoting his steed, and started back, apparently to circle around and up. The others of the gang appeared uncertain. They yelled hoarsely at Shadd, who halted on the steep slant some twenty paces above them. He spoke and made motions that evidently meant the climb was easy enough. It looked easy for him. His dark face flashed red in the rays of the sun.

At this critical moment Shefford decided to fire. He meant to kill Shadd, hoping if the leader were gone, the others would abandon the pursuit. The rifle wavered a little as he aimed — then grew still. He fired. Shadd never flinched. But the fiery mustang, perhaps wounded, certainly terrified, plunged down with piercing horrid screams. Shadd fell under him. Shrill yells rent the air. Like a thunderbolt the sliding horse was upon men and animals below.

A heavy shock — wild snorts — upflinging heads and hoofs — a terrible trampling, thudding, shrieking mêlée — then a brown, twisting, tangled mass shot down the slant over the rim!

Shefford dazedly thought he saw men

running. He did see plunging horses. One slipped and fell, rolled, and went into the chasm.

Then up from the depths came a crash — a long, sliding roar. In another instant there was a lighter crash — and a lighter sliding roar.

Two horses, shaking, paralyzed with fear, were left upon the narrow level. Beyond them a couple of men were crawling along the stone. Up on the slope stood the two Indians, holding down frightened horses and staring at the fatal slope.

Shefford lay there under the cedar, in the ghastly grip of the moment, hardly comprehending that his ill-aimed shot had been a thunderbolt. He did not think of shooting at the Paiutes. They, however, recovering from their shock, evidently feared ambush, for they swiftly drew up the slope and passed out of sight. The frightened horses below whistled and tramped along the lower level, finally vanishing. There was nothing left on the bare wall to prove to Shefford that it had been a scene of swift and tragic death. He leaned from his covert and peered over the rim. Hundreds of feet below he saw dark growths of piñons. There was no sign of a pile of horses and men, and then he realized that he could not tell the number that had perished. The swift finale had been as stunning to him as if lightning had struck near him.

Suddenly it flashed over him what state of suspense and torture Fay and Jane must be in at that very moment. Leaping up, he ran out of the cedars to the slope behind, and hurried down at risk of limb. The sun had set by this time. He hoped he could catch up with the party before dark. He went straight down, and the end of the slope was a smooth low wall. The Indian must have descended with the horses at some other point. The cañon was about fifty yards wide, and it headed under the near slope of Navajo Mountain. These smooth, rounded walls appeared to end at its low rim.

Shefford slid down upon a grassy bank, and, finding the tracks of the horses, he followed them. They led along the wall. As soon as he assured himself that Nas-Ta-Bega had gone down the cañon, he abandoned the tracks and pushed ahead swiftly. He heard the soft rush of running water. In the center of the cañon wound heavy lines of bright green foliage, evidently a rocky brook. The air was close, warm and sweet with perfume of flowers. The walls were low and shelving and soon lost that rounded appearance peculiar to the wind-blown slopes above. Shefford came to where the horses had plowed down a gravelly bank into the clear swift water of the brook. The little pools of water were still muddy. Shefford drank, finding the water cold and sweet, without the bitter bite of alkali. He crossed and pushed on, running on the grassy levels. Flowers were everywhere, but he did not notice them particularly. The cañon made many leisurely turns and its size, if it enlarged at all, was not perceptible to him yet. The rims above him were perhaps fifty feet high. Cottonwood trees began to appear along the brook and blossoming buck brush in the corners of wall.

He had traveled perhaps a mile when Nas-Ta-Bega, appearing to come out of the thicket, confronted him.

"Hello!" called Shefford. "Where is Fay . . . and the others?"

The Indian made a gesture that signified the rest of the party were beyond a little way. Shefford took Nas-Ta-Bega's arm, and, as they walked and he panted for breath, he told what had happened back on the slopes.

The Indian made one of his singular speaking sweeps of hand, and he scrutinized Shefford's face, but he received the news in silence. They turned a corner of wall, crossed a wide, shallow, boulder-strewn place in the brook, and mounted the bank to a thicket. Beyond this, from a clump of cottonwoods, Lassiter strode out with a gun in each hand. He had been hiding.

"Shore I'm glad to see you," he said, and the eyes that piercingly fixed on Shefford were now as keen as formerly they had been mild.

"Gone! Lassiter . . . they're gone," broke out Shefford. "Where's Fay . . . and Jane?"

Lassiter called, and presently the women came out of a thick brake. Fay bounded forward with her swift stride, while Jane followed with eager step and anxious face. Then they all surrounded Shefford.

"It was Shadd . . . and his gang," panted Shefford. "Eight in all, three or four Paiutes . . . the others outlaws. They lost track of us. Went below the place . . . where they shot at us. And they came up . . . on a bad slope."

Shefford described the slope and the deep chasm and how Shadd led up to the point where he saw his mistake, and then how the catastrophe fell.

"I shot and missed," repeated Shefford, with the sweat in beads on his pale face. "I missed Shadd. Maybe I hit the horse. The horse plunged . . . reared . . . fell back . . . a terrible fall . . . right upon that bunch of horses and men below. In a horrible wrestling, screaming tangle they slid over the rim! I don't know how many. I saw some men running along. I saw three other horses plunging. One slipped and went over. I have no idea how many, but Shadd and some of his gang went to destruction."

"Shore thet's fine!" said Lassiter. "Mebbe I won't get to use these guns, after all."

"Hardly on that gang." Shefford laughed. "The two Paiutes and what others escaped turned back. Maybe they'll meet a posse of Mormons . . . for, of course, the Mormons will track us, too . . . and come back to where Shadd lost his life. That's an awful place. Even the Paiute got lost. Couldn't follow Nas-Ta-Bega. It would take any pursuers some time to find how we got in here. I believe we need not fear further pursuit. Certainly not tonight or tomorrow. Then we'll be far down the cañon."

When Shefford concluded his earnest remarks, the faces of Fay and Jane had lost the signs of suppressed dread.

"Nas-Ta-Bega, make camp here," said Shefford. "Water . . . wood . . . grass, why this's something like. . . . Fay, how's your arm?"

"It hurts," she replied simply.

"Come with me down to the brook and let me wash and bind it properly."

They went, and she sat on a stone, while he knelt beside her and untied his scarf from her arm. As the blood had hardened, it was necessary to slit her sleeve up to the shoulder. Using his scarf, he washed the blood from the wound and found it to be merely a cut, a groove, on the surface.

"That's nothing," Shefford said lightly. "It'll heal in a day. But there'll always be a scar. And when we all get back to civilization and you wear a pretty gown without sleeves . . . people will wonder what made this mark on your beautiful arm."

Fay looked at him with wonderful eyes.

"Do women wear gowns without sleeves?" she asked.

"They do."

"Have I a . . . a beautiful arm?"

She stretched it out, blue-veined, the skin fine as satin, the lines graceful and flowing, a round, firm, strong arm.

"The most beautiful I ever saw," he replied.

But the pleasure his compliment gave her was not communicated to him. His last impression of that right arm had been of its strength — and his mind flashed with lightning swiftness to a picture that haunted him: Waggoner lying dead on the porch with that powerfully driven knife in his heart.

Shefford shuddered through all his being. Would this phantom come often to him like that? Hurriedly he bound up her arm with the scarf and did not look at her and was conscious that she felt a subtle change in him.

The short twilight ended with the fugitives comfortable in a camp that for natural features could not have been improved upon. Darkness found Jane and Fay asleep in a soft mossy bed, a blanket tucked around them, and their faces still and beautiful in the flickering campfire light. Lassiter did not linger long awake. Nas-Ta-Bega, seeing Shefford's excessive fatigue, urged him to sleep. Shefford demurred, insisting that he share the night watch. But Nas-Ta-Bega, by agreeing that Shefford might have the following night's duty, prevailed upon him.

Shefford seemed to shut his eyes upon darkness and to open them immediately to the light. The stream of blue sky above, the gold tints on the river, the rosy brightening colors down in the cañon were proofs of the sunrise. This morning Nas-Ta-Bega proceeded leisurely, and his manner was comforting. When all was in readiness for a start, he gave the mustang he had ridden to

Shefford and walked, leading the pack animal.

The mode of travel here was a combination of the best levels, the best places to cross the brook, the best banks to climb, and it was a process of continual repetition. As the Indian picked out the course and the mustang followed his lead, there was nothing for Shefford to do but take his choice between reflection that seemed predisposed toward gloom and an absorption in the beauty, color, wildness, and changing character of Nonnezoshe Boco.

Assuredly his experience in the desert did not count in it a trip down into a strange, beautiful, lost cañon such as this. It did not widen, although the walls grew higher. They began to lean and bulge, and the narrow strip of sky above resembled a flowing blue river. Huge caverns had been hollowed out by some mark of nature, what he could not tell, although he was sure it could not have been wind. When the brook ran close under one of these overhanging places, the running water made a singular, indescribable sound. A *crack* from a hoof on a stone rang like a hollow bell and echoed from wall to wall. The *croak* of a frog — the only living creature he had so far noted in the cañon — was a weird and melancholy thing.

Fay rode close to him, and his heart seemed to rejoice when she spoke, when she showed how she wanted to be near him, yet, try as he might, he could not respond. His speech to her — what little there was — did not come spontaneously. He suffered a remorse that he could not be honestly natural to her. Then he would drive away the encroaching gloom — trusting that a little time would dispel it.

"We are deeper down than Surprise Valley," said Fay.

"How do you know?" he asked.

"Here are the pink and yellow sago lilies. You remember we went once to find the white ones? I have found white lilies in Surprise Valley, but never any pink or yellow."

Shefford had seen flowers all along the green banks, but he had not marked the lilies. Here he dismounted and gathered several. They were larger than the white ones of higher altitude, of the same exquisite beauty and fragility, of such rare pink and yellow lines as he had never seen. He gave the flowers to Fay.

"They bloom only where it's always summer," she said.

That expressed their nature. They were the orchids of the summer cañons. They stood up everywhere star-like out the green.

433

It was impossible to prevent the mustangs from treading them under hoof. As the cañon deepened, and many little springs added their tiny volume to the brook, every grassy bench was dotted with lilies, like a green sky star-spangled. This increasing luxuriance manifested itself in the banks of purple moss and clumps of lavender daisies and great clusters of yellow violets. The brook was lined by blossoming buck brush. The rocky corners showed the crimson and magenta of cactus; ledges were green with shining moss that sparkled with little white flowers. The *hum* of bees filled the air.

By and by this green and colorful and verdant beauty, the almost level floor of the cañon, the banks of soft earth, the thickets and the clump of cottonwoods, the shelving caverns and the bulging walls — these features gradually were lost, and Nonnezoshe Boco began to deepen in bare red and white stone steps, the walls sheered away from one another, breaking into sections and ledges and rising higher and higher, and there began to be manifested a dark and solemn concordance with the nature that had created this rent in the earth.

There was a stretch of miles where steep steps in hard red rock alternated with long levels of round boulders. Here one by one the mustangs went lame. The fugitives, dismounting to spare the faithful beasts, slipped and stumbled over these loose and treacherous stones. Fay was the only one who did not show distress. She was glad to be on foot again, and the rolling boulders were as stable as solid rock for her.

The hours passed; the toil increased; the progress diminished. One of the mustangs failed entirely and was left, and all the while the dimensions of Nonnezoshe Boco magnified and its character changed. It became a thousand-foot walled cañon, leaning, broken, threatening, with great yellow slides blocking passage, with huge sections split off from the main wall, with immense dark and gloomy caverns. Strangely it had no intersecting cañon. It jealously guarded its secret. No unusual formations of cavern and pillar and half arch led the mind to expect any monstrous stone shape left by avalanche or cataclysm.

Down and down the fugitives toiled. Now the streambed was bare of boulders and the banks of earth. The floods that had rolled down that cañon had here borne away every loose thing. All the floor was bare white and red stone, polished, glistening, slippery, affording treacherous foot hold. The time came when Nas-Ta-Bega abandoned the streambed to take to the rock-strewn and cactus-covered ledges above.

Jane gave out and had to be assisted upon the weary mustang. Fay was persuaded to mount Nack-Yal again. Lassiter plodded along. The Indian bent tired steps far in front. Shefford traveled on after him, foot-sore and last.

The cañon widened ahead into a great, ragged, iron-hued amphitheater and from there apparently turned abruptly at right angles. Sunset rimmed the walls. Shefford wondered dully when the Indian would halt to camp. He dragged himself onward with eyes down on the rough ground.

When he raised them again, the Indian stood on a point of slope with folded arms, gazing down where the cañon veered. Something in Nas-Ta-Bega's pose quickened Shefford's pulse, and then his steps. He reached the Indian and the point where he, too, could see beyond that vast, jutting wall that had obstructed his view.

A mile beyond all was bright with the colors of sunset, and spanning the cañon in the graceful shape and beautiful lines of a rainbow was a magnificent stone bridge.

"Nonnezoshe!" exclaimed the Navajo with a deep and sonorous roll in his voice.

Chapter Eighteen

The rainbow bridge was the one great natural phenomenon, the one grand spectacle that Shefford had ever seen that did not at first give vague disappointment, a confounding of reality, a disenchantment of contrast with what the mind had conceived. This thing was glorious. It silenced him, yet did not awe or stun. His body and brain, weary and dull from the toil of travel, received a singular and revivifying freshness. He had a strange, mystic perception of this rosy-lined, stupendous arch of stone, as if in a former life it had been a goal he could not reach. This wonder of nature, although all-satisfying, all-fulfilling to his artist's soul, could not be a resting place for him, a destination where something awaited him, a height he must scale to find peace, the end of his strife. Yet it seemed all of these. He could not understand his perception or his emotion. Still, here at last, apparently, was the rainbow of his boyish dreams and of his manhood — a rainbow magnified even beyond those dreams, no longer transparent and ethereal, but solidified, a thing of ages, sweeping up majestically from the red walls, its iris-hued arch against the blue sky.

Nas-Ta-Bega led on down the ledge, and Shefford plodded thoughtfully after him. The others followed. A jutting corner of wall again hid the cañon. The Indian was working around to circle the huge amphitheater. It was slow, irritating, strenuous toil, for the way was on a steep slant, rough and loose and dragging. The rocks were as hard and jagged as lava, and the cactus further hindered progress. When at last the long half circle had been accomplished, the golden and rosy lights had faded.

Again the cañon opened to view. All the walls were pale and steely and the stone bridge loomed darkly. Nas-Ta-Bega said camp would be made at the bridge, which was now close. Just before they reached it, the Navajo halted with one of his singular actions. Then he stood motionless. Shefford realized that Nas-Ta-Bega was saying his prayer to this great stone god. Presently the Indian motioned for Shefford to lead the others and the horses on under the bridge. Shefford did so and, upon turning, was amazed to see the Indian climbing the steep and difficult slope on the other side. All the party watched him till he disappeared behind the huge base of cliff that supported the arch. Shefford selected a level place for camp, some few rods away, and here, with Lassiter, unsaddled and unpacked the lame, drooping mustangs. When this was done, twilight had fallen. Nas-Ta-Bega appeared, coming down the steep slope on this side of the bridge. Then Shefford divined why the Navajo had made that arduous climb. He would not go under the bridge. Nonnezoshe was a Navajo god, and Nas-Ta-Bega, although educated as a white man, was true to the superstition of his ancestors.

Nas-Ta-Bega turned the mustangs loose to fare for what scant grass grew on bench and slope. Firewood was even harder to find than grass. When the camp duties had been performed and the simple meal eaten, there was gloom gathering in the cañon and stars had begun to blink in the pale strip of blue above the lofty walls. The place was oppressive and the fugitives mostly silent. Shefford spread a bed of blankets for the women, and Jane at once lay wearily down. Fay stood beside the flickering fire, and Shefford felt her watching him. He was conscious of a desire to get away from her haunting gaze. To the gentle good night he bade her, she made no response.

Shefford moved away into a strange, dark shadow cast by the bridge against the pale starlight. It was a vivid black belt, where he imagined he was invisible but out of which he could see. There was a slab of rock near the foot of the bridge, and here Shefford composed himself to watch, to feel, to think the unknown thing that seemed to be inevitably coming to him.

A slight stiffening of his neck made him aware that he had been continuously looking up at the looming arch, and he found that insensibly it had changed and grown. It had never seemed the same any two moments, but that was not what he meant. Near at hand it was too vast a thing for immediate comprehension. He wanted to ponder on what had formed it — to reflect upon its meaning as to age and force of nature, yet all he could do at each moment was to see white stars hung along the dark curved line. The rim of the arch seemed to shine. The moon must be up there somewhere. The far side of the cañon was now a blank black wall. Over its towering rim showed a pale glow. It brightened. The shades in the cañon lightened. Then a white disk of moon peeped over the dark line. The bridge turned to silver, and the gloomy, shadowy belt it had cast blanched and vanished.

Shefford became aware of the presence of Nas-Ta-Bega. Dark, silent, statuesque, with inscrutable eyes unlifted, with all that was spiritual of the Indian suggested by a somber and tranquil knowledge of his place there, he represented the same to Shefford as a solitary figure of human life brought out the greatness of a great picture. Nonnezoshe Boco needed life, wild life, life of its millions of years — and here stood the dark and silent Indian.

There was a surge in Shefford's heart and in his mind, a perception of a moment of incalculable change to his soul. At that moment Fay Larkin stole like a phantom to his side and stood there with her uncovered head shining and her white face lovely in the moonlight.

"May I stay with you . . . a little?" she asked wistfully. "I can't sleep."

"Surely you may," he replied. "Does your arm hurt too badly, or are you too tired to sleep?"

"No . . . it's this place. I . . . I . . . can't tell you how I feel."

But was the feeling there in her eyes for Shefford to read? Had he too great an emotion — did he read too much — did he add from his soul? For him the wild,

441

starry, haunted eyes mirrored all that he had seen and felt under Nonnezoshe, and for herself they shone eloquently of courage and love.

"I need to talk . . . and I don't know how," she said.

He was silent, but he took her hands and drew her closer.

"Why are you so . . . so different?" she asked bravely.

"Different?" he echoed.

"Yes. You are kind . . . you speak the same to me, as you used to. But since we started, you've been different, somehow."

"Fay, think how hard and dangerous the trip's been! I've been worried . . . and sick with dread . . . with . . . oh! you can't imagine the strain I'm under. How could I be my old self?"

"It isn't worry I mean."

He was too miserable to try to find out what she did mean; besides, he believed, if he let himself think about it, he would know what troubled her.

"I . . . I am almost happy," she said softly.

"Fay! Aren't you at all afraid?"

"No. You'll take care of me. . . . Do . . . do you love me . . . like you did before?"

"Why, child! Of course, I love you," he replied brokenly, and he drew her closer. He had never embraced her, never kissed her. But there was a whiteness about her then — a wraith — a something from her soul, and he could only gaze at her.

"I love you," she whispered. "I thought I knew it that . . . that night. But I'm only finding it out now. . . . And somehow I had to tell you here."

"Fay, I haven't said much to you," he said hurriedly, duskily. "I haven't had an chance. I love you. I . . . I ask you . . . will you be my wife?"

"Of course," she said simply, but the white, moon-blanched face colored with a dark and leaping blush.

"We'll be married as soon as I've got you out of the desert," he went on. "And we'll forget . . . all . . . all that's happened. You're so young. You'll forget."

"I'd forgotten already, till this difference came in you. And pretty soon . . . when I say something more to you . . . I'll forget all except Surprise Valley . . . and my evenings in the starlight with you."

"Say it then . . . quick."

She was leaning against him, holding his hands in her strong clasp, soulful, tender, almost passionate. "You couldn't help it. . . . I'm to blame. . . . I remember what I said."

"What?" he queried in amaze.

" *'You can kill him!'* I said that. I made you kill him."

"Kill . . . who?" cried Shefford.

"Waggoner . . . my husband. I'm to blame. . . . That must be what's made you different. And, oh, I've wanted you to know it's all my fault. . . . But I wouldn't be sorry if you weren't. . . . I'm glad he's dead."

"You . . . think . . . I . . . ?" Shefford's gasping whisper failed in the shock of the revelation that Fay believed he had killed Waggoner. Then with the inference came its staggering truth — her guiltlessness — and a paralyzing joy held him stricken.

A powerful hand fell upon Shefford's shoulder, startling him. Nas-Ta-Bega stood there, looking down upon him and Fay. Never had the Indian seemed so dark, inscrutable of face. But in his magnificent bearing, in the spirit that Shefford sensed in him there was nobility and power, and a strange pride. The Indian kept one hand on Shefford's shoulder, and with the other he struck himself in the breast. The action was that of an Indian, impressive and stern, significant of an Indian's prowess.

"My God," breathed Shefford, very low.

"Oh, what does he mean?" cried Fay.

Shefford held her with shaking hands, trying to speak, to fight a way out of these stultifying emotions. "Nas-Ta-Bega . . . you heard . . . she thinks . . . I killed Waggoner!"

All about the Navajo then was dark and solemn disproof of her belief. He did not need to speak. His repetition of that savage, almost boastful blow on his breast added only to the dignity and not to the denial of a warrior.

"Fay, he means he killed the Mormon," said Shefford. "He must have, for I did not."

"Ah," murmured Fay, and she leaned to him with passionate, quivering gladness. It was the woman, the soul born in her that came uppermost then. Now, when there was no direct call to the wild and elemental in her nature, she showed a heart above revenge, the instinct and the saving beauty of right, of truth, as Shefford knew them. He took her into his arms and never had he loved her so well.

"Nas-Ta-Bega, you killed the Mormon," declared Shefford, with a voice that had gained strength. No silent Indian suggestion of a deed would suffice in that moment. Shefford needed to hear the Navajo speak — to have Fay hear him speak. "Nas-Ta-Bega, I know . . . I understand. But tell her. Speak so she will know. Tell it as a white man would."

"I heard her cry out," replied the Indian

in his slow English. "I waited. When he came, I killed him."

A poignant — "Why?" — was wrenched from Shefford.

Nas-Ta-Bega stood silently for a moment. *"Bi-nai!"* When that sonorous Indian name rolled in dignity from his lips, he silently stalked away into the gloom. That was his answer to the white man.

Shefford bent over Fay, and, as the strain on him broke, he held her closer and closer, and his tears streamed down and his voice broke in exclamations of tenderness and thanksgiving. It did not matter what she had thought, but she must never know what *he* had thought. He clasped her as something precious he had lost and regained. He was shaken with a passion of remorse. How could he have believed Fay Larkin guilty of murder? Women less wild and less justified than she had been driven to such a deed, yet how could he have believed it of her, when for two days he had been with her, had seen her face and deeply into her eyes? There was a mystery in his very blindness. He cast the whole thought from him forever. There was no shadow between Fay and him. He had found her. He had saved her. She was free. She was innocent. Suddenly, as he seemed delivered from contending tumults within, he became aware that it was no unresponsive creature he had folded to his breast.

He became suddenly alive to the warm, throbbing contact of her bosom — to her strong arms clinging around his neck — to her closed eyes — to the rapt whiteness of her face. He bent to cold lips that seemed to receive his first kisses as new and strange, but tremulously changed, at last, to meet his own, and then to burn with sweet and thrilling fire.

"My darling, my dream's come true," he said. "You are my treasure. I found you here at the foot of the rainbow! What if it is a stone rainbow, if all is not as I had dreamed? I followed a gleam. And it's led me to love and faith!"

Hours afterwards, Shefford walked alone to and fro under the bridge. His trouble had given place to serenity. But this night of nights he must live out wide-eyed to its end. The moon had long since crossed the streak of star-fired blue above and the cañon was black in shadow. At times a current of wind, with all the strangeness of that strange country in its hollow moan, rushed through the great stone arch. At other times there was silence such as Shefford imagined dwelled deeply inside this rocky world. At still other times an owl hooted, and the sound was nameless, but it had a mocking echo that never ended — an echo of night, silence, gloom, melancholy, death, age, eternity.

The Indian lay asleep with his dark face upturned, and the other sleepers lay, calm and white, in the starlight. Shefford saw in them the meaning of life and the past — the illimitable train of faces that had shone under the stars. There was a spirit in the cañon, and whether or not it was what the Navajo embodied in the great Nonnezoshe, or the life of the present, or the death of the ages, or the nature so magnificently manifested in those silent, dreaming, waiting walls — the truth for Shefford was that this spirit was God.

Life was eternal. Man's immortality lay in himself. Love of a woman was hope — happiness. Brotherhood — that mystic and grand *bi-nai* of the Navajo — that was religion.

Chapter Nineteen

The night passed, the gloom turned gray, the dawn stole, cool and pale, into the cañon. When Nas-Ta-Bega drove the mustangs into camp, the lofty ramparts of the walls were rimmed with gold and the dark arch of Nonnezoshe began to lose its steely gray.

The women had rested well and were in better condition to travel. Jane was cheerful, and Fay radiant one moment and in a dream the next. She was beginning to live in that wonderful future. They talked more than usual at breakfast, and Lassiter made droll remarks. Shefford, with his great and haunting trouble ended forever, with now only danger to face ahead, was a different man, but thoughtful and quiet.

This morning the Indian leisurely made preparations for the start. For all the concern he showed, he might have known every foot of the cañon below Nonnezoshe. Yet, for Shefford, with the dawn had returned anxiety, a restless feeling of the need for hurry. What obstacles, what impassable gorges might lay between this bridge and the river! The Indian's inscrutable serenity and Fay's trust, her radiance, the exquisite glow upon her face sustained Shefford and gave him patience to endure and conceal his dread.

At length the flight was resumed with Nas-Ta-Bega leading on foot, and Shefford walking in the rear. A quarter of a mile below camp the Indian led down a declivity into the bottom of the narrow gorge where the stream ran. He did not gaze backward for a last glance at Nonnezoshe, nor did Jane or Lassiter. Fay, however, checked Nack-Yal at the rim of this descent, and turned to look behind. Shefford contrasted her tremulous smile, her half-sad and half-happy good bye to this place, with the white stillness of her face when she had bade farewell to Surprise Valley. Then she rode Nack-Yal down into the gorge.

Shefford knew that this would be his last look at the rainbow bridge. As he gazed, the tip of the great arch lost its cold dark stone color and began to shine. The sun had just arisen high enough over some low break on the wall to reach the bridge. Shefford watched. Slowly, in wondrous transformation, the gold and blue and rose and the pink and purple blended their hues, softly, mistily, cloudily, till once again the arch was a rainbow.

Ages before life had evolved upon the earth, it had spread its grand arch from wall to wall, black and mystic at night, transparent and rosy in the sunrise, at sunset a flaming curve limned against the heavens. When the race of man had passed, it would perhaps stand there still. It was not for many eyes to see. Only by toil, sweat, endurance, blood could any man ever look at Nonnezoshe. So it would always be alone, grand, silent, beautiful, unintelligible. Shefford bade Nonnezoshe a mute, reverent farewell. Then, plunging down the weathered slope of the gorge to the stream below, he hurried forward to join the others. They had progressed much farther than he had imagined they would have, and this was owing to the fact that the floor of the gorge afforded easy travel. It was gravel or rock bottom, tortuous but open, with infrequent and shallow downward steps. The stream did not now rush and boil along and tumble over rock-encumbered ledges. In corners the water collected in round, green, eddying pools. There were patches of grass and willows and mounds of moss. Shefford's surprise equaled his relief, for he believed that the violent descent of Nonnezoshe Boco had been passed. Any turn now, he imagined, might bring the party out upon the river. When he caught up with them, he imparted this conviction that was received with cheer. The hopes of all, except the Indian, seemed mounting, and, if he ever hoped or despaired, it was never manifest.

Shefford's anticipation, however, was not soon realized. The fugitives traveled miles farther down Nonnezoshe Boco, and the only changes were that the walls of the lower gorge heightened and merged with those above, and that these upper ones towered ever loftier. Shefford had to throw his head straight back up at the rims, and the narrow strip of sky was now, indeed, a flowing stream of blue.

Difficult steps were met, too, yet nothing compared to those of the upper cañon. Shefford calculated that this day's travel had advanced several hours, and more than ever now he was anticipating the mouth of Nonnezoshe Boco. Still another hour went by. And then came striking changes. The cañon narrowed till the walls were scarcely twenty paces apart, the color of stone grew dark red above and black down low, the light of day became shadowed, and the floor was a level, gravelly, winding lane with the stream meandering slowly and silently.

Suddenly the Indian halted. He turned his ear down the cañon lane. He had heard something. The others grouped around him listened, but did not hear a sound except the soft flow of water and the heave of the mustangs. Then the Indian went on. Presently he halted again. Again he listened. This time he threw up his head, and upon his dark face shone a light that might have been pride.

"*Ise-ko-n-tsa-igi,*" he said.

The others could not understand, but they were impressed.

"Shore he means somethin' big," drawled Lassiter.

"Oh, what did he say?" queried Fay in eagerness.

"Nas-Ta-Bega, tell me," said Shefford. "We are full of hope."

"Grand Cañon," replied the Indian.

"How do you know?" asked Shefford.

"I hear the roar of the river."

But Shefford, listen as he might, could not hear it. They traveled on, winding down the wonderful lane. Every once in a while Shefford lagged behind, let the others pass out of hearing, and then he listened. At last he was rewarded. Low and deep, dull and strange, with some quality to incite dread, came a roar. Thereafter, at intervals, usually at turns in the cañon and when a faint stir of warm air fanned his cheeks he heard the sound, growing clearer and louder.

He rounded an abrupt corner to have the roar suddenly fill his ears, to see the lane extend straight to a ragged vent, and beyond that, at some distance, a dark, ragged, bulging wall, like iron. As he hurried forward, he was surprised to find that the noise did not increase. Here it kept a strange uniformity of tone and volume. The others of the party passed out of the mouth of Nonnezoshe Boco in advance of Shefford, and, when he reached it, they were grouped upon a bank of sand. A dark red cañon yawned before them and through it slid the strangest river Shefford had ever seen. At first glance he imagined the strangeness consisted of the dark red color of the water, but at the second he was not so sure. All the others, except Nas-Ta-Bega, eyed the river blankly, as if they did not know what to think. The roar came from around a huge, bulging wall downstream. Up the cañon, half a mile, at another turn, there was a leaping rapids of dirty red-white waves, and the sound of this, probably, was drowned in the unseen but nearer rapid.

"This is the Grand Cañon of the Colorado," said Shefford. "We've come out at the mouth of Nonnezoshe Boco. And now to wait for Joe Lake!"

They made camp on a dry level sandbar, under a shelving wall. Nas-Ta-Bega collected a pile of driftwood to be used for fire, and then he took the mustangs back up the side cañon to find grass for them. Lassiter appeared unusually quiet and soon passed from weary rest on the sand to deep slumber. Fay and Jane succumbed to an exhaustion that manifested itself the moment relaxation set in, and they, too, fell asleep. Shefford patrolled the long strip of sand under the wall, and watched up the river for Joe Lake. The Indian returned, and went along the river, climbed over the jutting sharp slopes that reached into the water, and passed out of sight upstream toward the rapid.

Shefford had a sense that the river and the cañon were too magnificent to be compared with others. Still, as all his emotions and sensations had been so wrought upon, he seemed not to have any left by which he might judge of what constituted the differences. He would wait. He had a grim conviction that before he was safely out of this earth-riven country that he would know. One thing, however, struck him, and it was that up the cañon, high over the lower walls, hazy and blue, stood other walls, and beyond and above them, dim in purple distance, upreared still other walls. The haze and the blue and the purple meant great distance, and likewise the height seemed incomparable.

The red river attracted him most. Since this was the medium by which he must escape with his party, it was natural that it absorbed him, to the neglect of the gigantic cliffs. The more he watched the river, studied it, listened to it, imagined its nature, its power, its relentlessness, the more he dreaded it. As the hours of the afternoon wore away, and he strolled along and rested on the banks, his first impressions, and what he realized might be his truest ones, were gradually lost. He could not bring them back. The river was changing, deceitful. It worked upon his mind. The low, hollow roar filled his ears and seemed to mock him. Then he endeavored to stop thinking about it, to confine his attention to the gap upstream where sooner or later he prayed that Joe Lake and his boat would appear. But although he controlled his gaze, he could not stay his thought and augmented his strange, pondering dread of the river.

The afternoon waned. Nas-Ta-Bega came

back to camp and said any likelihood of Joe's arrival was past for that day. Shefford could not get over an impression of the reality presented to his naked eyes. These lonely fugitives in the huge-walled cañon waiting for a boatman to come down that river! Strange and wild — those were the words, which inadequately at best, suited this country and the situations it produced.

After supper he and Fay walked along the bars of smooth red sand. There were a few moments when the distant peaks and domes and turrets were glorified in changing sunset hues. But the beauty was fleeting. Fay still showed lassitude. She was quiet, yet cheerful, and the sweetness of her smile, her absolute trust in him stirred and strengthened his spirit anew. Yet he suffered torture when he thought of trusting Fay's life, her soul, and her beauty to this strange red river.

Night brought him relief. He could not see the river; only the low roar made its presence known out there in the shadows. There being no need to stay awake, he dropped into heavy slumber.

Shefford was roused by hands dragging at him. Nas-Ta-Bega bent over him. It was broad daylight. The yellow wall high above

457

was glistening. A fire was crackling, and pleasant odors were wafted to him. Fay and Jane and Lassiter sat around the tarpaulin at breakfast.

After the meal, suspense and strain were manifested in all the fugitives, even the imperturbable Indian being more than usually watchful. His eyes scarcely ever left the black gap where the river slid around the turn above. Soon, as on the preceding day, he disappeared up the ragged, iron-bound shore. There was scarcely an attempt at conversation. A controlling thought bound that group into silence — if Joe Lake was ever going to come, he would come today.

Shefford asked himself a hundred times if it were possible, and his answer seemed to be in the low, sullen, muffled roar of the river. As the morning wore on toward noon, his dread deepened till all chance appeared hopeless. Already he began to have vague and unformed and disquieting ideas of the only avenue of escape left — to return up Nonnezoshe Boco — and that would be to enter a trap.

Suddenly a piercing cry pealed down the cañon. It was followed by echoes, weird and strange, that clapped from wall to wall in mocking concatenation. Nas-Ta-Bega appeared high on the ragged slope. The cry had been the Indian's. He swept an arm out — pointing upstream — and stood like a statue among the iron rocks.

Shefford's keen gaze sighted a moving something in the bend of the river. It was long, low, dark, and flat with a lighter object upright in the middle. A boat and a man!

"Joe! It's Joe!" yelled Shefford madly. "There! Look!"

Jane and Fay were on their knees in the sand, clasping each other, pale faces toward that bend in the river.

Shefford ran up the shore toward the Indian. He climbed the jutting slant of rock. The boat was now fully in the turn — it moved faster — it was nearing the smooth incline above the rapid. There! It glided down — heaved darkly up — settled back — and disappeared in the muddy roughness of water. Shefford held his breath and watched. A dark, bobbing object showed — vanished, showed again to enlarge — to take the shape of a big flatboat — and then it rode the swift, choppy current out of the lower end of the rapid.

Nas-Ta-Bega began to make violent motions, and Shefford, taking his cue, frantically waved his red scarf. There was a five-mile-an-hour current right before them, and Joe must needs see them so that he might sheer the huge and clumsy craft into the shore before it drifted too far down.

Presently Joe did see them. He appeared to be half naked. He raised aloft both arms, and bellowed down the cañon. The echoes loomed from wall to wall, every one stronger with the deep hoarse triumph of the Mormon's voice, till they passed on, growing weaker, to die away in the roar of river below. Then Joe bent to a long oar that appeared to be fastened to the stern of the boat, and the craft drifted out of the swifter current toward the shore. It reached a point opposite to where Shefford and the Indian waited, and, although Joe made prodigious efforts, it slid on. Still, it also drifted shoreward, and halfway down to the mouth of Nonnezoshe Boco Joe threw the end of a rope to the Indian.

"Ho! Ho!" yelled the Mormon, again setting into motion the fiendish echoes. He was naked to the waist; he had lost flesh; he was haggard, worn, dirty, wet. While he pulled on a shirt, Nas-Ta-Bega made the rope fast to a snag of a log of driftwood embedded in the sand, and the boat swung to shore. It was perhaps thirty feet long by half as many wide, crudely built of rough-hewn boards. The steering gear was a long pole with a plank nailed to the end. The craft was empty save for another pole and plank, Joe's coat, and a broken-handled shovel. There were water and sand on the flooring.

Joe stepped ashore, and he was gripped first by Shefford, and then by the Indian. He was an unkempt and gaunt giant, yet how steadfast and reliable, how grimly strong to inspire hope.

"Reckon most of me's here," he said in reply to greetings. "I've had water aplenty. My God! I've had *water!*" He rolled out a grim laugh. "But no grub for three days. Forgot to fetch some."

How practical he was! He told Fay she looked good for sore eyes, but he needed a biscuit most of all. There was just a second of singular hesitation when he faced Lassiter, and then the big strong hand of the young Mormon went out to meet the old gunman.

While they fed him and he ate like a starved man, Shefford told of the flight from the village, the rescuing of Jane and Lassiter from Surprise Valley, the descent from the plateau, the catastrophe to Shadd's gang — and, concluding, Shefford without any explanation told that Nas-Ta-Bega had killed the Mormon, Waggoner.

"Reckon I had that figured," replied Joe, "although, first off, I didn't think so. And

Shadd went over a cliff. That's good riddance. It beats me, though. You never knew what that Paiute was like with a horse. And he had some grand horses in his outfit. Pity about them."

Later, when Joe had a moment alone with Shefford, he explained that during his ride to Kayenta he had realized Fay's innocence and who had been responsible for the tragedy. He took Withers, the trader, into his confidence, and they planned a story, that Withers was to carry to Stonebridge, that would exculpate Fay and Shefford of anything more serious than flight. If Shefford got Fay safely out of the country at once, that would end the matter for all concerned.

"Reckon I'm some ferry boatman, too . . . a *fairy* boatman . . . haw! haw!" he added. "And we're going through. Now I want you to help me rig this tarpaulin up over the bow of the boat. If we can fix it up strong, it'll keep the waves from curling over. They filled her four times for me."

They folded the tarpaulin three times, and with stout pieces of split plank and horseshoe nails from Shefford's saddlebags and pieces of rope they rigged up a screen around bow and front corners.

Nas-Ta-Bega put the saddles in the boat.

The mustangs were far up Nonnezoshe Boco and would work their way back to green and luxuriant cañons. The Indian said they would soon become wild and would never be found. Shefford regretted Nack-Yal, but was glad the faithful little mustang would be free in one of those beautiful cañons.

"Reckon we'd better be off," called Joe. "All aboard!"

He placed Fay and Jane in a corner of the bow, where they would be spared sight of the rapids. Shefford loosed the rope, and sprang aboard last.

"Pard," said Joe, "it's one hell of a river! And now with the snow melting up in the mountains, it's twenty feet above normal and rising fast. But that's well for us. It covers the stones in the rapids. If it hadn't been in flood, Joe would be an angel now!"

The boat cleared the sand, lazily wheeled in the eddying water, and suddenly seemed caught by some powerful gliding force. When it swept out beyond the jutting wall, Shefford saw a quarter of a mile of sliding water that appeared to end abruptly. Beyond lengthened out the gigantic gap between the black and frowning cliffs.

"Wow!" ejaculated Joe. "Drops out of sight there. But that one ain't much. I can tell by the roar. When you see my hair stand up straight . . . then, look out! Lassiter, you look after the women. Shefford, you stand ready to bail out with the shovel, for we'll sure ship water. Nas-Ta-Bega, you help here with the oar."

The roar became a heavy, continuous rumble. The current quickened. Little streaks and ridges seemed to race along the boat. Strange gurglings rose from inside the bow. Shefford stood on tiptoe to see the break in the river below. Swiftly it came into sight — a wonderful, long, smooth red slant of water, a swelling mound, a huge back-curling wave, another and another, a sea of frothy uplifting crests, leaping and tumbling and diminishing down to the narrowing apex of the rapid. It was a frightful sight, yet it thrilled Shefford. Joe worked the steering oar back and forth, and headed the boat straight for the middle of the incline. The boat reached the round run, gracefully dipped with a heavy sop, and went shooting down. The wind blew wetly in Shefford's face. He stood erect, thrilled, fascinated, frightened. Then he seemed to feel himself lifted. The curling wave leaped at the boat. There was a shock that laid him flat, and, when he rose to his knees, all about him was roar and spray and leaping muddy waves.

Shock after shock jarred the boat. Splashes of water stung his face. Then the jar and the motion, the confusion and roar gradually lessened till Shefford rose to see smooth water ahead and the long tumbling rapid behind.

"Get busy, bailer!" yelled Joe. "Pretty soon, you'll be glad you have to bail . . . so you *can't* see!"

There were several inches of water in the bottom of the boat, and Shefford learned for the first time the expediency of a shovel in the art of bailing.

"That tarpaulin worked powerful good," went on Joe. "And it saves the women. Now if it just don't bust on a big wave! That one back there was little."

When Shefford had scooped out all the water, he went forward to see how Fay and Jane and Lassiter had fared. The women were pale, but composed. They had covered their heads.

"But the dreadful roar!" exclaimed Fay.

Lassiter looked shaken for once. "Shore I'd rather taken a chance meetin' them Mormons on the way out," he said.

Shefford spoke with an encouraging assurance that he did not himself feel. Almost at the moment he marked a silence that had fallen in the cañon, then it broke to a low, dull, strange roar.

465

"Aha! Hear that?" The Mormon shook his shaggy head. "Reckon we're in Cataract Cañon. We'll be standing on end from now on. Hang to her, boys!"

Danger of this unusual kind had brought out a peculiar levity in the somber Mormon — a kind of wild, gay excitement. His eyes rolled as he watched the river ahead, and he puffed out his cheek with his tongue.

The rugged, overhanging walls of the cañon grew sinister in Shefford's sight. They were iron jaws. And the river — that made him shudder to look down into it. The little whirling pits were eyes peering into his and they raced on with the boat, disappeared, and came again, always with the little hollow gurgles.

The craft drifted swiftly, and the roar increased. Another rapid seemed to move up into view. It came to a bend in the cañon. When the breeze struck Shefford's cheeks, he did not this time experience exhilaration. The current accelerated its sliding motion and bore the flatboat straight for the middle of the curve. Shefford saw the bend, a long, dark, narrow, gloomy cañon, and a stretch of contending waters, then, crouching low, he waited for the dip, the race, the shock. They came — the last stopping the boat —

throwing it aloft — letting it drop — and crests of angry waves curled over the side. Shefford, kneeling, felt the water slap around him, and in his ears was a deafening roar. There were endless moments of strife and hell and flying darkness of spray all about him and under him, rocking the boat. When they lessened — ceased in violence — he stood ankle deep in water, and then madly he began to bail.

Another roar deafened his ears, but he did not look up from his toil. When he had to get down to avoid the pitch, he closed his eyes. That rapid passed, and with more water to bail he resumed his share in the manning of the crude craft. It was more than a share — a tremendous responsibility to which he bent with all his might. He heard Joe yell — and again — and again. He heard the increasing roars one after another till they seemed one continuous bellow. He felt the shock, the pitch, the beating waves, and the lessening power of sound and current. That set him to his task. Always in these long intervals of toil he seemed to see without looking up the growing proportions of the cañon. The river had become a living, terrible thing. The intervals of his tireless effort, when he scooped the water overboard, were fleeting, and the rides through rapid after rapid were endless periods of waiting terror. His spirit and his hope were overshadowed by the rush and roar and fury.

Then, as he worked, there came a stretch of river that seemed quiet after chaos — and here for the first time he bailed the boat clear of water.

Jane and Fay were huddled in a corner with the flapping tarpaulin now half fallen over them. They were wet and muddy. Lassiter crouched like a man dazed by a bad dream and his white hair hung, stained and bedraggled, over his face. The Indian and the Mormon, grim, hard, worn, stood silently at the rear.

The afternoon was far advanced, and the sun had already descended below the western ramparts. A cool breeze blew up the cañon laden with a sound that was the same, yet not the same, as those low, dull roars that Shefford dreaded more and more.

Joe Lake turned his ear to the breeze. A stronger puff brought a heavy, quivering rumble. This time he did not vent his gay, wild defiance to the river. He bent lower — listened. Then, as the rumble became a strange, deep, reverberating roll, as if the monstrous rim were rolling huge stones down a subterranean cañon, Shefford saw with dilating eyes that the Mormon's hair was rising stiffly upon his head.

"Hear that!" said Joe, turning an ashen face to Shefford. "We'll drop off the earth now. Hang on to the girl, so if we go, you can go together . . . and, pard, if you've got a God . . . *pray!*"

Nas-Ta-Bega faced the bend from whence that rumble came and he was the same dark, inscrutable, passive Indian as of old. What was death to him?

Shefford felt the stinging, rushing love of life surge in him, and it was not for himself, he thought, but for Fay and the happiness she merited. He went to her, patted the covered head, and tried with words choking in his throat to give hope. He leaned with hands gripping the gunwale, with eyes wide-open, ready for the unknown.

The river made a quick turn, and from around the bend rumbled a terrible uproar. The current racing that way was divided or uncertain, and it gave strange, whirling motion to the boat. Joe and Nas-Ta-Bega shoved desperately upon the oar, all to no purpose. The currents had their will. The bow of the boat took the place of the stern. Then, swiftly as the head of a curved incline, it shot beyond the bulging wall.

Shefford saw an awful place before them.

The cañon had narrowed to half its width and turned almost at right angles. The huge clamor of appalling sound came from under the cliff where the swollen river had to pass and where there was not space. The rapid rushed in gigantic swells right upon the wall, boomed against it, climbed and spread and fell away, to recede, and gather new impetus, to leap madly down the cañon.

Shefford went to his knees, clasped Fay, and Jane, too. But, facing this appalling thing, he had to look. Courage of despair came to him at the last. This must be the end. With long, buoyant swings the boat sailed down, shot over the first waves, was caught and impelled straight toward the cliff. Huge whirlpools raced alongside and from them came a horrible, engulfing roar. Monstrous bulges rose on the other side. All the stupendous power up that mighty river of downward rushing silt swung the boat aloft, up and up, as the swell climbed the wall. Shefford, with transfixed eyes and harrowed soul, watched the wet, black wall. It loomed down upon him. The stern of the boat went high. Then, when the crash that meant doom seemed imminent, the swell spread and fell back from the wall, and the boat never struck at all. By some miraculous chance it had been favored by a strange and momentary receding of the huge, spent swell. Then it slid back, was caught and whirled by the current into red, frothy upflung rapids below. Shefford bowed his head over Fay and saw no more or felt or heard. What seemed a long time after that the broken voice of the Mormon recalled him to his labors.

The boat was half full of water. Nas-Ta-Bega scooped out great sheets of it with his hands. Shefford sprang to aid him, found the shovel, and plunged into the task. Slowly but surely they emptied the boat. Then Shefford saw that twilight had fallen. Joe was working the craft toward a narrow bank of sand, to which eventually they came, and the Indian sprang out to move to a rock.

The fugitives went ashore, and weary and silent and drenched they dropped in the warm sand.

Shefford could not sleep. The river kept him awake. In the distance it rumbled, low, deep, reverberating, and near at hand it was a thing of mutable mood. It moaned, whined, mocked, and laughed. It had the soul of a devil. It was a river that had cut its way to the bowels of the earth and its nature was destructive. It harbored no life. Fighting its way through those dead walls, cutting and tearing and wearing, its heavy burden of silt was death, destruction, and decay. A silent river, a murmuring, strange fierce, terrible, thundering river of the desert! Even in the dark it seemed to wear the hue of blood.

All night long Shefford heard it, and toward the dark hours before dawn, when a restless, broken sleep came to him, his dreams were dreams of a river of sounds. All beautiful sounds he knew and loved he heard — the sigh of the wind in the pines, the mourn of the wolf, the cry of the laughing gull, the murmur of running brooks, the song of a child, the whisper of a woman, and there were the boom of the surf, the roar of the north wind in the forest, the roll of thunder. There were the sounds not of earth — a river of the universe rolling the planets, engulfing the stars, pouring the sea of blue into infinite space.

Night with its fitful dreams passed. Dawn lifted the ebony gloom out of the cañon, and sunlight far up on the parapets renewed Shefford's spirit. He rose, and awoke the others. Fay's wistful smile still held its faith. They ate of the gritty, water-soaked food.

Then they embarked. The current carried them swiftly down and out of hearing of the last rapid. The character of the river and the cañon changed. The current lessened to a slow, smooth, silent, eddying flow. The walls grew straight, sheer, gloomy, and vast. Shefford noted these features, but he was listening so hard for the roar of the next rapid that he scarcely appreciated them. All the fugitives were listening. Every bend in the cañon — and now the turns were numerous — might hold a rapid. Shefford strained his ears. He imagined the low, dull, strange rumble. He had it in his ears, yet there was the growing sensation of silence.

"Shore this's a dead place," muttered Lassiter.

"She's only slowed up for a bigger plunge," Joe replied. "Listen! Hear that?"

But there was no true sound. Joe only imagined what he expected and hated and needed to hear.

Mile after mile they drifted through the silent gloom between those vast and magnificent walls. After the speed, the turmoil, the whirling, shrieking, thundering, the never-ceasing sound and change and motion, this slow, quiet drifting, this utterly absolute silence, these eddying stretches of still water below, worked strangely upon Shefford's mind, and he feared he was going mad.

There was no change to the silence, no

help for the slow drift, no lessening of the strain. The hours of the day passed as moments, the sun crossed the blue gap above, the golden lights hung on the upper walls, the gloom returned, and still there was only the dead, vast, insupportable silence. There came bends where the current quickened, ripples widened, long lanes of little waves roughened the surface, but they made no sound. Then the fugitives turned through a V-shaped vent in the cañon. The ponderous walls sheered away from the river. There was space and sunshine, and far beyond this league-wide open rose vermilion-colored cliffs. A mile below, the river disappeared in a dark, box-like passage from whence came a rumble that made Shefford's flesh creep.

The Mormon flung high his arms and let out the stentorian yell that had rolled down to the fugitives as they waited at the mouth of Nonnezoshe Boco, but now it had a wilder, more exultant note. Strange how he shifted his gaze to Fay Larkin!

"Girl! Get up and look!" he called. "The ferry! The ferry!"

Then he bent his brawny back over the steering oar, and the clumsy craft slowly turned toward the left-hand shore, where a long, low bank of green willows and cottonwoods gave welcome relief to the eyes. Upon the opposite side of the river Shefford saw a boat, similar to the one he was in, moored to the bank.

"Shore, if I ain't losin' my eyes, I seen an Injun with a red blanket," said Lassiter.

"Yes, Lassiter!" cried Shefford. "Look, Fay! Look, Jane! See! Indians . . . hogans . . . mustangs . . . there above the green bank!"

The boat glided slowly shoreward. The deep, hungry, terrible rumble of the remorseless river became something no more to dread.

Chapter Twenty

Two days' travel from the river, along the saw-toothed range of Echo Cliffs, stood Presbrey's trading post, a little, red-stone, square house in a green and pretty valley called Willow Springs. It was nearing the time of sunset — that gorgeous hour of color in the Painted Desert — when Shefford and his party rode down upon the post.

The scene lacked the wildness characteristic of Kayenta or Red Lake. There were wagons and teams, white men and Indians, burros, sheep, lambs, mustangs saddled and unsaddled, dogs, and chickens. A young, sweet-faced woman stood in the door of the post, and she it was who first sighted the fugitives. Presbrey was weighing bags of wool on a scale, and, when she called, he lazily turned, as if to wonder at her eagerness. Then he flung up his head, with its shock of heavy hair, in a start of surprise, and his florid face lost its lazy indolence to become wreathed in a huge smile.

"Haven't seen a white person in six months!" was his extraordinary greeting.

An hour later Shefford, clean-shaven, comfortably clothed once more, found himself a different man, and, when he saw Fay in white again, with a new and indefinable light shining through that old haunting shadow in her eyes, then the world changed, and he embraced perfect happiness.

There was a dinner such as Shefford had not seen for many a day and as Fay had never seen, and that brought to Jane Withersteen's eye the dreamy memory of the bountiful feasts which, long years ago, had been her pride. There was a story told to the curious trader and his kind wife — a story with its beginning back in those past years, of riders of the purple sage, of Surprise Valley then and now, of Fay Larkin as a child and then as a sealed wife, of the flight down Nonnezoshe Boco and the cañon, of a great Mormon and a noble Indian.

Presbrey stared with his deep-set eyes and wagged his tousled head and stared again. Then with the quick perception of the practical desert man he said: "I'm sending teamsters into Flagstaff tomorrow. Wife and I will go along with you. We've light wagons. Three days maybe . . . or four, and we'll be there. Shefford, I'm going to see you marry Fay Larkin!"

Fay and Jane and Lassiter showed strangely against this background of approaching civilization. Shefford realized more than ever the loneliness and isolation and wildness of so many years for them.

When the women had retired, Shefford and the men talked a while. Then Joe Lake rose to stretch his big frame.

"Friends, reckon I'm all in," he said. "Good night." In passing, he laid a heavy hand on Shefford's shoulder. "Well, you got out. I've only a queer notion how. But *Someone* beside an Indian and a Mormon guided you out! Be good to the girl. Good bye, pard!"

Shefford grasped the big hand and in the emotion of the moment did not catch the significance of Joe's last words.

Later Shefford stepped outside into the starlight for a few moments' quiet walk and thought before he went to bed. It was a white night. The coyotes were yelping. The stars shone, steadfast, bright, cold. Nas-Ta-Bega stalked out of the shadow of the house and joined Shefford. They walked in silence. Shefford's heart was too full for utterance, and the Indian seldom spoke at any time. When Shefford was ready to go in, Nas-Ta-Bega extended his hand.

"Good bye, *bi-nai!*" he said strangely, using English and Navajo in what Shefford supposed to be merely good night. The starlight shone fully upon the dark, inscrutable face of the Indian. Shefford bade him good night, and then watched him stride away in the silver gloom.

But next morning Shefford understood. Nas-Ta-Bega and Joe Lake were gone. It was a shock to Shefford. Yet what could he have said to either? Joe had shirked saying good bye to him and Fay, and the Indian had gone out of Shefford's life as he had come into it.

What these two men represented in Shefford's uplift was too great for the present to define, but they and the desert that had developed them had taught him the meaning of life. He might fail often, since failure was the lot of his kind, but could he ever fail again in faith in man or God, while he had mind to remember the Indian and the Mormon? Still, although he placed them on a noble height and loved them well, there would always abide with him a sorrow for the Mormon, and a sleepless and eternal regret for that Indian in his lonely cedar slope with the spirits of his vanishing race calling him.

Willow Springs appeared to be a lively place that morning. Presbrey was gay, and his sweet-faced wife was excited. The teamsters were a jolly whistling lot. The lean mustangs kicked and bit at each other. The trader had brought out two light wagons for the trip, and after the manner of desert men desired to start at sunrise. Far across the Painted Desert towered the San Francisco Peaks, black-timbered, blue-cañoned, purple-hazed, with white snow, like the clouds, around their summits.

Jane Withersteen looked at the radiant Fay and lived again in her happiness. At last excitement had been communicated to the old gunman.

"Shore we're goin' to live with Fay an' John, an' be near Venters an' Bess, an' see the blacks again, Jane. An' Venters will tell you, as he did me, how Wrangle run Black Star off his legs!"

All connected with that early start was sweet, sad, and hopeful.

So they rode away from Willow Springs, through the green fields of alfalfa and cottonwood, down the valley with its smoking hogans and whistling mustangs and scarlet-blanketed Indians, and out upon the colorful desert with its bare ridges toward the rosy sunrise.

Epilogue

On the outskirts of a little town in Illinois there was a farm of rolling pastureland, and here a beautiful meadow, green and red in clover, merged upon an orchard, in the midst of which a brown-tiled roof showed above the trees.

One afternoon in May, a group of people, strangely agitated, walked down a steady lane toward the meadow.

"Wal, Jane, I always knew we'd get a look at them hosses again. I shore knew," Lassiter was saying, in the same old cool, careless drawl, but his claw-like hands shook a little.

"Oh! Will they know me?" asked Jane, turning to a stalwart man — no other than the dark-faced Venters, her rider of other days.

"Know you? I'll bet they will. What do you say, Bess?"

The shadow brightened in Bess's somber

blue eyes, as if his words had recalled her fun in a rash and memorable past.

"Black Star will know her surely," replied Bess. "Sometimes he points his nose toward the west and watches as if he saw the purple slope and smelled the sage of Utah! He has never forgotten. But Night has grown deaf and partly blind of late. I doubt if he'll remember."

Shefford and Fay stood arm-in-arm in the background.

Out in the meadow two horses were grazing. They were sleek, shiny, long-maned, long-tailed, black as coal, and, although old, still splendid in every line.

"Do you remember them?" whispered Shefford.

"Oh, I only needed to see Black Star," answered Fay, her voice quivering. "I can remember being lifted on his back. How strange! It seems so long ago. . . . Look, Mother Jane is going out to them."

Jane Withersteen advanced alone through the clover, and it was with unsteady steps. Presently she halted. What glorious and bitter memories were expressed in her strange, poignant call!

Black Star started and swept up his noble head and looked. But Night went on calmly grazing. Then Jane called again — the same strange call, only louder, and this time broken. Black Star raised his head higher, and he whistled a piercing blast. He saw Jane; he knew her as he had remembered the call; he came pounding toward her. She met him, encircled his neck with her arms, and buried her face in his mane.

"Shore I reckon I'd better never say any more about Wrangle runnin' the blacks off their legs thet time," muttered Lassiter, as if to himself.

"Lassiter, you only dreamed that race," replied Venters with a smile.

"Oh, Bern, isn't it good that Black Star remembered her . . . that she'll have him . . . something left of her old home?" asked Bess wistfully.

"Indeed, it is good. But Bess, Jane Withersteen will find a new spirit and new happiness here."

Jane came toward them, leading both horses.

"Dear friends, I am happy. Today I bury all regrets of the past. I shall remember only . . . my riders of the purple sage."

Venters smiled his gladness. "And you . . . Lassiter . . . what shall you remember?" he queried.

The old gunman looked at Jane and then at his claw-like hands and then at Fay. His eyes lost their shadow and began to blink. "Wal, I rolled a stone once, but I reckon now thet Wrangle. . . ."

"Lassiter, I said you dreamed that race. Wrangle never beat the blacks," interrupted Venters. "And you, Fay . . . what shall you remember?"

"Surprise Valley," replied Fay dreamily.

"And you . . . Shefford?"

Shefford shook his head. For him there could never be one memory only. In his heart there would never change or die memories of the wild uplands, of the great towers and walls, of the golden sunsets, or the cañon ramparts of the silent, fragrant valleys where the cedars and the sago lilies grew, of those starlit nights when his love and faith awoke, of grand and lonely Nonnezoshe, of the red, sullen, thundering mysterious Colorado River, of a wonderful Indian and a noble Mormon — of all that was embodied for him in the meaning of the rainbow trail.

About the Author

Zane Grey was born Pearl Zane Gray at Zanesville, Ohio in 1872. He was graduated from the University of Pennsylvania in 1896 with a degree in dentistry. He practiced in New York City while striving to make a living by writing. He married Lina Elise Roth in 1905 and with her financial assistance he published his first novel himself, *Betty Zane* (1903). Closing his dental office, the Greys moved into a cottage on the Delaware River, near Lackawaxen, Pennsylvania. Grey took his first trip to Arizona in 1907 and, following his return, wrote *The Heritage of the Desert* (1910). The profound effect that the desert had had on him was so vibrantly captured that it still comes alive for a reader. Grey couldn't have been more fortunate in his choice of a mate. Trained in English at Hunter College, Lina Grey proofread every manuscript Grey wrote, polished his prose, and she effectively managed their financial affairs. Grey's early novels were serialized in pulp magazines, but by 1918 he had graduated to the slick magazine market. Motion picture rights brought in a fortune and, with 109 films based on his work, Grey set a record yet to be equaled by any other author. Zane Grey was not a realistic writer, but rather one who charted the interiors of the soul through encounters with the wilderness. He provided characters no less memorable than one finds in Balzac, Dickens, or Thomas Mann, and they have a vital story to tell. "There was so much unexpressed feeling that could not be entirely portrayed," Loren Grey, Grey's younger son and a noted psychologist, once recalled, "that, in later years, he would weep when re-reading one of his own books." Perhaps, too, terrible to suggest, Zane Grey may have wept at how his attempts at being truthful to his muse had so often been essentially altered by his editors, so that no one might ever be able to read his stories as he had intended them. It may be said of Zane Grey that, more than mere adventure tales, he fashioned psycho-dramas about the odyssey of the human soul. If his stories seem not always to be of the stuff of the mundane world, without what his stories do touch, the human world has little meaning — which may go a long way to explain the hold he has had on an enraptured reading public ever since his first Western novel in 1910.